Maoism in India

Maoism in India

Arun Srivastava

PRABHAT
PRAKASHAN

Published by
PRABHAT PRAKASHAN PVT. LTD.
4/19 Asaf Ali Road,
New Delhi-110 002 (INDIA)
e-mail: prabhatbooks@gmail.com

ISBN 978-93-5186-513-1
MAOISM IN INDIA
by Arun Srivastava

Edition
2025

Price
₹ 500.00 (Rupees Five Hundred only)

Printed at
R-Tech Offset Printers, Delhi

To

Pushpa

Author's Note

One cannot expect that Maosim or Marxism-Leninism will follow the same path, or have the same paradigmatic structure in all countries, as experimenting with ideologies primarily depends on the demographic, economic and cultural variables and realities. But the fact is after near 50 years of its birth, the Naxalite movement is in a bind; searching for a compatible ideological format and base to accomplish revolution. The ideological polemics and analysis of the character of the state have obliterated.

Paradoxically, forty odd Naxalite factions are behaving more like small grocery shops in the villages. This is manifestation of the lack of political-economic urgency to combat neoliberal economy. Old social order perpetuates. No serious effort is visible to amalgamate armed struggle, parliamentary struggle and mass movement.

Notwithstanding Maoists flexing their muscle and showing armed power, the fact is the movement lacks mature leadership who can look beyond and find out the reason for dilution of the difference between the productive forces and the production relations.

The most interesting development in recent years has been drawing a dividing line between Maoism and Marxism-Leninism (M-L). While the state machinery applies a single yardstick to club them together, Maoists are unwilling to accept M-L as a revolutionary outfit. While Mao Zedong believed in and propagated Marxist-Leninist theory and described his own ideology as Mao Zedong's Thought, the Indian Maoists have projected Mao Zedong's Thought as

Maoism. They try to distance from Marxism-Leninism. Most of the recent actions are in fact part of the strategy to reinforce the supremacy of their line.

Money and gun power has emerged as the focal point of this strategy. This has in fact eroded the base of the Maoists. In Lalgarh (West Bengal), the Maoists are working at cross purposes. The blast of the Gyaneshwari Express is an example. This situation has put the rank and file in the state of amnesia. They are caught between two confusing scenario; state repression and indifferent leadership. The fact is the movement without a mass movement has been depending on terror tactics for its survival.

The fall out is visible on the ground level. Never before during the 48 year of Naxalite movement such large number of Naxalites or Maoists had surrendered or were arrested as was witnessed during last couple of years in Bihar and Jharkhand; the region which gave a new dimension to the Naxalite movement in seventies. Not less than two dozens of hardcore activists, mainly of the rank of commanders (zonal commanders, sub-zonal commanders) and state level leaders besides hundreds of cadres laid their arms. The statement of sub-zonal commander of Sone-Ganga-Vindhyachal zone, Sudama Oraon provides an insight. He and his 21 comrades were enlightened due to the kindness of the police chief of Rohtas. He said: "We have seen enough of the Naxalite double standard. Now we want to leave our past behind and join the mainstream." They made no secret that they were disenchanted with their top leadership.

Most of those surrendered Naxalites nurse the view that the guerilla actions do not conform to the basic concept of Guerilla Warfare. In most of the cases, the whim of the leadership prevailed over the ground realities. They often ignore Mao Zedong's ideological spirit. They are also aggrieved at the reluctance of the leadership to follow the path of political mobilization of the general mass. They find it hard to justify recent guerilla actions as in most of the cases no class enemy was at the target.

Ground level cadres also nurse the view that Andhra Pradesh centric leadership lacks the basic knowledge of other states. Wide ranging disagreement persists within the top leadership on the issue of territory and funds. Most of the leaders in Bihar, Jharkhand, West Bengal, Odisha, Chhattisgarh are feeling isolated. What is interesting is factional stakes are visible even within the territories.

Significantly, the Nitish Kumar Government's 'Shikaria Model', mechanism to bring back the Maoists into the mainstream has caught the imagination of the Maoist naxalites. Shikaria a village in Jehanabad, the region which witnessed worst massacres in seventies and eighties between Naxalites and Ranavir Sena, is the birth place of MKSS which had launched the revolutionary movement for change. After coming to power, Nitish handed over the development funds to the people at the ground. They were to identify the priorities and undertake the development. The Naxalite who used to collect levies from local bigwigs are getting the funds from the government. Relatives of the Naxalites have turned contractors. During last seven years, the region has not witnessed any significant Naxalite armed action. They are also using this money to finance their operations in other places.

Contents

1

Inside India's Red Corridor

If what the Maoists claim or the media reports is true that India's 'red corridor' covers a substantial chunk of the country, with more than 200 of its 640 districts under Maoist control, then the half of the country should have been under the direct control of the Maoists and these areas should have been witnessing peoples' upsurge. As the Maoists mention in their programmes and strategy, protracted class war or civil war already have been waged in the entire region under its control to throw out the so-called reactionary and anti- people governments. But this has not happened. Paradoxically the bourgeoise-controlled governments have been ruling the states in the region demarcated as the red corridor.

The term 'red corridor' has been used for the entire naxal-infested region that includes, Chhattisgarh, Odisha and Jharkhand as well as parts of Andhra Pradesh, Bihar, West Bengal and Maharashtra. Interrogations of arrested cadres reveal that it meant a narrow but contiguous strip that runs from the southern tip of Chhattisgarh to central Jharkhand – the two key theatres of naxal violence. 'Red corridor' gives them easy movement and safe passage through three states. What the government calls the 'red corridor' – could really be called the 'natural resources corridor'. These state are the crown jewels of modern 'progress'.

In sharp contrast to the economic and political realities, a sustained effort is being made to create a skewed impression about the 'red corridor'. The main players of course are the media and the bureaucracy. Their campaign obviously gives rise to the question; why after all they are determined to create this picture of red-terror? In reality, it is simply not more than a small strip being used by the Maoists to deflect the police action. Why then it is blown out of proportion? There must be some reason. Going by its present character it cannot at all be described as the base area of the Maoists. The Maoist idea of mobile warfare and a red corridor is that of better trained military companies should be able to operate from anywhere.

The Maoists advocate armed agrarian revolution to establish a classless society and have their roots in the Naxalbari uprising of the 1967. But they have taken myriad and often diametrically opposited paths. In fact, the media and the bureaucracy have helped their cause to a major extent. While the media is interested in publishing hot and exclusive stories, the bureaucrats and police have been using the Maoist and red corridor bogey to get elevated in their position and make easy money.

Fighting Maoism has attained the character of a big industry. The government spends thousands of crores of unaccounted money on the operation. The State Governments as well as the central agencies actually do not have a properly audited expenditure statement. On the plea of eradicating Maoist insurgency even an officer at the lower level could spend a big amount without any significant accountability. In some of the cases, the police pay to some Maoist leaders. The Shikaria experiment was launched on the strength of this secret fund. At least a dozen of 'so- called' Maoists are regularly paid. Patronising the police-source, the informers, and paying them is the old game.

Sometime back, the then Union home minister Shriprakash Jaiswal had accused the Arjun Munda-led BJP Jharkhand Government of misusing funds allotted to Jharkhand for fighting the Naxalites. Criticising the government for misusing funds, Jaiswal had said: "The Munda Government used the funds meant for fighting the Naxalites to buy swanky vehicles for the ministers and senior bureaucrats. It had nothing to do with the police modernisation programme. A huge amount earmarked for the purpose also remained unspent over the years." Jaiswal said there was a significant decline in the acts of the rebels after the change of guard in the state and also praised the prompt police action. Blaming poverty for the rebel menace, Jaiswal said the State Government should focus on land reforms and ensure strict implementation of the Centre-sponsored poverty eradication schemes like Pradhan Manthri Gram Sadak Yojana and Rojagar Guarantee Yojana. He had said, "Our government believes in police modernisation through advanced training, sophisticated weapons and competent officials. We have given the rebel-ravaged states choppers on several occasions in the past to carry out air surveillance. But aerial attacks will be our last option. My government is competent enough to flush out rebels without stringent laws like POTA. We have already set an example by restoring normal situation in Mizoram without POTA or the likes."

Even the former Union minister P. Chidambaram had told the MPs from 34 Left-wing-insurgency hit districts to properly utilise development funds provided by the Central Government to help curb Maoist insurgency. Chairing a meeting to review the steps needed for integrated development of Maoist infested districts, Chidambaram cited statistics to suggest that funds released for these districts were not utilised properly. He had said, "a plan would be worked out on the basis of concrete suggestions received from the MPs and be presented to chief ministers of Maoist-hit states."

A Planning Commission task force had reported after the Dantewada massacre that development work was slowest in the areas with huge Maoist presence. The report found that in Dantewada, claims for land made under the Forest Rights Act had not been given. Only 46 percent of the funds meant for roads had been used and nearly 63 percent of the healthcare money had been spent. The government is focusing on connectivity in these terrains, which has been the biggest disadvantage faced by security forces during the anti-Maoist operations. Similarly, nearly 5.86 percent funds for ashram schools has been utilised, while 72 percent given under an electricity scheme was used, 86 percent for education, 80.35 percent for the job guarantee scheme and 87 percent for drinking water supply. Unfortunately, the MPs did not care for Chidambaram's advice. No concrete suggestions were placed by them before the government. While so much noise is being created over the possible threat from the Maoists, no substantive effort is being made for improving the live of the crores of the poor people, proletariat and tribals.

In this connection, the observation of the Comptroller and Auditor General (CAG) of India is worth mentioning. It rapped the Odisha Government for its failure to utilise the funds allocated under the Centrally-sponsored Security-Related Expenditure (SRE) scheme. An estimated ₹ 137.96 crore was surrendered by the State Government on March 31, 2012. The State Government failed to utilise the funds sanctioned by the Union Government under the scheme from 2009 to 2012, the CAG report revealed. The SRE scheme, launched in 1996 and revised in February 2005, is being implemented in nine vulnerable districts with an objective to supplement the State's efforts in dealing with the Maoist menace effectively by way of reimbursing expenditure incurred by the State on security-related activities. SRE funds were provided in State Budget on the basis of the proposals.

The entire approach to fighting Maosim conjures one to believe that the administration and state machinery do not view Maoism and Maoists as the potential threat. Since their areas of operations are localized and confined to some pockets, they are not in a position to pose a serious security threat. If the Maoist threat was real, the governments would certainly have utilized the fund to effectively counter them. We have the example of Bengal of seventies before us; how the government combated the Naxalites. Since there was no threat perception no effort in fact was made to follow the 2004 instruction of the then Prime Minister, Dr Manmohan Singh to intensify the development process at the grass-root level. In Odisha, Annual Action Plan prepared by the State

Home Department and submitted to the Government of India for approval. Pending the Centre's approval, expenditure was incurred through the State Budget and the Home Department claimed reimbursement under the scheme from the Centre against the spending by the Drawing and Disbursing Officers. The CAG expressed his displeasure over the improper assessment of the requirement and management of funds under the SRE scheme to deal with the Maoist problem. As per the CAG report, budgetary estimates were not realistic as the expenditure ranging from 46 percent to 75 percent indicating the provisions made both in IAP and in the Budget estimates were unrealistic.

During the period 2009-10 and 2011-12, the audit report pointed out, the State Government could not utilise the budgetary amounts of 26 percent in 2009-10, 28 percent in 2010-11 and 55 percent in 2011-12. The CAG report said shortcomings in budgetary control, advance release of funds to the executing agency and delayed payment of rehabilitation packages to the extremists who surrendered affected the implementation of the SRE scheme and defeated its objective. The CAG has recommended to the government to complete the works under the SRE scheme within the stipulated time, pay rehabilitation package as per rule and put in place an effective monitoring mechanism system for successful implementation of the scheme.

Though the State Government failed to utilise the funds, it made an additional provision of ₹ 13.91 crore in its Supplementary Budget for 2011-12, which was also surrendered along with savings of ₹ 73.78 crore of the year. The audit report also pointed out that the State Government too incurred expenditure on office equipments and establishment expenses of the training institutes meant for the Special Operation Group (SOG) deployed to curb Maoist activities in violation of the SRE. During 2012, the government spent ₹ 5.19 crore violating the guidelines. Besides, the Centre had disallowed ₹ 15.60 crore due to incurring of expenditure on inadmissible items during 2009-12, the report said.

Obviously, these imply that the ruling elite were not at all interested in countering the Maoism. Instead it was using the Maoists bogey for its selfish gain. The statistics furnished about the areas under their control and strength of their armed wing were also confusing. The armed wing of the Maoists, the PLGA (Peoples Liberation Guerrilla Army) is estimated to have around 9,500 armed cadres. In 2007, it was estimated that Naxalites were active across 'half of the India's 28 states' which accounts for about 40 percent of India's geographical area; an area known as the 'red corridor', where, according to estimates, they controlled 92,000 square kilometers. In 2009, Naxalites were active across approximately 180 districts in ten states. The Naxalites operate in 60 districts mainly in the states of Odisha (five affected districts), Jharkhand (fourteen affected districts), Bihar (five affected districts), Andhra Pradesh, Chhattisgarh (ten affected districts), Madhya Pradesh (eight affected districts), Maharashtra (two affected districts) and West Bengal (eight affected districts). In West Bengal, areas west of Howrah are affected by the insurgency. Chhattisgarh is the epicentre of the conflict (2007).

Paradoxically, even after spending crores of money on information collection, the government agencies are not in possession of the actual cadre strength of the Maoists. Whatever figures are catered to the media or to the officials are simply based on speculations of some fertile intelligence mind. The bigger the number of cadres, the bigger is the flow of fund. Interestingly, a study of the Observer Research Foundation, Delhi, estimates the Maoists now have 9,000-10,000 armed fighters, with access to about 6,500 firearms. There are perhaps a further 40,000 full-time cadres. In nearly 1,600 violent incidents involving Maoists last year, 669 people died. There have been spectacular attacks across a big area: a train hold-up involving 250 armed fighters, a jailbreak freeing 350 prisoners, a near-miss assassination attempt in 2004 against a leading politician. Maoists now affect some 170 of India's 602 districts – a 'red corridor' down a swathe of central India from the border with Nepal in the north to

Karnataka in the south and covering more than a quarter of India's land mass.

Naxalites *vs* Maoists

It is strange that scholars and experts who have been projecting the Maoist threat as the major stumbling block for development fail to differentiate between Maoists and Naxalites. They use the word Naxalite for the Maoists. Sometime back it was pointed out that the Maoists carry out detail socio-economic surveys before starting operations in a target area, helping to identify grievances they can exploit. They also say that the Maoists have been among the most principled of terrorist groups in selecting their targets. Their attacks are not random; though, because they so often use crude landmines, they may kill the wrong people. Their leaders are thinking far into the future, taking a 20-year to 25-year view of their struggle. 'Liberated' areas, such as their part of Dantewada, would be expanded until they pose a threat even to India's cities. But a closer look at the Maoists actions does not corroborate the observations of these experts. Most of their actions have been erratic and irresponsible and for this they had to receive flaks. Even former Naxalites leaders, the founders of the movement in 1967 had criticised this approach and whimsical action of the Maoists. If they really had carried out some detail surveys then in that case they would certainly not have created such infantile blunders.

Ashim Chatterjee, one of the founder members of the Naxalbari movement holds, "Without taking up the responsibility of organising the class struggle, if you launch an armed struggle, it will inevitably become terrorism. It degenerated into a terrorist campaign. I've given it a name; it's an exercise in socialism in words, and terrorism in deeds." Maoists once had a reasonably successful political movement, but it was fractured by a crisis of identity and a battle within. It is unclear whether the young, fighters, deep in the jungles of Odisha or Chhattisgarh even know what it means to be a Maoist or what Mao Zedong stood for.

It is significant that during these years in Odisha, the number of districts affected by Maoist activities has been reduced from 17 to 9, as claimed by the Director General of Police (DGP) on December 30, 2012. In February 2009, the Union Government announced a new initiative, the 'Integrated Action Plan' (IAP) for broad, co-ordinated operations to deal to with the Maoist problem in Karnataka, Chhattisgarh, Odisha, Andhra Pradesh, Maharashtra, Jharkhand, Bihar, Uttar Pradesh, and West Bengal. This plan included funding for grass-root economic development projects in Maoist-affected areas, as well as increased special police funding for better containment. In August 2010, after the first full year of implementation of the national IAP program, Karnataka was removed from the list of affected states. In July 2011, the number of Naxal-affected areas was reduced to (figure includes proposed addition of 20 districts) 83 districts across nine states. In December 2011, the government reported that the number of Naxalite-related deaths and injuries nationwide had gone down by nearly 50 percent from 2010 levels.

This was happening when the then Prime Minister was harping constantly on the need for hastening up the development agenda of the government. Ironically, every one remembered and quoted his 2006 observation that Maoists were the greatest threat to the country and its development, no one recalled what he had said in June 2004. He had said, "Development is the master remedy to win over people", adding that the government was "strengthening the development work in the 60 Maoist-affected districts." In September 2009, Dr Singh had admitted that the Maoists had growing appeal among a large section of Indian society, including tribal communities, the rural poor as well as sections of the intelligentsia and the youth. He added that "Dealing with left-wing extremism requires a nuanced strategy – a holistic approach. It cannot be treated simply as a law and order problem." In the first half of 2009, 56 Maoist attacks were reported. The South Asia Terrorism Portal reported 998 killed in the conflict: 392 civilians, 312 security forces and 294 rebels. In 2010, even Home Secretary, Gopal Krishna Pillai had acknowledged that there are legitimate grievances regarding local people's access to forest land and produce and the distribution of benefits from mining and hydro power developments.

In this backdrop, the revelation that Maoists have established a red corridor is beyond comprehension. Shrinking of the base and also depletion of rank and file does not commensurate with the official and media claim that the Maoist red corridor was becoming a potential threat to the security of the country. The trajectory of the Communist Party of India-Maoist (CPI-Maoist) movement demonstrates conflicting trends which gives, great relief to the state.

Since 2010, there has been significant geographical and operational decline of the movement. This has resulted in drop in fatalities, declining incidents of Maoist violence, and a retreat from a number of areas notwithstanding their aim to make new inroads and "extend the people's war throughout the country." In 2008, the ministry of home affairs (MHA) had indicated that a total of 223 districts across 20 states were affected by the Maoist movement. This assessment had dropped to just 182 districts as on October 31, 2011 in 20 states. Data compiled by the South Asia Terrorism Portal (SATP) confirms these broad trends, with total affected districts dropping from 194 in 2008 to just 141 in 2011. Significantly, SATP enumerates just 48 of these districts in the Highly Affected Category in 2011, down from 58 in 2008; another 47 and 46 districts, respectively, were listed in the moderately and marginally affected categories in 2011, as against 54 and 83 districts in these categories in 2008.

Quite significantly, all the states in the red corridor zone have recorded a decline in the number of affected districts, even as reverses have been registered in several of the newer 'extension' areas. Andhra Pradesh which was already on the mend in 2008 has seen the most dramatic recovery, with affected districts down from 22 to 11. SATP data indicates that just two Khammam and Vishakapatnam of the affected districts in the state are currently in the 'highly affected' category. Uttarakhand has seen a drop from 12 affected district to just 4. There is troubling news from the Northeast, with Assam registering a rise from 4 to 10 affected districts; Arunachal Pradesh has one new entrant; and Tripura maintains 2 districts. Haryana, Karnataka, Kerala, Tamil Nadu, Rajasthan and Gujarat, again, lying outside traditional areas of Maoist activity, have registered a decline in the numbers of districts affected. Intelligence sources indicate that the Maoists are exerting particular efforts to set up bases on the tri-junction of Karnataka, Kerala and Tamil Nadu.

From 1,005 Maoist-related fatalities in 2010 according to MHA (1,180 according to SATP), total fatalities in 2011 had dropped sharply to 606. The most significant decline was recorded in West Bengal, which had highest number of incidents and fatalities in 2010. Killings dropped from 258 in 2010 to just 41 in 2011. The spike in fatalities in West Bengal in 2009-10 was the consequence of the alliance of opportunity between the Trinamool Congress (TC) and the Maoists formed to unseat the (CPI-M) Government that ruled the state for the 34 years, before it was routed in the elections of April-May 2011. With the installation of the TC Government in Kolkata, a ceasefire – part of the pre-election deal between the Maoists and the TC – brought violence down to a trickle. However, an upward trend was again visible towards the end of the year, as the deal between the TC and the Maoists collapsed. West Bengal recorded just three Maoist-linked fatalities in 2007, 26 in 2008, and 158 in 2009.

Home Ministry data indicates that even in Chhattisgarh incidents of fatalities have declined. The state recorded 202 fatalities in 2011, down from 343 in 2010. The year 2011 also witnessed decline in incidents in other states: 182 fatalities in Jharkhand; 64 in Bihar, 54 in Maharashtra, and 53 in Odisha. Fatalities in Maoist-related violence dropped from 285 in 2010 to 142 in 2011; while civilian fatalities fell from 720 to 464 over the same period. The number of major incidents (involving three or more fatalities) also registered a significant decline, from 60 such incidents in 2010, to 47 in 2011.

The most significant reverses suffered by the Maoists were in the arrest and killing of their top leadership. While total Maoist fatalities have registered significant declines, from 219 in 2009, through 172 in 2010, to 99 in 2011, the attrition at the top has been devastating. Of the 16-member Politburo of 2007, 2 have been killed, while another 7 are in custody. This has left just Muppala Lakshman Rao alias Ganapathy, the party General Secretary, Prashant Bose alias Kishan Da, Nambala Keshavarao aka Ganganna, Mallojula Venugopal Rao aka Bhupathi, Katakam Sudershan aka Anand, Malla Raji Reddy aka Sathenna and Misir Besra aka Sunirmal, still underground and active out of the Politburo members.

Of the 39 member Central Committee (including the Politburo), 18 have been neutralized – with 5 killed, and 13 in custody. This has weakened the regional, state and district level leaderships, sending the movement into a defensive tailspin. As many as 1,972 Maoists have been arrested in 2011, adding to 2,916 in 2010 and 1,981 in 2009; and another 393 surrendered in 2011, as against 266 in 2010 and 150 in 2009. Significantly, sizeable proportion of top leadership has been neutralized across the country due to the intelligence-based operations led by the Andhra Pradesh Police and, in particular, the State's Special Intelligence Branch.

Meanwhile responses from the Maoist state units have also shifted track. After the Chintalnad incident of April 2010, in which 76 security forces personnel were killed, the 'area domination' approach was discarded, as the disconnect between objectives and capabilities became obvious. The MHA has shifted its rhetoric to a 'holistic' approach emphasising development and the responsibility of the states for 'law and order' operations. The latest thrust has been on 'capacity building' and the 'containment of violence' rather than emphasising on wiping out the Maoists in their areas. The Government intend to involve NGOs through livelihood programme. The emphasis has also been on financial allocations to the states under the Integrated Action Plan. The states have embraced this approach, shifting the emphasis from operational successes and 'kills', to the developmental interventions under 'integrated action plans'. Ironically, evidences from states reveal that implementation of these plans is riddled with corruption and irregularities, and only a tiny proportion of the allocations actually reach intended beneficiaries in the Maoist-affected areas, and at least a significant fraction of these actually flows into Maoist coffers.

Most of the states under the red corridor have increased police recruitment, and have improved police-population ratios. According to the National Crime Records Bureau, the all India average remained at 133 between 2009 and 2010. However, Andhra Pradesh recorded an increase from 128 per 100,000 to 131; Chhattisgarh from 164 to 170; and Jharkhand from 139 to 151. Bihar, with the worst ratio in the country, went up from an abysmal 62 to just 64; and West Bengal, from 93 to 95. Maharashtra actually dropped from 166 to 164; and Odisha from 108 to 106. The Maoists have suffered tremendously as a result of their wrong strategy. The visible decline in a range of parameters of Maoist activities coincides with the effort to recover from the reverses of the recent past. The fatalities in Chhattisgarh were significantly down from 2007. Similarly, Andhra Pradesh, the state with the most Maoist activity a few years ago, has improved security with a corresponding drop in fatality rates. Unfortunately, as conditions have improved in Chhattisgarh and Andhra Pradesh, the Maoist forces seem to have shifted their operations to the state of Odisha where conditions have worsened. South Asia Terrorism Portal's fatality count across the six states that saw the majority of the fighting (Bihar, Odisha, Jharkhand, Maharashtra, Chhattisgarh, and Andhra Pradesh) was 794. This included 399 civilians, 221 security force personnel and 174 insurgents.

Emergence of at least a dozen Maoist splinter groups in Jharkhand is testimony to the fact that the organisation has lost its touch and appeal. Most of the second rank leaders have left the parent organization owing to fundamental ideological and programmetical differences and have floated their own groups. One of them the Tritiya Prastuti Sommittee indeed commands a significant following among the tribals.

The TPC, meaning the Third Preparatory Committee, was formed in 2002 after a number of cadres of the Communist Party of India-Maoist (CPI-Maoist) in Jharkhand walked out of their parent outfit complaining of the domination of the Yadav caste in the decision-making process of CPI-Maoist. The TPC cadres were mostly from the Dalit (downtrodden) Bhokta, Turi, Badai, Oraon, and Ghanju castes. Since its inception, the outfit has indulged in fratricidal clashes with the CPI-Maoist and other Maoist outfits including the Jharkhand Liberation Tigers (JLT). The TPC has declared that its "main enemy is not the police machinery, but the CPI-Maoist."

The TPC has its strongholds primarily in the Latehar, Chatra and Palamu districts of Jharkhand. In July 2007, the outfit's sub-zonal commander of Palamau district, Girijai claimed that the outfit has established units in each of the 22 districts of Jharkhand. The charge of the TPC against the Maoists is: "They have diverted from their original principle and are involved in petty activities. And to successfully wage armed struggle against the Maoists, there is an imperative need to strengthen our own organisation. The results of our expansion would give us positive results in near future."

TPC has been active in Chatra, Gaya, Ramgarh, Latehar, Aurangabad, Palamu, West Singhbhum, Lohardagga and Simdega districts. It has some presence in Kolkata, Howrah and Hooghly districts. Sometime back, the district in-charge Kolkata, Howrah and Hooghly Rabindranath Dasgupta was arrested from Changrabandha in Mekhliganj of Cooch Behar district in West Bengal. The TPC broke away from the Maoists towards the end of 2004 over differences about the merger of the MCC and PW to form the CPI-Maoist. Another major bone of contention was the dominance of Yadavs in Maoist leadership. TPC mainly comprises cadres of Ganju, Oraon and Bhokta communities. The TPC is one among the 12 Maoist groups operating in Jharkhand. A November 2007 assessment by the Jharkhand Police put the cadre strength of the outfit at 70. Extortion from development projects and contractors are the main source of income for the TPC. Coal traders are specifically targeted by the outfit.

Caste element in fact played a major role in Maoist split. Recently, TPC shot dead ten hard core Maoists in Jharkhand. The killings were a result of 'caste war' between the two groups. While the TPC is dominated by Ghanju tribe and people belonging to the Scheduled Caste, the CPI(Maoists) mostly comprises of Yadavs. The two groups have been engaged in turf wars for the past couple of years. There have been regular instances of Maoists killing TPC men. The recent incident was a show of strength by the TPC. The Maoists killed by the TPC were first poisoned and then shot dead from a close range, the official said. In Jharkhand, the CPI(Maoists) is headed by Prashant Bose alias Kishen Da and Arvind. While most of the politburo members or the top 20 cadres of CPI(Maoists) belonged to Andhra Pradesh, these two leaders have started their independent operations in the state.

Disillusioned with the leadership, some of the Maoists have also joined the electoral process as independents. Girija Singh alias Giriji, a former sub-zonal commander of the Tritiya Prastuti Committee (a Maoist breakaway faction), is set to fight it out with Vinod Sharma, an ex-Maoist zonal commander, in Daltonganj. In this matter, some NGOs have also been quite active. Girija has been fielded by Nawjawan Sangarh Morcha led by former minister Bhanu Pratap Shahi. Former Maoist Marshal Turi's wife, Salomi Turi, and Mahadev Ravinath Pahan, brother of Maoist zonal commander Kundan Pahan are also in the fray. Salomi is fighting on a JMM ticket while Mahadev is a JVM-P candidate. Considering their past, police are keeping a close watch on them so that they do not take support from their former organizations. Dissatisfied with extremism, Giriji has decided to join mainstream politics to help the poor. It simply manifest the nature and amount of disillusionment.

Though the Maoists claim to strive for building mass movement and agitations, the truth remains that they have been quite dependent on the gun power and muscle power. Even in small incidents, they resort to use of physical force. Tuku Manjhi described how he was almost beaten to death by Maoist fighters who suspected him of treason: "They did not tell me anything, they grabbed me along with two others and took us away. They had taken my elder brother earlier and tied him up and after that they took me and tied me as well. You can see I still have the rope marks. We were three of us who were beaten, I survived and the others died." Whether it is Jharkhand or Odisha or Chattishgarh most adivasis don't support the Maoists for the cause of creating a communist raj. The poor adivasi does not know anything about Marxism or the Maoist slogan *Lal Qila pe Lal Nishan Mang Raha hai Hindustan*; it is an alien word for them. In fact, most of them even do not know the name of the capital of their states.

In fact, Maoists have forced them to succumb to their authority and follow their dictates. They have been doing this through use of brutal gun power. This has been giving rise to panic and threat of the red corridor. To enforce their rule and authority, the Maoists have been resorting to attacks on the trains or on the JCB machines of the contractors. The offices and equipments of the private companies and contractors are not out of class compulsions attached but to force them to fall in line and abide by their diktat. Significantly, analysts have drawn attention to increasing Maoist attacks on infrastructure. P. Ramana, research fellow at the Delhi-based Institute for Defense Studies and Analyses, pointed out that 62 telecommunication towers were damaged by the Maoists in the states of Andhra Pradesh, Bihar, Chhattisgarh, Jharkhand, Maharashtra and Odisha in from 2005 to 2008, with 43 of these occurring in 2008. These attacks are aimed at disrupting communication amongst the security forces, as well as between 'police informants' – who have been provided cellular telephones – and the security forces. Nevertheless how could Maoists ignore the fact that while security forces have other mode of communication facilities and channels, the common people are the prime user of these towers? Any amount of clarification and explanation cannot exonerate them of the charge of committing injustice and perpetuating crime the common people. The Maoists have also been blowing up power lines and service towers. In May 2007, they blew up three 132 kVA high-tension towers in the Bastar region, plunging six districts into darkness for a week and disrupting normal power distribution for a fortnight. "Functioning of hospitals, communication systems and rail traffic, besides iron ore mines was badly affected," Ramana points out. In June, two 220 KVA towers were blasted depriving 15,000 villages of electricity. These machinations being used by the Maoists to terrorise the common people as well administration, are in fact proving to the counter productive

Quite significantly the Communist Party of India-Maoist, in its September 10, 2014 message to the Milan International Conference in Solidarity with the People's War in India confessed that its earlier assessment, that the 'countrywide movement is facing a very difficult condition' was a correct evaluation of the ground situation. The party, however, expressed confidence to fight back. In the message it mentioned, "We are striving hard for revival of the movement in some of the areas from where we had to retreat. In areas where we have weakened the party is trying to face the situation with Bolshevik spirit."

The message also underlined, "Facing heavy odds and losses, we are opening up a new war front in the Sahyadri (Western Ghats) border region of Karnataka-Kerala-Tamil Nadu." It ought to be mentioned that effort to spread the Maoist movement in the Southern States had miserably failed. The people of the region were not in the mood to repose their trust in the Maoists. Nevertheless, this has not deterred the Maoist from trying.

This move has come to the notice to the Ministry of home affairs which is obvious as the MHA in a six-page letter sent to 13 states in 2013 cautioned, "The CPI-Maoist is trying to develop the tri-junction of Karnataka, Kerala and Tamil Nadu as a suitable operational base." With the view to consolidate their position in Kerala, CPI-Maoist and the

Communist Party of India (Marxist Leninist Naxalbari) merged on May 1, 2014, with the CPI-Maoist. Though they have not carried out any major act of violence in the state, they have been visible around; there is significant evidence of their mobilisation. On September 22, 2014, regional television channels in Kerala showed video clips of CPI-Maoist leader Roopesh, contemplating to launch armed struggle in the state.

In the message to the Milan International Conference, the CPI-Maoist claims: An exceptional contribution of the party is that of arousing the women who are half the sky and developing their capacities in political, organisational, military, cultural and other spheres so that they can lay claim to their share in struggle. Today around 40 percent of the fighting force of the PLGA (People's Liberation Guerrilla Army) consists of women, though the percentage varies in various guerrilla zones. Women are commanders at the platoon level and members of company level party committees. If the media are to be believed while women constituted around 25 percent of Maoist cadres in 2008, this has increased to 40 percent by 2010 and may have risen to 60 percent by the beginning of 2013, with Chhattisgarh leading among the Maoist-hit states.

According to Intelligence Bureau (IB), about 60 percent women cadres were recruited at lower ranks in Maoist camps in the first few months of 2013, while women comprised 50 percent of the 'area and divisional committees' and 25 percent in 'zonal committees'. In Bastar, around 27 'divisional committees' were operating under the 'Dandkaranya Special Zonal Committee', of which at least 20 were being led by women. Even police officers like Deputy Inspector General, R.P. Kalluri, who commanded operations in the Maoist-hit Bastar region in 2013 confessed: "The woman cadres are more brutal and ferocious. We cannot rule out their increasing numbers in the movement in Bastar. We have to psychologically deal with the issue."

Eyewitnesses to the May 25, 2013, Darbha Valley (Bastar District) massacre in which 31 Congress leaders were slaughtered by the Maoists reveal that women cadres played a crucial role. After killing Mahendra Karma, the leader of Salwa Judum, women Maoists had sung and danced near his body. The number of Maoist attacks in which woman cadres played significant roles is long. Earlier women were either recruited to assist men or for ordinary tasks. Now the scenario has changed. With most of the men rebels quitting the movement, it has prompted the Maoist to change their recruitment strategy. They are giving more preference to females.

Sujata who has been active over the past several years in the region, is now said to be heading the Dandakaranya 'state military commission'. Accompanying her are Niti (chief of the north Bastar 'divisional committee'), Madhvi (west Bastar 'divisional committee), and Kosi (Mangler 'area committee'), among a rash of other women operational commanders.

Replying to a question in the Lok Sabha on August 13, 2013, the then minister of state for home affairs, R.P.N. Singh had observed: "In recent incidents of Naxalite attacks, participation of a substantial number of female cadres has been observed. A large number of female cadres have also died in exchanges of fire with the Security Forces."

Despite this increasing operational prominence, it is shocking to learn that allegation are being levelled by some former Maoists that women in Maoist camps are exploited sexually. Women cadres who have surrendered disclose incidents of exploitation by male cadres and leaders. A teenage Maoist cadre, who surrendered on September 11, 2014, alleged that a zonal commander of the 'South Chhotanagpur Division', raped her and threatened to kill her and her mother if she complained: "I moved from one place to another in the forest with top Maoists and cooked for them, along with some adult girls. Sometime in 2013, when I was sleeping alone in one of the camps in Khunti forest, one of the leaders came and raped me. He warned to kill my mother and me if I opened my mouth." Three Maoists, including two women who surrendered on August 25, 2014, in Bastar (Chhattisgarh) stated that they were frustrated due to discrimination and exploitation of lower level cadres and women by senior cadres from Andhra Pradesh.

Tribals, who are the principal subject of the Maoists' 'liberation struggle' in India, have also suffered at the hands of their 'saviours'. Of the 4,955 civilians killed by the Maoists between 2004 and July 15, 2014, an "overwhelming majority are tribals." This was revealed by the Minister of State for Home Affairs Kiren Rijiju in a written reply to Lok Sabha on August 5, 2014.

Though the Maoists claim to recognize their vulnerabilities and mistakes, apparently there is no indication that they have undertaken purification drive even while they celebrate their organisational and operational successes. They accept decimation of their leadership, the "destruction of our urban networks (and) destruction of the infrastructure built up through the collective labour of the masses", but refrain from analysing the reason for the malaise. It would not be exaggeration to say that this step is anti-Maoist. This is the result of over dependence on the strike power and guerilla units of the organizations. Absence of a political commisseur and lack of a sound mass political base often gives rise to such revisionist trends. The Maoists may succeed in setting up their units in Western Ghat but whether they would acquire the character of a liberating force is in doubt. They may exercise their rights on the minerals and nature, but that is not going to usher into revolution.

They ought to remember that the "enemy who was successful in damaging the leadership and cadre in the urban and plain areas is now targeting the leadership in forest areas." The Maoists in their message to Milan also admit "While the tightening blockades, combing and attacks brought out the steel in the vast majority of our ranks, it has also exposed the rotten elements that had remained hidden among us. Liquidationists who pretend that protracted people's war is not suited to our conditions, cowards who flee under different pretexts hopelessly trying to cover up their defeatism, traitors who sell out the people for the pittance thrown to them by the enemy – these trying times have uncovered them, one after the other. Among the masses some have 'surrendered' under enemy brute force. Repeated and heavy attacks have caused great harm to the party structures in the villages and consequently to the RPCs (Revolutionary People's Committees) and mass organisations too. A section of the masses have become passive."

Over the preceding 15 months, moreover, the message concedes, the Maoists' principal efforts have been "to preserve our movement and leadership amid intensified enemy offensive", suggesting a principally approach, though a Tactical Counter-offensive also "destroyed road building equipment, vehicles, guest house and camp offices of the government and the big construction and mining companies."

Despite the enormous reverses of the recent past, the Maoists continue to believe that it can recover and revive the party organization and its 'military capabilities', to inflict eventual defeat on the India state.

Graveyard of Security Personnel

The Indian Air Force is planning a new base near Bhilai in Chhattisgarh. The base could well be the 61st in the country and the newest in Chhattisgarh, which is currently embroiled in a bloody war with Maoist rebels that has left thousands dead mostly paramilitary troops. The last time Chhattisgarh had any kind of base for the armed forces was during World War II, since then, there has been nothing of the nature or magnitude that is currently being contemplated. It is indeed beyond comprehension as the Maoist movement has been on the wane, even conceded by the Central Government, then what is the rationale for large-scale military intervention in the Maoist-infested regions? If it has business and administrative value and importance then the government must clarify. It should not link it to Maoist activity. Interestingly, the IAF has been looking at having an airbase in this part of the country since 2009. The proposed base will have Gwalior in Madhya Pradesh to its north and Nagpur in Maharashtra to its west.

The observation of Dr Michael Kugelman, a scholar and expert on South Asia, is worth mentioning. While he described the Maoists a 'bona fide threat' to India, he also cautioned that since the number and intensity of Communist attacks have decreased in recent years, "I think it's wrong to describe it, as New Delhi does, as India's most serious internal security challenge." Dr Kugelman explained that the Naxalites flourish in India because they exploit the very sharp class divides and economic inequalities most discernable in India's hinterland. "Many tribal peoples in Chhattisgarh and elsewhere in central and eastern India resent how the Indian Government and private corporations engage in heavy resource extractions. These areas of India are so poor and underdeveloped, and that these resource extractions are not shared equitably with locals, helps fuel the insurgency."

According to the 2001 Census, about three-quarters of Dantewada's 1,220 villages are almost wholly tribal; 1,161 have no medical facilities; 214 have no primary school; the literacy rate is 29 percent for men and 14 percent for women. Most of the inhabitants are subsistence farmers eking a meagre cash income from selling forest products such as tendu patta. Markets in the forest have been closed. A big iron mine, Bailadilla, on the edge of the forest, employs few local people. A railway has been built to take the ore to the sea. The government blames the Maoists for blocking development. But the Maoists tell people that roads are intended simply to help the state plunder the forests and take wealth out, not bring it in. Many believe them.

Apart from the CPI(Maoist), which is the focus of official attention, there are other groups whose methods of functioning differ on the extent of mobilisation of the people, role of the armed underground cadre, etc., though they all agree on the need for revolutionary change. Some of them are represented in elected bodies such as panchayats and legislative assemblies. Mass participation in militant protests has always been a feature of Naxalite mobilisation. But the

Maoists have not been giving much credence to it. They believed in the strike power of the gun and which is why they could not make the tribals rally behind them.

Tribal and Scheduled Caste youths of Naxal-infested Malkangiri district showed enthusiastic response towards police constable recruitment drive despite threats and lures of Maoists. This has been happening in spite of Maoists diktat to the tribal and dalit youths of the district not to join the police force. The Maoists had even given the lure that they would provide more money than the police constable's if they joined their People's Liberation Guerilla Army (PLGA). Citing their recent actions, they claimed that they had an upper hand over the police and tribal youths should join them rather than the police force. It is revealed that there were more candidates from Scheduled Tribe and Scheduled Caste community than general candidates. It was a good response as the literacy rate is quite low in Malkangiri district. On July 20 during his visit to Malkangiri district after the landmine blast near a village which had killed 17 policemen, the Chief Minister Naveen Patnaik had declared that around 2,000 local tribal youths would be recruited in Naxal-infested districts of the state.

The CPI (Maoists) have introduced structural changes in their organisation, particularly in forest areas of Jharkhand-Bihar. Formation of East Bihar Eastern Jharkhand Special Area Committee (EBEJSAC) for four districts of Santhal Pargana division including Dumka, Godda, Pakur and Jamtara of Jharkhand and Bhagalpur, Banka, Jamui Lakhisarai and Monghyr of Bihar is a part of the strategy adopted during the fourth-central committee meet of the CPI (Maoists) held in 2013.

The EBEJSAC leaders confess that to establish dominance over areas where the revolution was gaining ground, the party decided to form new special area committee. But the bare fact is the party has failed to live upto the expectations of the people, especially the tribals. There has been a noticeable hatred and revulsion among the tribal peasantry against ruling classes in Santhal region but the

Maoists could not provide a concrete direction to it. Obviously, the question arises why the Maoists failed? The reason is too simple, they failed to mobilize the masses notwithstanding party deciding to dismantle Bihar Jharkhand North Chhattisgarh Special Area Committee (BJNCSAC) to restore the old organisation EBEJSAC with the motto to concentrate upon smaller areas and opt for mass mobilisation. There are potentialities for the movement to advance.

In fact, the resolution adopted at the 4th CC reads, "We should implement the tactics. We should once again mobilize and consolidate the party forces where they had become dispersed; we should strengthen in the areas where we have weakened and we should expand to new areas and spheres basing on this consolidated strength." But their actions do not endorse their resolutions. Soon after reorganisation the Maoists carried out two major attacks in the region; attack on convoy of Pakur SP Amarjeet Balihar in July 2013 in which nine people were killed and a landmine blast during the 2014 Lok Sabha elections in Dumka in which eight people were killed on April 24. Jharkhand police have identified at least six Maoists active in the region which includes Pavitar Da alias Nandlal Manjhi, Pravil Da alias Hirendra Murmu, Shahdeo Ravi alias Tala Da, Kanchan Yadav alias Mota, Daud Hembram alias Vimal Da and Joseph Hansda to be leading the activities in the region. Experts emphasise that the red corridor is simply a hoax and not a real threat. They also allege that the Maoist leaders have been using this to coerce and extort money.

Relying on the statements of surrender Maoists, the government allegis that Maoism has now become an organized business worth ₹ 1500 crore in the form of 'levy'. The CPI(Maoist) and especially its splinter groups hardly pump the money back for running the movement. Instead they use it to maintain luxurious life style. The Naxal literature and documents seized have revealed intricate details of 'levy' extorted by groups which run in several hundred crores every year. The 'levy' is not only paid by the contractors working in the areas but also by the industrial houses. If a conservative estimate is taken of the income generated from 'levy' in the seven most states—Jharkhand, Chhattisgarh, Andhra Pradesh, Odisha, Bihar, West Bengal and Maharashtra—security agencies feel the collection from these areas, which are commonly referred to as 'red corridor', amount to nearly ₹ 1,500 crore.

The Maoists have even come out with a card, which shows the exact amount of 'levy' to be paid by contractors, petrol pump owners and land owners. It usually ranges from 10 percent of the project cost for those making unpaved roads to five percent for small bridges and others. Besides the fixed levy, the left-wing extremists groups also demand money from industries functioning in the areas 'as and when they need' and even issue receipts for the same. Interestingly, it is not just the Maoists who approach contractors for money but in some cases even the contractors approach the Maoists with money.

Sometime back, in fact a senior party functionary Mihir Besra had told police that the CPI-Maoist collected over 10 billion in 2007 through their state committees and had set a target of 11.25 billion for 2008. Available information suggests that, increased levies were imposed on the state committees. Some prominent Maoist leaders such as Andhra Pradesh state committee secretary Konapuri Ilaiah aka Sambashivudu raised over ₹ 80 crore alone and Muppala Lakshman Rao alias Ganapati, the 'general secretary' of the party, raised ₹ 285 crore in 2007, Besra told to the police. He had further revealed that all the leaders operated their own bank accounts, funded their units and operations but reported to the central committee. For collecting the fund, the Maoists target road contractors, forest products (tendu patta, bamboo and wood, etc.) contractors, small and large enterprises such as spinning mills, beedi units, rice and flour mills, grocery, medical and liquor shops and private doctors. They are also coerced to pay to private school operators. Apart from these, the Maoists collect taxes from government officials in rural areas. A senior Maoist leader in the Bihar-Jharkhand area, Narla Ravi Sharma, arrested in Bihar in October 2009, told the authorities that these companies regularly pay the Maoists. Another major source of funding for the Maoists is poppy or opium cultivation. According to the Narcotics Control Bureau in India, the Maoists thrive on money earned through this illicit cultivation. Its 2007 report found out that of the total quantity of marijuana seized in the country, a disproportionately high percentage came from Maoists-controlled pockets in the States of Madhya Pradesh, Maharashtra, Chhattisgarh and Andhra Pradesh.

Maoists collect 10 percent of their total funds from Chhattisgarh. Essar group, and other big companies pay regular levies to the Maoists in the state. Situation of extortion in Jharkhand is worst. From here, the annual collection is nearly ₹ 320 crore, this is 20 percent of total annual budget of CPI(Maoist). Illegal mining is another source of income for Maoists in mineral rich Jharkhand. In Bihar also the Maoists extort roughly ₹ 300 crore every year. The Maoists have a sizeable presence in Gaya, Aurangabad, Rohatas, Kaimur, Arwal, Bhojpur, Munger, Lakhisarai, and Sheikhpura. West Bengal is one of those states where Maoists are effectively active. Here stone crushers, coal businessmen, coal mafias, and government officials are the main target of extortion.

The Maoists spend the funds in various programmes including buying arms. The arrested senior leader Mihir Besra has told the police that the Maoists spend a large amount on procuring weapons, ammunitions and explosives. The Maoist arsenal has almost all kinds of modern weapons including AKs, UMGs, MMGs, LMGs, Picca, Sniper rifles, INSAS, Carbines, SL ₹ 303 rifles.

If officials are to be believed the Maoists spent over ₹ 175 crore in 2007 for purchase of weapons, landmines and rocket launchers. This amount has now been increased and it is over ₹ 200 crore. Vehicles, uniforms and medicines are another major component of expenditure. The Maoists have acquired motor cycles. They also pay monthly salaries to its cadres. The cadres are paid monthly salaries that range from ₹ 2000 to ₹ 3000. The party spend 20 percent of its total funds in cadre's welfare activities such as weddings and other cultural fests. 20 percent goes to treatment of injured cadre. Spokesperson of Madhya Zonal Committee of CPI(Maoist) says treatment of cadre in hospitals is a costly affair. Whenever a cadre got injured in a gunfight, he can't be taken to a nearby health centre. He must be sent outside for treatment. Maoists spend 60 percent of total funds in running the party and procuring arms and ammunitions.

Narla Ravi Sharma, in-charge of Bihar Jharkhand Special Area Committee, arrested in October 2009 revealed that big corporations doing business in Maoist areas are the most important sources of funds for the Maoists. These industries, which are mainly into mining, manufacturing, metals, etc., have only the options of either paying what the Maoists demand or closing their businesses in those areas. The companies give their excuse that the government does not provide adequate security and therefore they have to succumb to Maoist demands. The Maoists blew up the guest house of mining corporation Essar in Malkangiri for the same reason. Abhijit Group, another private company into power generation in Jharkhand, claims that they were attacked and four of their security guards were killed for refusing to pay the Maoists. Jharkhand which contributes the major share to the Maoist exchequer has the bulk of the corporations including Rungta Mines, Usha Martin, Torian Iron & Steel, etc. which have allegedly paid ₹ 25 lakhs each, the Birla Bauxite Company in Palamau which paid ₹ 80 lakhs, Latehar-based Tetaria Mines which has paid ₹ 2 lakhs to the Maoists in 2007-08 and many more. As it happened with Hindalco in Jharkhand, the Maoists even abduct the employees of defaulters.

The arrest of Kanchan, the state committee secretary of CPI(Maoist) revealed that they have a broad urban network in Kolkata and other cities. He revealed that the urban workers stay in rented houses paying upto ₹ 10,000 per month. The party spends a huge fund on propaganda as on conferences and seminars they conduct every month in big cities like Delhi and the numerous Maoist websites and publications.

Wikileaks reported that a leading Indian business house regularly pays money (kind of protection money) to Maoist leaders to safeguard their business interest in the so-called red-corridor. It has been widely reported that the Maoist cadre regularly blow-up infrastructural facilities in the adivasis region. In their zeal for undermining the Indian Government, Maoist fighters have torched construction equipment, bombed government schools and de-railed passenger trains, killing hundreds. In the name of state security, several activists who have supported the Maoists have been jailed and tortured. Innocent people have also been implicated on false charges. These are often intimidation tactics used by the government to discourage people from having any contact with the Maoists.

The uprising by Maoist fighters and its suppression by the Indian Government, has claimed more than 10,000 lives since 1980, and displaced 12 million people. Many of the victims are not even associated with either side. They are simply caught in the crossfire. And the violence is escalating as both sides mount offensive after counter-offensive. If one has to calculate dispassionately, how many adivasis have been killed by Maoists forces or by government forces during last decade or so then the number of adivasis killed by both would be on a very high side. Ashim Chatterjee in an interview to Al Jazeera said: "They are the judges and the executionists who take lives of poor tribals." He lamented that the Maoists have degenerated into "socialism in words and terrorism in deeds."

The Maoists claim to uphold the cause of the tribals and fight for them. But this is not entirely true. It is an open secret that commercialisation and corporatisation of forest resources has reduced the access of tribals to them. Alienation of tribal land and control of it by richer non-tribal elements from outside is a significant factor in tribal unrest. The governments have not willing to accord right to property to the adivasi women. Though displacement due to the construction of large dams and other industries has been going on for decades, no significant effort has been made by the successive governments to rehabilitate the poor tribals. The result is the tribals have tured beggars in their own land. Most of them who migrated to other states have been languishing. No doubt this has strengthened their demand for tribal self-governance.

The most surprising aspect has been the passive attitude of the Maoists. They could have easily built a democratic mass movement on this issue but they did not do so. The reason has been it was a reformist measure. Strange enough. An insight into their political actions would reveal that most of the village development programmes have been basically reformist in content and character. There is no denying the fact that the Maoists have never been serious to the tribal question and problem.

B. Mungekar, member, Planning Commission, has prepared a report showing that between 1951 and 1990, 40 million people were displaced as a result of development projects. Of these, 40 percent were tribal people. Only 25 percent of the displaced have so far been 'rehabilitated'. The adequacy and quality of the rehabilitation has come into serious question especially in the context of the controversy over the Sardar Sarovar Project. In the light of this, it is not surprising that the Maoist have found support among a section of tribals who became victims of development.

The conflict between economic progress and aboriginal land rights continues to fuel the Maoist activities. Their strongest bases are in the poorest areas of India. They are concentrated on the tribal belt such as West Bengal, Odisha, and Andhra Pradesh where locals experience forced acquisition of their land for developmental projects. The alienation that is being exploited by the Maoists has a social, communal and regional dimension. The battle can also be described between India's most neglected people and the nation's most powerful industrial businesses. The adivasis make up about 8.4 percent of the population and live in severe poverty. They live in remote areas where government administration is weak and there is a lack of government services. These indigenous people have the lowest literacy rates in the country and highest rates of infant mortality.

Dearth of Future Leaders

It is a paradox that in spite of having the image of a militant fighter and emancipator of the poor, the Maoists are not getting fresh recruits. The party badly suffers due to utter lack of youth leaders. It has to depend on the old and aged hands. With a large number of senior leaders either eliminated by the police or are in jails or have surrendered, the party is being run by a skeleton leadership. This certainly does not go well with the claim of the party that it has launched protracted war. For guiding a protracted war, it is imperative that the party ought to have a strong and dedicated band of second leaders. There is no denying the fact that the Maoists are facing acute dearth of second-rank leadership. The youths from the tribal community or from the rural poor families are unwilling to join them. The CPI(Maoist) is really in a precarious condition. With unable to motivate the tribal youths and other extremely poor section to join them, the organization is stagnating notwithstanding their claim of spreading the protracted war zone. The Naxalites whether it was CPI(ML) Liberation or other group never had this problem. Ironically, the Maoists are in a vulnerable position with recruitment of cadres having gone down significantly in the recent years. Their popularity among the tribals and poor rural people has also hit low.

According to some stray reports, some youths from Tinsukia, Dibrugarh and Sivasagar districts of Upper Assam, who had gone outside the state for employment, might have joined the Maoists for financial gains. Young people from Jharkhand, Bihar and Odisha are getting caught up in the Maoist insurgency for financial rather than ideological reasons. In spite of suffering at the hands of the government officials and middlemen, these youths are not getting attracted in large numbers to the Maoists, which should have been the only course in normal manner. These youths instead have opted to migrate and do some petty work to sustain their families. The paramilitary forces have been trying to recruit these youths but they too not have succeeded to that extent. There is a lingering suspicion in the minds of these youths towards the security forces. After clearing his tenth standard school leaving board exam two years ago, Swapan Murmu, a boy from the Santhal tribe, began doing farm jobs to help his family.

The village of Madhupur, where he lives, is tucked away at the end of a 6 km, unpaved road in a remote corner of West Bengal's West Midnapore district. Swapan is one of a few dozen tribal boys who have been working odd jobs since leaving their school-level studies or dropping out of college. Madhupur is well known to anti-insurgency force commanders of the region. Some underground Maoist guerrillas hail from the village, and security forces have raided it many times in recent years, looking for them. A few days later, some 15 boys from Madhupur, including Swapan, turned up at the nearby CRPF camp and said they were interested to take the test. The government jobs will open avenues of sustainable livelihood for the youths. If the tribal boys find that it's not difficult for them to get government jobs, Maoists call will fail to have any impact on them. Most tribal youths join the Maoists primarily for financial reasons, and not for ideological understanding or commitment. Maoists have also been advising the tribal and also Nepali youths not to join the security force and wage a war against their own persons.

After their previous setback, the Maoists have been trying to regroup in Jangalmahal in West Bengal. This time the youths of the villages in the region are at their focus. Reports suggest that Maoists are attempting to replenish their cadres by visiting villages in West Bengal. They have been urging the youth from the forest areas to join their squads. For making them join, they have been narrating how the Trinmool failed to live upto its assurances and promises made to the tribals. They are coming down from hills and moving from door to door. Small groups are fanning out to remote areas to interact with youths to 'share their pain', an activity not witnessed since the death of their leader Kishenji. TMC panchayat and block level leaders who had fought against Maoists in the past are the focus of attacks. Despite their efforts, the Maoists have failed to get a positive response to their appeal from the youths of the region.

Maoists believe in Mao Zedong theory of "political power comes from the barrel of the gun." But, for the Indian Maoists, the guns have lost their charm. They are more dependent on explosives and bombs. But this is their compulsion. In the past, they used to loot the police armory and get guns from other sources. But now this avenue is closed. DG CRPF Dilip Trivedi is on record: "In the past couple of years, Maoists have not been able to loot weapons from the police station or armoury. Many of their arms and ammunition manufacturing units have also been neutralized by the security forces. Thus has led to top brass passing order and instructions to cadres to use explosives and bombs instead of looking for guns."

Most of the setbacks the Maoists received in the recent past have been primarily due to the absence of a strong second line of leadership. Just a day after the Chhattisgarh Chief Minister, Raman Singh, assured the delegation of National Security Advisory Board (NSAB), "The day is not far when Chhattisgarh will become Naxal-free, thanks to the joint efforts of State Government and Centre in wiping out the Maoist menace," the Maoists struck back killing 14 Central Reserve Police Force (CRPF) personnel, including two officers, in Sukma district of Chhattisgarh on December 1, 2014. At least 15 personnel have been injured – five are reported to be in a serious condition. The incident took place deep in the forest, around 10 km southwest of the last police camp at Chintagufa. The security forces were inside the forest for an operation when the Maoists ambushed them. This speaks of the dare devilry of the Maoists. They were not scared of the presence of huge team of over 550 CRPF and state personnel in the surrounding areas. The incident took place in the same region where seven personnel were injured by Maoist just a week back. The attack has come at a time when Chhattisgarh has been claiming record Naxal surrenders in the last six months. When he was sworn-in as Chief Minister of Chhattisgarh for the third time in December 2013, Raman Singh vowed that his government would sternly deal with the Left-wing extremism and uproot it. Incidentally, the number of security personnel, policemen and civilians who have been killed since then has risen. In more than half a dozen attacks between February and March of 2014, the Maoists have already killed 22 security personnel and civilians. Sukma is considered to be a 'liberated zone'. Surprisingly, the forces have rarely been able to venture into this area. It is beyond comprehension why the security forces have failed to curb the Maoist activities in this zone. On 25 May 2013, Maoists attacked a convoy of Indian National Congress leaders in the Darbha Valley under Sukma in which at least 27 leaders and common people, including that of former state minister Mahendra Karma and Chhattisgarh Congress chief Nand Kumar Patel were killed. Vidya Charan Shukla, a senior Congress leader also later succumbed to his injuries. In the police parlance, Sukma is a part of the 'red corridor', the belt affected by the Maoist insurgency. This region has been under continuous attack by the Maoists, who have been targeting police personnel and political leaders.

The then Union Home Minister P. Chidambaram had proposed to carry out counter offensive in the entire Bastar region but had to call off because of opposition from party leaders including Digvijaya Singh and some members of the National Advisory Council headed by Sonia Gandhi. The latest incident makes it explicit that the police administration has failed to take lessons from the last year's murderous attack. The attack has come at a time when Chhattisgarh has been citing record Naxal surrenders in the last six months. Probably, the main motto behind this action of the Maoists was to celebrate the foundation day of their guerilla army. The attack was carried out a day before the People's Liberation of Guerrilla Army of the CPI(Maoist) was set to begin its foundation week, from December 2-8. The reiteration of the Union Home Minister Rajnath Singh, "It is a challenge for the country. I am personally hurt by this incident," is not enough. One thing is also clear that the security forces are finding it tough to challenge their supremacy. After last year's massacre the CRPF did not evolve a concrete action plan to counter them. In this background, the government should intensify the socio-economic programmes for the empowerment of the tribals and poor people of the zone. This is the only tenable way out to fight the Maoist.

Paradoxically, the party leadership never tried to cultivate and build the second line of leadership. Interestingly, some who were there with the party till a couple of years back have now left it to float their own organization or returned to the mainstream life. Undeniably, they are on the backfoot. They even did not launch their counter-offensive actions against the security forces. This they have been doing every year during the months of January to June. The success of the security forces in their operations against the Maoists also owes to the fact that there is no second-rank leadership to challenge and counter security offensive.

In recent years the younger people across the country tend to keep away from the left political parties and the political spectrum. This is in sharp contrast to what was seen in seventies and even in early nineties. Youths of today are socially more progressive, and are looking for an activist government. Unlike the youth of early decades, today's youth support social spending and they are in favour of higher taxes if it means better public services. They desire to have an active participation in the power dynamics.

In 1991 when Laloo Yadav took to fighting against the hegemony of the feudal and upper caste people, the youths of the backward castes were at the forefront of the movement. They rallied behind him. These youths responded to Laloo's call only on the lines of the caste affinity and identification. Even during those years, the Left parties utterly failed to entice and enroll this huge population of the youths. It is worth recalling that the hard core Naxalite belonging to the Yadav caste elected to the state assembly on the ticket of the CPI(ML) switched their political allegiance and loyalty to Lalu and joined his RJD since it represented the power dynamics of the Yadav caste.

This simply manifested the end of the Indian youths Romance with Communism. The youth have come to nurse the opinion that the communism has lost relevance in the post-liberalization era. Maoists at their recent Congress emphasized to reach out to the youths. The party utterly lacks new blood and young faces. Maoists ought to do serious introspection as to why the youths were not willing to join them. It is historically correct that youths were the main force for the left in India. The roots of the communist movement in India go back to 1920's when Communist Party of India was founded as an alternative to the existing Congress-led anti-imperialist movement. The movement was angst-driven against the economic injustice of the rich and wealthy class.

The youths lapped up the new idea of change and power dynamics. What is the reason that the Maoists fail to attract them? In trying to bring about radical change, the idea missed the opportunity of changing things at the margin. The disillusionment of the youths also owes to failure of the communist in enforcing a revolution. Thousands of youths sacrificed their lives, they were either killed by the police or by the private goons. The left leaders in fact betrayed these youths by not spear heading the movement on the correct political line.

Roots of Communism persisted only in Kerala and Bengal, where aspirations of the youths matched with the ideologies of the Left. Ironically even in these states the left parties have lost support of the youths. In Bengal the youths have preferred to rally behind Mamata Banerjee or BJP. The primary reason is again the same; youths perceive these organisations as the symbol of the power dynamics.

Yet another factor that ought to be mentioned is the youths of the bourgeoning middle class are not inclined to lose their economic gains and comfort life by embracing the ultra left. They have learned the futility of aligning with them. Eminent left intellectual Prabhat Patnaik felt that the appeal of the Communist movement among the youth and society at large had waned, and identified three factors that contributed to it; "One is the ploy of neo-liberalism supporters to direct the failings of the system towards a person or a political party instead of the basic idea itself. For instance, the huge corruption and mis-governance by the UPA is projected as the incompetence of either prime minister Manmohan Singh or that of the dynasty of the Congress". Secondly, unlike in the past, today's agitated youth have to face many issues. This is a major factor that contributed to the lack of interest among the youths in the Communist movement in the country. Finally the Communists should understand that they could still build a social revolution in a country that long had had been mired in social evils like caste system. No doubt some parties are emerging from social movements, it is only that the Left parties can convince people that they alone can provide space for both social movement and power dynamics, be a governing option.

The elections in India have been a sort of manifestation of the social protest against the failure of the party in power. The left parties, unfortunately, could not accomplish the task of channelizing this mood of the people. The reason is the left, particularly the Maoist and Naxalite, leaders failed to connect with the common people. After Charu Majumdar, it was Vinod Mishra, general secretary of the CPI(ML) who could articulate the feelings of the people and connect with them. The IPF could win a number of seats in the state assemblies, or even the parliament due to this factor. Why did the Left parties, particularly the Naxalites fail to get those votes? It is a mistake to narrow down the answer to just one reason. But it must be remembered that the Left's thrust are not especially popular today.

The left has also failed to provide a platform to those who are actively looking for a party, who want parties to be relevant to their lives and to the power dynamics. Little doubt that India's communists are not losing their touch with the people, and the fast changing world around them. Have not people stopped believing them?

Somewhere down the line in a fast-changing world, the communists, the Naxalites and the Maoists have begun losing their way. After the first wave of farm reforms exhausted its potential, they needed fresh ideas. This has become more imperative in the background when the government resorted to cut back on spending, and private capital was touted as the main driver of growth and jobs. Land reforms had run short of fresh ideas; it has remained a mere rhetoric and farm produce prices are falling. Like the urban middle class, the peasants now also aspire for better lives.

With the growing influences of market forces in the national economy and increasing competition between states to attract private capital, the communists are in state of confusion to match its anti-corporate, anti-globalisation rhetoric with the practice of competitive federalism. People prefer to repose their trust in the regional parties. The decline of the communists possibly means that the "party-society" is now unraveling. Nevertheless, functioning in a democracy, the Communist Parties have resembled like social democrats with Stalinist tendencies.

□

2

Oasis of Junglemahal

History of modern revolutions is replete with evidences that political violence focused on seizure of state power alone is ultimately harmful for toiling masses. It makes people passive. Revolutionary terror always devoured its own children when the minority tried to impose their will and vision of change. French and Russian Revolutions are replete with such examples.

The extent of physical violence needed in the destruction of the old state and its socio-political props depend on the response of the state, its armed forces and private armies of its stakeholders. In India, the revolution is yet to come to that stage where the need for the subjective mobilization of revolutionary forces should be defined. The defining aspects of a revolutionary party should not be its military muscle but ideological and political appeals and synergy with the masses. Nevertheless, the revolutionary groups which have been active are reluctant to take lessons from the past and continue to behave in a manner which is not in conformity to the Marxist-Leninist or Maoist doctrine.

A revolutionary party must strive to practise non-coercive methods to achieve hegemony on public opinion. Unfortunately during the 50 years of the Naxalite movement, what we have seen is the use of coercive tactics in the name of furthering class struggle. In recent times, this is being practised by the CPI(Maoists) in the States of Andhra Pradesh, Jharkhand, West Bengal, Chhattisgarh and in Odisha. The leadership of the party has forgotten that innovative and sustained moves will ensure popular mobilization of revolutionary classes and masses and also a clear mechanism for people's control on the revolutionary party and its army.

In Indian situation, the revolutionaries are not interested in convergence of the old and new, instead they intend to perpetrate their diktats through guns. For them old has lost its relevance; it is obsolete. Had it not been the case, the Maoists should have taken lessons from the old struggles. This convergence provides the opportunity to look at the degree of development and ought to be done to achieve the desired goal: It struggles for power and creates alternative structures.

The revolutionary forces must realise and also understand that the seizure of power alone can't ensure revolutionary transformation of a bourgeoisie state into a people's state. Revolutionary states also faced blockades and subversion from the global capital and compromised in many situations like their nationalist and state socialist variations. Like other post-colonial states, they too need capital for industrialization and social sector spending. They ought to remember that in the age of liberalization and globalization and where the reforms are the guiding motivation for economic resurgence this is bound to have its impact on the decision-making process even at the lowest level of the administration. The Union Government has already implemented a number of reform programmes. The Lok Sabha election of 2014 makes it explicit that urban middle class which strives to shape the future polity has decisively voted for reforms. Though still 70 per cent of the population is dependout on agriculture, the 30 per cent urban middle class managed to change the political contour of India. In this background, any communist party or revolutionary group aspiring to bring about revolution must be well versed with the implications and nuances of the mechanism of reforms and also understand the intensity of the impact comprehensively and then decide to evolve its own set of radical programmes.

The manner in which the Maoists have been behaving and operating in their so-called base areas simply gives the impression that they have ignored these home truths. Their lack of respect for those who 'differ' and their 'intolerance' to criticism, which also manifest their 'political weaknesses', stem from their refusal to accept the revolutionary problem and think over them.

No doubt, the CPI(Maoist) as the inheritor of Naxalite 'spiritual legacy' have earned people's respect for their sacrifice, devotions and commitment to the poorest of the poor and oppressed, but their reckless violence and killing of innocent people has made them suspect in the eyes of even sympathizers about their ideological commitment and political honesty. The Naxalite movement's moral appeal in the society has been much larger than collective political impact and much lesser organizational presence. But there is no denying the fact that of late due to the whimsical killings, even the people travelling in the trains, the innocent people, by the Maoists has lowered this moral appeal. People now look at the Maoists, with element of suspicion and disdain. They do not differentiate between Naxalite and Maoist, for them every one is Naxalite and the movement gains a bad name.

Maoists are credited with catapulting the issue of tribal dispossessions at the political centre-stage of Indian developmental discourse and gaining widespread support from these most oppressed communities but this is not the whole truth. In fact, the CPI(ML) ever since its inception in 1967 has been laying extra stress on mobilising the tribals and working amongst them. Most of the senior leaders had spent long years working amongst them. Despite this claim, the fact remains that they have no noteworthy base among working class, large section of urban poor and middle class, dalits and minorities. If the leadership thinks that the party's political-social isolation as well as its absence in rest of the country can be undone only through the extension of the areas of armed struggle and supportive urban infiltration, they are horribly mistaken.

Asim Chatterjee, one of the founders of the CPI(ML), also holds the view that the Maoists are not pursuing the right line. He mentioned that "The present-day development of the political scenario in Junglemahal is astonishing. That the Maoists are facing severe setbacks is no secret. The Maoists have lost their mass base and are actually on the run. The loss of Kishenji is a clear pointer to this disaster. One may wonder over the real reason for this debacle. Some think that this disaster denotes the success of the operations of the joint forces deployed in Junglemahal. The real reason however for this disaster lies with the Maoists. The Maoists themselves are responsible for it. Deviations inherent in the political line pursued by the Maoists are the real factors. The correctness or incorrectness of the political line decides the fate of any struggle. What are the deviations? Long ago many, including myself, pointed out these deviations."

The deviations could be categorised: First, over-dependence on modern weapons. Arms, no doubt, are necessary, but over-dependence on arms leads to non-reliance on the people. Significant Mao had pointed out that revolutionary war is the war of the masses. A revolutionary war can only survive by unleashing the initiative, activity and creativity of the masses. Second, over-dependence on the forest terrain. The question of the terrain is, no doubt, important, but its role is never determining. Third, establishment of party hegemony by force over mass organization. One can cite the case of People's Committee against Police Atrocities or PCPA of Junglemahal as an instance. PCPA initially was a vibrant organization consisting of different groups and parties opposed to police atrocities in which Maoists were the only armed group. The Maoists later drove out all other parties. As a result, PCPA became a rubber stamp organization of the Maoists, in the process PCPA lost the effectiveness in mobilizing the people. Experience shows that whenever revolutionary war degenerates into a war of party supremacy instead of war of the masses, it becomes suicidal for the war as well as for the party. Fourth, in the name of the fighting revisionism, the Maoists carried out annihilation of lower-rank CPI(M) cadres and supporters, mostly poor tribal peasants. The fight against revisionism is a political struggle and not a military war. The culture of seeking a military solution for any contradiction among people is self-defeating and suicidal. Fifth, there was weakness in their approach to the class question. Maoists often ignored the class question, as it became evident from the class analysis of the victims of their execution. Most of them were poor people who had been executed according to the verdict of the kangaroo courts where the Maoists played the role of prosecutor, judge and executioner.

Little doubt Maoists have inherited this. The PWG or CPI (Party Unity) before their merger and floating of CPI(Maoists) believed in indiscriminate use of violence and killings. They, in the first stage, had started targeting the cadres of the CPI(ML) Liberation in Patna, Gaya, Jehanabad and Aurangabad districts of Bihar. Due to this armed policy of the PWG or Party Unity, the movement in fact lost a number of good cadres. After formation of the Maoist party, the cadres and workers are finding it hard to abandon their past habit and they still continue to practise the same policy of giving credence to armed action over political action. In fact, the mindset of the Maoist rank and file has been framed in such a manner that does not understand any alternate or new experiment. A communist revolutionary ought not to forget that armed struggle is the product of development of class struggle. Maoist talk of flexibility and openness to friendly criticism are largely tactical and unconvincing. In fact, they share the CPM's big brotherly arrogance. All gestures of openness end whenever others question their claims to the leadership of left and democratic forces. But experiences showed that communists' intolerance had been the worst stumbling bloc for any genuine, broad-based and united peoples' movements.

Maoist leadership is yet to show any signs of change in the percepts and practices. Recently, six jailed members of the CPI(Maoist) politburo and central committee have identified the fight against the nexus of Indian neo-liberal elite and imperialists as the uppermost task and appealed to party's critics in people's movements for reciprocal tolerance and recognition as well as broad unity of all resistance forces. But so far it is not clear whether the top party leadership outside jail endorsed the call and moved in that direction.

Rectification drive is the key to survival of a communist party. Even the communist parties of Russia and China used this mechanism to cleanse the party. But it appears that the rectification programme has lost meaning as well as relevance for the Maoists, though they officially conduct rectification programme. It is really surprising even after this how could they continue to commit the same mistake years after years? It was in 1972, while Charu Majumdar was still alive that the issue of selective annihilation was raised and a general opinion prevailed in the party that peoples' mass movement should precede any such armed action. As mentioned earlier even leader like Asim Chatterjee had criticised this tendency.

A closer look at the armed actions of the Maoists would make it abundantly clear that they resorted to indiscriminate killings not for ideological compulsions but to satisfy the ego of their trigger hungry leadership. Maoists' new circular on rectification points out:

(a) In some areas, the lands occupied from the landlords in the past are lying fallow due to government repression; when the landlords try to sell these lands, the rich peasants and middle peasants are purchasing them. On such occasions, instead of bringing pressure through the agricultural labourers and poor peasants, who occupied those lands, on those who purchased the lands and stopping the sale, the squads themselves have been thrashing the rich and middle peasants who purchased the lands.

(b) In the struggle for eradication of the bad habits like liquor consumption educating the people with a long-term view is lacking in the struggle to obstruct the manufacture of arrack, instead of rallying the people, especially the women, prominence is being given to squad actions only. Physical punishments are being imposed disregarding class basis.

(c) When problems arise in man-woman relations, especially in matters relating to marriage, judgments are being given without taking into view the social problems women face.

(d) In various kinds of peoples' panchayats instead of listening to the versions of both sides apart from gathering the needed information from others in the village also, one-sided judgements are delivered under the effect of sectarianism.

(e) When some among the people commit mistakes when they oppose the mass organizations, on whom they are suspected to be working as informers, punishment much beyond their wrongs are being imposed.

This circular on rectification was issued by a Maoist committee in Dandakaranya. It provides ample indication that the leadership did not prefer to take political action. There are many other aspects which are not incorporated herein. The squad members behave like gods and every thing of the areas should be at their command. The firepower has made the cadres mercenaries. Squads have progressed to platoons and companies and now they are talking of raising battalion. It is intriguing how could the political commissenar allow this to happen? It obviously implied that the Maoists have a very fragile political institution. It is encouraging to note that in recent times the Dandakarnya unit of the Maoists has been laying considerable emphasis on political initiative and the situation has undergone a major change. But it is intriguing why did the Maoists' leadership experiment with the success story in other states? They have left these states to the armed squads to act in whimsical manner.

The most interesting development in recent years has been drawing a dividing line by the Maoists between Maoism and Marxism-Leninism (M-L). While the state machinery applies a single yardstick to club them together, Maoists are unwilling to accept M-L as a revolutionary outfit. While Mao

Zedong believed in and propagated Marxist-Leninist theory and described his own ideology as Mao Zedong's Thought, the Indian Maoists have projected Mao Zedong's Thought as Maoism. They try to distance from Marxism-Leninism. Most of the recent actions are in fact part of the strategy to reinforce the supremacy of their line.

Notwithstanding Maoists flexing their muscle and armed power, the fact remains the movement lacks mature leadership who can look beyond and find out the reason for dilution of the difference between the productive forces and the production relations. Since this polemics is not clear to the rank and file, they primarily prefer to indulge in killing the innocent. Only in some areas where the individual political leadership has been strong, as has been the case in Dandakaranya that the squads could be put under some check and fundamental mass movement-oriented programmes be undertaken. Maoists have not succeeded to put a check on in Andhra Pradesh, their stronghold.

The situation in Bengal, Bihar and Jharkhand has been worse. The border areas of these three states have been the hot bed of the Maoists activities. But the fact remains that the leadership has failed to build a popular mass movement. What they have been doing in the name of keeping aloft the revolutionary flag is to blow train, railway bridges, schools and kill innocent people. What is worse is the Maoists operations in these areas have been taking place on the caste line. The Maoists leadership is badly divided on Yadav-Mahato caste line. Yadav belonged to erstwhile MCC. They are primarily confined to Gaya, Aurangabad and Jehanabad areas of Bihar.

Significantly, the Nitish Kumar Government's 'Shikaria Model', a mechanism to bring back the Maoists into the mainstream has caught the imagination of the Maoists. Shikaria, a village in Jehanabad, the region which witnessed worst massacres in seventies and eighties between Naxalites and Ranavir Sena, is the birthplace of MKSS which had launched the revolutionary movement for change. After coming to power, Nitish ensured participation of Maoist in the utilisation of Development fund. They were to identify the priorities and undertake the development. The Naxalite who used to collect levies from local bigwigs started getting the funds from the government. Close relatives of the Naxalites performed the task of contractors. During last seven years, the region has not witnessed any significant action. They are also using this money to finance their operations in other places.

In its message to the People of Lalgarh, the Maoist on June 15, 2009 had hailed the annihilation of the poor people of the area on the plea of being class enemies. It said we hail your glorious struggle as your mass upsurge inspires millions to spread the red flame of Lalgarh to every corner of the country. Interestingly, the people of Bengal who had been witness to Naxalbari uprising of sixties did not see any uprising in 2009. Nevertheless, the message read: "Your revolt, with arms in hands, has risen like a storm against decades of social fascist neglect, misrule and terror. You have stormed the police camps, CPM offices – the centres of state terror – and chased them out of the area. For over seven months you and your comrades from the surrounding areas have practically paralysed the whole administration in a vast region. Not only that, while exposing the hoax of so-called development of three decades of the social-fascists, you have yourselves undertaken numerous development works through *shramdan*, like health projects, irrigation, roads, schools, etc. It is indeed an inspiring example of new forms of struggle for all of us to learn from resulting in the call to build thousands of Lalgarhs in every corner of the country!"

It further read: "Terrorised by your mass upheaval, the central and state forces, along with the *Harmad bahini goonda* force of the social fascists, have launched massive attacks on the entire people of your area. With wide-scale anti-propaganda the government turned your area into a war zone. Armed people, with traditional weapons, have heroically resisted the attack launched by 40 companies of central para-military forces, the special forces of the Cobras, Helicopters, along with State forces and the CPM *goonda bahini.*

"It is known to all that there was resentment of the people against the handing over of 4,000 acres of forest land to the Jindal plant, on which it is you and you alone that have the rights. It is you, the villagers of the area, who alone have the rights over this land, and not the government. After the attack on the convoy of the Chief Minister and others while returning from the inauguration of this plant and the terror then unleashed by the police, your movement took a political shape with thousand and thousand of masses mobilised against the police and administration. Along with the heroic mass resistance against the police and para-military attacks, this mass upsurge has created a big political impact over the entire country arousing a hope and inspiration amongst the toiling masses fighting against all kinds of exploitation, repression and injustice. This has had the added political impact to thoroughly expose the social fascist face of the CPM revisionists and accelerated the process of polarisation of the forces of revolution and reaction.

"The Politburo of the CPI(Maoist) hails your glorious mass uprising and strongly condemns the cruel repression unleashed on the masses in your area by the central and state forces. It calls on the whole Party and PLGA, its mass organisations and each and every section of the revolutionary masses, to come forward in support of your movement and rise against the brutal attack on the struggling and fighting people of Lalgarh. We further call on the Party and people in the surrounding areas to take proper actions and conduct necessary activities in support of your great uprising. We vow to lend you all support in every possible way, particularly the support of the oppressed masses throughout the country.

"The most significant aspects of the struggle from which we can all learn and emulate throughout the country are:

(i) Yours was a truly armed mass movement which drew into it the entire masses of the area with the ability to keep out the entire reactionary state machinery for a full seven months.

(ii) Your form of mass organisation of constituting a committee in every village comprising five men and five women was a truly new example of a real mass-based democratic organisation which can mobilise and organise the vast masses of the people.

(iii) Yours was not a movement for mere economic interests but a political upsurge for your political rights and self-respect of the adivasi and non-adivasi toiling masses.

(iv) Your movement was an example of how to truly build a united front of all forces drawing in all sections of the masses and also involving the progressive and intellectual forces of the cities as well, combining a skilful balance between reform work, political agitation and armed resistance against the state and government.

"Comrades, our entire Party will learn from this heroic experience, vow to spread Lalgarh-type movements throughout the country, propagate your movement throughout the country and lend your movement all kinds of necessary assistance."

The deviation of the rank and file in Jharkhand region has been underlined in a report carried by the *People's March* in the issue of October 2005-September 2005. The report indicts certain practices followed by the Maoists in Jharkhand. It reads: In recent years large-scale relief and reform programmes launched by the government have created a huge battery of contractors and middlemen in the rural area. They are the social basis of various groups of ruling class parties. Locally, they maintain links with organizers (comrades at zone and even higher levels), appease them assure block officials and engineers that they can manage the new government and get hold of contracts. During the polls, these are the elements who wean away people to polling stations. That relation with such type of contractors has been maintained by party organisers is a matter of concern. Some of our comrades use such contractors not only for various works but also for the most secret work of the party and they also share their joys and sorrows. The tiffs between contractors over this or that contract has become a cause for contradiction between our cadres. For example in Chatra the so-called contradiction between Yadavs and Ganjhus is not a contradiction between toiling masses of these two castes, but between contractors and middlemen of these two castes."

The Naxalites – or 'Maoists' as they have now come to be described – have the explicit aim of establishing a 'people's democratic state under the leadership of the proletariat', which requires 'smashing the reactionary autocratic state'. The party programme of the Communist Party of India (Maoist) goes on: This new democratic state will be the people's democratic dictatorship exercised by the united front comprising the proletariat, peasantry, petty-bourgeoisie and the national bourgeoisie class under the leadership of the proletariat based upon the worker-peasant alliance. The state will guarantee real democracy for the vast majority of people while exercising dictatorship over the tiny minority of exploiters. The Maoists argue that the pursuit of parliamentary democracy is an exercise in futility and explain the necessity for armed struggle against the present 'reactionary autocratic state' given the strength of its armed machinery.

The Lalgarh area of West Medinipur in West Bengal, came to international attention when a massive police action began there (on 18-19 June 2009). It was recognised that Lalgarh had experienced an insurrection against the Left Front Government of the state and the region was described as a 'Maoist-run state within the state'. Inevitably, the Government of West Bengal sought to re-establish its authority over the area and called upon the assistance of the paramilitary forces of the Central Government in order to do so. But, was there 'a Maoist-run state' in Lalgarh?

Maoists' secret terror operations often make the people suspect them. They express total indifference to human lives, their arms deals lead them, inevitably, into shady transactions with corrupt power brokers. They engage in a killing spree, discredit the independent tribal movement, and then they leave, after giving the state authorities a splendid excuse for crushing it.

The Maoists have been at the helm of the movement in Lalgarh right from its inception. Even as they organised the resistance to state repression, they placed forward an alternative programme of development based on the people's initiative and their voluntary labour. So, what was going on in Lalgarh? Lalgarh is a forested, hill area in the Jungalmahal of West Bengal that extends to Jharkhand. It is an area of small landholdings and of poor, rainfed agriculture. The major source of income is from collection of saal leaves (for making leaf-plates) in the forests, an activity carried on by women. According to the report of the All-India Fact Finding Team of April 2009, 'The area had a history of neglect and discrimination. The landscape of bleak wretchedness is dominated by the bizarre splendour of the party offices of the Communist Party of India (Marxist) [CPI(M)] and the houses of local party leaders.'

On 2 November, there was a mine explosion near Medinipur town while the then West Bengal Chief Minister Buddhadeb Bhattacharya and the then Union minister Ram Vilas Paswan were returning from the inauguration of a steel works. The circumstances of the blast remain mysterious, but it was immediately followed by reprisals by the state police, accompanied by armed CPI(M) volunteers, targetting villagers in Lalgarh for harbouring Maoists. The police actions were so brutal that it spontaneously forced the people to resort to mass movement against the police repression.

Pulish Santrash Birodhi Janasadharanar Committee (PSBJC or People's Committee Against Police Atrocities [PCAPA]) resolved to keep the police and state administration out of their area. On 6 November 2008, the PSBJC began setting up road blocks and barricades, and thereafter successfully held government forces at bay for six months. During these months, the activists implemented livelihood and welfare programmes, including some minor irrigation projects and the establishment of primary healthcare centres.

But unfortunately the PSBJC's spokesman and leader, Chhatradhar Mahato, was branded a 'Maoist', though he was associated with the Trinamul Congress. The PSBJC movement had a democratic character, and included women.

Maoist general secretary Ganapathy strongly argued that they did not 'derail' a popular movement but 'showed it the way' and pioneered the alternative path of development with which people in Lalgarh were experimenting before the crackdown. Ganapathy says: "The Lalgarh story illustrates, I think, major questions about the Maoist movement. There is no doubt of the connection between the Maoists and the people living in marginal hill and forest areas who have gained little if anything from government programmes and who have often suffered from repressive acts by state functionaries."

The chances of land reforms being carried out in India by intervention from above now seem remote as there is no significant pressure for reforms from below in the major agricultural regions of the country. Moreover, the major left parties have chosen not to focus on marginal areas where the land issue is still alive. The Maoist organisations have filled the gap. Their major contribution to Indian politics is that they have kept alive the agrarian demands of the rural poor through persistent peasant struggles. Their emphasis, on armed resistance to oppression by Junkers landowners and has appealed to many of these oppressed people.

In sixties when the Naxalite movement was launched, founder leaders Asim Chatterjee and Santosh Rana chose Gopiballavpur, Debra and Baharagora in West Medinipur as their struggle zone because of the sharp feudal contradictions in these areas. But the Maoists chose Lalgarh. From the very beginning they have entered into Bengal with the aim to spread their area of operation on the strength of their fire power not on class struggle.

Party Unity and MCC cadres and leaders were active in Junglemahal for many years. After launching of CPI(Maoists), they made a significant penetration in the region as other Naxalite groups did not exit. In the initial stage of entry, they carried out reformist programmes like setting up of medical dispensaries, construction of rainwater reservoirs and making provisions for drinking water. State Government has denied these basic facilities to the adivasis. Maoists had launched their programme as a part of their long-term strategy to capture state power by guerilla warfare. It is also a fact that their bases were confined to some isolated narrow terrains.

Soon the Maoists could prepare a strong base in Lalgarh-Junglemahal. But they could not hold on to it. Their sectarian approach to the adivasi issues and haste to implement their own plan proved to be suicidal. They have no regard for the traditions and culture of the adivasis. Their political strategy was a great divider. After partial withdrawal of the government forces, the armed squads of the Maoists had a free run. During 2009 and 2010, at least 300 activists and cadres of CPI(M) were killed by the Maoists. Ironically, almost all were poor adivasis and not class enemies. Even in some cases the families were not allowed to lift and cremate the dead bodies. In fact, the Maoists re-enacted the CPI(M) policy of wiping out the social and political opposition through armed action. The Maoists also hijacked the programmes of the Peoples Committee against Police Action. They maneouvered and removed some of the key persons from the PCPA. The hijacking of the peoples' resistance movement against police atrocities by the Maoists and projecting this as their own and killing of innocent adivasis started working against the Maoists. Maoists began to lose popular support as the people of Junglemahal and Lalgarh did not accept their version of politics of violence. The fact remains that Maoists under Kishenji were isolated from the people of Junglemahal and the state administration took advantage of this situation to eliminate him through encounter.

Even Kishenji had admitted that 52 persons were killed in just seven months during January-July 2009. These executions were carried without the sanction from 'higher courts' in accordance to the constitution of the Maoists' Janatam Government. The party did not bother to explain these killings and also the justice system involved. It is not clear if these killings were of political opponents or of those who had committed heinous crimes against the people. This is not how political differences can be resolved. Today if Maoists have been virtually vanquished in Junglemahal, it is not due to the superior war machinery of the State but in no small measure due to their own conduct which alienated sections of people with some turning against them. Years of selfless and painstaking work carried out by them for nearly two decades stands crushed.

Money and gun power emerged as the focal point of this strategy. This has in fact eroded the base of the Maoists. In Lalgarh, the Maoists are working at cross purposes. The blast of the Gyaneshwari Express was an example. This situation put the rank and file in the state of amnesia. They were caught between two confusing scenario: state repression and indifferent leadership. The fact was the movement without a mass base was depending on terror tactics for its survival. Their actions also underlined the poor quality of their understanding of the class struggle and class enemy. It is indeed ridiculous to believe, according to them, Gyaneshwari Express symbolized the power of the state and the passengers travelling in it were class enemies!

It is not clear who is the authority to decide about the actions: at what level does it get decided when, where and how an action is to be carried out? Is it decided by the party or the squad? If a squad carries out an action without the party's permission, especially one in which a dastardly act is committed what punishment is meted out? If there is a great deal of autonomy given to the armed squads, then how does the party maintain discipline to ensure that their strategic objective does not get jeopardized by tactical errors? Though the Maoists have been presenting the façade of a unified command, the fact remains that the leadership/cadres of the party unity or people war are free to take their own decisions and so is the case with the erstwhile MCC guys.

A document of the party however throws enough light on the Maoist operation in Lalgarh. The party was not fully involved in the operation. The document made explicit that

Kishenji was the sole individual to plan, guide and execute the actions. This obviously raises questions on the efficacy of the party's claim of launching revolution in Lalgarh and thereby implying whole of Bengal. The document reads: "Revival of the Combative Spirit of Naxalbari in West Bengal brings us to the Lalgarh movement, which was led by Kishenji on behalf of the CPI(Maoist). The West Bengal Government had handed over some 4500 acres of forest land to the Sajjan Jindal business group at Salboni in the district of West Midnapore even as the government's land reform programme of allotting *pattas* (formal rights) for cultivable forest land and forest land under cultivation to poor tribal peasants was kept in cold storage. The reign of terror let loose on the adivasis – in the wake of the detonation of a landmine that narrowly missed the cavalcade of the then West Bengal Chief Minister Buddhadev Bhattacharjee on 2 November 2008 on the way back after a foundation stone-laying ceremony at the site of the Jindal project – was actively resisted, for, with Maoist backing led by Kishenji, their dignity could no longer be crushed. By mid-November, the Pulishi Atyachar-er Birudhhe Janasadharan-er Committee (People's Committee against Police Atrocities, the PCAPA) was formed to lead the mass struggle in Lalgarh and the adjoining areas. From December 2008 to June 2009, as long as Maoist politics was in command, what was really heartening were the direct forms of people's democracy in practice: each village now had a gram (village) committee with five women and five men on it; two persons, a man and a woman from each village, were a part of the central coordinating committee; the manner of taking and ratifying decisions was utterly democratic; officials were made to sit on the ground on hand-woven mats on equal terms to negotiate with the committees.

"And, with the meagre resources at its command, the PCAPA-led mass movement was able to run health posts with doctors from Kolkata coming in once a week, construct and repair embankments, dig ponds, set up tube wells, teach the local language in some schools, a lot of all this through shramdaan (voluntary labour). Spring, it seemed, was truly in the air. As long as it lasted, for seven months the PCAPA and the CPI(Maoist), led by Kishenji, together seemed to have struck an astute balance between political mobilization, armed actions, and social welfare/'development' activity. But when they destroyed the 'White House', a symbol of the 'ancient regime', the palatial house of Anuj Pandey, the Communist Party of India (Marxist) [CPI(M)] zonal secretary, at Dharampur on 14 June 2009, that was the last straw. The Joint Forces (JF) of the central and State Governments moved in like an occupation army, with the CPI(M) harmads acting as their local collaborators. The Maoist tactics of successfully combining mass political mobilization and armed struggle suffered a setback. Moreover, Kishenji erred in handling the contradictions between the CPI(M), then the ruling party, and the Trinamool Congress (TMC), led by Mamata Banerjee, then the main opposition party. And, his aggressive sectarian and ultra-left adventurist tactics cost the party and the mass movement dearly, for these acts brought on state repression a multiple of what it would have otherwise been. The contradictions between the Maoist revolutionaries and the social democratic CPI(M) at the local level need not have been escalated to the point of becoming intensely antagonistic. And, some of the (excessive) killings were the Maoists really annihilating class enemies? Ultimately, it was the Trinamool Congress who took advantage of the situation to defeat the CPI(M) candidates in the area in the assembly elections in April-May this year.

"As part of her promise of ushering in *parivartan* (change), Mamata Banerjee pledged the withdrawal of the JF that, for the adivasis, has been an occupying force since mid-June 2009, the unconditional release of all political prisoners, especially the hundreds of adivasis arrested and dumped into jail in the course of the JF operations, and a dialogue with the Maoists; but, on assuming power, she has now reneged on all of these pledges. Instead, the recruitment of some 10,000 special police havildars (constables), on the lines of the Salwa Judum in Chhattisgarh, is on the anvil. And, the TMC's own Bhairav Bahini has been assisting the

JF just like the CPI(M)'s harmads did as collaborators of that occupational force. Indeed, many of the harmads have shifted allegiance to the TMC's Bhairav Bahini. A 'development package' with 'surrender' sops, the re-deployment of the JF with the Commando Battalions for Resolute Action, the so called COBRA, at its core, the stepping up of training of the state's armed police in jungle warfare, a strengthening of the Naxalite section of the Intelligence Bureau on the lines of the Special Intelligence Bureau of Andhra Pradesh (APSIB), and the state's Counter Insurgency Force along the lines of the Greyhounds, all these are seen to have yielded results – a mood of triumphalism now prevails after the 'hunting' down of Kishenji."

In a strange manner, the party washed off its hands of the Lalgarh episode by saying: "Now, while much of the credit for the revival of the Maoist movement in the Jangalmahal area of West Bengal must go to Kishenji and his close comrades, like the late Sasadhar Mahato, they will have to bear much of the responsibility for the present setback there too." This is certainly not the manner in which a revolutionary party works. An operation, which the party claimed to be uprising, could not be left to the personal whim of an individual. Obviously, it underlined that the party leadership was not sincere in carrying out revolutionary work in Lalgarh.

The attitudes of Maoist top guns apparently confirm the repetition of worst traditions of communist movement both during war and peace; denial of wrong practices. They seemed to have inherited the tendency to put the blames on distant state units, lower rank and file while de-linking the past mistakes from the present. They refuse to make public admission of failure in the name of democratic centralism, cadre morale as well as in the larger interest of the revolution.

It is not the problems of mere deviations from the line of selective and deterrent violence instead it smacks of a cult of political violence aimed at coercive hegemony, a shortcut for painstaking political campaigns and mass movements. Kishenji had insisted that he had been following the CC line on the issue of killings. Dismissing the sentiments about sparing poor suspects considering their class background, he said: "Ask our CC if you think it is Kishenji line that we are practising in Junglemahal. We killed only 50 percent of those who should have been eliminated. Media may have portrayed me as a bloodthirsty person. But in my party, I am known as soft-minded".

It is sad that the Maoists have not evolved the mechanism to resolve the political differences. They have been behaving in the manner of a mercenary or a criminal don: every issue has to be settled through use of guns. But this cost them pretty high in Junglemahal. Today the Maoists have been completely vanquished in Junglemahal. To attribute this to the superior war machinery of the state would be wrong. They have been vanquished due to their own conduct and failings which alienated a large section of the adivasi people. How could an organisation and its leadership which had relentlessly carried so called painstaking work amongst the adivasis prefer to kill the socially respected adivasi leaders who have been fighting for their emancipation? A Kangaroo Court of the Maoists ordered killing of an honest human rights activists Niyamat Ansari in 2011 in the Manika block of Latehar in Jharkhand.

Though Kishenji was killed nearly two years back, so far the party has not come out with any self-critical analysis on the Lalgarh movement despite pointed criticisms of reckless killings in Junglemahal by friendly people. Sushil Roy (*TOI*, 18 October, 2012) and some CPI(Maoist) leaders blamed Kishenji for the miscarriage of the movement.

The latest example is the party's endorsement of the belly bomb that the PLGA men had planted inside the abdomen of a slain CRPF jawan in Jharkhand's Latehar after an encounter in January. Also they had booby-trapped another jawan's body, which exploded taking the toll of four innocent lives after the CRPF-Jharkhand Jaguar Joint Force had forced villagers to pick up the dead uniformed men at gunpoint. Rights activists as well as a section of the civil liberty bodies condemned the 'bestial deeds'; the desecration of the dead bodies by the Maoists and use of civilians as human shields by the forces of the government and described them both as war crimes.

Sometime back, the PUDR in a statement had criticized the CPI(Maoist) for doing disservice to the resistance to state-corporate joint plunder of minerals in Jharkhand by such crimes and wanted its leadership to own up the 'command responsibility' for these acts. It observed: "CPI(Maoist) through such deeds does its own cause harm apart from weakening the resistance to government's growth obsessed and FDI driven policies, which is resulting in development of underdevelopment. Instead of occupying higher moral ground for their 'people's war', Maoist combatants are showing propensity towards regression. We need to know from CPI(Maoist) if they accept the principle of command responsibility for this act? What action have they taken so far to find out who was responsible for this act which was not possible without some planning and preparation?"

Kondapalli Seetharamaiah, a former CPI(ML) leader, in April 1980 formed the CPI(ML) People's War that became known as People's War Group (PWG) that constitutes the other major part of the biggest Maoist party today. PWG gave Maoism in India a new life and new characteristics. Seetharamaiah again was mainly following Mazumdar's approach of armed strife but was eager expanding the struggle to economy and politics by mobilizing the masses and establishing front organizations that worked over ground. But unfortunately the present leadership is not keen to follow his path.

The success of the Maoist movement is deeply rooted in the weakness of the Indian state to fulfill its functions and responsibilities. Although India, in comparison to other former colonized states, was able to develop a powerful apparatus of state, its control remains in large parts precarious in terms of its conception. State administration is especially in those areas is sparsely developed which are most affected by Naxalite violence. This fact is reflected by small state budgets, low bureaucratic efficiency as well as prevailing corruption. There are even some remote areas where state domination is almost completely absent (*Mainstream* 2008).

The rank and file of the party and even a section of the West Bengal state unit of the Maoist party was vertically split on the role and approach of their polit bureau member Kishenji. Though Kishenji was an old hand, his stand on having working relation with Trinmool Congress particularly Mamata Banerjee was disliked by many. Some of them even felt that he was committing the same mistake which Azad had committed earlier in Andhra Pradesh. Interestingly, the latter events proved them right.

Kishenji had described the Lalgarh movement as second Naxalbari movement. But while Naxalbari movement had evoked strong political reaction throughout the country and helped polarize the political parties and forces, no such impact of Lalgarh movement was visible. Instead the role of the Maoists created suspicion in the mind of adivasis and also among the common people about the democratic character of the Maoist movement. This was the reason that the movement failed to isolate the ruling class and Left Front.

Those opposed to Kishenji's line say that adivasis and others had initiated a movement in and around Lalgarh. This was essentially a peoples' affair. Though during the Left Front rule the CPI(M) gained a kind of mastery in applying the policy of area domination, particularly in the rural areas of West Bengal after Nandigram setback, the Left Front government could not muster enough courage to intervene in the tribal affairs and fight the adivasis in Lalgarh. But unfortunately the opportunity was provided by the Maoists. The Maoists who by now had already formed their base in Lalgarh carried out a blast on the convoy of the Chief Minister Buddhadeb Bhattacharya. The CPI(M) and Left Front government seized the opportunity and launched a massive action in Lalgarh and Jangalmahal. The motto was to liberate Lalgarh from Maoists. The situation deteriorated to such an extent that intellectuals and writers had to come to the streets protesting against the CPI(M) assault.

The CPI(M) applied its vast party machinery skillfully combining it with the state machinery, over which it had established a vicious grip, to achieve its absolute supremacy over the village society. The TMC fought with the CPI(M) during its emergence in the state political scene in the 1998-2001 in the countryside of West Medinipur, Hooghly and Bankura districts to successfully bring rural areas under its domination. The policy of area domination at that time found expression in the battle to physically capture villages after villages with marauding armed gangs attacking and counter-attacking each other's territory, burning and looting houses, killing and injuring people, thereby bringing immense misery to the people of the affected area. The Maoists though having a different ideological make-up, hardly lagged behind in following this policy of area domination. One may recollect that almost during the same period the CPI(ML) (People's War) and MCC, the very parties united to form the Communist Party of India (Maoist), fought among themselves for area domination in the forest areas of West Bengal, leave aside such instances of fratricidal fighting between various revolutionary parties raging for long in Andhra Pradesh, Bihar and Jharkhand.

The CPI(M) would not have been washed out of Lalgarh if the TMC of Mamote had not joined hands with Maoists. Primarily the dominance of TMC made the people response their faith in TMC and in the process Maoists were marginalised. Though Maoists claim to follow Maoism, as an ideology, a look at the political development would make clear that it was no better than a bourgeoise political party. Their actions gave the impression that they were politically bankrupt. Else, how could a party which hates the parliamentary system of the country repose its faith in the Trinmool Congress? Their entire action was in sharp contrast to their claim of being a revolutionary communist party.

The Maoists utterly lacked the political perspective was evident from their joining hands with CPI(M) in Garebeta after they killed one local BJP leader in Sandhipur village of Garbeta I block. They carried out the operation for simply demoralising the TMC and BJP combine in the area. TMC in retaliation killed the brother of the Maoist leader Asit

Sarkar. Eliminated his nephew and blinded his brother-in-law. After the 1998 panchayat elections, the TMC-BJP combine got an upper-hand over their rival CPI(M) in some areas as they succeeded in capturing a number of panchayats. After the Maoists started their organizational work in the plain lands of Garbeta I and Garbeta II blocks of West Medinipur, they had to face stiff opposition from the forces loyal to the TMC-BJP combine. After these incidents, series of clashes took place in Garbeta and surrounding areas between the Maoists and the TMC-BJP. However, the Maoists succeeded in putting the TMC-BJP combine in a tight corner by dint of their training in guerrilla warfare including their skill in using long-range fire-arms. Strangely, the CPI(M) leaders of the area who were made to flee from the region by the TMC-BJP forces, extended helping hand to the Maoists by providing food and shelters to defeat their common enemy. But things once again turned against Maoist once the TMC-BJP combine began to retreat from the area in face of the Maoists' guerilla attack.

But once the TMC began retreating from the area, the CPI(M) immediately started attacking the Maoists for re-capturing their lost territory. Significantly, some TMC supporters, evicted from their villages by the CPI(M), joined the Maoists forces to resist the fast expanding CPI(M) and for returning to their homes. The Maoists depending on the support received from their enemy of yesterday, formed a bigger armed squad (platoon in the Maoist parlance) to counter the CPI(M) attacks. Unfortunately, for the Maoists this time they did not get the crucial support of the SC-ST people which they had received earlier while fighting against the TMC-BJP forces. In the ensuing fight between the Maoists and the CPI(M), the subaltern people in the war-zone of Garbeta became largely neutral and refused to provide shelter to the Maoist forces that they required badly to keep their hide-outs secret from enemy forces.

This task was undertaken by TMC-turned-Maoist supporters. They offered the Maoist force shelter in Chhoto Angaria. But the shelter was soon exposed to the CPI(M) that had already 'captured' that area. The CPI(M) mobilised their forces, surrounded the 'shelter' and burnt the house after killing at least five squad members of the Maoists. The owner of the house fled to Kolkata to inform the TMC leadership about the carnage. Being informed, Mamata Banerjee promptly claimed that her supporters were killed by the CPI(M) in Chhoto Angaria. After that gory incident, the Maoists retreated from that area once for all and instead concentrated their activities in the forest areas of the South Bengal districts. That was their first intervention in the battle for area domination. The CPI(M) tactfully used Maoists to regain its domination over a certain area.

The Maoist movement got a fillip with the outbreak of Lalgarh movement. The CPI(M), though maintained a low profile initially, tried to re-establish its stranglehold over the area at the later stage by setting up a number of armed camps bolstered and supported by the anti-Maoists operations of the joint forces (state police plus central paramilitary forces). During this crucial phase, the Maoists failed to mobilize the local people. People's mobilization against armed camps could have possible as was amply demonstrated by the Natai incident where CPI(M) gangs opened fire on the agitating villagers killing nine of them. The Maoists instead concentrated in organizing armed squads and conducting raids in the houses of CPI(M) cadres and supporters and also on the joint forces. In the offensive launched by them, scores of CPI(M) supporters, mostly poor and middle class village people, and a number of personnel of the state forces were killed. The Junglemahal really turned into a war-zone where killings and counter-killings became the order of the day for quite sometimes.

Once the assembly elections were announced, political equations began to change with the entry of the TMC as a contending power in Junglemahal. Realignment of political forces began to take shape in the area with the Maoists and the TMC coming to terms, though unofficially in a desperate bid to beat the CPI(M) and defeat the Left Front. This time in Junglemahal the alignment of political forces took a reverse shape as the TMC was extended generous support by the Maoists who even filled grounds with their supporters for the TMC leaders to address public rallies. The declaration of the top Maoists leader Kishenji that he wanted to see Mamata Banerjee as the Chief Minister of West Bengal paved the way for the alliance. The TMC, which did not have substantial presence in Junglemahal earlier, was quick to seize the opportunity and infiltrated in a big way in the People's Committee against Police Atrocities (PCPA) and Adibasi-Mulbasi Committee that had been spearheading the Lalgarh movement and hence were the targets of state repression. For Maoists presence of TMC people in these organizations was a boon as it would dissuade the state forces at least to some extent from attacking them and act as a safeguard to their own supporters working in these organizations. But in the tactical maneuver to use each other in the opportunist alliance, the TMC ably organized its own organizational base cutting across the Maoist support-base throughout the Junglemahal.

After TMC won with a thumping majority, the basis for TMC-Maoist alliance evaporated and the ground was set for a new battle to establish supremacy in the Junglemahal of West Bengal. This time the battle-line was drawn between the TMC and the Maoists, each trying to consolidate and expand their bases. It is forgone conclusion that the TMC would use the state forces at its disposal to suppress any resurgence of the Maoists. Anyone closely following the developments in the Junglemahal of West Bengal should not harbour the illusion that the new government would negotiate peace with the Maoists. Negotiation between the state and insurgent groups could materialize only when the insurgent group is strong to be defeated by force and/or there is some room for the latter to be accommodated in the present state set-up.

So it was no wonder that peace talk between the state and the Maoists did not materialise in West Bengal. The TMC Government put the agenda of peace talks by appointing interloculators, but did not fulfill its pre-poll promises of withdrawal of joint forces and release of political prisoners (and withdrawal of previous political cases). The anti-Maoist operations of the joint forces continued. Besides joint forces operations considerable number of leaders and activists of PCPA in West Medinipur district and Adibasi-Mulbasi Committee in Purulia were persuaded to join the TMC. With the help of these elements, the TMC organized resistance groups to thwart the movement of the Maoists in the villages.

This enraged the Maoists who in retaliation once again resorted to individual killings. In one incident, the Maoist squad came in search of an erstwhile leader of the Adibasi-Mulbasi Committee in Purulia who had joined the TMC and killed his brother and father while failing to apprehend him. Such killings gave the government the required ground to start the joint operation in full-fledge. Because of the substantial infiltration by the TMC inside the Maoist network, the Maoists became vulnerable to the operations of the joint force as never before.

A senior leader of the CPI(Maoist) said, "the circumstances in which Kishenji was killed may remain a mystery, but the incident itself was indication of receding influence of the Maoists in the Junglemahal. The new rulers strategically used the promise of withdrawal of joint force and release of political prisoners to win over the support of the Maoists in the crucial assembly election and then used the peace-initiative to divide and penetrate the Maoist ranks and extend its hegemony over the area. The Maoists had become victim of their own politics by first forming opportunist alliance with a ruling class party, then misreading the ground situation of Junglemahal and probably being unguarded for a while by over-emphasizing the peace-initiative and above all undermining as always the necessity to conduct political-ideological struggles to counter the influence of the state and parliamentary parties and almost entirely replacing it by their brand of 'armed struggle', which principally took the form of individual assassinations."

He further said, "Thus it seems that to both the sides, peace has not been a real issue to negotiate with and both wanted to use the same tactically to gain an upper-hand over the other in the concrete conditions of Junglemahal. In the game of one-upmanship, the state and the ruling party has scored over the Maoists at least for the time being. The principal problem for both the sides seems their utter disrespect to the democratic norms and aspirations of the people. The new ruling party went back on its own pre-poll promises to withdraw the joint forces, release political prisoners and withdraw political cases of the earlier regime. Rather the new government resumed the policy of 'encounter' killings to physically eliminate the Maoist threat. The Maoists on their part did not cease their policy of individual killings of political opponents. Both sides seem more than ever eager to establish their exclusive domination over Junglemahal. With such scanty regard to democracy, the society cannot rid of the cycle of violence and peace hardly gets a chance."

One thing which ought to be underlined is the failure of the Maoist leadership in countering the situation. Since they always relied on their strike power, they paid little attention to build a mass movement and in Lalgarh too their main focus was on use of arms power. This was the reason that could not counter the assault of the CPI(M) and Left Front Government. Initially, there were two forces; one led by the CPI(M) and joint security forces and second the Maoists and the Peoples' Action Committee Against Police Torture. The Trinmool Congress of Mamata entered into the picture as the third force. Since the CPI(M) was the common enemy of the TMC and Maoists, they joined hands against it. It produced some good results. A section of the TMC accepted the leadership of Maoists. The Maoists were also of the view that joining hands with the TMC would provide them cover against police action. But they had erred. Taking advantage of this situation, the Maoists rank was infiltrated by the intelligence men. They succeeded in having a major say in the party. Then the style of functioning of Kishenji was yet another factor. He came to repose his faith in these new entrants. If party's insiders and some top leaders are to be believed, Kishenji sidelined some of the key persons. After the elections, when the TMC won, the scene changed. The TMC was no more sympathetic to the Maoists, notwithstanding appointing interlocutors and lobbying by some independent individuals to open peace dialogue with the Maoists. Significantly, Kishenji had extended full cooperation and help of the party to the TMC in winning the elections. Those who know would vouch that TMC was never a force in Lalgarh. It was the leverage provided by Maoists and particularly by Kishenji that made it a force in the Junglemahal.

In these regions, high castes people, landlords and loan sharks dominate the rural population and benefit from their exploitation. The rural development programs in these areas have not reached the bottom of the society and instead contributed to the persistence of landlordism. The state has never bothered to comply with its basic responsibilities; guaranteeing security, providing basic amenities as well as ensuring social upward mobility (Frontier). Acute malnutrition is prevalent. Basic services such as roads, sanitation and electricity are not provided in the regions dominated by the poor, dalit and adivasis. Public institutions such as schools, health care centers and police stations are underdeveloped. Even Planning Commission had admitted that public administration is frequently affected by corruption and because of that, in conjunction with inefficient administration, funds that are assigned for the minor developed parts of India, do not reach the poor.

This led to the frustration and loss of confidence in the state by the residents of the respective areas. Due to this, the influence and control of the state is marginal. These circumstances enable the Maoist to take influence easily on large parts of the society. The people expect that the state would provide basic needs to them but it generally fails. Under these conditions, the population reacts with a lot of gratitude towards the efforts of the Naxalites. In the process, the state loses its turf to the Maoists as it was not able to address the basic needs of the population (*Mainstream* 2008).

Due to the fact that the Maoists were able to spread their influence into several pockets within the Indian state, there exist parallel claims to power over respective regions. This fact, and the direct violent attacks against the agents, institutions and symbols of the state, apparently challenges the inherent ideals of the state, namely sovereignty and monopoly on the use of force. Hence, the state's legitimacy is in crisis. The coercive reaction by the Indian state on the Naxalite challenge instead contributed to alienate large parts of the population living in the conflict zone even more from the state. Since the general election 2009, the degree of violence has increased. That is because the state initiated Operation Green Hunt, a wide-scale military offensive against the positions of the Maoists. The task of the security forces is to engage the Naxalites into fights and expel them from their areas of influence.

In 2008, the Planning Commission received from an expert group a well-researched 95-pages extensive report that addressed the socio-economic root causes of the Naxalite movement. But the government turned away from its suggestions and neither Prime Minister Manmohan Singh nor Home Minister P. Chidambaram has referred to the report in their statements. The report did not only mention the social and economic causes for the rise of Maoism in India like displacement, unequal land distribution, discrimination or socio-economic deprivation but also addressed the weakness of the state in the remote areas and questioned the dominant approach by the government that is based on force and maintenance of law and order (Planning Commission 2008, especially p. 56 onwards).

Moreover, various departments of Ministry of Home Affairs have repeatedly called attention to the socio-economic root causes of the Naxalites movement but due to institutional flaws this view was not able to prevail. Instead the main source of information for the Central Government and especially the MHA remains the Intelligence Bureau (IB) that has only a limited capacity regarding the analysis of social and economic issues and its perspective is dominated mainly by the security aspect.

□

3

Marxism-Leninism and Maoism

Moving around the jungles of Latehar and Palamau in Jharkhand and plains in Gaya and Jehanabad of Bihar, I met adivasi and Yadav cadres of the CPI(Maoist). During interaction, they were quite candid in admitting their operational mistakes and confess that killings of the people often do not conform to the ideological spirit of the movement. When confronted, they accepted that they do not have any choice and have to obey the dictates coming from above.

They don't have any say in the decision-making process. They are simply to carry out the orders without assessing whether it was wrong or right. Most of the cadres have not met their top leaders or had the opportunity to convey their feelings or information from the ground zero. The compulsion of hierarchy prevents them from meeting their top leaders. Their immediate bosses, either the junior commanders or joint commanders often betray the same feelings. This is practised to maintain the sanctity of the hierarchy and also the needs of the secret operations. They have participated in number of operations and have killed people. But all such actions were planned by the top leaders. Nevertheless, these cadres nurse the feeling that most of those killed did not fit into the framework of class enemy. The classical example is of Gyaneshwari train blast episode. They still feel that train killing was a wrong decision. But then the direction was from the top. They had to execute.

What attracts the adivasi youth to the Maoists – even though they have not read and understood the party documents, its ideological approach, its programme, strategy and tactics – is really intriguing. However, the youth put it this way: "See when everyone is out to exploit us it is heartening to see Maoists coming forward to defend us. They carry arms. But nowadays every one, even a member of the civil society carries arms. At least this sends the message that they are ready to take to arms for us. In today's world, arms has its importance and it cannot be denied." Their idea and perception of party line and ideology is if not blurred it is certainly skewed. Most of them are even not aware that party has an important document like strategy and tactics.

Party's reliance on gun power goes back to the days of the formation of the CPI(ML). Even in 1969, some leaders under the banner of Dakhin Desh had opposed the Marxist-Leninist line and advocated to present Maoism as the only ideology of the Naxalite movement. Though the leader Charu Majumdar was for class annihilation and taking to arms, it was the emphasis on mass movement that the Dakhin Desh group rebelled. But they failed to muster support and their move could not succeed. Later they formed Maoist Communist Centre and advocated their line. They in fact had some base in Gaya and Aurangabad districts of Bihar. The Party Unity also believed in this line but with some moderation. The party was not out right opposed to mass mobilization. The MCC was purely for military intervention.

When the Communist Party of India (Marxist-Leninist) was being formed in 1969, some groups retained their separate identities. One such group was Dakshin Desh, named after its publication. Dakshin Desh meant 'Southern Land' (implied that India was the 'Southern land' whereas China was the 'Northern land'). Amulaya Sen and Kanai Chatterjee were the leading figures of the Dakshin Desh group. In contrast to the CPI(ML) policies of armed struggle and individual annihilation, the Dakshin Desh group upheld that mass mobilisations were essential for engaging in armed struggle. It was Kanai Chatterjee's innovative thinking that made him critical of Charu Mazumdar's CPI(ML) and it's tactical line of individual annihilation. Kanai Chatterjee believed that the time was not appropriate for formation of the party. He felt there had to be greater development in the revolutionary movement to form a party. In his view, first an agrarian revolutionary movement had to be launched.

From 1967 to 1969 the then Dakshin Desh group built up the movement in Kolkata, Howrah, Hoogli, Midnapur, Bardhwan, Birbum and 24 Parganas, together, with some work in Assam and Tripura. They built the peasant movement firstly in Sonarpur and then in Kanksa in Bardhwan district. Thereafter, they established some contacts in Bihar. In October 1969, the Maoist Communist Centre was formed. Kanai Chatterjee laid the basic line in the very first issue of *Lal Pataka* in 1969. The important topics dealt with were: (a) the importance of Maoism (then called 'thought') in the present era, (b) in the present situation, the tactical line and tactical slogans, (c) the correct policy towards the participation in elections and a correct analysis of the boycott of elections, saying that though it was a question of tactics, it acquires the significance of strategy in the concrete conditions of India, (d) the correct line regarding the armed agrarian revolutionary war, that is, protracted people's war including army building and base areas, (e) correct orientation towards forms of struggle (open and secret, legal and illegal, peaceful and armed), (f) the programmes, tactics and methods of the peasant struggle, (g) approach and method towards the UF, (h) political propaganda, (i) on the women's question, the student movement and the nationality question in India, and (j) methods of leadership. (*Peoples March*, Nov-Dec 2004 issue).

One thing was quite significant, the Dakshin Desh did not claim at that stage that Maoism was an ideology or gun power was the only means to achieve revolution. The developments indicate that the leadership was in favour of building strong mass movement and held Mao Zedong line as his thought.

Later K.C. chalked out a path for the MCC whereby he formulated a strategy of his own. The methods of work they adopted resembled Mao Zedong's Red Army in the revolutionary war. The group began armed activities in the Jungalmahal area, Burdwan district, West Bengal, where dalits and adivasis constituted large sections of the local population. The territory was covered with deep forests, considered ideal for guerrilla warfare. The group formed political militia squads, which moved around in the villages and conducted political activities to mobilise local peasants. The squads were often made up by recruits from Calcutta. The squads looted grain storages, captured firearms and assassinated landlords and perceived police informers. By 1973 it was estimated that the group had 37 squads in the area, with a combined membership of 106. However, in spite of several years of political and armed activities, the group failed to make a breakthrough in the Jungalmahal area. In 1976, it decided to expand its activities to other parts of the country. Soon it began activities in eastern Bihar, and for this purpose an apex Bengal-Bihar Special Area Committee was set up by the MCC.

Chatterji died in 1982. Following his death, MCC was riddled by internal divisions. Chatterji's successor, Siveji, and his deputy, Ramadhar Singh, disagreed over the policy of individual annihilations. Singh broke away and joined Kanu Sanyal's group. In the mid- and late-1980, leadership of MCC was taken over by Sanjay Dusadh and Pramod Mishra. At this point, the influence of the group had spread to the central parts of Bihar. The group now counted with 500 wholetime cadres and 10,000 members. Mass organizations of MCC included Krantikari Kisan Committee (Revolutionary Peasants Committee), Jana Suraksha Sangarsh Manch (People's Defence Struggle Bloc), Krantikarai Buddhijevi Sangh and Krantikari Chhatra League (Revolutionary Students League). The armed wing of the party was called Lal Raskha Dal (Red Defence Force).

In rural Bihar, the party had become a major force to reckon with in some areas. In the pockets of its influence, the party ran a parallel judicial system, with a system of people's courts. The expansion of the party occurred as it became one of several caste-based armed groups in the area.

In September 1993, MCC, Communist Party of India (Marxist-Leninist) People's War and Communist Party of India (Marxist-Leninist) Party Unity decided to coordinate their struggles. As a result, the All India People's Resistance Forum was formed, with the participation of cadres from the three parties. AIPRF held a mass rally, with around 1,00,000 participants, on March 21, 1994. The founding documents of the MCC stressed the importance of base areas in the revolutionary process. "If we are to build armed-agrarian revolution, a people's army and red base areas, we will always have to remain firm on some basic principles regarding their inter-relation. The building up and consolidation of the armed, agrarian revolution, people's army and base areas – these tasks are related to each other. 'If we are to build up an agrarian revolution no people's army can be built up. Similarly an agrarian revolution cannot be built up without a people's army. Again without a people's army no base area can be built up. Similarly without base areas the very existence of people's army cannot be maintained. It is only through agrarian revolutionary guerilla struggle and the establishment of the people's army that a red base area can be built up. Again through this work alone the revolutionary high tide can be accelerated throughout the country, and depending on the base area and with the help of the peoples army, the agrarian revolution also can be consolidated, deepened and expanded." This statement was the chief demarcating factor of the MCC with the CPI(ML).

The July-Oct 1997 issue of *Vanguard* mentioned about polemical differences of MCC with Peoples War Group. Kanai Chatterjee had said: "It is wrong to say that Dakshin Desh Group left the AICCR because of it's differences on the issue of immediate formatting of the party. AICCR did not recognize any group with a separate identity like the Dakshin Desh Groups as it's constituents. No representative of this group was a member of the East Bengal Co-ordination Committee. Or of the AICCR."

The MCC made the following criticism of the CPI(ML): "Naturally as the party was formed without following the revolutionary process, method and style, some known degenerated elements could capture some posts in the leadership from he beginnings. This facilitates undeclared groups and a tendency of group mentality and bureaucratism replacing democratic Centralism."

Kanai Chatterjee stated that "We have to give utmost importance on organising extensive political campaign and political exposure campaign on a large scale. Only this will take us towards the path of People's War and inspire the masses to politics of socialism, people's democracy and armed people's dictatorship under the leadership of the working class. In view of the present semi-colonial and semi-feudal society of India, the exposure of the economy and politics at present and the propogation of the politics of agrarian evolution or peoples democratic revolution.

The first phase can be stretched from 1964 to 1968 and began when the revisionist line was established at the first Congress of the CPI(M): (i) drawing a clear line of demarcation with the revisionists in the political and organizational fields, (ii) linking the daily revolutionary practice of Indian revolution to the theory, (iii) developing a political and tactical line not merely as a formality, but giving it a concrete structure in various spheres of activity, and (iv) based on these revolutionary policies, style and method, and in the course of revolutionary struggles and guided by a revolutionary theory, to build a revolutionary party. The second phase, which stretched from 1969 to 1978, was a period of implementation of the party's line, policies and plans. It was a period of gaining practical experience towards the path of establishing the 'Red Agrarian Revolutionary Resistance War.' Work was begun on this basis in the Sundarbans, 24 Parganas, Hoogli, Midnapur, Kanksa, Gaya and Hazaribagh. Of these experiences, the most encouraging was that of Kanksa and Hazaribagh. Here, a wide movement was built on issues like wage hike, seizure of crops, fertiliser problem, confiscation of grains from landlords and against various forms of political and social oppression. Also, a wide mass movement was built, some notorious landlords punished and steps were taken towards disarming of the enemy and arming the people.

Although claiming to defer from Charu Mazumdar's line in their actual working process, their practice was virtually the same. The Maoist Communist Centre also deployed the tactic of "Individual Annihilation of the Class Enemy." It was Kanai Chatterjee who made a rectification of the line where the formation of mass organizations and building of mass movements was indispensable. The MCC did not build separate peasant organization but had a strategy to build the Krantikari Kisan Commitees. These committees tried the landlords and re-distributed land to the landless peasants. Punishments were awarded to guilty landlords. Mass fronts were also built in the student, youth women and cultural front. The Nari Mukti Sangh, a mass organization of women led a significant movement. It was in 1978 when the MCC made a self-correction and decided to form mass organizations like the Revolutionary Peasants Committee. The mistakes of the past were analysed. The third phase, which stretched from 1979 to 1988, was a period of taking the lessons, both positive and negative, of the second phase and enriching both the theory and practice. In this phase, the MCC focused on Bihar; and with the perspective of building a people's army and base area, the Bihar-Bengal Special Area Committee was established, the 'Preparatory Committee for Revolutionary Peasant Struggles' was formed and soon Revolutionary Peasant Councils emerged. In this phase, militant struggles developed and the landlords' authority smashed, thousands of acres of land seized and distributed to the landless.

It has been a long and arduous path of over two decades of discussions between the two parties that finally culminated in formation of the CPI(Maoists) with the merger of the MCC and People's War. The process witnessed many ups and downs. It saw even some dark periods. But finally it emerged triumphant. The first ever meeting between the latter two parties began in 1981, when the then leaders, comrade Kanai Chatterjee of the then MCC and comrade K. Seetharamiah of the then CPI(ML)(PW) met for over 12 days. After this very first meet both leaders, though belonging to different streams, stated that the grounds to merge are strong as both were basically traversing a similar path. Both parties set out the procedure for preparation of the documents and then merger. In later years, one development was quite prominent inside the party. It became an organization of the Yadavs. The entire party was under the control of the Yadavs. The reason was in Gaya, Jehanabad and Auangabad belt the land dispute and animosity was mainly between the Yadavs and Rajputs. The Yadavs were also soft towards RJD of Lalu Prasad Yadav. During those days it was said that the activists of MCC were Yadavs during the day and Maoists during the night.

Then in 1998 the two major parties within the M-L trend, the PW and the PU, merged to form a single party of this trend. But already the situation at the ground level in Bihar had deteriorated and after 1998 the clashes between PW and the MCC continued and intensified. Then the two parties entered the period now referred to as the 'Black Chapter' of the Indian revolution. Large numbers were killed from both the sides. This situation caused much damage to the revolutionary movement. This process continued even when various genuine supporters of the movement opposed the retaliatory methods adopted by both the parties. Many intellectuals and progressive elements who support revolution appealed to both the parties to stop these clashes. Different communist revolutionary groups and parties in the country appealed to resolve the clashes. Many South Asian Maoist parties, and other international Maoist forces also appealed to stop the clashes. In due course, the process of rethinking was already going on inside the MCC. At the time of the PW/PU unity itself the PW took a decision to unilaterally stop clashes, but neither did it make it public nor convey it to the MCC, so it had little impact. In this overall backdrop, the MCC took the initiative in openly declaring a unilateral ceasefire in January 2000. Thereafter, PW also responded to stop the clashes. Hence, the negative relation between the two parties started turning into a positive one. In the meantime, the PW held its 9th Congress in August 2001. Also the MCCI had to face a major two line struggle with a small faction from within on certain ideological-political and o ther issues.

Finally, the process of talks between the two parties was once again started in August 2001. The other important reasons for the growing closeness of the two were the decisions of the PW Congress which rectified some of its earlier understandings and also adopted Maoism in place of Mao Thought. In the very first meeting, the delegations of the two parties offered a serious self-criticism, and decisions were taken to initiate joint activities at the Bihar/Jharkhand level. The written self-criticisms were taken publicly throughout the rank and file of the Bihar/Jharkhand party and the situation further developed in the positive direction. Throughout the period of the latter part of 2001 and entire 2002, major joint activities were taken in Bihar-Jharkhand including the successful three-day economic blockade of the two states in protest against POTA. Talks also continued between these two parties through this period. Finally, it was in the important Feb. 2003 bilateral meeting that a decision was taken to take concrete steps for starting discussion on ideological-political issues of line with the clear direction and purpose of merger of the two parties. In this meeting, a serious and extensive self-criticism was put forward by both the parties for the 'Black Chapter' and this too was carried publicly. Both parties vowed never to repeat clashes with class friends no matter how severe the difference. At this meeting, the grounds were also laid to advance and finalise the process of merger. They were, firstly, on the ideology of the party – Marxism-Leninism-Maoism. The other documents decided to be drafted were on the programme, strategy and tactics, political resolution on the international and domestic situation, and the party constitution. The task of drafting the five documents was divided amongst the two parties. Then, in four rounds of negotiations, between the high-level delegations of the two parties and the respective CCs, final agreement was reached after detailed discussions on these documents on all major issues at a joint meeting of the two CCs in Sept. 2004. The documents were adopted and decided to be translated into about 10 regional languages to be discussed throughout the party. Some minor differences that remained were referred for further discussion and study to be clinched at a later date. Finally, the joint CC meeting of both, parties took the decision of merger and a central committee (provisional) was established.

One of the most famous actions carried out by the MCC was in Dalelchak Baghaura in Aurangabad on May 29, 1987. The Yadav activists of the Maoist Communist Centre slaughtered 42 Rajputs in retaliation for murders. Aurangabad is a feudal centre. The landlords launched an attack on Seshani village on April 19, 1987. This was in retaliation to the policies of the Krantikari Kisan Commitees which banned the sale of 150 acres of land owned by the Mahanta of Jnibigha village. This land was however bought by Lootan Sinh. The Kisan Committee destroyed the office of Babu Lootan and his tractors were burnt. A red flag was hoisted over his land. The landlords were also enraged by an earlier clash with the MCC and the fact that hundreds of Mahua trees were owned by the Kisan Samiti. The landlords launched an attack on MCC activists in Seshani, killing eight activists and two children.

Following this the Red Defence Corpes launched an attack on Dalelchak Baghaura. That area historically had the most notorious landlords like Satyendra Narayan Singh, Ram Narseh Singh and Lootan Babu. Triveni Singh, Samresh Singh and Abhan Singh were other tyrants. It was the Krantikari Kisan Committees that challenged their might. Another similar incident took place in Bara village in Gaya district on February 12, 1992, when 37 upper caste members of the Bhumihar caste were hacked to death. According to Prakash Singh (Former Inspector General of Police in his book *The Naxalite Movement in India*), "The party has built an armed wing known as the Lal Raksha Dal and managed to stockpile about seven to eight hundred firearms of different descriptions, including a couple of A-K 47 Rifles...."

In Jharkhand, the MCC led a famous movement. In Jharkhand the MCC waged many a famous struggle, seizing and re-distributing landlord's land. They defended the formation of separate state of Jharkhand but only when it was connected to the overall class struggle. Sibu Soren was unsympathetic but Vinod Mahato was impressed with the MCC. Between 1987 and 1990, over 7000 acres of land in Chatanpur were re-distributed among the villagers. Forest offices were attacked. In 1991, the landlords formed the Sunlight Sena in retaliation. The MCC retaliated. Their armed squads liquidated the entire Sena in the region.

Assessment of the Maoist Communist Centre

The most important question of historical assessment was their original difference with the original CPI(ML) and later why it developed serious differences with the Peoples War Group or Party Unity Group to the extent that even inter-group clashes occurred on a wide scale. This reflected the defective military line of both the erstwhile Peoples War Group and the MCC. True they resolved it ultimately but did they analyse the root cause of the clashes and rectify those aspects of the line that caused them?

One theoretical weakness of the Maoist Communist Centre was it was replacing the term 'Mao Zedong Thought', with 'Maoism'. Even the CCP did not replace Mao Tsetung Thought with Maoism in the Socialist and Cultural Revolution Period. This denies the fact that it is the 'era of imperialism' as profounded by Comrade Lenin. It also joined the Revolutionary Internationalist Movement, a Communist International Organization, which was prematurely formed, without adequate development of the World Communist Movement. There is a debate in the Revolutionary Camp on the question of whether Maoism can replace the term Mao Tsetung Thought. One section states that only the term Maoism can correctly credit his contribution, the other condemns this replacement as it feels that it replaces the era of 'Leninism'. Even after the triumph of the Revolution in 1949, the CCP called the ideology Marxism-Leninsm and the

Thought of Mao Tsetung. In the Great Proletarian Cultural Revolution launched in 1966 period the CCP termed it Marxism-Leninism-Mao Tsetung Thought.

After the merger of MCC and People's War group, the new formed outfit CPI(Maoist) adopted this as their official line. The strategy and tactics of the party makes its explicit that the political line to present Maoism as the ideology has prevailed over accepting Marxism-Leninism. This was done more out of operational compulsion rather than political need. If they would have accepted the general line that Maoism was a thought process and Marxism-Lenisism was the ideology, in that case they would have to be part of the greater organization CPI(ML). Since they had to keep afloat their own outfit, they indulged in projecting Maoism and specifically its military action. A closer look however makes it explicit that factional feud and bourgeoise politics of one-upmanship have been primary reasons for CPI(Maoist) resorting to mercenary type military actions; indiscriminate killings of innocent people and over dependence on arms power.

In the early phase of Naxalite movement, there were two sets of major differences which in recent times has crystalised; depending primarily on mobile guerilla actions and mass mobilization. Open functioning and mass mobilization is better exemplified by CPI(ML) and Maoists represent the second one, the mobile guerilla action. Incidentally, this was one of the main points of difference in the undivided CPI during the Telengana movement as well the reason for formation of the CPI(M). Despite the fact the Indian economy has undergone a major change and other number of changes has taken place in the body politic, the Maoists are still reluctant to change their stance and continue to treat themselves as the inheritor of the original line and ideology.

During the seventies and eighties, the Maoists made the CPI(ML) their target of attack and killed their some of the key members. The CPI(ML) in their latest document says: "In the course of the rise and spread of our movement and organization in Bihar, we have historically had to face hostilities from different quarters: the feudal forces, the state and from Maoists. In the Magadh region of central Bihar (specially in the districts of Patna, Jehanabad, Arwal, Gaya, Aurangabad) where the predecessors of today's Maoists too had pockets of operation and influence, we had to withstand a spate of attacks and killings unleashed by both the MCC and the Party Unity Group.

"Till date we have lost no less than 224 comrades including our supporters, activists and leaders in these attacks. In Jehananbad-Arwal alone 127 comrades have lost their live, at least 70 in Patna, 17 in Gaya and 7 in Aurangabad. The attacks and killings did stop for a while after 2005 but of late we have again lost 5 comrades in East Champaran and most recently a long standing comrade and member of party's Barachati block committee Comrade Arjun Patel Yadav was gunned down by Maoists in Gaya. In Jehanabad Arwal COC (Party Unity) killed 60, MCC 21 and PWG 40 of our comrades. They have perpetrated 16 massacres claiming the lives of 85 people, 48 in 7 massacres in Jehananbad Arwal, 31 people in 7 massacres in Patna, 3 in Gaya and 3 in Champaran."

Maoists have killed many eminent persons owing allegiance to CPI(ML). There documents say: The list of comrades killed includes popular cultural activists like peoples' poet Virendra Vidrohi (killed on 30 January 1993 in Jehanabad). He had blackened the face of Congress Chief Minister Bhagwat Jha Azad in late 1980's. They also killed comrades like Rajeshwar Mochi (block pramukh of Dulhiunchak), Vijendra Prasad (Mukhiya, Poonpoon), Raju Singh (Mukhiya, Masaurhi), Yogendra Bind (Mukhiya, Jehanabad), Rajeshwar Prasad (DCM, Patna), Jaipal Singh Yadav (member Paliganj Area Committee).

The CPI(ML) also alleged in their latest publication that "when land struggle erupted under our leadership in Gaya and our organization began to expand in the district, the MCC in collusion with feudal forces sought to block up by unleashing violence. They killed our activists Chandra Deo Prasad, Ram Narayan Yadav, Shibbali Mistri as well as septuagenarian parents of comrade R.N. Yadav. The CPI(ML) also undertook political action and mobilized ideologically the rank and file against these actions of MCC." It strongly feels that since the party was devoid of any concrete approach to mass movement, they indulged in indiscriminate killings which later became the ideology of the Maoists.

The strategy and tactics of a Communist Party is the most sacred document. It defines the basic character of the party. Maoist documents on strategy and tactics say: "in the concrete conditions of semi-colonial, semi-feudal India where bourgeoise revolution too has not been completed and uneven social, economic and political condition exist, the objective conditions permit the proletarian party to initiate and sustain armed struggle in the vast country side.

"No peaceful period of preparation for revolution is required in India unlike in the capitalist countries where the bourgeoise democratic revolution were completed and armed insurrection is the path of revolution."

Maoists should realize that Indian economy has undergone a major change and India is no longer a simply semi-colonial and semi-feudal state. Moreover, this is not an immutable statement. The revolutionary situation of China could not be equated with India. Moreover, India is the biggest democracy in the world and this fact cannot be denied also. Naturally, the bourgeoise revolution in the classical Marxist concept will not occur in India; it will undergo a change; the face and tactics of the revolution would have to be changed. Maoists must realize that operating in a certain pocket is quite different from unleashing armed insurrection in all the states that too at all India level.

Maoists are wrong when they say, "No peaceful period of preparation in required." The fact remains that they do not have any work in urban areas of the states where they are active. Almost all the important comrades in Patna have been arrested. In Calcutta, they do not have any base. They even cannot aspire to have a base in Raipur and Ranchi or Bhubneshwar. Any preparation for long-drawn revolutionary process needs time. How do the Maoists propose to work in towns, cities and easily accessible plain areas which have strong networks of the state and where the masses, while engaging in drab everyday struggle are not yet ready for an armed showdown with the state? One thing is absolutely clear that Maoists have no clear concept of the Indian state. It uses greyhound, cobra and other dreaded paramilitary forces against the Naxalites, but never speaks in favour of using the army to contain them.

The Leadership Crisis

The lack of senior leaders and rank and file members, coupled with intensifying counter insurgency operations and desertion by members, has led to a crisis in the Communist Party of India (Maoists). Significantly, Muppalla Laxmana Rao alias Ganapathy, General Secretary, Communist Party of India (Maoist) confessed to a crisis within the party in a 7000-word letter to party members. The crisis according to Ganapathy is not just due the lack of leaders at the top, but also within the party ranks.

The number of members – earlier between 10,000 to 12,000 – has decreased. The ratio of men and women has also changed with women constituting 60 percent of the cadre. A good number of them have surrendered or joined mainstream politics or joined vigilante groups or formed bands of extortionists in several places. Vigilante groups have 'surrendering ceremonies' where Maoists lay down arms and join the groups to help catch their former comrades. Ganapathy pointed out that only three central committee members working outside guerilla zones were free as of now. The rest have been killed or are in custody. When the last party congress, the Ninth or Unity Congress, was held in 2007, the CPI(Maoist) had around 40 central committee members and 14 politburo members. Now, only 20 central committee and 7 politburo members are free.

Ganapathy's letter comes at a time when the Maoists' morale is already low because of the recent killing of Maoist sub-zonal committee chief Madhav alias Gollu Ramullu in Odisha. In the letter, Ganapathy asked for top Maoist leaders in jail to be freed – either by bailing them out or through prison breaks. He cited the jail break of three Maoists leaders from Chaibasa in January 2011, where slain politburo leader Kishenji's close aides – Girish 'Mangru' Mahato, Raghu Hembrom and Motilal Soren – broke the bars of their cell and escaped the jail. After the escape, they returned to the 'liberated' zone of Saranda and set up a massive training camp with Kishenji. Last year, there was a well-planned attack on a prison van in Giridih, Jharkhand in which several Maoist militia leaders were freed. In 2009, politburo member, Misir Besra escaped from a court in Bihar.

On the desertion of party members, Ganapathy said, "Instead of firmly adhering to our general political line and firmly implementing it creatively in the conditions where the enemy onslaught is seriously increasing and we are suffering losses, some individuals brought forth opportunistic arguments and left the party. Let us be cautious towards such opportunistic trends that that may also arise in future and fight them back. Let us get rid of sectarian and bureaucratic trends in internal party relations that are harming the unity of the party, isolating us from the masses and helping the enemy."

One of the leaders who left the party is Sabyasachi Panda, Secretary, Odisha State Committee, and Zonal Commander. Panda, who had grievances against two central committee members – Manoj 'Modem' Balakrishna and Ramakrishna RK – both his superiors, exposed the sectarian conflict within the party. Following his exit, the Maoists have not been able to recruit cadres, especially of Odiya origin. Panda was not alone. Members have also left the party in Chhattisgarh, Jharkhand and Bihar over minor issues and joined vigilante groups. With government offering attractive surrender policies, a large number of Maoists left the party in the Gaya-Palamu area of Jharkhand-Bihar Special Area Committee in the last few years and joined mainstream politics.

Many members are unhappy with the leadership and regional differences are brewing within the party. This puts the CPI(Maoist) – which was a merger of the Maoist Communist Centre (MCC), the People's War Group (PWG) and other parties – at risk. However, Prashant Bose, second in the Maoist hierarchy and chief of the erstwhile MCC, is quiet about the differences. Several of the ex-MCC cadres in CPI(Maoist) are unhappy with how Andhra leaders treat them. For instance, Ajay Mahato – the Sub-Zonal Commander of Giridih in Jharkhand, who had led a raid on a prison van to free Maoist cadres – had been asking for arms, but got none from his superiors.

Despite the dearth of leaders, there is no consensus yet on the elevation of junior members to the central committee. Besides, the positions of the jailed central committee members have been left vacant since their return is expected. Ganapthy said that he was looking forward to the movement gaining momentum through the youth and students who had joined them. The Maoists rely on the support of intellectual and frontal groups in urban areas which follow the Maoist ideology. Ganapathi hopes that the students of various colleges in Kolkata and Delhi will help revive the revolutionary movement in Kolkata. "They helped organise and sustain it in Lalgarh between 2008 and 2011," he said. This statement is in line with the government's suspicion that several students and professors of colleges in these two cities are involved with the Maoists.

Significantly, the CPI(ML) which recently joined hands with the Maoists has also been critical of the Maoists' indiscriminate actions. Following the death of Koteshwar Rao alias Kishenji in an encounter, they had issued a statement and also had criticized the approach of CPI(Maoist) on the question of 'peace talks'. They had requested the leadership of the CPI(Maoist) "to take lessons from these erroneous steps which have caused grievous losses, to re-examine their line and to join with the revolutionary forces to mobilize the masses for putting an end to this hated, anti-people ruling system." The CPI(ML) held that though CPI(Maoist) is claiming that it is working for the overthrow of the reactionary

Indian state, it is pursuing an anarchist line which is harming them as well as the revolutionary movement.

The merger of the Party Unity with the Maoist Communist Center (MCC) and formation of CPI(Maoist) led to its 2004 Congress adopting more dogmatic positions, including the acceptance of Maoism in place of Mao Tsetung Thought, as its ideological guideline. The differences between these two concepts are basic. According to the understanding upheld by the Marxist-Leninist forces, Mao developed the theory and practice of People's Democratic Revolution based on the teachings of the Communist International and applied it in the concrete conditions of China successfully. Mao later led the socialist revolution in China in the concrete conditions there. During the course of his long-revolutionary practice, he developed the understanding about the dialectical approach towards contradictions in a given situation. He developed the ideological-political struggle against the capitalist roaders who had usurped power in Soviet Union through the Great Debate documents, and in the course of the struggle against the capitalist roaders within the CPC developed the concept of Cultural Revolution, the theory and practice of developing class struggle under the dictatorship of the proletariat, based on the Marxist-Leninist teachings. The Cultural Revolution had reached a peak by 1967 with the removal of Liu Shaochi and Deng Tsiaoping from all positions of authority and people's communes as centers of people's political power were coming up all over China challenging the authority of the capitalist roaders.

It is by summing up these contributions of Mao, the Marxist-Leninist stream which had emerged at the international level in the course of struggle against the capitalist roaders who had usurped power in socialist Soviet Union and degenerated it to a social imperialist power, colliding and contending with US imperialism for world hegemony, had put forward Mao Tsetung Thought as their guiding ideology. But with the publication of the book, *Long Live the Victory of People's War*, by Lin Biao in 1966, a sectarian line started emerging in China, which was 'waving the red flag to destroy the red flag'. While claiming to uphold Cultural Revolution, it suppressed the mass upsurge developing as a part of it based on Mao's call, using the military. In the course of the tortuous class struggle developing in this period, the correctness of the Leninist teaching that the right and left deviations are two sides of the same coin and both ultimately serve the imperialists and their lackeys was being proved once again.

This book characterized the state and society in all Asian, African and Latin American countries as semi-colonial, semi-feudal, similar to pre-revolutionary China. It started advocating that the era of Leninism, the era of imperialism and proletarian revolution which was upheld by the Marxist-Leninist forces until then is over, and a new era of 'total collapse of imperialism and worldwide victory of socialism' had emerged, with Mao Tsetung Thought as the Marxism-Leninism of the new era. The Chinese Path of people's war, which Mao and the CPC leaders had repeatedly explained till then as a practice developed in the unique conditions of China was put forward as the strategic line applicable for all these countries. Following Naxalbari Uprising, the *Beijing Daily* published the article 'Spring Thunder over India' advocating this line.

Marxism-Leninism versus Maoism

Maoism, as advocated by the CPI(Maoist), is nothing but an aberration, a deviation from the basic understanding about Marxism-Leninism. Presently, UCPN (Maoist) of Nepal, in spite of upholding Maoism in name, has basically changed its practice and has criticized the CPI(Maoist) for its sectarian line. Again, it is reported that because of the sectarian approach of the 'front organizations' of CPI(Maoist), they are now expelled from the International League of People's Struggles (ILPS) led by the Communist Party of Philippines, which is also upholding Maoism, but practicing mass line to a great extent.

Unfortunately, under this concept, Marxism is reduced to a dogma. Marxist classics are reduced to idols. So the

Maoists do not find any need for analyzing the reasons for the degeneration of all the erstwhile socialist countries to capitalist path or the degeneration of most of the erstwhile communist parties to revisionism. Abandoning Bolshevik style of party and class/mass organization building, relying only on the supremacy of the squads and their fire power, it has reduced revolution to a game of heroes. If Lenin taught "Revolution is the festival of the masses" and Mao declared "Masses, masses alone are the creators of history", according to the Maoists it is the heroes who create history.

The CPI(Maoist) has repeatedly used word neo-liberal in its documents. But they have not put forward any analysis of transformation that has taken place in the forms of imperialist exploitation. An analysis of the present Indian situation put forward by CPI(Maoist) is that it is difficult for anyone to explain why the present mass upsurges are taking place. Even when big mass movements emerge in different areas and when they get an opportunity to influence any of them as happened in the Lalgarh area of W. Bengal, they reduce it to an area for deploying their guerilla squads and to organize actions like the derailing of Gyaneswari Express which killed many and inconvenienced millions for nearly two years, as the railway department stopped plying trains through that route in the night in the name of lack of security.

In Chhattisgarh, the Maoists are calling the forest areas of Dantewada district as their liberated area. But Jan Myrdal in his book *Red Star Over India* actually writes something else. When the earlier Congress Government tried to privatize the Shivnath river and later when the BJP Government declared a Special Economic Zone (SEZ) in Rajnandgaon district, a powerful mass movement was organized under the initiative of CPI(ML) due to which the latter's implementation was truncated and the latter had to be abandoned. Similar mass movements are taking place against other neo-liberal projects also. But in Dantewada, a corporate group like Essar has constructed a more than 200 km long pipeline to loot the rich iron ore of that area. The same is the case of other so-called Maoist-controlled areas in Jharkhand, Lalgarh in

Bengal and Odisha-AP border areas also. Instead of mobilizing the masses and throwing out the MNCs, corporate houses and mining mafias, often Maoists are serving as their mercenaries after taking huge sums from them. The Communist Parties built under the guidance of the Communist International based on Bolshevik Principles had a great tradition of building the party surrounded by the class and mass organizations. They collected money from the people and the mass organizations besides the levy from the party members and sympathizers.

The CPI(ML) alleged that the method of 'levying' adopted by the Maoists, especially when they are in the infantile stage of their growth has corrupted their own cadres. Combined with the sectarian practice of 'money actions' followed by many groups and splinter factions in many areas corruption has become rampant among these sections including the Maoists as there is no accounting of the money collected or no principles are followed in collection. In areas of AP and some other states, money is demanded to become cadres. The spirit of depending on the masses is alien to many of them. Maoists are justifying it in the name of huge amounts required to purchase sophisticated arms and to maintain hideouts. But whatever may be the justification, this practice has led to a deterioration of communist values among the cadres.

In India, whatever may be the claims of the Maoist leaders and the propaganda of the state, they are a dwindling force. Not only that, all the former socialist countries have degenerated to capitalist path. Just by waging few squad actions in highly a big country like India with more than 1.25 billion people and with organized and centralized oppressive state machinery, how can the revolution be led forward? If the CPI(Maoist) leadership, impervious to all these factors, continue its suicidal path, can anyone justify them?

The task before the communist force is to take lessons from the past, reorganize the party and lead the People' Democratic Revolution forward mobilizing all the revolutionary classes and sections for it. We appeal to their cadres to come out of this anarchist politics and join the revolutionary Marxist-Leninist camp.

In 1984, the Revolutionary Internationalist Movement (RIM) was founded, grouping together the Maoist revolutionaries' world over who were determined to fight for a world without exploitation and oppression and without imperialism. The Indian Maoists coinciding with the Mao Tsetung Centenary declared that their guiding ideology is Marxism-Leninism-Maoism.

The Declaration of the RIM upholds the proletarian revolutionary ideology and on that basis it addresses the tasks of the revolutionary communists in different countries. The declaration stresses "Mao Tsetung's qualitative development of the science of Marxism-Leninism" and affirms that he raised it to "a new stage." However, the use of the term "Marxism-Leninism-Mao Tsetung Thought" in our declaration reflected a still incomplete understanding of this new stage. In the last nine years our movement has been engaged in a long, rich and thoroughgoing discussion and struggle to more fully grasp Mao Tsetung's development of Marxism.

Maoism is not just the sum of Mao's great contributions. It is the comprehensive and all-round development of Marxism-Leninism to a new and higher stage. Marxism-Leninism-Maoism is an integral whole; it is the ideology of the proletariat synthesized and developed to new stages, from Marxism to Marxism-Leninism to Marxism-Leninism-Maoism. Marxism-Leninism-Maoism is a universally applicable, living and scientific ideology.

What has been most unfortunate is that the Indian Maoists have forgotten the golden words of Mao; experiment with the Marxism-Leninism in the prevailing condition of the country. The Maoist's rhetorics simply conveys the message that they are not competent at all to experiment the Marxism-Leninism theory in the Indian context. They are simply paying lip service to the greatest revolutionary. They ought to realize that Marxism-Leninism-Maoism is the enemy of all forms of revisionism and dogmatism. It is all-powerful because it is true.

Maoism is the elevation of Marxism-Leninism to a new and superior stage in the development of socialism. Marxism-

Leninism-Maoism combines to form a whole. One of the objectives of the Chinese revolution was to create a “new democracy” that would differ from the Western industrial and Soviet democratic models. The revolution resulted in the establishment of a socialist state. Politically, the “new democracy”, was marked neither by a bourgeois dictatorship nor by a dictatorship of the proletariat but by a joint dictatorship of all the revolutionary classes. In the “new democracy”, the state sector was to constitute the leading force behind the national economy.

Quite often people fail to differentiate between Maoists and Naxalites and use the two terms (Maoists and Naxalists) as synonym. Media which claims to know all about Maoism is simply not only creating confusion but is in fact oblivion over the two widely used terms and use them in their reports leading to impression that both are same with two different names. The basic difference between Maoists struggle and the Naxalite movement is, though both trace their origin in the Naxalbari Uprising of 1967, but while the Naxalite Movement thrives on the original spirit of Naxalbari; the Maoist struggle is an aberration of the 1967 Uprising.

Naxalism originated as a rebellion against marginalization of the poor. It began in 1967 with an armed peasant uprising in Naxalbari village of Darjeeling district in West Bengal. The term ‘Naxal’ came from the name of the village. The Naxals are considered left radical communists who support Maoists political ideology. The origin of the Naxals was a result of the split that took place in the Communist Party of India (Marxist) in 1967. It led to the formation of Communist Party of India (Marxist and Leninist). West Bengal being the centre of the movement initially, Naxalism spread to the lesser developed areas like Jharkhand, Odisha, Chhattisgarh and Andhra Pradesh. The CPI-ML has been fighting elections in several states. Prominent among these groups are the CPI-ML (Liberation), CPI-ML (Kanu), CPI-ML (Jan Shakti), CPI-ML (New Democracy) and others. However, a section of communist rebels retained separate identity. Along with Marxism and

Leninism, a new concept of Maoism emerged in India. Around 1966, Maoist Communist Centre (MCC) was formed in West Bengal. The group shot into prominence in Bihar in mid-1980s when they killed 54 Rajputs in Dalelchak-Bhagaura village of Aurangabad. Another violent struggle was started by the People's War Group (PWG) in Telangana. The MCC and the PWG merged to form the Communist Party of India (Maoist) later, which is posing a big challenge to India.

There are two fundamental differences between the Naxalites and Maoists. While the Naxalites pursue the policy of organizing peoples' movement at the grass-root level on various socio-economic issued and strive to organize and consolidate them and participate in the democratic process, Maoists have been primarily dependent on the use of the fire power. They do not support the electoral politics as it smacks of revisionism. The Naxalites have armed wing but they do not use it indiscriminately while the existence of the Maoists primarily depends on their armed militia. Maoists cannot think of surviving without the reckless use of armed power.

A façade works to differentiate Marxism-Leninism from Maoism. It is argued that Maoism has a more rural bent than the Marxism-Leninism. One argument is also put forward that the Soviet version of communism is suitable to urban workers who should form the revolutionary vanguard, Mao Zedong. On the other hand, the Communist revolutions, the Maoists are for peasantry, who would later join with their proletariat comrades in the cities to form classless paradises.

This is the most unfortunate development to creep in the Naxalite movement. Mao Zedong thought at no stage rejects Marxism-Leninism as urban ideology. Under the guidance of Mao Zedong, the greatest Marxist-Leninist practitioner, revolutionary groups from inside the old communist parties have been breaking away politically from the revisionist leadership of these parties. The study of Marxism-Leninism and the thought of Mao Zedong is important for the building of these new Marxist-Leninist parties. The most important task for the newly emerging Marxist-Leninist parties is to arm their respective parties with correct theory. This means to arm them with the theory of Marxism-Leninism. The study of Marxism-Leninism must also include the study of the Thought of Mao Zedong which is the Marxism-Leninism of the modern era.

Lenin used to say that Marxism is composed of the following three integral parts: (1) philosophy, (2) political economy, and (3) the theory of class struggle. When we study the Thought of Mao Zedong, we can see how he developed these three component parts of Marxism. Mao Zedong solved these questions with the aid of Marxist dialectics. In this way, he gave an important exposition of Marxist dialectics. He stressed in detail the relation between motive and effect. Mechanical materialists pay attention only to effect but not to motive.

The Thought of Mao Zedong has really creatively developed Marxism-Leninism. It has been elevated to a higher level. Juxtaposing Maoism against Marxism-Leninism would simply amount to negating the basic tenet of Maoism. Mao Zedong has systematically studied the laws of the Marxist-Leninist dialectics and has developed Lenin's thesis contained in his work *On the Question of Dialectics*. Mao Zedong does not deny the law about quantitative and qualitative change or the law of the negation.

Let us look at how Mao Zedong developed the Marxist-Leninist theory of the class struggle. Mao divided the history of development of Marxism-Leninism into three stages. To quote: "Marx and Engels founded the theory of scientific socialism, Lenin and Stalin developed Marxism, solved a series of questions of the proletarian revolution in present era and solved the theoretical and practical questions of carrying on the revolution under the dictatorship of the proletariat. These are three monumental milestones in the history of the development of Marxism."

Mao Zedong developed this Marxist-Leninist theory of revolution and the dictatorship of the proletariat and carried out the revolution of the proletariat in his own country. The dictatorship of the proletariat became a reality in China, a country with a population of 700 million people. He also solved the question of how to make revolution in the present era in which imperialism is heading for total collapse and socialism is advancing to worldwide victory. He has also solved the question of how to make revolution under conditions of the dictatorship of the proletariat.

Undeniably, Mao Zedong is the greatest Marxist-Leninist. He inherited, defended and developed Marxism-Leninism with genius and raised Marxism-Leninism to a completely new stage. Mao's thought is Marxism-Leninism in which imperialism is heading for total collapse and socialism is advancing to world-wide victory. It is the guiding principle for all the work of our party and country.

Often the Dr. Manmohan Singh as the prime minister had to face flak for not adopting a strong and aggressive approach and posture towards the Maoists notwithstanding the fact that they have been inflicting heavy losses to the security forces and common people. In the wake of the Bastar massacre of Congress leaders, everyone accused him of being too soft towards the Maoists and not adopting an aggressive approach. Only once he had used hard language and described Naxalism as a threat to the country, otherwise he is known to use moderate language against them. Even after Dantewala massacre of 2010 in which 76 CRPF personnel were shot dead by Maoists, Manmohan Singh did not appear to be aggressive. He told Chief Ministers of Naxalites-affected states on July 14, 2010: "For far too long have our tribal brothers and sisters seen the administration in the form of a rapacious forest guard, a brutal policeman, a greedy patwari. It is time that we provided a better delivery of services, one which is sensitive and caring to the needs and concerns of the tribal population." His speeches on April 16, 2012, Feb 1, 2011, Feb 7, 2010 and August 17, 2009-during UPA 2 lacked aggression. The Indian state unlike other imperialist countries does not primarily depend or rely on its strike power. In September 2004 speaking to the Chief Minister in Hyderabad, Prime Minister had specifically advised them to treat the matter as socio-economic issue. But the indiscriminate killings of the innocent people provided the opportunity to the state to strike back.

The overreliance on guns has reached to such a stage that the Maoists are unable to find an alternate measure to reach solution. Even their New Circular on Rectification underlines that in the struggle for the eradication of bad habits like liquor consumption, educating the people with the long-term view is lacking; in the struggle to obstruct manufacture of arrack, instead of rallying the people, especially the women, prominence is given to squad actions only. Squads have progressed to platoons and companies and now they are talking of raising battalions. The message is clear for the rank and file: The road to revolution is through guns.

One has to be pragmatic about evaluating and defining the Indian state. Rhetoric is not sufficient. It should be based on concrete objective as well subjective analysis of the existing scenario. The general secretary of the Maoists in an interview to the *Open* magazine, October 2009, had said: "It is true that our movement is stronger in the forests than in the plains and urban areas. This focus is linked to our path of protracted peoples' war. But it is not correct to say that we have ignored the plain areas." It would be expected of the Maoists to name the urban areas where they have a movement. Significantly, they don't have any work in urban areas. They are mainly confined to the tribal belts as they know that they lack the perspective of mass organization. Interestingly, the People's War Group set up by Seetharamaiah which now strictly adheres to the culture of guns, had in the initial stage emphasized on mass mobilization. But the new leadership discarded it as mass mobilization needed more in-depth study of the ground situation and application of correct Maoist thoughts.

What the revolutionary gain the Maoists achieved after carrying out 2010 Dantewala massacre in which 76 CRPF personnel were killed? The May 25 massacre of 29 Congress leaders is nothing but simply a revenge killing. There is no ideology involved in it. Even their document released after the brutal killing reiterate it.

On May 25, 2013, a detachment of the People's Liberation Guerilla Army of the CPI(Maoist) carried out the most gruesome attack in Sukma of Chhattisgarh in which at least 27 Congress leaders, activists and policemen including Mahendra Karma, the Salwa Judum leader of the state were gunned down. The Maoists have legitimized the killing as according to them Karma represented the oppressive face of the state administration. The handout released by the Maoists after the massacre claimed that it was legitimate response to the inhuman atrocities, brutal murders and endless terror perpetrated on the adivasis of Bastar.

Describing the attack as historic, the Maoists claimed that it took place when the Congress Party leaders were touring in Bastar region as part of their 'Parivartan Yatra' program (i.e. March of Change) keeping their eye on forthcoming assembly elections. Obviously, this implied that this attack was neither a classical revolutionary action nor a people's intervention. The attack was basically a military action devoid of an ideological base and approach. Karma has been at the target of the Maoists for pretty long time. But the Maoists could not muster courage to attack earlier. On Saturday when he was participating in the Parivartan Yatra the Maoists shot him dead. Polemically, this action does not fit into the Maoist philosophy or ideology.

Maoists claim that goal of the attack was mainly to eliminate Karma and some other reactionary Congress top leaders. Then why other innocent people, junior Congress workers, security personnel, activists were killed. What is the explanation of the revolutionaries? The Maoists even did not apologise for their crime. Dandakaranya Special Zonal Committee of Communist Party of India (Maoist) simply expressed regrets, condolede and offered sympathy to the families of the bereaved. This is the highest form of averseness towards the precious lives of the innocent persons. As if they have demolished and defeated the state apparatus, they also congratulated the guerilla activists.

The Maoist document claimed: "Dandakaranya Special Zonal Committee of Communist Party of India (Maoist) takes absolute responsibility for this attack. We send our revolutionary greetings to the PLGA commanders who led this daring ambush, to the red fighters who contributed in this success, to the people who took part in it by lending active support and to the entire revolutionary masses of Bastar region. This attack has once again proved the historic fact that those fascists who perpetrate violence, atrocities and massacres on the people, will never be forgiven and they would inevitably be punished by the people."

Hatred towards Mahendra Karma was quite perceptible and was the sole reason for carrying out the operation. No ideology was involved. The document read: "The so-called tribal leader Mahendra Karma was born into a feudal manjhi family. Both his grandfather Masa Karma and father Bodda Manjhi were notorious harassers of the people in their times and were acted as trusted agents of colonial rulers. His family's entire history is known of inhuman exploitation and oppression of adivasis. Mahendra Karma's political life was started in 1975 as a member of AISF while he was studying the law. He was elected as MLA from CPI first in 1978. Later in 1981, when he was denied ticket by CPI, he joined Congress. In 1996, he had gone with a breakaway faction of Madhavrao Scindhia and became member of Indian Parliament as an independent candidate. Later he rejoined the Congress Party.

"In 1996, a massive movement took place in Bastar demanding the implementation of Sixth Schedule. Though mainly CPI had led that movement, our party – it was CPI(ML) [People's War] then – also took active part in that movement mobilizing the masses on a large scale. But Mahendra Karma took bitter stand against that movement proving himself as representative of the selfish urban business people, who had come to Bastar as settlers and had accumulated massive wealth. Then only his anti-adivasi and pro-comprador nature was clearly exposed before the people. Since the 1980s, he had strengthened the bonds with big business and capitalist classes in Bastar.

"Then in 1999, Karma's name was exposed in a big scam called 'Malik Makbuja'. A Lokayukta report revealed that in the period of 1992-96, Mahendra Karma hand in glove with timber black-marketeers had made millions of rupees by cheating adivasi people and colluding with revenue and forest officials and the district collector. Though a CBI probe was ordered into this scam, nothing harm was done to the culprits as always happen.

"Mahendra Karma was minister of jails in undivided Madhya Pradesh. Later became industries and commerce minister in Ajit Jogi's Government when Chhattisgarh State was carved out of it. At that time a forceful land acquisition took place in Nagarnar for the proposed steel plant by Romelt/NMDC. While the local people refused to give up their lands, Mahendra Karma took stand against the people and in favor of the capitalists. He played a key role in forcibly taking away the lands by suppressing the people with support of brutal police force. The people who lost their lands in Nagarnar received neither compensation nor the employment as government had promised till now. They were forced to disperse.

"From the very beginning, Mahendra Karma stood as an arch enemy of the revolutionary movement. The reason is clear – hailed from a typical feudal family and 'grown up' as an agent of big business and bourgeois classes. The first Jan Jagaran ('awareness') campaign was launched in 1990-91 against the revolutionary movement. The revisionist CPI had participated in that counter-revolutionary campaign. Karma and many of his relatives belonged to the landlord classes had actively participated in it. The second Jan Jagaran campaign was launched in 1997-98 led by Mahendra Karma himself. This was started in Mahendra Karma's own village Faraspal and its surrounding villages and spread up to Bhairamgarh and Kutru areas. Hundreds of people were tortured and arrested and sent to jails. Many an incident of looting and setting fire to houses took place. Womenfolk were raped. However, under the leadership of our party and mass organizations people came together and strongly countered this counter-revolutionary onslaught.

"Within a short time, this campaign was defeated. Later the revolutionary movement became more consolidated. Anti-feudal struggles were intensified in many areas. Landlords like Podia Patel, the brother of Mahendra Karma, and some close relatives of him were killed as part of mass resistance actions. In many villages, the power of feudal forces and bad gentry was thrown out and the process of establishment of People's Revolutionary Power organs began. The feudal forces including Mahendra Karma were very furious as their lands were redistributed among the poor and landless peasants and the customs like unjustly forcing the people to pay penalties to the landlords were stopped. They opposed the progressive changes like stopping of forced marriages of women, discouraging polygamy, etc. also. And at the same time, the revolutionary movement was seemed as a hurdle by the corporate houses like Tatas and Essars who started their attempts to plunder away the natural resources of Bastar region. So, they naturally colluded with the counter-revolutionary elements like Mahendra Karma.

"They fed him with millions of coffers in order to create conducive atmosphere for their arbitrary depredations. On the other hand, after the emergence of CPI(Maoist) as a country-wide consolidated party as an outcome of the merger between the genuine revolutionary organizations, exploitative ruling classes intensified their counter-revolutionary onslaught in the guidance of the imperialists so as to crush the revolutionary movement. Thus, a brutal attack in connivance with the Congress and the BJP has started in Bastar region, namely 'Salwa Judum'. So many followers and relatives of Mahendra Karma like Soyam Muka, Rambhuvan Kushwaha, Ajay Singh, Vikram Mandavi, Gannu Patel, Madhukarrao, and Gota Chinna, etc. emerged as key leaders of Salwa Judum."

This is something like patting their own back. Maoists have been trying to hide behind the façade of self-eulogy. Karma was corrupt, anti-people element but this does not mean that he should be killed in this manner; an action of deceit. Maoists should have taken to mass movement and organized the people of his constituency to expose his anti-adivasi and pro-comprador nature. In sharp contrast to Maoist operation, Karma in fact went to the people and prepared them to fight against them. Maoist handout confesses: "from the very beginning, Mahendra Karma stood as an arch enemy of the revolutionary movement. The first Jan Jagaran ('awareness') campaign was launched in 1990-91 against the revolutionary movement. The revisionist CPI had participated in that counter-revolutionary campaign. Karma and many of his relatives belonged to the landlord classes had actively participated in it. The second Jan Jagaran campaign was launched in 1997-98 led by Mahendra Karma himself. This was started in Mahendra Karma's own village Faraspal and its surrounding villages and spread up to Bhairamgarh and Kutru areas." No peace-loving people or concerned with the rights of the tribals would endorse creation and launching of Salwa Judum by Karma. This utterly violated the fundamental rights of the adivasis and was a mechanism to perpetrate worst nature of torture on them. Basically, this was the reason that Supreme Court had ordered the state to disband it.

Maoists claim: "one can hardly find any examples in the history to compare the severity of the devastation and barbarity caused by Salwa Judum to the lives of the Bastar people. It killed more than one thousand people in cold blood; torched 640 villages into ashes, robbed thousands of houses; ate or took away chickens, goats, pigs, etc.; forced more than two million people to be displaced; dragged more than 50 thousand people into staterun 'relief' camps. Thus, the Salwa Judum became anathema to the people. Hundreds of women were gang raped. Many women were murdered after rape. Massacres took place in many places." The question arises what did the Maoists do mobilize this suffering humanity against Karma? Nothing, they simply relied on their arm power. In such a situation when the people are finding it arduous to survive no force on the earth could have prevented them to join the ranks of Maoist and launch mass movement. But it did not happen.

In fact, the attack on the Congress leader was extension of their policy to attack the security forces. No one should be under illusion that the Maoists are serving the interest of the poor. They are, in true sense, turning them more vulnerable to the retaliatory actions. The reason for this digression is wrong application of the ideology. This has been going on the days Kanai Chatterjee was the leader of the Maoist Communist Centre. They did not believe in Marxism-Leninism and based their edifice of revolutionary struggle on Maoism. Ironically, they treated tactics as strategy. This has given birth to militarism and distancing from the mass mobilisation.

Basically, this was the ideological difference for Kanai Chatterjee that he kept away from the Marxist-Leninist parties and policies. The Maoists believe in one philosophy that devoid of a political ideology they can reach to their destination through assertion of their gun power. But they are completely wrong. They must thank Raman Singh Government of Chhattisgarh for their survival in the state. Look at the manner they have been flushed out of Andhra Pradesh. If tomorrow the state decides to have its presence in the dense forests of Chhattisgarh, they will be simply helter skelter for survival. Wielding gun is simply a romance and the Maoists must learn to. They must look at the Democratic Centralism as one word and not as two separate words having different meaning. They must realize that their over dependence on arms and using the arms power in this indiscriminate manner will simply jeopardize the interest of the tribals for whom they claim to fight for.

Barely twenty days after the Bastar massacre, the Maoists carried out another bloody operation in Bihar on June 13, 2013. If in Bastar Mahendra Karma was their target, in Bihar it was Patna-Dhanbad Intercity Express, a railway train. They brutally killed three people including one sub-inspector of Bihar police, an employee of private firm and a constable of RPF. Over hundred Maoist guerillas, many of them women, attacked the train. First their comrades stopped the train by pulling the chain at an isolated place in Jamui and then indiscriminately fired at the passengers. They looted the passengers and left for the forest. In Patna, the police said the aim of the attack was to loot weapon from the escorting policemen.

The police headquarter might be right in its assertion. But a closer look at the nature and style of the attack made it explicit that it was a well-planned tactics to reinforce their authority, reflect the element of area control and domination and try to regain their lost influence in the region. In no way the Dhanbad-Patna Intercity Express could be described as a legitimate military target in a war situation. There was no troop movement in the train except the presence of five to six armed RPF and RPSF jawans who were on duty to guard the passengers from train robbers and other miscreants. Though armed Maoist cadres reportedly succeeded in snatching three weapons from the railway force, the attack on a passenger train can't be justified on military ground. Even if the three lives were lost in the crossfire, Maoists can't be absolved from the crime of murdering the three passengers, one of them was an off-duty policeman. Three weapons at the cost of three lives! What a great symmetry in the revolutionary means and the end!

The passengers' versions in the media pointed to indiscriminate firing towards AC and non-AC coaches from outside while the outnumbered RPF/RPSF men retaliated from inside. How did the People's Liberation Guerilla Army chose to make the passenger train a military target risking so many civilian lives? There was no warning to the passengers from the Maoist side either to lie down or get off the train which had happened in earlier occasions. In fact, the attack sets a dangerous precedence even by the Maoist version of war norms. Earlier, Maoist leadership used to apologize for attacks on passenger trains or buses and assured no repetition of such 'mistakes'.

In one such incident, a public transport bus was ambushed in Chhattisgarh. Some civilian passengers including tribals got killed along with the targeted members of Koya commondos who were also traveling by the same bus. Maoist leadership later sought public apology, though critics attributed it to the party's fears of adverse impact of the attack on its core support base. Similar regret was expressed during an earlier attack on a passenger train, probably in Andhra.

In those days, even the security mandarins credited the guerrillas for caring for civilian lives.

The ferocity of the war between government forces and Maoists has given an alarming rise to barbarity at both sides in recent months in complete disregard to war norms codified by Geneva Convention or valued in our indigenous martial tradition.

The use of tribal villagers as human shields by the government forces and booby-trapping of slain jawans' bodies by Maoists in Jharkhand's Latehar few months back led to the loss of five innocent lives including a teenager. The bizarre justification of their respective actions by the state police and Maoists made it clear that similar fate awaits civilians and dead in uniforms more and more. The civilian fatalities in Bihar-Jharkhand region since 2010 included the death of eight persons when a bomb, allegedly planted by Maoists exploded in Pachokhar village in Aurangabad District. The victims included 5 children while 11 others sustained injuries. In another incident, at least 12 villagers, including three women and one child, were killed when nearly 150 heavily-armed Maoist cadres attacked Phulwariya village in Jamui District. It was initially justified as a retaliatory killing but was regretted later.

Maoists ought to do some soul searching. They have formed the habit of talking and claiming too much. It is not that people do not make out of what they say. They should not remain under any illusion that people do not know about them. They must adopt a realistic approach. On May 1, 2014, the CPI(ML) Naxalbari merged with the CPI(Maoist). This merger is a major moral booster for the Maoists as it has come at a time when the Maoists were facing flaks and were feeling insecure with a major section of the rank and file deserting it against the wrong handling of the situation by the party leadership. Obviously, the Maoists claimed that it would strengthen the vanguard of the Indian proletariat. The merger was announced by Abhay and Krantipriya, spokespersons of the respective parties. Like the Maoists the CPI(ML) Naxalbari were making serious efforts to unify all Maoist forces.

Maoists claimed that as a culmination of the merger processes the two parties the CPI(Maoist) has been further strengthened. This unification has proved beyond doubt that, on the one hand, by mobilising oppressed masses in Protracted People's War against the ruling classes and imperialism and, on the other, by adhering to Marxism-Leninism-Maoism and the revolutionary line of the party and waging persistent struggle against the revisionists and liquidationists, all the genuine Maoist forces can unite into a single party, however long a process it might be. The Maoists pledged, "Our party shall continue the task of unifying all the genuine revolutionary forces functioning in various ML groups."

The Maoists made it clear that the unified party takes Marxism-Leninism-Maoism as its guiding ideology and deepens its understanding by upholding, defending and applying it creatively. The unity now achieved gives a boost to the capacity of the CPI(Maoist) to better fulfill its role as the vanguard of the Indian revolution. Over decades of arduous struggle, sacrificing thousands of lives of great communist leaders, red fighters and oppressed masses, the CPI(Maoist) has developed the people's war in India to the level where guerilla bases and red political power, in the form of Revolutionary Peoples Committees, have been established in central and eastern India, protected by the People's Liberation Guerilla Army and the People's Militia.

One thing is obvious Maoists projecting this as the biggest achievement is primarily a part of their psychological war against the trend of desertions that has gripped the party. The manner in which senior leaders and commanders of its guerilla squads have been surrendering has unnerved the leadership. In fact, to hide its failures and weaknesses, the leadership has been harping on the success of their military actions and government military action against them. The statement which announced the merger also mentions that in India the government has deployed four lakhs of its mercenary forces in central and eastern India, where the class struggle has reached the stage of intense revolutionary civil war, emerging as a revolutionary alternative, which is inspiring vast oppressed masses towards revolution and is concretised in the formation of People's Liberation Guerrilla Army (PLGA) and the new democratic state in its embryonic form. It is stepping up militarisation of Western Ghats to crush the budding revolutionary armed struggle.

But the fact of the matter is their claims are simply hyperboles and nothing more than that. The central and eastern India even does not have façade of a sustained movement least to speak of class struggle and civil war. Their organization has been petered away in this region except in Dandakaranya. In Bihar and Jharkhand, the existence of the party fully depends on some stray violent actions. As they claim that the eastern India is witnessing civil war, obviously the landed gentry of the region ought to not muster courage to touch the dalits. On the contrary, the feudal landlords and their private musclemen have been ruling the roost and perpetrating torture on the rural poor and proletariat.

How will the Maoists explain the fleeing away of the harijans and dalits from the village Pura in Gaya? What is their explanation for Ranbir Sena goons raping six harijan girls and women in Bhojpur? Maoists claim they have been spearheading a civil war in eastern India. If it is true these sordid incident must not have taken place. How could the feudal mercenaries dare to challenge the military power of the Maoists?

The victory of BJP and installation of Narendra Modi as the Prime Minister has witnessed the new trend of consolidation of the feudal forces and intensification of exploitation, oppression and fascism. It has surfaced in the ugliest form in the plains of Bihar, where the Maoists claim to work and spearheading a civil war. Five dalit women rag-pickers, including some minors, were raped by Ranbir Sena goons on October 8 night at village Kurmuri in Bhojpur district of Bihar. The incident happened when these women had gone to sell scrap to Kurmuri village. The incident took place when nine rag-pickers from nearby Dumaria village reached a scrap yard called at Maa Saraswatiji Enterprises to sell the scrap they had collected. Scrap yard owner

Neelnidhi, his brother Jayprakash Singh and their associate Guddu allegedly kept the payment on hold on the excuse that it would take time to arrange the change.

The total value of scrap sold by the nine was ₹ 1000. As it was already past 6 pm and the team had to walk 8 km back to their village, the rag-pickers kept insisting on prompt payment. There were three married women, two girls, two minor girls and two minor boys in the group. Neelnidhi Singh allegedly flashed a gun at the mushahar women to terrorise them into staying back at the shop. Guddu Pandit is said to have brought pouches of country liquor and the three reportedly forced the women and girls to drink the alcohol. The two minor boys are reported to have been tied with ropes. Six women and girls, including two minors, were then allegedly raped at an orchard near the thatched scrapyard. The victims, who came to their full senses by midnight, jumped into a drain to reach an approach road and escape to the Dumaria village. One of the girls, aged around 7, was spared and returned with the victims. One of the victims later reported the matter to Sikarhatta police on Thursday. The victims have also alleged that the perpetrators forced them to drink liquor before being raped.

The police have lodged a case against three persons Nilnidhi Singh, his brother Jai Prakash Singh and an employee, Jaggu. Nilnidhi Singh is the former area commander of the banned upper caste private army Ranvir Sena. The main accused, Neelnidhi is already facing 18 criminal cases and was on bail. Kurmuri, a village of 4,000 people dominated by upper-caste Bhumihars, is just one of many villages in Bhojpur which has been witnessing recurring caste tension since the killing of former Ranbir Sena chief Barmeshwar Mukhiya in June 2012. The Sena activities have picked up in the area after Narendra Modi became the Prime Minister. Taking serious view of the alleged rape of dalit women the then Chief Minister Jitan Ram Manjhi directed Bhojpur District Magistrate and Superintendent of Police to take stern action against the accused men.

A week back, over 300 dalit villagers ran away from Pura village under Tekari police station in Gaya district after a threat from some upper caste strongmen. They took shelter in a government building at the block headquarters for three days, before being persuaded to return after assurance of safety by the district administration. The incident took place while the then Chief Minister, Jitan Ram Majhi, himself a mahadalit, was speaking to the laureate of London School of Economics about the 'Bihar Model of Development'. Hundreds of mahadalits of the Pura village in the CM's own home district Gaya, were forced to flee after the murder of mahadalit Arjun Majhi, to intimidate his brother Vakil Majhi and prevent the latter from filing nominations in the elections for the post of the President to the Primary Agriculture Cooperative Society (PACS). The mahadalits of Pura village, Tekari police station, Gaya, have been forced to flee en masse, fearing a massacre by strongmen from the dominant community.

The police are yet to arrest most of the named accused in Arjun Majhi's murder, and have also made no move to arrest those who are openly threatening to massacre the mahadalits. Just imagine the audacity and courage of the upper caste goons. Even while Bihar is administered by mahadalit Chief Minister, the upper caste mercenaries are least bothered of the law of the land. The emergence and consolidation of the upper caste strike power could be understood from the simple fact that a dalit man's kin can be killed to punish him for wanting to file nominations for an election, and the dalits in the CM's own home district continue to face the very real fear of a massacre.

An insight into the Pura incident underlined that Bihar Governments, police administration, from the Lalu era to the present JD(U) rule, have colluded with the perpetrators of organized violence against the dalits and oppressed castes. The state machinery nurses a regimented view towards the mahadalits. Significantly, Nitish Kumar, the JD(U) supremo has been harping on organizing and empowering the mahadalits. They are the major vote of Nitish.

In the 1990s, the police and administration under the Lalu and Rabri Governments, failed to prevent the Bathani Tola, Laxmanpur Bathe and other massacres, and then proceeded to scuttle evidence in order to protect the Ranveer Sena perpetrators. Lalu Yadav openly declared his willingness to collude with the Ranveer Sena in order to counter the assertion of the poor and oppressed who rallied around the CPI(ML).

Nitish Kumar's first act as the Chief Minister in 2004 was to disband the Amir Das Commission which was about to submit its findings into the political mentors of the Ranveer Sena. The motivation was obvious, the political mentors included a large number of top JD(U) and BJP leaders. The serial acquittals of the Ranveer Sena members convicted for the Bathani Tola, Bathe and other massacres, also exposed how the Lalu-Rabri and Nitish regimes alike had acted to protect the perpetrators and perpetuate the injustice against the dalits and oppressed castes. The Nitish Government further exposed its true character when it allowed the Ranveer Sena supporters to run amok and unleash violence on dalits and on public property after the killing of the Ranveer Sena chief Brahmeshwar Singh.

On Independence Day last year, dalits in Baddi village in Rohtas were attacked by feudal forces. The Nitish Government refused to order a CBI enquiry into the murders of mukhiya Chhotu Kushwaha and CPI(ML) leader Bhaiyyaram Yadav by feudal forces.

As if these incidents were not enough proof of communalization of Bihari society, a chilling revelation was made by the then Chief Minister of Bihar, Jeetan Ram Majhi. Recently, he expressed his shock that a temple he had visited in Madhubani had been washed after his visit, presumably to 'purify'. The mahadalit CM has polluted the temple. Ironically, after his exposure Majhi became the target of criticism. Political leaders cutting across the political colour denied the incident. It was even argued that this nature of incidents could not take place in Bihar. Some even accused of Majhi to don limelight with hurling such accusations. Some cabinet colleagues of the CM even opined that the CM was misinformed, and perhaps this is why no case has yet been filed against the temple authorities.

After the murder, a CPI-ML Liberation team visited Pura and Tekari where Arjun Manjhi was murdered. The team noted that after the murder and subsequent intimidation, several mahadalit families of the Pura village had fled from the village fearing their lives. The team visited these families who are currently sheltering along with their children in Tekari. The team held that this attack on the mahadalit Musahar caste by feudal forces in Pura was to restrain them from participating in the electoral process. Vakil Manjhi of the Musahar caste was standing as a presidential candidate in the PACS elections. The powerful people of the village could not tolerate the fact that a person of the Musahar caste was standing for PACS elections. These feudal forces threatened Vakil Manjhi not to stand for the elections but Vakil refused to budge. Subsequently, on the night of 19 September, they attacked the Musahar toli. They could not find Vakil Manjhi but they abducted his brother Arjun Manjhi and killed him.

These incidents speak loud that the feudal fascist forces have been once again trying to raise their ugly fangs. It would be naive to believe that these forces were weeded out of Bihar. They were simply buying time. NDA's clear majority in the Parliament under Modi, absence of a strong parliamentary opposition, and most importantly emergence of RSS as the most potent communal Hindutva force simply helped the feudal mercenaries to resurrect. It did not take long for BJP and RSS to reveal its fascist, pro-imperialist, anti-federal and Indian expansionist face while using the people's mandate to justify its anti-people actions. Workers, peasants, Muslims, dalits and other exploited masses are already finding themselves amidst growing persecution as Modi Government reveals its fascist face.

It is really sad that the Maoists have not succeeded in working out an alternate mechanism to counter the emergence of RSS-BJP's fascism. To effectively implement the neo-liberal policies, imperialists and their allies seek to establish neo-fascist forms of rule. This is a challenge before the revolutionary and democratic forces.

During last couple of years, Maoists have lost considerably in Bihar, Jharkhand and Bengal. Killing of Kishenji is an example. They are taking to resorting to armed action to retrieve their lost ground. Maoists have suffered serious setback during these years and their rank and file has also depleted due to surrender, arrest and death of cadres. Significantly, Bihar and Jharkhand witnessed large number of arrests and surrenders. Obviously, at some level, it implied that some insider was feeding the police about the movement of the leaders. The party is not completely united. There are large-scale fissures. Instead of expanding in more fresh areas, the base of the Maoists was gradually shrinking in these states. The Bihar police has even succeeded in demolishing their training centres. This is a major jolt to the party. In some cases, the leaders have to desert their safe sanctuaries as these have come at the target of the police. Party insiders maintain that the party has suffered immense loss in these states.

A senior leader Anup Thakur revealed to the police that the lower-level leaders and cadres are not willing to hand over the money collected as levy to the top leadership. He said in Koel-Sankha zone nearly ₹ 5 crores is realized as levy but there is accountability of the money; who realized the money and where it went. A serious controversy has gripped the organisation. A tendency has also developed to keep the levy money with the individual leaders and not to deposit it to the concerned person. He even accepted that significant number of leaders and cadres have left the organization to float some parallel organization. The May 25 attack in Dandakaranya and June 13 strike in Bihar are primarily aimed at boosting the sagging morals of the cadres and make them feel that the party was control of the situation; Maoist movement has not lost its relevance and intensity.

Before the June 13 strike, the last significant attack was carried out in March 2005 when the ultras tried to derail Rajdhani Express in Aurangabad. Same year the Maoists carried out a successful jail break at Jehanabad and managed to release 398 prisoners and looted the entire armoury. It is not that no other action took place. But their intensity was quite minimal. Moreover, they were smaller and scattered. Interestingly, their main were the road construction companies. The companies had to face their revolutionary wrath for delaying or denying to pay the levies and extortion money. One wonders how could government property or for that matter the railways become the class enemies of the Maoists. They never spelt out their strategy behind targeting them. In order to boost the operation, the party had also decided to depute a couple of politbureau or central committee members in this region and intensifying their actions. The situation has also complicated for the Maoists with the State Government taking a number of steps to strengthen policing in the region.

It was with the aim of breaking this logjam; they enacted the June 13 operation. But this raises the question how long Maoists would take to guns to assert their might and presence? It is a fact that they have failed to match the strike power of the state police. No doubt they have ambushed and killed some paramilitary forces, but it does not in any way is enough to prove that they have much powerful strike rate than the state. Indian state is most ruthless as was seen in seventies when it mercilessly finished the Naxalites. Same thing happened again in the case of Khalistan. For fear of alienating the common people and particularly the rural poor, the government was refraining from resorting to excessive use of armed forces. If this was not the case, the government would not have hesitated to go all out against the Maoists. They must not be under any illusion of possessing immense strike power. They have been pushed out of Andhra Pradesh and Bengal and are now facing the heat in Bihar, Jharkhand and to some extent in Odisha. The Maoists are contemplating to carry out some major actions to break the present empasse. They are now eyeing the border areas for their next attack. They have based their plan on the presumption that Nepali Maoists would help them. This would also once again revive the theory of red-corridor which of late has lost some relevance.

Revolution is a social process of radical change and a revolutionary party can steer it only by undertaking 'concrete analysis of concrete (social) conditions' described by Lenin as 'the most essential thing, the living soul of Marxism'. However, examination of the Indian Maoists' theory and practice would reveal wide gap in their understanding of the present Indian realities with that of pre-revolution China. The Maoists' strategy and tactics in India is based on the Chinese path of revolution largely ignoring deep-rooted changes that had taken place in post-colonial India. It is astonishing how the Maoists could conveniently forget the capitalist development that has taken place during last thirty years. The Indian state is technically now more a semi-feudal and semi-colonial. How could the Maoists ignore the bourgeoning middle class. When the Naxalbari movement took place at that the population of the middle class was in few crores. Now it is 30 percent, around 45 crores, of the Indian population. This middle class is now the axis of the political functioning. This section which has been the patron of the capitalist economy now decides the mode of the politics.

During the phase of reforms and globalization, significant capitalist penetration has taken place in agriculture, in transport and in communications. The character and face of the working class has undergone a significant make over. Though the number of rural poor has increased substantially during this phase, the Maoists have not done any thing substantive to reach out to them. They are in their make believe world. Revolutionary ideology needs particularly to be updated to radically expand the horizon of democracy transcending the monolithic way thinking and functioning.

Marxism is the only revolutionary ideology which is marked by the term 'scientific'. Mao Zedong explained the 'science of Marxism' in the following words, "It was not until the modern proletariat emerged along with immense forces of production (large-scale industry) that man was able to acquire a comprehensive, historical understanding of the development of society and turn this knowledge into a science, the science of Marxism" So the science of Marxism is supposed to be as dynamic as any other branch of science and is subject to developing according to the development of society and man's understandings of the same. When Lenin applied his understanding of Marxism to the concrete situations of Russia, he developed it substantively and in the process clearly departed from Marx's formulation that proletarian revolution would take place first in developed capitalist countries.

Inspired by Mao's revolutionary thoughts, Communist Party of India (Maoist) claims in its party programme to follow 'the most scientific and developed ideology of Marxism-Leninism-Maoism'. According to the Strategy and Tactics document of CPI(Maoist), "The path followed by the Chinese Revolution is also applicable in semi-colonial semi-feudal India due to basic similarities in the conditions between India and pre-revolutionary China." This characterization of India to have basic similarities with pre-liberation China and on that basis determining the path of Indian revolution to be the Chinese Path seems contradictory to the methodology that Lenin and Mao followed while formulating the paths of revolution in their respective countries. This method was summed up by Lenin when he criticized the Hungarian Communist Bela Kun saying that he "gives up the most essential thing in Marxism, the living soul of Marxism, the concrete analysis of concrete conditions." Mao did a lot of library works studying China's history of development before writing series of articles explaining the socio-economic-political structure prevailing in pre-liberation China. But the Indian Maoists during their very birth as a force arrived at the formulation that 'Chinese path is our path' without commendable research work and since then it seems to have become a kind of dogma blocking any initiative on their part to take up the task of concrete analysis of concrete Indian conditions. As they think that the problem of determining the path of revolution has been solved once for all, they never thought it necessary to enter into the painstaking job of undertaking the vast theoretical task.

There is a vast reality gap between the Indian Maoists perception and the prevailing ground realities of India. The

Maoists must realize and understand that remarkable changes have taken place ever since the days of Naxalbari movement. Moreover, instead of finding out similarities between the Chinese condition and Indian scenario, the Maoist should focus on the area of dissimilarities and based on that finding that should chalk out strategy and tactics afresh. When the Indian Maoists find 'basic similarities in the conditions between India and pre-revolutionary China', any person will wonder how the Indian situation in the 21st century can have 'basic similarities' with China of the first half of the last century. Did India remain the same as it was in the first half of 20th century?

Besides India is having highly centralized state machinery where the State Governments might have their separate domains, but work in unison with the Central Government particularly on the question of dealing with anti-state insurgency. At the same time, a growth of organized strikes by the workers and of insurrections by the peasants in the countryside under the leadership of the Maoists is not happening in India, although the Maoists are working in India for quite a long time. Nevertheless, it is evident that both objective conditions in India and subjective preparations of the revolutionaries do not match to that of pre-liberation China.

Leave alone creating liberated Red areas, the phenomena of peasant uprisings against landlords that once shook Indian countryside (during Tebhaga and Naxalbari) can hardly be seen in today's India. Struggles centring the land question are still taking place (as witnessed in Nandigram and other areas of India), but there the peasants are struggling to defend their land from being confiscated by the state and big bourgeoisie. When the fragmented peasantry is straightaway fighting against the state and corporate houses to defend their land, the Maoists are imagining that old type anti-feudal struggles would break through in the Indian countryside. It does not mean that feudal exploitations have cease to exist in India, but questions the formulation of the Maoists that in India the 'contradiction between feudalism and the broad masses is the principal contradiction at present'. Though landlords are there in the rural areas, they hardly wield direct political power today. During last 30 years, spectacular changes have taken place in the power structure of India, where dalit power was established in Uttar Pradesh and OBCs like Jadavs and Kurmis are dominating the political scene of Bihar, both the states known for upper-caste landlordism.

In West Bengal, the principal ruling party, having considerable base among the lower caste poor peasantry, control rural power with an iron hand so much so that every contradiction with power tends to take the form of anti-CPI(M) struggle. The latest examples of Nandigram and Lalgarh movements can be examined in this regard. In Nandigram, the anti-state land movement turned into a bitter struggle for the peasantry to thwart waves of attacks by the armed marauders of the ruling party. In Lalgarh, Maoist actions are hardly directed against any landlord, while scores of poor and middle-class people belonging to the CPI(M) fell to their bullets. Whether these actions can be justified is one question, but how do they anyway match with the Maoists' rhetoric of anti-feudal agrarian revolution?

When the Maoists in Nepal took the decision to enter into electoral competition, the Indian Maoists promptly condemned the decision sticking to the slogan of 'election boycott' basing on the assumption that "all parliamentary institutions and parliamentary system itself, including all the parliamentary parties of the ruling classes, stand exposed before the masses more than ever." But at the peak of the Lalgarh movement one CPI(Maoist) leader Shekhar admitted at a press meet, "The People's Committee against Police Atrocities (PCPA) wants to participate in (parliamentary) election to defeat the CPI(M) party. Though our policy is to boycott the elections, we are supporting this stand in view of the aspirations of the broad people towards election." Thus, the party's policy on parliamentary elections did not correspond to the ground reality. More confusing was the statement of Kishenji who wanted "to see Mamata Banerjee as the Chief Minister of West Bengal."

The two aspects regarding agrarian revolution and election boycott, key to the Indian Maoists' ideological position, might be suffice to realize the extent of reality gap that exist between their ideological position and ground realities.

The Strategy & Tactics document of CPI(Maoist) mention that "...revolution will suffer if we fail to take into account the specific characteristics and peculiarities while formulating the guiding principles of our revolutionary path." But in the whole document no effort is ever made to take into account of the specific characteristics and peculiarities that Indian realities pose before the revolutionaries. Only in one paragraph these peculiarities are mentioned only to brush aside the same in one stroke. The paragraph reads, "Some people argue that in India it is impossible to establish liberated areas, to build the red army and to carry out protracted people's war because there is relatively more industrial development, capitalist relation in agriculture and better transport and communication facilities, and the Indian government has a strong centralized administrative system with a modern army when compared to pre-revolutionary China. These arguments are wrong." The Maoist document seems to agree that the above characteristics are peculiar to Indian situation, but does not clarify what implications these specific characteristics might have on Indian revolution.

While the Maoists condemn parliamentary democracy as hoax, they are keen to use political parties, elections, media and human rights bodies. The CPI(Maoist) has come out to express the party's view on media, judiciary, cultural, religious and human rights organizations as its spokesman Azad extended their arguments against accepting multi-party democracy even after revolution, "Then there will be several institutions like the judiciary, the election commission, the media, various artistic, cultural and even religious bodies, non-government organizations, and also human rights organizations some of which are floated by the ruling classes, and so on. If one slips into the quagmire of the so-called multiparty democratic republic, one cannot escape from upholding these so-called independent institutions. Many of these can become hideouts of the reactionary forces and work for counter-revolution in diverse subtle ways"

The Maoist strategy and tactics says: "The CPC led by Com. Mao made historic and comprehensive analysis of the development of Mao Thought (now Maoism), through its 9th Congress, held in 1969. It summed up Mao Zedong Thought as a completely new and higher stage of Marxism-Leninism. Thus, Mao Zedong Thought, whose historic significance began to be recognized by the Marxist-Leninist forces worldwide ever since The Great Debate, became established as a qualitatively higher stage in the development of the proletarian ideology by the time of the 9th Congress of the CPC. Maoism is not just the sum total of Mao's great contributions. It is the most comprehensive and all-round development of the science of Marxism-Leninism that had taken shape in the period of the tremendous changes and great upheavals that had occurred in the world since the time of Com. Lenin, namely the emergence of the Socialist camp following WW II; the upsurge of the national liberation struggles throughout the world leading to a new phase of neo-colonial control and exploitation; and the restoration of capitalism in the Soviet Union and Eastern Europe with the usurpation of power by the modern revisionist Khrushchov clique. Marxism-Leninism-Maoism is an integrated whole. Maoism is Marxism-Leninism of the present-day. To negate Maoism is to negate Marxism-Leninism itself. In our understanding, there has never been a Chinese wall between Marxism-Leninism-Mao Thought and MLM. Yet the term Maoism is a more precise and scientific explanation for Mao's contribution. In addition since modern revisionism is belittling Mao Thought and negating or denying the historical and international significance of Mao Thought, it will be more correct and appropriate to use the terminology Maoism in lieu of Mao Thought in order to draw a clear line of demarcation with them."

Mindless killings rather than following the Marxist-Leninist line of mass mobilization has witnessed a major split in the CPI(Maoist) in Jharkhand. A number of senior leaders and cadres opposed to the politics pursued by the party have come together to float a parallel Maoist outfit, Triteeya Sammelan Prastuti Committee. The organization believes in Maoist ideology but is strongly opposed to their style of functioning. This year in March they killed at least ten Maoists who were planning to carry out some action in Chatara. The TPC has gained acceptance in the local people. While they are against the government, trying to build popular movement on local issues, but they like Maoists are not against development works. In fact, they provide protection to the government authorities and contractors from Maoists. TPC is in control of the areas in Palamau, Latehar and some other districts in Jharkhand they have wider network in Jharkhand-Bihar border areas.

A closer look at the split would reveal that former MCC members have started leaving the CPI(Maoist). The party was formed in 2004 following the merger of Maoist Communist Centre and People's War Group. MCC was active in Bihar, Jharkhand and Bengal and PWG had base in Andhra Pradesh. It is significant that most of the leaders are comparatively young and in their forties. It is not that they are easily accessible. They live like a guerilla revolutionary in their base areas. But the Maoists pretensions are not there. They mix with the people freely of course they have their hideouts. They have been carrying out armed action but strictly adhering to the ideological needs and norms. There is no room for indiscriminate and mindless killings.

A visit to the areas wrested from the Maoists and now under their control would reveal a different reading and understanding. There is no basic difference between the lifestyle of a Maoist and TPC leader. But the commitment to ideology and common people is of high order. They don't terrorise or exploit the local people. Though a banned organization, its leaders and members have contested local body elections and also openly interact with the other political party leaders. Though they find fault with the election system and over dependence on elections, they are at the same time not in the favour of election boycott. They believe gun power should be subservient to the people's power.

TPC's Jharkhand Commander, Akraman is quite candid: "Just see by announcing war Maoists have been trapped in quicksand. They should make their target clear; who is the class enemy? Against who have they launched their attack? Maoists must understand this is not the time to fight. The prime task should have been to awaken the mass and prepare them for long drawn struggle. How could you achieve the goal of liberating the people without awakening them? Their main task to use violence against anyone has weakened them considerably. They have been ironically misusing their energy on wrong priorities."

Akraman who joined the MCC at an early age of 12 has been the main brain behind the TPC. He claimed that it was his platoon which killed 10 Maoists and held 25 others as hostages in Lakadmanda village in Chatra. He was the zonal commander when he left the CPI(Maoists).

TPC chief Brajesh Ganjhu feels: "Maoists have deviated from their path and have been indulging in simple violence devoid of a mass movement, the people's struggle. Though they talk of Mao and Lenin, in practice, they don't subscribe to their values and teachings. They claim that Jana Adalats usually penalize a guilty but in reality it is the whim of some leaders that dictates the course of action. When the PWG and MCC talks were in the final stage, several comrades left the MCC in Bihar and Jharkhand on ideological ground. Ironically, the Maoists began killing the comrades who had left the MCC. After 2004 they had emerged as a stronger outfit. Maoists killed 200 of our people from 2002 to 2004. Those who were alive finally decided to form TPC. What was interesting a good number of leaders and cadres of Maoist also deserted their party and joined the TPC."

While the Maoists describe the TPC leadership as traitors and police dogs, they also accuse the TPC leaders of pursuing a sectarian line of caste war between Yadavs and Ganjhus. Most of the Yadavs who were originally with the MCC are now with Maoists. They also allege that they are creation of police and are a non-political organization. But the matter of fact is the TPC has been experimenting with the Marxist-Leninist ideology as propounded by Mao Zedong. Sagar says: "We have come to hear about this allegation from some other source. But it is not new allegation. The Maoists have the habit of maligning their rivals. Undeniably, we have been using police. We are a small outfit and we are still making our inroads. If we take up fight with the police at this stage then that will harm us immensely. Our people are elected people's representatives. Naturally, they have to interact with all kind of people, including the police and have some understanding them. But we do not bother what Maoists say about us. We are clear what we have to do."

Akraman is more clear, "this is a canard being spread by the Maoists. When I was leaving the MCC at that time the Maoists have killed five persons of my squad. None of them was a Ganjhu. Even police was spreading this canard against us. They have dubious design. The areas under control of TPC have been quite peaceful. Even the Maoists do not dare to enter into these areas and carry out any operation. Local people say that development is the main focus of TPC." He says: "we are for mitigating the poverty and exploitation of the rural poor. Since the government has launched various programmes for helping the poor, why not to take advantage of those programmes. Why to deprive the poor people of the benefits of these programmes by obstructing them."

The number of such splinter groups is around a dozen. Some of them which have fire power as well as cadre strength include TPC, People's Liberation Front of India, Jharkhand Liberation Tigers and Jharkhand Jana Mukti Parishad. TPC was initially led by Bharatji, a front ranking leader of erstwhile MCC. After he left for Bengal the outfit is led by Brajesh Ganjhu. PFLI formed in 2007 and led by Dinesh Yadav has been active in Khunti, Ranchi, Gumla and Simdega.

The split and formation of groups primarily owe to mutual mistrust and caste domination. These groups accuse the Maoists of disruptive politics. Though the Maoists spokesman

Prashant alias Manas accuses the Jharkhand Government of propping up these groups and using them against the Maoists, the fact remains that these groups have many fundamental differences with the Maoists. The extortion and levy has been one of the issues on which these groups frequently clash.

Maoists have been accusing the government of not following the resolutions of Geneva Convention. But the reality is that they themselves can be held responsible for violating it. In January 2013 bodies of some CRPF jawans with crude bombs planted inside their abdomen were detected in Latehar. This was the misdeed of the Maoists. Incidentally, the Maoists who had planted the bomb was arrested last month from a nursing house in Patna. They have been killing the policemen even without provocation. These actions were against the spirit of Geneva Convention which makes it clear that no side in an armed conflict can mutilate combatant's body.

Recently, a very senior Maoist leader Vijay Kumar Arya observed that they were resorting to armed action in self-defence. He may be right in his presumptions. But none of actions carried out by the Maoists justify his observation. One thing is quite significance is that he admits that the party has been striking for broadening its base; put a check on the shrinking support base. He claims that efforts are on to bridge the gap between terrain and plain, but refrains from giving detail information. Arya also admitted the fact that Chatra district in Jharkhand which was once supposed to be Jaffna for the Maoists has been lost to the splinter groups.

□

4

When Suicide is Salvation

The general secretary of the Communist Party of India (Maoist) Muppala Lakshmana Rao, alias 'Ganapathy' holds, "revolutionary prospect and the situation in India are excellent; the social contradictions in country are sharpening; people of India are fighting a bitter struggle against feudalism, imperialism and comprador bureaucratic capitalism under his party's leadership and it is impossible for the Government of India to permanently suppress the Maoist, democratic, progressive, patriotic forces and national liberation struggles. The more they try to suppress it, the more they will rise up."

Ganapathy's perception may be true. But in the eyes of a farmer, the peasant, particularly those committing suicide he is wrong. Subjective as well as objective conditions being mature for a revolutionary struggle surrounding the poor peasantry who are committing suicides, the party has miserably failed to exploit the ground situation and work amongst them. The party's 9th Congress had also adopted a resolution on farmers' suicides which states that the number of peasants committing suicides has increased phenomenally. This is particularly so in Vidarbha, AP and Punjab. In past 10 years, several thousand peasants all over the country have committed suicide. In Maharashtra alone the number is almost 7000. From June 2006 to end of December 900 peasants had committed suicide. Cotton cultivators have been particularly affected. Though the

Maoist's Congress adopted a resolution, it did not work out a strategic approach to organize them and dissuade them from committing suicide. After all a Maoists is not a pessimist element or individual.

The real cause for suicides is the globalisation, liberalisation and privatisation policies pursued by the governments together with the continuing semi-colonial and semi-feudal relations. There is a general perception that Indian economy has transformed but the fact remains that even in the era of reforms and liberalisation the semi-colonial exploitation and relations continue to exist. The government has been pursuing new liberal policies but at the base of the programme lies the basic structure of semi-colonial and semi-feudal relation. These policies have led to the reduction of subsidies for agricultural inputs and low prices for agricultural products.

It is true that most farmers who have committed suicides have outstanding loans against them. The fact is that farmers who do not commit suicide also have outstanding loans against them. What do the farmers who commit suicide have in common? Those who have taken their lives were deep in debt – peasant households in debt doubled in the first decade of the neoliberal 'economic reforms', from 26 percent of farm households to 48.6 percent. National Sample Survey data reveals it. But in the worst states, the percentage of such households is far higher. For instance, 82 percent of all farm households in Andhra Pradesh were in debt by 2001-02. Those who killed themselves were overwhelmingly cash crop farmers – growers of cotton, coffee, sugarcane, groundnut, pepper, vanilla. (Suicides are fewer among food crop farmers; growers of rice, wheat, maize, pulses.) The brave new world philosophy mandated countless millions of Third World farmers forced to move from food crop cultivation to cash crop (the mantra of 'export-led growth'). For millions of subsistence farmers in India, this meant much higher cultivation costs, far greater loans, much higher debt, and being locked into the volatility of global commodity prices. That's a sector dominated by a handful of multinational corporations.

The suicides have exposed many myths. There has been a general perception that cash crops ensure better future for the farmers. But what we saw in Vidarbha; it was the cash crop that was the villain. It is said that subsistence farming is not sustainable and farmers often commit suicide. But this theory is also not tenable. Basically, inequality was the great man-eater among the 'Emerging Tiger' nations of the developing world. The commercialization of the countryside devastated all other aspects of life for peasant farmer and landless workers. Health costs, skyrocketed. Many thousands of youngsters dropped out of both school and college to work on their parents' farms. The average monthly per capita expenditure of the Indian farm household was just ₹ 503 by early this decade. Of that, 60 percent roughly was spent on food and another 18 percent on fuel, clothing and footwear.

According to a study conducted by the Indira Gandhi Institute of Development Research, Mumbai, the major reasons for farmers' suicides are debt, crop failure and low return, illness of family members, failure to arrange marriage of daughters and a lack of alternative sources of income. The farmers perceived suicides as a complex interplay of eleven reasons which cover social, political and environmental constraints. Some scholars have identified eleven reasons for farmers' suicide: (1) debt, (2) addiction, (3) environmental problems, (4) poor prices for farm produce, (5) stress and family responsibilities, (6) government apathy, (7) poor irrigation, (8) increased cost of cultivation, (9) private money lenders, (10) use of chemical fertilizers, (11) crop failure. Participants perceived that the human activities such as excess use of chemical fertilizers and use of genetically modified seeds cause a loss of land biodiversity and repeated crop failure, which subsequently lead to high costs of cultivation and debt. It was aggravated by government policies related to market prices, exploitation by private moneylenders and its ultimate health consequence was frustration leading to suicide.

Undeniably, the growing crisis is the result of ambiguous path of capitalist development that India pursued over the past two decades. Indian economy has not undergone basic transformation. Whatever change that has taken place is cosmetic in nature. The private sector has been using these jargons to fulfill its liquidity needs. It is also due to the way the global capitalism brought in or introduced new methodology to link the autonomous farmers or the social categories with the larger market.

The lopsided of development has increased the disparity between the urban and rural areas. Poverty percentage over the past two decades has declined between the urban and rural areas, but the disparity has widened. NSSO has counted that between 1977-78 and 1999-2000, the percentage of people living below the poverty line has declined from 51.3 percent to 26.1 percent, while in absolute number, it has declined from 328.9 million to 260.3 million. This does not mean that urban-rural disparity has declined; rather it has increased. In fact, the rural poverty ratio is still relatively high in Odisha, Bihar and the North Eastern States.

The exercise for measuring poverty has been typically mechanical in nature. Though the statistics undoubtedly reinforces the fact that poverty has declined it does not properly reflect upon the fact the disparities continue to exist. Even the measurement of the poverty level is not factual.

Let us take the basic figure of child nutrition to check the variations in poverty. The reduction in malnutrition among children has been very slow when compared to rapid economic growth in the post-reform period. International studies show that the rate of decline in child undernutrition tends to be around half the rate of growth of per capita GDP. As Angus Deaton and Jean Drèze said, in India's case, per capita GDP of about 4.2 per cent during 1990 and 2005 was expected to reduce malnutrition by about 2.1 per cent per annum or 27 per cent during this period. Compared to this, the decline in malnutrition among children was only 10 per cent.

Inspite of significant progress in the last eight years, a lot of work has to be done in order to reduce malnutrition in India. This also poses challenges at the global level because figures released by UNICEF show that in 2011, 55 million out of 102 million underweight children under five in the world — or 54 per cent of the global total — live in India. Similarly, 62 million out of 166 million stunted children of the world are from India (37 per cent). In other words, one out of two underweight children and two out of five stunted children are in India. It is true that with recent progress, the absolute numbers of children with malnutrition will come down. If the poverty has indeed declined then there was no reason that the purchasing power of the poor would not have increased. This minimum decline in malnutrition only endorses the fact that the poverty has declined only on papers.

The World Bank's Global Monitoring Report for 2014-15 on the Millennium Development Goals says India has been the biggest contributor to poverty reduction between 2008 and 2011, with around 140 million liberated from the clutches of poverty. But the matter of fact is poverty continues to haunt the rural poor, particularly the agricultural labourers and poor peasants. Had this been not the case such large number of suicides in the agriculture ought to not to have taken place. The farmers are unable to meet their fiscal demands. No doubt since early 1950s, Indian government has been putting in schemes to help the poor attain self-sufficiency in food production but the measures like giving ration cards and price controls over the supply of basic commodities have failed to have major impact. These efforts prevented famines, but did little to eliminate or reduce poverty in rural or urban areas. Klonner and Oldiges, in a 2012 study, underlined that MGNREGA helps reduce rural poverty gap (intensity of rural poverty), seasonal poverty, but not overall poverty.

The Indian government's definition of poverty in 2009 was questioned by United Nation's World Food Programme. It wondered if 11 kilograms of grains per month per person (24 lbs) is sufficient. The political debate that followed launched India's National Food Security Act, 2013, that guarantees food grains at very low costs to 820 million of the poorest Indians. Various sources have questioned whether India should continue anchoring its definition of poverty around food or money. If really India has been witnessing rapid economic growth it is unlikely that a major section of the rural population would prefer to migrate toward cities, making the issue of urban poverty more important.

There is no denying the fact that India should focus on Human Development Index (HDI) for a composite statistic of life expectancy, education, and income indices. Poverty in India is widespread, and a variety of methods have been proposed to measure it. Some semi-economic and non-economic indices have also been proposed to measure poverty in India; for example, the Multi-dimensional Poverty Index placed 33% weight on number of years spent in school and education and 6.25% weight on financial condition of a person, in order to determine if that person is poor.

The different definitions and different underlying small sample surveys used to determine poverty in India, have resulted in widely different estimates of poverty from 1950s to 2010s. In 2012, the Indian government stated 21.9% of its population is below its official poverty limit. The World Bank, in 2011 based on 2005's PPPs International Comparison Program, estimated 24.6% of Indian population, or about 300 million people, lived below $1.25 per day on purchasing power parity. According to United Nation's Millennium Development Goal (MGD) programme 270 millions or 21.9% people out of 1.2 billion of Indians lived below poverty line of $1.25 in 2011-2012. The World Bank reviewed and proposed revisions in May 2014, to its poverty calculation methodology. According to this the world had 872.3 million people below the new poverty line, of which 179.6 million people lived in India. In other words, India with 17.5% of total world's population, had 20.6% share of world's poorest in 2011.

The total amount of debt of the farmers who committed suicide was not uniform. It varied between ₹ 5000 to ₹ 50000.

Many of them had borrowed loan on short-term basis. The reasons for the rural indebtedness may be located elsewhere such as the cumulative crop losses, or the inadequate rainfall, drying up of institutional credit for small and marginal farmers, sharp increase in the cost of production, declining prices of agricultural commodities, withdrawal of subsidies to agricultural sector, or the exclusion of large number of farmers from the safety net as well as from public distribution system. Significantly, most of those committed suicide had borrowed money from the moneylenders, who would charge an interest at a rate of anything between 36 percent and 60 percent per annum. This shows that the institutionalised credit system has failed to address the issues of rural indebtedness.The nationalised banks or Gramin Banks have also failed to reach out to the farmers and peasant. Had it not been the case.They would not have borrowed from money lenders.

Facing losses, peasants were forced to take loans, first from banks. When banks stopped giving loans, they turned to moneylenders. More than 75 percent of loans are from private moneylenders charging exorbitant interest rates. Failure of MNC Monsanto's BT Cotton Seeds was the final blow. A section of farmers' leaders like Sharad Joshi had already betrayed the peasants by supporting globalisation. Disheartened farmers have turned to suicides. These are in reality killings by a government acting in the interests of the imperialists.

Why Farmers Commit Suicide?

Farmer suicide in India is the intentional ending of one's life by a person dependent on farming as their primary source of livelihood. The farmers suicide rate in India has been in 1.4 to 1.8 per 100,000 range over a 10-year period through 2005. Farmer suicides account for 11.2 percent of all suicides in India. Activists and scholars have offered a number of conflicting reasons for farmer suicides such as monsoon failure, high debt burdens, genetically modified crops, government policies, public mental health, personal issues and family problems. The National Crime Records Bureau of India reported in its 2012 annual report that 135,445 people committed suicide in India, of which 13,754 were farmers (11.2 percent). Of these, 5 out of 29 states accounted for 10,486 farmers suicides (76 percent) – Maharashtra, Andhra Pradesh, Karnataka, Madhya Pradesh and Kerala.

In 2011, a total of 135,585 people committed suicide, of which 14,207 were farmers. In 2010, 15,963 farmers in India committed suicide, while total suicides were 134,599. In 2012, the State of Maharashtra, with 3,786 farmers' suicides accounted for about a quarter of the all-India total. Farmer suicides rates in Bihar and Uttar Pradesh – two large states of India by size and population – have been about 10 times lower than Maharashtra, Kerala and Pondicherry. In 2012, there were 745 farmer suicides in Uttar Pradesh.

Farmer's suicide is a matter of great concern. While a comprehensive all-India study is yet to be undertake, the fact remains that most suicides occurred in developed states of Andhra Pradesh, Maharashtra, Karnataka, Kerala and Punjab. The situation was so grim that the Maharashtra Government set up a office to deal with farmer's distress. Attempts were made to create the impression that cotton grower farmers were committing suicides, especially those from Vidarbha. However, a deeper look made it abundantly clear that it was not just the cotton farmer but farmers as a professional category were suffering, irrespective of their holding size. Moreover, it was not just the farmers from Vidarbha but all over Maharashtra who showed a significantly high suicide rate.

In 2004, in response to a request from the All India Biodynamic and Organic Farming Association, the Mumbai High Court required the Tata Institute to produce a report on farmer suicides in Maharashtra, and the institute submitted its report in March 2005. The survey cited "government apathy, the absence of a safety net for farmers, and lack of access to information related to agriculture as the chief causes for the desperate condition of farmers in the state."

However, a 2012 study pointed to debt, alcohol addiction, environment, low-produce prices, stress, family responsibilities, apathy, poor irrigation, increased cost of cultivation, private moneylenders, use of chemical fertilizers and crop failure as the potent reasons. Left economists like Utsa Patnaik, Jayati Ghosh and Prabhat Patnaik nevertheless suggest that structural changes in the macro-economic policy of Indian Government that favoured privatisation, liberalisation and globalisation is the root cause of farmer suicides. Others dispute such views.

The Bt Cotton theory was challenged. In 2008, a report published by the International Food Policy Research Institute, an agriculture policy think-tank based in Washington DC, stated that there was no evidence for an increased suicide rate following the 2002 introduction of Bt Cotton. The report stated that farmer suicides predate the official commercial introduction of Bt Cotton by Monsanto Mahyco in 2002 (and its unofficial introduction by Navbharat Seeds in 2001) and that such suicides were a fairly constant portion of the overall national suicide rate since 1997.

In 2011, a review of the evidence regarding the relationship between Bt Cotton and farmers' suicides in India was published in the *Journal of Development Studies*, which said, "Available data show no evidence of a 'resurgence' of farmer suicides. Moreover, Bt Cotton technology has been very effective overall in India." However, the most common reason for suicide in south India are social issues, interpersonal and family problems, financial difficulties, and pre-existing mental illness.

The government appointed a number of inquiries to look into the causes of farmer's suicide and farm-related distress in general. Krishak Ayog (National Farmer Commission) visited all suicide-prone farming regions of India, then in 2006 published three reports with its recommendations. Subsequently, the then prime minister Manmohan Singh visited Vidarbha in 2006 and promised a package of 110 billion. The government set up a dedicated group to deal with farm distress in 2006 known as the Vasantrao Naik Sheti Swavlamban Mission, based in Amravati. A group to study the farmer's suicides was also constituted by the Government of Karnataka.

However, investigations by researchers from the Cambridge University's Department of Sociology and University College London's Department of Political Science have found that rates of suicide are highest in areas with the most debt-ridden farmers who are clinging to tiny small holdings – less than one hectare – and are trying to grow cash crops such as cotton and coffee that are highly susceptible to global price fluctuations. Farmers at highest risk have three characteristics: those that grow cash crops such as coffee and cotton; those with 'marginal' farms of less than one hectare; and those with debts of ₹ 300 or more. States in which these characteristics are most prevalent had the highest suicide rates. These characteristics accounted for almost 75 percent of the variability in state-level suicides. The researchers said their study points to a vicious cycle of Indian small holders forced into debt due to market fluctuations.

The research supports a range of previous case studies that point to a crisis in key areas of India's agriculture sector following the liberalization of the nation's economy during the 1990s. Researchers said that policy intervention to stabilize the price of cash crops and relieve indebted farmers may help stem the tide of suicide that has swept the Indian countryside. A recent Lancet study by researchers from the London School of Hygiene and Tropical Medicine which showed Indian suicide rates to be among the highest in the world. "Many believe that the opening of markets and scaling back of state support following the liberalization of the Indian economy led to an 'agrarian crisis' in rural India – which has resulted in these shocking numbers of suicide among Indian agricultural workers," said Jonathan Kennedy.

"Small-scale farmers who cultivate capital-intensive cash crops – which are subject to massive price fluctuations – are particularly vulnerable to accruing debts they can't repay. Many farmers who are traditionally responsible for a household's economic well-being resort to suicide because they can't support their families," Kennedy added. The researchers found that suicide rates tend to be higher in states with greater economic disparity but inequality as a predictor of suicide rates paled in comparison with cash crops and marginalized, indebted farmers.

Significantly, Kennedy pointed out, West Bengal which has high numbers of small holders has a very low suicide rate. This was because the CPM – who have an 'unrivalled commitment' to improving the condition of poor farmers – had a strong political influence over the past four decades.

"The liberalization of the Indian economy is most often associated with near-double digit growth, the rise of India as an economic powerhouse and the emergence of wealthy urban middle classes. But it is often forgotten that over 833 million people – almost 70 percent of the Indian population – still live in rural areas," Kennedy said. Researchers analyzed suicide figures of 18 states as well as national crime with census statistics and surveying done by the Ministry of Agriculture to create data models that investigated whether case studies of 'farmer suicide' that concentrate on a few suicide hotspots could be generalized across India.

Since 2001, one Indian farmer has committed suicide every half hour. Is climate change to blame for it? Like most modernizing countries, India has seen a decline in the number of individuals who engage in agriculture for a living. In the decade between 2001 and 2011, for example, the government estimates the number of Indian farmers declined by 9 million people, which marks the first absolute decline in this segment of the population since 1971. As a percentage of the total populace, farmers declined by 7 percent during the last decade, and they now constitute less than a quarter of India's population.

After all, a decline in the agrarian population could be a sign of increased productivity, or simply greater opportunities in the urban population. But this is not the case in India. The primary reason is the agriculture operation and production has been of subsistence nature. It has not been creator of assets. The farmers have simply been surviving except in developed states of Punjab and Haryana.

One of the more authoritative studies on the subject, 'Farmers' Suicides in India: Magnitudes, Trends and Spatial Patterns', examined farmer suicides in India between the years of 1997 and 2006. According to the study, "Going by the official data, on average nearly 16,000 farmers committed suicide every year over the last decade or so. It is also clear from the table that every seventh suicide in the country was a farm suicide." This was, the study's author noted, if anything a drastic underestimation of the problem. That is because, according to the author, many police officers only counted someone who had committed suicide as a farmer if they owned the title to their land, which an increasing number of Indian farmers do not. Additionally, as in many cultures, many parts of India consider suicide taboo and therefore family members are likely to report the cause of death as something else.

According to the 2011 census, farmers committed suicide at a rate of 16.3 per 100,000 farmers. This was slightly higher than the 15.7 per 100,000 farmers in 2001. But the real shock comes when one compares the numbers to the Indian population at large, which has also experienced a rising suicide rate in recent years. An average of 11.1 Indians per 100,000 killed themselves in 2011. Thus, India's farmers committed suicide at a rate 47 percent higher than the rest of the population. The problem has become so bad that some states stopped keeping track of the suicide rate among farmers.

A 2008 study by the International Food Policy Research Institute found indebtedness among Indian farmers can be linked to numerous causes, including a lack of reliable credit, changes in government policies, cropping patterns, plant and insect resistance to pesticides, and even shifts in the crops planted on the farm. The Council for Social Development's (CSD) June 2012 study, Socio-Economic Impact assessment of Bt Cotton in India, identified the key reasons leading to farmer suicides as lack of irrigation facilities, unavailability of timely credit and fluctuating cotton prices over the years. No doubt, Government of India has been taking steps to address the problems of the farmers' suicides, but these are not sufficient and adequate. Often the political interventions prevails. The official figure is actually 270,000 since 1995.

One of the most disquieting developments in the era of the neo-liberal policy in India has been widespread occurrence of farmers' suicides in different parts of the country including not only in the drought-prone areas of Andhra Pradesh, Karnataka and Maharashtra but also in a state of having sufficient rainfall like Kerala, as also in Punjab with large areas under irrigation. With the government occupied with the economic growth and promotion of the private sector, the agricultural and rural development sectors were neglected. The government and the Finance Minister would become restive whenever the stock exchange registered a fall and elated when the stock exchange rose. Ironically, the Reserve Bank, instead of honouring its commitment and responsibility to the agricultural and rural sector, has been more concerned of the market and market forces.

The causes of farmers' suicides are both economic and social. The economic causes are:

(i) growing expenditure, specially on bought inputs
(ii) low productivity
(iii) inadequate prices of agriculture produce
(iv) difficulties in marketing and marketing hazards
(v) natural hazards caused by drought
(vi) absence of proper crop planning
(vii) unsatisfactory agriculture credit
(viii) accumulated burden of debt.

Amongst the social causes are:

(i) the drinking habit which atrophies the productivity of the farmer

(ii) extravagant expenditure on marriages

(iii) bad health and illness and inability to meet the necessary expenditure on medicine and health services.

Resolution on Farmers' Suicides

The number of peasants committing suicides has increased phenomenally in recent years. The scenario is quite harrowing in Vidarbha, AP and Punjab, all the most developed regions and states of the country. In past 10 years several thousand peasants all over the country have committed suicide. In Maharashtra alone the number is more than 10000.

In a welfare state, it is the responsibility of the State and Central governments to protect the interest of its people. But both the Maharashtra and the Government of India were found wanting to come to the help of the distressed people. Instead of looking at the suicides from human perspective, the bureaucrats looked at the deaths from the narrow prism of farm loan. What was most unfortunate was that they did not view it as a capitalist hegemony to exploit the poor farmers by supplying sub-standard seeds. Ironically, the governments are diverting attention by placing the blame on loans for wasteful expenditure, poor crop/output, family and other psychological tensions. The financial package of the Union Government was nothing but a cunning attempt of the finance department to fool the masses. While the peasants did not get a paisa, the money went to cooperative banks.

It is most unfortunate that the governments have been taking the voice and stand of leaders like Sharad Joshi as the stand and understanding of the common farmers. It ought to be borne in mind that the farming class is horizontally split in capitalist farmers, middle peasant and poor or small peasant.

The 9th Congress of the Maoists had opposed the pro-imperialist policies of the government, expressed its sympathies with the peasants and appealed them to wage militant struggle. But it did not volunteer to spearhead the peasant movement. The 10th Congress called upon the peasants to demand that debts be waived, agricultural subsidies be restored, investments in irrigation and other agricultural needs be increased, proper prices for agricultural products should be paid and MNCs like Monsanto and their GM seeds should be banned. But ironically the Maoists did not organize any political protest movement against these malaises. They decided to oppose the policies of liberalisation, privatisation and globalisation. In fact, even after recent setbacks the Maoists have not come out of their mental block of depending on armed action.

They say that only New Democratic Revolution will solve the problems of the peasantry. But they are personally not sure how the country will usher into New Democratic Revolution. Will it directly descend from the sky or the Maoists strive to achieve it? They are talking like a political leader of a bourgeoise political party who are not tired of mesmerizing the people with utopian offers. It is quite interesting to read their pledge to organise the vast masses of the peasantry to intensify the armed struggle to overthrow this semi-colonial, semi-feudal system. They plan to achieve it by organizing some stray armed actions in Dandakaranya and Jharkhand!

Farmers' suicides in Vidarbha are caused by the complex interplay of social, political and environmental constraints. Hence, a comprehensive intervention to ensure self-reliance and capacity building among farmers in modern farming techniques, monitoring and support system for vulnerable farmers, a village-level, transparent system for disbursement of relief packages is required to prevent farmer suicides in the near future. Apart from this, there is a need to strengthen the National Mental Health Program at primary health-care level to offer support and counseling to vulnerable farmers in rural area.

In the absence of institutionalized finance, the farmers normally resort to borrowing from private moneylenders. Significantly, the loans taken from the private moneylenders are difficult to repay with the period due to high interest rates. Hence, the government should ensure adequate institutional finance and crop insurance to small farmers. Maharashtra State Government plans to alleviate debt, ensure fresh crop loans for both small and big farmers, disburse loans through the farmers' Self-Help Groups, provide subsidy of the crop insurance premium, encourage the promotion of agro-processing industry, provide financial assistance for community marriage and encourage organic farming. Ironically it is yet to move in a concrete manner.

Five things have been changed with Monsanto's entry. First, Indian companies were locked into joint ventures and licensing arrangements, and concentration over the seed sector increased. In the case of cotton, Monsanto now controls 95 percent of the cotton seed market through its GMOs. Second, seed which had been the farmers' common resource became the 'intellectual property' of Monsanto, for which it started collecting royalties thus raising the costs of seed. Third, open-pollinated cotton seeds were displaced by hybrids, including GMO hybrids. A renewable resource became a non-renewable patented commodity. Fourth, cotton which had earlier been grown as a mixture with food crops now had to be grown as a monoculture, with higher vulnerability to pests, disease, drought and crop failure. Finally, Monsanto started to subvert India's regulatory processes, and in fact started to use public resources to push its non-renewable hybrids and GMOs through so-called public-private partnerships (PPP).

According to data from the Indian Government, nearly 75 percent rural debt is due to purchased inputs. Farmers' debt grows as Monsanto profits grow. It is in this systemic sense that Monsanto's seeds are those of suicide. An internal advisory by the Agricultural Ministry of India in January 2012 had this to say to the cotton growing states in India: "Cotton farmers are in a deep crisis since shifting to Bt Cotton.

The spate of farmer suicides in 2011-12 has been particularly severe among Bt Cotton farmers."

The Lancet study notes: "Most public attention [on suicide] in India has focused on suicide in farmers." A significant number of ethnographies, case studies, government reports, and newspaper articles claim that the opening of markets and scaling back of state support that followed the liberalization of the Indian economy in the early 1990s led to an 'agrarian crisis' and an increase in farmers' suicides. So-called 'marginal farmers' with landholdings of less than one hectare, who cultivate capital-intensive cash crops that are subject to price fluctuations such as coffee and cotton, are most likely to have debts that they are unable to pay back, and are, therefore, at greater risk of committing suicide. This research concentrates on states that have some of the highest suicide rates in the country such as Andhra Pradesh, Kerala, Karnataka and Maharashtra. Thus, when taken as a whole this body of research suggests that inter-state variation in suicide rates can, at least to some extent, be explained by the characteristics of the rural political economy. The Lancet study does not, however, correctly operationalize the mechanism that many case studies identify as linking farmers to increased suicide rates.

A lawsuit has been filed against the company that is responsible for farmer suicide every 30 minutes, five million farmers are now suing Monsanto. The farmers state that Monsanto has been unfairly gathering exorbitant profits each year on a global scale from 'renewal' seed harvests, which are crops planted using seed from the previous year's harvest. The practice of using renewal seeds dates back to ancient times, but Monsanto seeks to collect massive royalties and put an end to the practice. Why? Because Monsanto owns the very patent to the genetically modified seed, and is charging the farmers not only for the original crops, but the later harvests as well.

The Indian Government's response to the crisis – largely in the form of limited debt relief and compensation programes

– has, by and large, failed to address the magnitude and scope of the problem or its underlying causes. The government has long been alerted to the cotton farmer suicide crisis, yet has done little to adequately respond. Cotton exemplifies India's general shift toward cash crop cultivation, a shift that has contributed significantly to farmer vulnerability, as evidenced by the fact that the majority of suicides every thirty minutes: farmer suicides, human rights, and the agrarian crisis in India are committed by farmers in the cash crop sector. The cotton industry, has also been dominated by foreign multinationals that promote genetically modified seeds and exert increasing control over the cost, quality, and availability of agricultural inputs.

A combination of India's economic reforms, the influence of multinationals in the cotton farming sector, and poor climate conditions have all led to a deepening agrarian crisis. As a result, smallholder farmers are trapped in a cycle of debt. During a bad year, money from the sale of the cotton crop might not cover even the initial cost of the inputs, let alone be sufficient for paying the usurious interest on loans or provide adequate food or necessities for the family. The only way out might be to take on yet more loans and buy yet more inputs, which in turn can lead to even greater debt. As noted above, indebtedness is a leading factor in farmer's suicides. The farmer may see little hope in this situation and, ironically, many take their lives by ingesting the very pesticide which they went into debt to purchase.

Farmer indebtedness is put in even starker relief, and poses an even more insurmountable burden, when the farmers have daughters whose marriages require the payment of dowry. Farmers who pay these dowries fall further into debt – or face the social stigma of being unable to pay – and may commit suicide as a result. Even more startlingly, in Andhra Pradesh, unmarried daughters, wracked with guilt over their fathers' deaths, have committed suicide themselves.

The abnormal suicides should have provided the right opportunity and platform to the Maoists to grow and expand in Maharashtra, Karnataka and other states. But the fact remains that they continue to be confined in some tribal-dominated areas. This ought to be viewed and analysed in proper perspective. The fact remains that ever since their birth, party unit and MCC, have been active in the tribal areas. Unlike other Naxalite parties, they failed to build a strong base in other areas, specially in non-tribal areas. Do the Maoists think that they can bring about revolution in India on the support of tribals only? Else, what is the reason that they are not willing to expand? One of the reasons may be their shyness to penetrate into the urban areas where they will have to confront the bourgeoning middle class. Notwithstanding their claims of being a revolutionary party, they are in fact scared of sharing the ground and exposing themselves to the new social and cultural scenario.

Their resolution also makes it clear that their understanding of the Indian farmers and peasantry has been poor. It's official now: India has witnessed over a quarter of a million farmers' suicides between 1995 and 2010. The National Crime Records Bureau's report on 'Suicides in India' places the number for 2010 at 15,964. That brings the cumulative 16-year total from 1995 to 2,56,913. This is worst-ever recorded wave of suicides of this kind in human history. Maharashtra posts a dismal picture with over 50,000 farmers killing themselves in the country's richest state in that period. It also remains the worst state for such deaths for a decade now. Close to two-thirds of all farm suicides have occurred in five States: Maharashtra, Karnataka, AP, Madhya Pradesh and Chhattisgarh.

Significantly, Maharashtra in the past has been witness to strong Marxist movement. The state had produced some of the famous leftist leaders. But today with the economy undergoing a major shift, the leftist or Marxist movement has lost the touch or charm to the people of the state. They prefer to vote a dalit party but not eager to support a left party. Obviously at one level it also makes clear that Maoists have lost touch with the people of the state and more importantly evolve a strategy as to how to combat the menace of globlisation and reforms. Simply condemning the twin menaces would not do. For them it is much easier to carry out annihilations, blow a school or train, kill the police or seek extortion. In tribal belt, they do not have do much. It is the fire power that matters most. But the moment they start interacting with the globalised political and economic development, they find themselves handicap.

Ganapathy is also far from the truth when he says, "the people of India are fighting a bitter struggle against feudalism, imperialism and comprador bureaucratic capitalism under our party's leadership. We would be able to influence the situation in South Asia by defending ourselves against the enemy offensive and intensifying our People's War. Except some scarce and isolated pockets, the influence of the CPI(Maoist) is not uniform." It would not be an exaggeration to say that the government and basically the Union Home Ministry has made the Maoists a demon to be feared. The manner in which the home ministry and particularly P. Chidambaram has been harping on the Maoism that the people got scared of it and in turn they also became a big cat. If what Ganapathy says the people of the country have launched a struggle then it should have been visible in Maharashtra, Gujarat, Karnataka and in some pocket of Kerala. But no where the people were seen to rise against the government, on the issue of farmers' suicide. Probably, it was not a serious matter at all for the Maoists to pay enough attention.

The Maoists have been neglecting the peasants in their operational areas. The reason as laid down in the strategy and tactics documents of the party is "If the party organization is confined to the peasantry alone the development of the party along with the movement will be retarded." The strategy and tactics of the party makes it abundantly clear that the focus should not be on the peasantry whereas in an economy like India, the peasantry should be the main force for undertaking the revolution. Party nevertheless mentions that the leadership should review the situation from time to time with a strategic perspective and concentrate on expanding into the working class, students, youth, women, intelligentsia and other sections. Likewise, the leadership has to strive to maintain the balance in the party organization between strategic areas and other areas and between rural and urban areas. Special consolidation campaigns, education campaigns have to be taken up so as to increase the party membership in a big way.

Interestingly, the same document underlines, "our path is the path of protracted people's war, it is obvious that we have to mainly concentrate our work including party building on the rural areas. In order to strengthen the proletarian foundations in the party organisation, we have to pay special attention to building the party among the poor peasants and agricultural labourers in the rural areas also. In fact, the task to build up the party from among the workers and landless-poor peasants is the backbone or the basis of our party building. We have also to give importance to the task of building our party among the students who are a revolutionary force and who are subjected to grave injustice due to the unscientific and undemocratic education policy and face a dark future. To begin with, we must make efforts to educate and consolidate them in the rural and urban areas. The advanced among them should be sent to backward rural areas to integrate with the peasantry and adivasis. We have to give special importance to assimilate into the party organisation the unemployed youth living in the extensive rural areas and towns and cities. Similarly, we have to give importance to party work among teachers, intellectuals, employees in other fields, etc."

These two formulations make it clear that the party has certain amount of confusion about the role of the peasantry. They talk liberally about Mao Zedong and his revolution, but fail to appreciate the role of the peasantry, which constituted the main force. The CPI(Maoist) is confused is manifest in two contradictory resolutions on peasantry.

The attitude and approach of the party on the issue of leadership is also a revelation. It states, "party should take special steps to ensure that dalits develop into leadership positions at all levels of the party organisation. In the sphere of women, and particularly toiling women, the party must make special efforts and draw them into the ongoing armed agrarian revolutionary struggle as well as into struggles against social inequalities, oppression and patriarchy. We must pay attention to giving training to develop necessary political consciousness in them in order to develop them as able party cadre and to include them in various party committees including with all other committees and promote them to leadership positions." Its observation on dalit leadership is sectarian. A dalit is also a peasant or landless labourers. Why instead of identifying him on the basis of profession, a dalit should be chosen on the caste line? This only encourages the element of casteism. How could a party dedicated to the Maoism preach this political line? Moreover by implication it intends to send the message that the dalits are not capable to lead struggles on their own. Else what is the implication of saying that we must give training to develop political consciousness? The Maoist live under the illusion that they don't have political consciousness. It is worth mentioning that turn to the Bhojpur struggle of early seventies and find out the role played by the dalits and harijans. In fact, they led the Naxalite movement and revived it when it was virtually on the verge of decline.

The strategy and tactics also make it clear that the party has to make similar steps in relation to the adivasi masses. "The party must give special attention in the education and training of the party members hailing from Adivasi community in ideological, political, organisational and military matters. It is only through such special attention that we will be able to help these comrades overcome the handicaps which social oppression and backwardness has forced upon them. It is only such measures that will facilitate the quick development of Adivasi comrades in the various levels of leadership in the party and the PLGA. Just as we expand and develop the revolutionary movement to the higher stage, likewise we have to develop the party by increasing its membership extensively and consolidating it. It is only by increasing the party membership and consolidating the party that we will be able to develop the revolutionary movement to the higher stage and expand it further. Conversely, only when we expand and take the revolutionary movement to the higher stage, will it be possible to increase the membership of the party and consolidate it? It is only when we understand the dialectical relationship between these two aspects, we can develop the class struggle, the revolutionary movement and develop the party as a strong and experienced leader of the oppressed masses. It is very much necessary to concentrate on party building if the people's war has to advance in big leaps. There is a dialectical relationship between propaganda, agitation, struggle and organization." How could the leadership say so? It appears that they are ignorant of some of the famous adivasi rebellions. They claim to organize adivasis in Jharkhand, but they should know the past of the tribal movements and struggles. They must refrain from generalizing the issue.

Their contempt for the adivasis is also manifest in their evaluation of the roles of the adivasis in their movement. The strategy and tactics of the party underlines: "The adivasis, or the tribes residing in the hilly regions, forests or less-developed plains in India, constitute about 7 percent of the Indian population. Representing relatively more backward forces of production, their economy, society and culture differ significantly from those in the rest of India. The imperialists, comprador bureaucratic bourgeoisie, unscrupulous contractors, moneylenders, traders and government officials have deprived the adivasis of their land and other traditional means of livelihood. The process of breaking up of their traditional economies, society and culture and their forcible assimilation into the semi-colonial, semi-feudal setup by the Indian ruling classes serving imperialism is proceeding at an unprecedented pace particularly after the transfer of power. The attempts to convert adivasis into various religions with the backing of the state have been going on since a long time. Whereas during British rule, Christianity spread on a considerable scale into the vast tracts inhabited by the adivasis, after the transfer of power it is the Hindu chauvinist organisations that are aggressively spreading Hindu religion in these areas. As the regions inhabited by the adivasis are rich in mineral deposits and forest wealth, imperialists and comprador bureaucratic bourgeoisie are evincing special interest in exploiting these regions through mining, quarrying and such other activities. Some infrastructure too has been developed towards this end. The State and Central governments have been carrying on construction works, luring a section from the adivasis under the name of welfare schemes. In the main, tribal chiefs, are benefiting from government schemes and are trying to turn the people in favour of the government and, in some areas, a tiny section of adivasis have become rich and have developed themselves as local oppressors. Both of them constitute the social basis for the ruling class parties or parties in the name of welfare of various tribes and nationalities."

The party also mentions: "proper tactics have to be adopted to ensure the eradication of the influence on the Adivasi masses of this intermediary section which is divorced from labour, while at the same time proper tactics have to be adopted so that a strong unity within the toiling adivasi people could be achieved and also a strong unity between toiling people of tribals and non-tribals can be developed maintained."

Those regions have strategic importance for the Indian revolution from the military viewpoint due to their favourable terrain that facilitates the establishment of base areas. Hence, the party should organise adivasis with the slogans, 'Right over the forest belongs to people and adivasis', 'Political autonomy to the adivasi territories' and transform the territory as exploitation free territory, i.e. 'red land', 'don't be divided, be united' 'unite the real friends against the real enemies', 'right over all the resources including water, forest, etc.' 'right for protecting their own culture and development', and draw up a specific plan for work among them to mobilise them against economic, political, social and cultural oppression by imperialism, CBB and feudalism.

Agrarian Equations

India is an agrarian country with around 70 percent of its people depending directly or indirectly upon agriculture. Agriculture in India is often attributed as gambling with monsoons because of its almost exclusive dependency on precipitation from monsoons. The failure of these monsoons can lead to a series of droughts, lack of better prices, and exploitation of the farmers by middlemen, all of which have led to a series of suicides committed by farmers across India.

Initially, the government denied the reports of the suicides. As more and more suicides started taking place the government was left with no alternative but to accept the fact. Every 30 minutes a farmer in India commits suicide, crushed – say human-rights activists – by debt, moneylenders and the destructive policies associated with the introduction of expensive genetically modified cotton seed. Prince Charles has spoken of the "truly appalling and tragic rate of small farmer suicides in India, stemming in part from the failure of many GM crop varieties." Britain's *Daily Mail* called it 'The GM genocide'. Frankly speaking, the issue of farmer suicides is not just entirely a farmer issue, or rural issue, or a village issue – it is a much more broader political-economic problem. The issue of farmer suicides first gained media attention in 1995 as Maharashtra began reporting a significant rise in farmers killing themselves.

More than 17,500 farmers a year killed themselves between 2002 and 2006, according to experts who have analyzed the statistics. What has been most significant is that the farmers who committed suicides hailed from the rich states; most suicides occurred in States of Andhra Pradesh,

Maharashtra, Karnataka, Kerala and Punjab. In 2006, the State of Maharashtra, with 4,453 farmers' suicides accounted for over a quarter of the all-India total of 17,060, according to the National Crime Records Bureau (NCRB). NCRB also stated that there were at least 16,196 farmers' suicides in India in 2008, bringing the total since 1997 to 199,132. According to another study by the Bureau, while the number of farm suicides increased since 2001, the number of farmers has fallen, as thousands abandoning agriculture in distress. According to government data, over 5,000 farmers committed suicide in 2005-09 in Maharashtra, while 1,313 cases reported by Andhra Pradesh between 2005 and 2007. In Karnataka, the number stood at 1,003, since 2005-06 till August 2009. According to NCRB database, number of suicides during 2005-09 in Gujarat 387, Kerala 905, Punjab 75 and Tamil Nadu 26. In April 2009, the State of Chhattisgarh reported 1,500 farmers committed suicide due to debt and crop failure. At least 17,368 Indian farmers killed themselves in 2009, the worst figure for farm suicides in six years, according to data of the National Crime Records Bureau (NCRB).

The first state where suicides were reported was Maharashtra. It is said that the Maoists instead of finding out the reasons and analyzing them continued to blast the trains and schools. It clearly speaks of their lack of commitment to the peasantry. One thing ought to be mentioned here. Chairman Mao Zedong had depended on the peasantry to carry forward his struggle at a time when Chiang Kai Shek appeared on the Chinese scene. How could the followers of Mao tend to forget the great preaching of Mao which was to become the foundation stone for the New Democracy?

It's official now. India has witnessed over a quarter of a million farmers' suicides between 1995 and 2010. The National Crime Records Bureau's report on 'Suicides in India' places the number for 2010 at 15,964. That brings the cumulative 16-year total from 1995 to 2,56,913. This is worst-ever recorded wave of suicides of this kind in human history.

The data show clearly that the last eight years were much worse than the preceding eight. As many as 1,35,756 farmers killed themselves in the 2003-10 period. For 1995-2002, the total was 1,21,157. On average, this means the number of farmers killing themselves each year between 2003 and 2010 is 1,825 higher than the numbers that took their lives in the earlier period. Which is alarming since the total number of farmers is declining significantly. Compared to the 1991 Census, the 2001 Census saw a drop of over seven million in the population of cultivators (main workers). The corresponding census data for 2011 are yet to come in, but their population has surely dipped further. In other words, farm suicides are rising through the period of India's agrarian crisis, even as the number of farmers is shrinking.

In the beginning, it was believed that most of the suicides were happening among the cotton growers, especially those from Vidarbha. But the figures from the State Crime Records Bureau, however, indicated that it was not just the cotton farmer but farmers as a professional category were suffering, irrespective of their holding size. Besides not just the farmers from Vidarbha but farmers all over Maharashtra were committing suicide. Suicides also took place advanced state of Punjab. The rising number of farmer suicides in the Punjab region of India exposes the problem of extreme rural insecurity, which contradicts the notion of the fastest-growing national economies in the world. Punjab's agricultural output had increased manifold when the Central Indian Government chose the state as the site for the 'Green Revolution'. Now without any alternate source of employment, small and marginal farmers of Punjab continue to pursue the environmentally and economically unsustainable agrarian practices of the Green Revolution, while accumulating high agrarian debt. Though estimates vary, reports of a significant number of farmer suicides are emerging from the region known as India's 'bread basket'.

Even the then Prime Minister Manmohan Singh visited Vidarbha and promised a package of ₹ 110 billion (about $2.4

billion) to be spent by the government in Vidarbha. The families of farmers who had committed suicide were also offered an ex-gratia grant to the tune of ₹ 100,000 (about $2,000) by the government, though this amount was changed several times. But this gesture was not sufficient to check the process of suicides.

Those who killed themselves were primarily cash crop farmers; growers of cotton, coffee, sugarcane, groundnut, pepper, vanilla. One thing interesting to watch is suicides are fewer among food crop farmers, that is, growers of rice, wheat, maize, pulses. This ought to be studied and analysed seriously. The main reason for the suicides by the farmers mainly engaged in cash crop cultivation is huge amount of money involved in it. For millions of subsistence farmers in India, this meant much higher cultivation costs, far greater loans, much higher debt, and being locked into the volatility of global commodity prices. That's a sector dominated by a handful of multinational corporations.

Left Wing Extremism

Only 6 of Maharashtra's 35 districts are affected by Left Wing Extremism (LWE). The MHA designates Maharashtra as one of the states where LWE has been kept under control. But the number of incidents has not been less in comparison to the Naxalite-infested states. All the six LWE- affected districts in Maharashtra (Gadchiroli, Chandrapur, Bhandara, Gondia, Yavatmal and Nanded) are located in the eastern part of the state, in the economically backward Vidarbha region, sharing borders with Chhattisgarh and Andhra Pradesh. Geographical contiguity with, and the 'spill over' from, the Maoist-affected districts of Adilabad, Karimnagar and Nizamabad in Andhra Pradesh, as well as Rajnandgaon, Bastar, Kanker and Dantewada in Chhattisgarh, have been described as the principal reason for the extremism in Maharashtra.

The Maoists have also exploited the geographical conditions and terrain of these districts for their activities.

According to the Maharashtra State Forest Department, 47.08 percent of the total area in Gondia district is designated as 'forest'; in Gadchiroli the forest area is 90.96 percent; in Bhandara, 45.58 percent; in Chandrapur, 46.69 percent; in Yavatmal, 27.35 percent; and in Nanded, 11.35 percent. The scheduled tribe population – populations that have been highly vulnerable to Maoist mobilization – in these districts is also comparatively higher. With the state tribal percentage at 8.8 percent, Gadchiroli's tribal population is 38.3 percent; Yavatmal, 19.2 percent; Chandrapur, 18.11 percent; Gondia, 18 percent; Nanded, 8.8 percent; and Bhandara, 8.6 percent.

It is intriguing why the Maoists have not succeeded in making an effective intervention in the case of suicides in Vidarbha region. It was in the politically advantageous situation but lacked the will to make the political initiative. Yet another development also need to be looked into seriously is, though the region is in proximity to the Andhra Pradesh and Chhattisgarh, the arrests and surrenders of the CPI-Maoist cadres are said to have been a major accomplishment of the Anti-Naxal Cell. The Maharashtra police have also claimed to have curtailed the flow of cadres to Maoist ranks. Maoist recruitment in both Gadchiroli and Chandrapur districts is said to have been drastically reduced, forcing the outfit to wind up several of its dalams (armed squads) in the Gadchiroli and Gondia districts by June 2007 and shifting the existing cadres into Chhattisgarh. The dalams that have folded up include the Gamini, Kotagaon, Dhanora and Jimmalgatta.

Obviously, it makes clear that Maoist leadership failed to analyse the prevailing objective conditions at the ground level and implement the Maoist theory. Else, there is no reason that it should have failed in building a strong peasant struggle. In the past, this area has also been witness to CPI and CPI(M) movements. The Maoists attacked not only state police personnel, government offices and infrastructures, but he also carried out a campaign against 'police informers' and their own surrendered colleagues. In the first three months of 2007, at least eight surrendered Maoists were killed by their former comrades in Gadchiroli, Gondia and Chandrapur districts. At least four incidents of suspected police informers being killed by the Maoists were reported from Gadchiroli district in 2007.

Among the state's initiatives is the Gaonbandi (no entry to the villages) scheme that has been implemented since 2003, to prevent the Maoists from exploiting, mobilizing and recruiting the villagers. As part of the Scheme, any local village body or panchayat passing a resolution barring entry to the Maoists, is provided with ₹ 200,000, to be paid in two installments. Regrettably, the implementation of the scheme was skewed. Till the end of 2006, only 112 of the total of 324 Gaonbandi villages (villages that had banned Maoist entry) had been given the assured funds. Of these, only 73 villages received the full amount of ₹ 200,000. In November 2006, the Maharashtra Government increased the reward amount to ₹ 300,000, to be paid in one installment. However, the scheme continues to be marred by a poor record of disbursement of the promised funds.

The orientation of the anti-Maoist strategy in Maharashtra appears to be prejudiced heavily towards containing the violent potential of the outfit. Maharashtra police have invested substantially on augmenting the fighting capabilities of its force. At the forefront of anti-Maoist operations in the Vidarbha region is a Special Action Group (SAG) of 300 specially trained armed police personnel, raised in 2006 on the lines of the Greyhounds in Andhra Pradesh. Trained at the Unconventional Operations Training Centre (UOTC) at Hingana on the outskirts of Nagpur, SAG personnel have been deployed in Gadchiroli, Gondia and Bhandara districts. The Maharashtra police can rightly take credit for having contained Maoist violence within manageable limits, but there appears to be a bigger challenge at hand: countering the emerging Maoist potential to carry out urban operations. Three arrests in 2007 have brought this tactic into the open, as the Maoists consolidate capacities in urban centres to station their propaganda units and middle and senior level strategists.

Maoist mobilisation and networks have long been suspected in Maharashtra's urban centres, including Nashik, Pune and Mumbai. A large number of non-governmental organisations (NGOs) operating in these areas are believed to be funding and supporting the Maoists. In 2006, the state intelligence had blacklisted 59 such Mumbai-based NGOs. Operational successes by the police are, no doubt, significant. Much more will, however, be needed in terms of a strategy of containment and defence against the creeping Maoist consolidation in widening areas of the state, and to plug the unique vulnerabilities of a democratic system, compounded by the structural infirmities and lack of resources committed to policing in the state, and across the country. The recent police 'successes' provide little grounds for the euphoric statements. The Maoist challenge can be expected to hang heavy over Maharashtra for some time to come.

It is an irony that farmers have to spend a huge amount on food. Millions of small and marginal Indian farmers are net purchasers of food grain. They cannot produce enough to feed their families and have to work on the fields of others and elsewhere to meet the gap. Hunger among those who produce food is a very real thing. Add to this the fact that the 'per capita net availability' of food grain has fallen dramatically among Indians since the 'reforms' began: from 510 grams per Indian in 1991, to 422 grams by 2005. (That's not a drop of 88 grams. It's a fall of 88 multiplied by 365 and then by one billion Indians.) As Prof. Utsa Patnaik, India's top economist on agriculture, has been constantly pointing out, the average poor family has about 100 kg less today than it did just ten years ago – while the elite eat like it's going out of style. For many, the shift from food crop to cash crop makes it worse. At the end of the day, you can still eat your paddy. It's tough, digesting cotton. Meanwhile, even the food crop sector is coming steadily under corporate price-rigging control. Speculation in the futures markets pushed up grain prices across the globe earlier this year.

Even as incomes of the farmers crashed, so did the price they got for their cash crops. The battle over cotton subsidies alone destroyed cotton farmers not merely in India but in African nations such as Burkina Faso, Benin, Mali, and Chad. Ironically, all along, India kept reducing investment in agriculture (standard neoliberal procedure). Life was being made more and more impossible for small farmers. As costs rose, credit dried up. Debt went out of control. Subsidies destroyed their prices. A paradox indeed the largest number of farm suicides is in Maharashtra, home to the Mumbai Stock Exchange and with its capital Mumbai being home to 21 of India's 51 dollar billionaires and over a fourth of the country's 100,000 dollar millionaires.

An investigation into farmers' suicides in Yavatmal District by Meeta and Ravilochan in association with the Yashwantrao Chavan Academy of Development Administration (YASHADA) underlined that Yavatmal was the highest suicide rate in Maharashtra. Total number of suicides in Yavatmal was 640, 819, 832, 787 and 786, in 2000, 2001, 2002, 2003, and 2004, respectively. In each of these years, suicides of farmers and agricultural workers represented 23, 24, 23, 22, and 30 percent, respectively, of all suicides. A total of 148 case studies are presented in the book. To give a flavor of these case studies, two are very briefly described below. A 45-year-old farmer who committed suicide by consuming poison in 2004. He had three acres of land. There was a crop loan of ₹ 3,954 taken in 2001 from the Primary Agricultural Credit Society, which remained unpaid. In 2003-04, he spent ₹ 10,000 in treating his wife who was a psychiatric patient at a private clinic. In another case, a 50-year-old farmer committed suicide by consuming poison in 2004. He had 19 acres of land. There was an outstanding loan of ₹ 33,000 with the Bank of Maharashtra, and another outstanding loan of ₹ 8,000 from the Primary Agricultural Credit Society. In 2004, he spent ₹ 60,000 on the marriage of his second daughter. He used to drink alcohol and also gamble. He was having an affair with his bhabhi (sister-in-law). His affair had been discovered shortly before his suicide.

The findings made it amply clear that indebtedness was rampant. A much more plausible cause for cotton farmers' distress in Maharashtra is provided by Sharad Joshi, leader of the Shetkari Sanghatana. According to Joshi, the primary villain is the Maharashtra State Cotton Monopoly Procurement Scheme – a mechanism that makes the State Government the sole buyer of cotton in Maharashtra, and despite generous promises, usually pays farmers less than prevailing market prices. Cotton farmers in Gujarat, who, by contrast, enjoy better access to markets, a State Government that invests in infrastructure, and access to new technologies, are witnessing unprecedented prosperity.

According to Jean Dreze and Amartya Sen, the relevance of the suicide rate as a basic development indicator is far from clear. Indeed, many countries with high suicide rates (e.g. the Scandinavian countries) are doing extremely well in terms of overall social opportunities, and it would be quite odd to take their high suicide rates as a severe indictment of their development record. Suicide rates do correlate with specific social problems such as high rates of unemployment or divorce and it is quite possible that problems of this kind contribute to the high rate of suicide in Kerala. But these problems such as they are, do not detract from Kerala's achievements in other, more fundamental fields such as health and education.

These suicides also enforce one point very specifically and that is farming in India is not a particularly lucrative profession. It is thus no surprise that, according to a survey, nearly 40 percent of Indian farmers would like to give up farming if they had a choice. Farmer would not like to lose his land but it is a fact that they are literally scratching out a livelihood from their lands. They are the real masters of their profession. But lack of financial support has turned them alien in their own land.

A number of discourses have been taking place on how to ameliorate the economic and social condition of peasantry. But the bare minimum effort is not being made. What is needed is to increase opportunities to fully utilize their own talents and abilities. Since the markets have come to stay and influence their lives, efforts should also be made to regulate the markets in a more decent manner, friendly to peasants. Social safety nets must accompany free markets, so that people can survive occasional downturns and bad luck. Farming should be seen as an occupation like any other occupation. And farmers should be seen as economic creatures interested in earning a good income and not just in "feeding the population." We have formed the habit of looking at the peasants and peasantry in a more romantic manner than juding them on the class basis. It would be wrong to see farmers romantically as repositories of culture and tradition. In fact, farmers should be given economic freedom and opportunities for economic growth and upward mobility, just like engineers, doctors, businessmen, etc.

Meanwhile, the neoliberal model that pushed growth through one kind of consumption also meant re-directing huge amounts of money away from rural credit to fuel the lifestyles of the aspiring elites of the cities (and countryside, too). Thousands of rural bank branches shut down during the 20 years from 1993-2012. The average rural family today is eating nearly 100 grams less of food grains than six or seven years ago and the average per capita availability of food grains has declined sharply. In 1991, when reforms began, availability of food per person was 510 grams, today it has fallen to 437 grams. It is an explosive situation in India today as far as agriculture is concerned and the farmers are concerned with the employment rates in rural areas being the lowest since the late 1990s.

The fact of the matter is that the farmers are losing faith in the government due to its failure to design and implement pro-poor policies for the small farmers who survive on agriculture. Many states have offered financial relief packages only to the families of deceased farmers who were unable to manage payments on their bank loans. Provision of relief facilities alone is not sufficient. In the absence of institutionalized finance, the farmers normally resort to borrowing from private moneylenders. Significantly, the loans taken from the private moneylenders are difficult to repay due to high interest rates. If at all the government intends to protect the farmers, it must ensure institutional finance and crop insurance to small farmers.

How Big is the Problem?

The thrust of the development has been to transform India rapidly into a primarily urban, industrial society with industry as its main source of income. With neoliberal policies instituted in the 1990s; the government and society had become unconcerned about the condition of the countryside. The government has launched MNREGA for providing jobs to the extremely poor and landless labourers. But the fact is that it has not succeeded keeping in view the enormity of the situation. The Government officials, ironically, have been acting like middlemen and usurping the fund then depriving the poor labourers. Even those enrolled for the jobs are not getting the work on regular basis. The basic preamble of the scheme is that the labourer must get at least 100 days of work. But what about other 265 days? Moreover, like any other urban people he has his family problems, falling sick, educating kids and meeting the exigencies of the family. From where should he bring money to supplement his needs? The government has to be move sensitive and adopt a pragmatic approach in this matter.

One important aspect that was perceptible about farmers suicide is these are occurring at younger ages, particularly around the time that young adults join the workforce or get married, and it's really this context of social pressure that is most associated with suicide, not farming. It is a bare fact that openness of the economy has hurt the farm sector, so there should be more state intervention in agriculture. Farmer suicides proved to be a big hit among politicians.

Returns to cultivation have been quite poor. On an average, returns to cultivation per farmer household is ₹ 11,259 in 2002-03. At a time, when the Indian economy is growing the agrarian scenario is not doing well. At 1999-2000 prices, share of agriculture in gross domestic product is at 20 percent in 2004-05, down from 41 percent in 1972-73; whereas during the same period, the share of employment in agriculture using usual principal and subsidiary status declined at a much slower pace from 74 percent to 57 percent only. Ratio of worker productivity in agriculture to worker productivity in non-agriculture is about one-fifth. The agrarian sector is lagging behind. The most common thing was indebtedness (96 out of 111 cases, 87 percent). From all those indebted, 44 percent were harassed for repayment of loan and in 33 percent of cases the creditor insisted on immediate repayment. Next in importance is fall in economic position (74 percent). Indebtedness per se need not lead to economic downfall, but when repayment is difficult and the household may resort to sale of assets.

Crop loss can also happen due to excessive untimely rain, say, during the time of harvest. Crop failure can lead to economic downfall and make it difficult to repay existing loans. This will also increase the need for additional credit. Crop failure leading to fall in economic position is quite significant.

Increasing number of farmers suicide makes it clear that agrarias scenario utterly lacks peasants' movement. Interesting to watch during the decade of globalisation, no activist from the India committed suicide protesting against globalisation. Lee Kyung-Hae, a South Korean farmer and lawmaker in Cancun who was holding a banner that read, 'WTO Kills Farmers', was the first to commit suicide against globalisation. Lee was the former president of the Korean National Future Farmer's and Fisherman's Association, an agricultural lobbying group. Thus, one could discern that farmers' suicide was the result of deep or sharpening agrarian crisis emanating from the capitalist development in agriculture, although there are five important debates, which attempt to look at the issue of suicide differently. It cannot be denied that during last decade India has witnessed unprecedented agrarian distress. The per capita production of food grains has witnessed a decline, but more than that rural India has experienced a massive deflation. All India absorption of food grains per capita per annum has fallen by 22 kilograms between the three-year period of 1995-98 and that of 2000-03.

Growing crisis is the result of ambiguous path of capitalist development. The planners and the government simply borrowed the concept and implemented it without even trying to present in the Indian background and texture. The path of capitalist development has increased the disparity between the urban and rural areas.

□

5

Trajectory of Maoist Movement

Junglemahal and Lalgarh which were once the home of the Maoists and heralded rebirth of the Naxalbari movement, are now the burial ground for them. Maoists in spite of their claims have not succeeded in expanding to new areas, except anchoring into Dandakaranya. The situation in Bihar and Jharkhand has not been rosy either. The intellectuals and academics sympathetic to Maoists have been busy trying to find out the reasons for the demise of the Maoist movement in Bengal. They blame Mamata Banerjee of betraying them. One feels pity at them. How could they think that a bourgeoise political party, that too without any defined goal and objective, least to speak of ideology protect and patronise an ultra left outfit?

Kishenji instead of falling into the trap should have applied Marxist-Leninist postulates to find an answer to the issue. One wonders how could Kishenji, a politbureau member of the CPI(Maoist), repose his faith in Mamata and instead of pursuing his goal should give a call to install her as the chief minister? In September 2009, Calcutta's newspapers had published Kishenji's views on why he thought Mamata Banerjee was the fittest person to replace Marxist Buddhadeb Bhattcharya as the chief minister. It simply manifested the weakness of the Indian Maoist revolutionaries. The bourgeoise weakness to indulge in parliamentary politics was primarily responsible for this. Though they have been decrying elections and democracy and terming them as farce, the fact remains that they have been very much a part of the

Indian political establishment. In Andhra Pradesh, they extended support to TDP and even to the Congress. In Bihar and Bengal, they followed the same path. In Bihar during the Lalu era Maoists belonging to MCC were widely known as RJD during the day and Maoists by night. In many places, they used to mobilise votes and manage booths for RJD candidates while trying to damage the prospect of rival contestants, CPI(ML) nominees in particular. Acting in collusion with the then ruling RJD and the local administration, they attacked the CPI(ML) office at Paliganj, barely six months before the February 2005 Assembly Elections. In Jharkhand, the CPI(Maoist) squads allowed themselves to be used by the BJP and the notorious SP of Giridih in gunning down the CPI(ML) legislator Mahendra Singh during election campaign.

Their reluctance to practise democratic functioning and refraining from taking to mass-based politics primarily owe to their fear of losing identity. They nurse the view that they can survive if they continue to practise arms line. Under the garb of Maoism, the Maoists were simply carrying out killings. Their actions lacked political maturity and dimension. Maoists have not made any substantial effort to arouse the political conscious of the rural poor, the tribals, precisely the proletariats.

Maoists claim to follow Maoism. But an analysis of their political actions and developments in Bihar and Bengal would make explicit that they acted like a bourgeoise party. They were confused of their future moves and steps. Else, how could they repose faith in Trinmool Congress or join hands with the CPI(M)? Their actions were in sharp contrast to the actions of a revolutionary communist party. The Maoist utterly lacked the political perspective was evident from their joining hands with the CPI(M) in Garbeta after they killed one local BJP leader.

In India, there is huge space for the Maoists to fill the way the political parties are losing peoples support and sympathy. But they have miserably failed to use and exploit the situation. What are the factors for their failures? One has to look into the objective and subjective conditions and backgrounds of their failure. While the protagonists claim the party is expanding and getting new faces every day, the fact is otherwise. The party in fact is losing its support base and cadres. No new cadres are joining them. The proletariats are in a state of confusion.

Manik, the secretary of the West Bengal State Committee of CPI (Maoists) who resigned in protest against party pursuing the line of arbitrary use of violence and resorting to mindless killings, has mentioned in his note to the party Congress that spontaneity (bourgeoise values and sentiments) was the principal weakness of the party. He said the weakness should be searched more deeply than it is in the circular. The circular with the aim of conducting rectification campaign had identified four trends as main weaknesses besides the element of spontaneity. He mentioned, "I feel that we should have a clear conception about class struggle to understand this problem of spontaneity. So I shall start my discussion from the class struggle and step by step advance to understand Lenin's explanation on spontaneity and how to understand the problems of West Bengal from this point of view."

Manik wrote: "Revolution is the festival of people. All the revolution in the history of world was advanced only with the participation of people. Our revolution cannot be an exception. This is not a fight of some people or groups against some other people or groups. Rather it is a struggle of one class against other class. It is a struggle to establish the power and authority of one class against other. Lenin had also said that our task was that of the organising proletarian class struggle. But what is class struggle. The struggle of the workers becomes a class struggle only when all the foremost representative of the working class of the whole country are conscious of themselves as a single working class and launch a struggle that is directed not against individual employer, but against the entire class of capitalists and against the government that support that class."

"The principal condition for the struggle of the workers and other working people to become a class struggle according to a Marxist outlook is the presence of political consciousness among those classes. The main task of the communist is to organise the class struggle of broad worker and peasant masses and the key to develop the class struggle is political consciousness among the oppressed classes. Only this political consciousness makes workers and peasants class conscious."

Manik challenged the very existence of the Maoists as communist. He made it clear that simply parroting the name of Mao or Marx would not make a party communist. He even mentioned, "the communists play the role of midwife in revolution. But how? How the workers and peasants should be organised so that they become class conscious? How political consciousness can be imparted among them? How the communists should fulfil their historical task?"

The problem of spontaneity arises from underestimating or neglecting the role of political consciousness in revolution. The communist should give importance to organise the spontaneous struggle; the economic struggle of the working class should try to impart political character in the economic struggle and build up economic struggle against the employers and the government. Only then the workers can be made class conscious and they could be mobilised in the revolution. Though there is resentment against exploitation and oppression among the working class and other oppressed people, ideologically, they are dominated by the ruling class ideology; bourgeoise ideology. So it is not enough to organise people in struggle against exploitation and oppression, their ideology has to be changed. The exploiting system will remain safe till there is domination of bourgeoise ideology on the people. So to liberate the workers and peasants, first they have to be liberated from this bourgeoise ideology. To mobilise the workers and peasants in revolutionary movement by developing their class consciousness political work should be the primary work of the communists.

Manik obviously intended to point out that the CPI(Maoist) was simply indulging in mindless killings and was not interested in political work among the proletariat. How could Maoists ignore the fact that to establish revolutionary theory among the people theory must correspond to the objective reality. It has to clearly explain all the peculiarities and all the changes in the social system. It must clearly enunciate the laws of social development. It should clearly explain how the development of productive forces is obstructed and what are the classes acting as main obstacle in this development. It should contain a clear-cut outline of the new system. It should be the duty of the leaders to gain an ever clearer insight into all theoretical questions to free themselves more and more from the influence of traditional phrases inherited from the old world outlook.

Quoting Lenin, "the widespread of Marxism was accompanied by a certain lowering of the theoretical level. Quite a number of people with a very little and even a total lack of theoretical training joined the movement because of its practical significance and its practical successes", Manik in his note said, "in our work also we could see that most of our cadres join our party being attracted by its practical work. Many of them work as full timers in our squads or mass organisations. They join the party organisationally but not ideologically. Lenin had asked to give theoretical training to all the cadres as it is they who apply theory in day-to-day life and spread it among the broad masses."

One thing is absolutely clear, without revolutionary theory there can be no revolutionary movement. Maoists have been harping on the revolutionary movement. But the fact remains that they do not any specific understanding of the revolutionary theory. Had it been not the case, they would not have resorted to mindless attacks and killings. They often come out with the explanation that they blast primary school buildings as the government stations the security forces in these premises. Fine. But at the same time they must realise that sooner or later the security forces would move out of the building. After that what will happen to the poor students who were denied of the basic education. The task to oppose stationing of the security forces in these buildings could have been performed by the front organisations. But it is not practised, since the Maoists do not have viable mass organisations. They are primarily scared of having mass organisations.

If a revolutionary party does not have theoretical work, it would become the victim of the bourgoise machinations. Practice will grope in the dark and peoples class consciousness will never develop. Party cadres will develop illusion on the narrow day-to-day partial activities. Leave aside the task of developing political consciousness among people, the consciousness of the cadres will go down to the level of trade union consciousness. The influence of economism will spread among the rank and file.

Yet another party functionary Shyam held the view: "If we go deep into our practice of last few years, it would be obvious that our party is lagging behind in political ideological matter, specially it is so, in the case of our leadership committee. If we deeply anaylse the words lagging behind then the words disinclination or neglect will be more appropriate than it. The disinclination towards political ideological matter will in the course of practice increase infatuation for daily activities or will occupy the central point. It will be apparent that due to the neglect and sense of helplessness towards ideological development, without our knowledge (theoretical level) we are preparing for ourselves a foundation for falling down to the trade union consciousness level of an ordinary worker who fight for immediate benefits."

Duty of a communist is to organise the class struggle. They fulfil this task principally by taking the scientific revolutionary ideology among the people. For this they have to develop scientific revolutionary theory through theoretical work. But it does not appear to be happening in the case of Maoists. Except carrying out violent actions, the Maoists cadres do not have other tasks. The party has become victim of spontaneity due to lack of clear theoretical knowledge about political work and political struggle. The Maoists are trying to develop revolutionary movement by giving militant shape to these movements and combing political propaganda with it. They are trying to organise the people initially through economic movements. Incidentally, based on this economic movement, they are trying to develop political consciousness of the people.

The Maoists formed a base in Lalgarh. But they did not try to analyse the ground realities prevailing in West Bengal. If they had carried out any analytical work, they should certainly not have erred in supporting Mamata Banerjee. Their approach makes it clear that the leadership did not pay sincere attention to class analysis. Two peculiarities of West Bengal make it necessary to look at the problems in different ways from other states. First, the total amount of land under big landlords is less than other states. Second, a long revisionist rule has divided people on party basis. The parties in power have spread their influences down to the grass-root level. Maoists ought to not to have ignored the fact that like other states Bengal too has undergone a change during last 40 years. The traditional class relations have taken new dimensions. The operation barga and functioning of panchayats have given a new dimension to the agrarian questions. Can the Maoists advance the movement without seriously looking into the prevailing socio-economic and also political scenario? A new class of middle peasantly has born out of these agrarias policies and programmes. The Maoist must not view the Bengal problem in the backdrop of Andhra Pradesh where they had to retreat under police action. Can it be told what are the enemy classes and what are the friendly classes? Which old production relation they want to break and what new relation they want to build? If these questions are not well defined, how could they aspire to mobilise peasantry in agrarian revolution? As they do not have theoretical clarity on these questions, they are neither finding a way to bring an upsurge of peasant revolution nor they are able to chalk a programme in this matter. They are running after whatever local issues they get in the rural areas.

The modus operandi of Maoists in Bengal reveal that they have not been able to identify class enemies. Maoists talk of Chinese revolution. But how could they forget that Chinese revolution advanced through series of peasant struggle. Ironically, the Maoists cannot cite single place in

India where they have developed peasant struggle. In China, peoples' army was built up but Mao did not allow them to dictate. They supplemented the political actions. Peoples' army was built up and base areas could be established by creating alternative power. Without a clear-cut perspective of seizure of power through revolution and a clear-cut planning to build a new system by destroying the present one, how the party inspire people in revolutionary politics? How could they be able to establish proletarian ideology over the people by destroying the influence of bourgeoise ideology? How could the movement be saved from becoming a victim of spontaneity?

Manik in his document urged, "the party should have developed the theoretical of the entire party system if it wants to work in the complex situation in Bengal. Till now we have not properly grasped the Marxist theory of social development. So the programme of socio-economic investigation taken up by the state committee will remain unfulfilled if we cannot give emphasis on developing the over all theoretical level of our state party. Secondly, our theory has to be implemented to develop revolutionary movement. Theory can get final shape only through development of real mass revolutionary struggle."

A dissenting document presented before the West Bengal state plenum however seeks to know: "When the movements of Andhra Pradesh and North Telegana are facing the danger of being oriented towards economism and revisionism, then what is the condition of our movement in West Bengal? How much our work in rural areas can be compared with the experience of Chinese revolution? If we judge our work in the light of the above lessons and experiences, we can find many similarities of our problems of work with that of AP and NT.

"Firstly, we have no such planning to conduct propaganda and agitation among the people on the basis of each and every incident of political repression. We have no clear idea about the importance of continuous propaganda campaign and political struggle necessary to make people politically conscious and arouse them in class struggle. The development of political consciousness among lakhs of peasants in Hunan as Mao described was not confined only to their local economic and political problems. This consciousness was anti- imperialist and anti-feudal and even in support of the socialist revolution in Russia. In our activity, how much political consciousness we could have developed among the broad peasant masses? What in fact has been the initiative in this direction?

"Secondly, we have no such organisation capable to conduct this type of political propaganda and political struggle. For conducting propaganda and agitation among the broad masses, we need party network at the village level and a very active mass organisation. We can see from the Hunan report comrade Mao is giving the main credit for conducting political propaganda and struggle to the peasant association. We do not have such efficient and politically conscious propagandist and agitators at the grass-root level."

The CPI(Maoist) claim to inherit the ideology of Mao and work accordingly but the facts make it clear that the party does not follow the Maoist doctrine. If the political propaganda and political mobilisation are seen in the background of the Maoist ideology, it would appear to be just a drop in the ocean. The Maoists do not attach significance to the two major issues. Their main approach has been to carry on mindless and indiscriminate killings. How to justify the killing of two labourers who were engaged under MANREGA to carry out some cleaning task? The Maoists killed them in Jharkhand. This is ridiculous. This trend also underlines that the Maoists are so enthusiastic of the concept of democracy and particularly to the Democratic Centralism.

There may be two reasons for the party not having relation to the democracy. First, either the party does not believe in internal democracy or second, it has failed to understand the meaning of the word in its entirety. The naxalite movement has been the oldest movement in the country, but so far it has not succeeded in becoming the main focal point of protest. The people have been opting for many smaller agencies and channels as Narmada Bachao Andolan,

Bachpan Bachao, etc. Why? It is basically due to the democratic character of the Indian state. People can ventilate their feelings and grievances. It is significant that the communist movement has failed to make breakthrough in countries consistently practising bourgeois democracy (as in western Europe) or pursuing parliamentary democracy for a fairly long time (as in India). Lenin's thesis that bourgeois democracy would be more advantageous to the proletariat (in advancing proletarian revolution) than the bourgeoisie apparently proved to the contrary in the world historic developments of the last one century. The question of democracy has assumed increasingly greater importance in the contemporary world. In the post-World War II situation, the movement for democracy seems to have engulfed the whole world. The national liberation struggles were simultaneously marked with the struggle for democracy and it was no wonder that most of the rulers of newly independent countries like India embraced democratic method of governance in the form of parliamentary democracy. Paradoxically, the parliamentary form of democracy was to some extent promoted and projected by the Western imperialist powers as a better form of governance in the post-colonial countries vis-à-vis the emergence of socialist system of governance at that point of time. The interests of the erstwhile colonial masters and the rulers of newly independent states converged on the common agenda to keep the communist threat at bay.

The last quarter of the twentieth century might be marked as a period of rapid spread of parliamentary democracy throughout the world accelerated by both the struggles against despotic rulers of Third World countries being propped up by the Western powers and the collapse of the socialist system of governance in most of the socialist-bloc countries. Most of the latter countries subsequently embraced the parliamentary path of democracy aided and abetted by the Western powers. When asked what democracy means, people of these former socialist-bloc countries emphasised three things: the freedom to do and say what you want; the choice of government by competitive elections; and a welfare state. Democracy as an ideal was endorsed in all the 13 countries.

Democracy seems to have won the battle against different forms of autocratic regimes, not only in the post-colonial countries, as also in countries of the erstwhile socialist-bloc. Wherever people have tasted democracy; 'the freedom to do and say what you want' coupled with 'the choice of government by competitive elections', though not always accompanied by a truly welfare state, the same people would probably reject any regime with a lesser freedom. Hence, it seems no wonder that people of countries where parliamentary democracy is operating for a fairly long time have not been attracted to communism anywhere in the world. Communist parties have been successful to capture power only in countries having autocratic regimes or under colonial rule. More than 100 years has passed since Lenin said, "The proletariat has nothing to lose but its chain, but with the aid of democratism it has the world to win. That is why the more consistent the bourgeois revolution is in achieving its democratic transformations, the less will it limit itself to what is of advantage exclusively to the bourgeoisie" (Lenin 1977: 78). He further clarified, "The more complete, determined and consistent the bourgeois revolution, the more assured will the proletariat's struggle be against the bourgeoisie and for socialism" (Lenin).

There is an inverse relationship between the advancement of the communist movement and the spread of democracy in the contemporary world. The communist movement failed to survive in a country which practices democracy. We ought to examine the question of democracy as it is posed in the contemporary Maoist movement in India. The immediate aim of the Maoist party has been "to accomplish the New Democratic Revolution in India by overthrowing imperialism, feudalism and comprador bureaucratic capitalism only through the Protracted People's War and establishes the people's democratic dictatorship under the leadership of the proletariat" [Constitution of the CPI(Maoist), Chapter 2, Article 4]. Here the goal of the Maoist party and the method of achieving the same have been spelt out in the same breath. While the goal is to establish people's democratic dictatorship, the method is 'only through protracted people's war'. How is this people's democratic dictatorship? The state under this new kind of dictatorship is supposed to "guarantee real democracy for the vast majority of the people while exercising dictatorship over the tiny minority of the exploiters" [Article 25 of the Programme of CPI(Maoist)].

Then how do the CPI(Maoist) party evaluate the parliamentary democracy functioning in India? The present parliamentary system of India is completely rejected by the party as "an outright fraud framed in the deceptive name of 'biggest democracy of the world' whereas all the institutions like parliament, legislative council and executive councils (including the so-called panchayati raj) are a thin cover for the autocratic rule representing the dictatorship of comprador bureaucratic dictatorship and feudal classes subservient to imperialism." Basing on this analysis, the party has formulated its slogan of 'election boycott', which though a question of tactics, "acquires the significance of strategy in the concrete condition of India."

The Maoists should not be under any illusion about Indian democracy and elections. Probably, they nurse the view that since the democracy in India is non-existent and does not have approval of the broader mass, it would not suit them to have support of the common mass and spread. They may be right in their perception, but this is certainly not the ground reality. Elections are more than festivals in India. It reflects the collective assertion of the section of the society which has been their rights. People love and enjoy participating in the election irrespective of the fact in the long run the elected representatives seldom prefer to take care of his voters and the people. In fact, people eagerly wait for the elections. In an average Indian household, the political awareness is of quite high order. Even in the dalit and harijan ghettos, the people are conscious of their rights.

It would be worth recalling one incident. After the decline of the Naxalbari movement, the party suffered fragmentation.

Fresh efforts were made to revive the Naxalbari movement in the plains of Bihar. The much-awaited opportunity was provided by the elections. Ram Naresh Ram was contesting as an independent from Sahar assembly constituency in 1967. Jagdish Mahato, the Master Saheb was campaigning for him. Master Saheb was in touch with some Naxalite leaders. Presence of Ram Naresh in the electoral fray was unacceptable to the upper caste people and the situation got further aggravated due to the campaigning of Master Saheb. They brutally assaulted Masterji in Ekwari and this proved to be the turning point in the plains of Bihar for the movement. The Naxalite movement which was later acknowledged as the Bhojpur movement emerged in a much stronger manner and form. Even the MCC owed its birth to the emergence of Bhojpur movement. Jagdish Mahato, a school teacher, led the protracted struggle against exploitative landlords. Since then 45 years have passed and the movement has spread to as many as 30 districts. The worst-effected area is the Central and South Bihar. It was the election which played very important role in organising the dalits and harijans. During these years, militant dalits and harijans fought many battles against the upper caste dominance in the plains of Bihar. The Maoists would have to take lessons from the past.

One thing is absolutely clear that Maoists do not have any pragmatic understanding of the existing situation. Else, how to explain the brutal killing of Superintendent of Police of Pakur and his four associates; three body guards and driver in an ambush in Kathikund forest of Dumka in Jharkhand on July 2, 2013? Within 39 days this was the fourth major assault carried out by the Maoists. SP Amarjit Balihar was returning from meeting with his DIG when his vehicle was attacked. The Maoists attacked the convoy from higher ground. Though Balihar was not in the mode of preparedness to take on any Maoist attack, for those who follow the Maoist movement this attack in Jharkhand did not come as surprise. Balihar was not prepared may be for the reason that this area has yet not featured on the Maoist map. This is a futile debate as the Maoists do not go by any ground level law not even the Geneva Convention. Like in Chhattisgarh after Pakur incident the police headquarters issued a general alert to all SPs in Jharkhand. But Balihar preferred to ignore it. And he paid the price. The DGP Rajeev Kumar was probably right when he said, "It looks like Maoists went after a soft target. They have suffered major losses in the past few months. We have a massive operation in Latehar and have made significant progress in Gumla."

And now when five policemen have lost their lives, the State Government has promised a harsher action against the Maoists. It would review its intelligence network too. Obviously, this situation would favour the Maoists. They would blame the government using state power against the poor adivasis. But at the same time they cannot absolve them of the charge that the situation was created by them. There was no use of carrying out any action against Balihar. Let Maoists enumerate the gains they have made out of this action. Significantly, the Union Government on July 3, told Naxal-hit states to brace for more such attacks particularly in the areas where deployment of forces has been quite thin. The government also asked them to go aggressive after the Maoists where they are comfortable.

Maoists ought to clarify their positions on democracy. Their attitude towards the parliamentary system in India, not only determines their position on the parliamentary elections, but the whole strategy of winning power 'only through the Protracted People's War'. The outright rejection of the parliamentary system of democracy has no doubt been the main attraction that draws a number of people, mainly from the younger generation, disgruntled with the system, to the Maoists movement. This rejection of the parliamentary system coupled with the call to rebel against the system, that has not been able to abolish hunger, unemployment and other socio-economic discriminations and deprivations, was the key to unleash the 'spring thunder' that once shook the Indian polity to the root. But later events proved that election boycott was not the right tactics or strategy and the party had to amend it. The [illegible]e of elections in Bihar also made it clear that the parliamentary system could be used to further the movement. It requires skill.

Political scientists and analysts have observed that through these political reforms, democracy in India has "struck deep roots and is empowering millions to demand a better life and greater dignity for themselves and the democratic process in India has come a long way in bringing under its influence the lives of the subaltern classes." Simultaneously, economic reforms have been instrumental in bringing forth new class relations in the Indian countryside, which is principally marked by the economic and political decline of the old-landed elite and the emergence of rural bourgeoisie. Of course, none of these reforms have changed the basic conditions of sufferings and deprivations of the Indian masses and there are certain zones in India where these state-sponsored reforms failed to bring substantial changes in the old order, but it would be naive to altogether ignore the implications of these changes in the body politic of our country and frame political strategy on the basis of old, pre-conceived ideas.

The Maoists seem to have undermined the implications of these political and economic reforms when they formulated their slogan of election boycott basing on the assumption that "all parliamentary institutions and parliamentary system itself, including all the parliamentary parties of the ruling classes, stand exposed before the masses more than ever." [Article 27 of Programme of CPI(Maoist)]. Such exposition fails to explain why people of India exercise their franchise in consecutive elections in so large numbers. It seems remarkable that people vote in larger numbers in a state like West Bengal, where people are more connected with organized politics and in the process have become more politicized. Moreover, in recent times people of this state successfully used their voting right in support of their struggle to thwart state and private repression and defend their right on land. Even at the peak of the recent Lalgarh movement, which the Maoist party has claimed to be leading, one CPI(Maoist) leader Shekhar admitted in a press meet in the forest of

Lalgarh, "The People's Committee against Police Atrocities (PCPA) wants to participate in (parliamentary) election to defeat the CPI(M) Party. Though our policy is to boycott the elections, we are supporting this stand in view of the aspirations of the broad people towards election." Thus, the party's policy on parliamentary elections did not correspond to the ground reality of a place where the people were agitating against the state for a long period and the Maoists had substantial influence on the local population.

In the 2013 panchayat elections, a large number of Maoists who had joined the Trinmool Congress have entered into the electoral fray in Lalgarh and Junglemahal. In fact, at least 15 of them have got elected unopposed. They used their reputation of being Naxalites. Significantly, while the Indian Maoists have been opposed to participating in the elections, their counterparts in Nepal, the Communist Party of Nepal (Maoist) entered into electoral competition not only in the existing system of governance, but expressed its commitment to multi-party democracy as 'a strategically theoretically developed position' of the party. Rebuffing the CPN(Maoist)'s position on multi-party democracy, the CPI(Maoist) spokesperson Azad observed, "by describing this decision on multiparty democracy as a strategically, theoretically developed position comrade Prachanda has brought a dangerous thesis to the fore – the thesis of peaceful coexistence with the ruling class parties instead of overthrowing them through revolution; peaceful competition with all other parliamentary parties, including the ruling class parties that are stooges of imperialism or foreign reaction, in so-called parliamentary elections;... opening the doors wide for the feudal-comprador reactionaries to come to power by utilizing the backwardness of the masses and the massive backing from domestic and foreign reactionaries or the comprador bureaucratic bourgeois and feudal and petty bourgeois forces to hijack the entire course of development of the society from the socialist direction to maintaining the existing system (even if in a new form) in the name of democracy and nationalism. Whatever may be our good intentions for building a more democratic system, the laws governing class struggle will not permit of such a system."

Azad talks utopian. He said after the seizure of power in the whole country, the Maoists will allow 'genuinely anti-imperialist anti-feudal parties' to function and that too as part of the power. It again implied that they have not accessed the real power of the state which so far by all standards and norms has been maintaining restraint. The CPI(Maoist) has so far failed to find a single ally, with whom it can build up 'an anti-imperialist anti-feudal united front' which is one of the key components of its Party Programme. Leave alone the numerous parliamentary parties; it does not find an ally in the other Naxalite parties. Sometimes, it has entered into bitter and bloody rivalries with these parties. One may recollect that the two parties, CPI(ML) (People's War) and Maoist Communist Centre, who have merged to form the present Maoist Party, had a long history of bitter fight among themselves which can be termed as a turf war to gain supremacy over each other in their common territory, particularly in Bihar. So the question remains whether any party would be left in the new power structure even to share power with the Maoist Party. The obvious conclusion one may arrive at is that all other parties, which have a meaningful existence in present India, will not be allowed to function once the Maoist Party captures power in the country.

The Maoists seem to have completely disregarded the impact of the democratic institutions on the broad public life in India today. All these institutions have become part and parcel of the public life and doing away with them would jeopardize whatever has so far been achieved by the long struggles of the Indian people. That some of these institutions may be used by 'reactionary forces' cannot be the cause to eliminate all such democratic institutions. Rather one would wonder what will happen to the democratic participation of the people "not only through voting but in the life of the political parties and civil society organizations, in the discussion of public policy issues, in communicating with and demanding accountability from elected representatives, in monitoring official conduct and in direct engagement with public issues at local level" (Diamond and Morlino 2004), which are seen as necessary to maintain the 'democratic quality' of a society.

It is not clear how do the Indian Maoists contemplate in their future scheme of things to deal with the democratic aspirations of the broad masses created by the functioning of multi-party democracy and other democratic institutions in India for such a long period? Or do they belong to the category of Socialist parties, which "simply espouse democracy if, as and when it serves their ideals and interests and not otherwise"? In brief, it seems that the Indian Maoists' theoretical position on democracy has left many questions than answers in the contemporary debate on the contentious issue.

The entire practice of the CPI(Maoist) Party in areas with favourable terrain is based on the assumption that "it is possible to go for armed form of struggle from the very beginning as it is the principal form of struggle in the entire period of New Democratic Revolution (NDR)" [Strategy and Tactics of CPI(Maoist), p. 59]. Here the pertinent point is that the party is determining the form of struggle basing on its formulation that "armed struggle is the principal form of struggle in the entire period of NDR," and not on the basis of people's level of consciousness in that particular area. This seems tantamount to denying the people the right to determine in which form they want to struggle against the rulers, if they want at all. With this target of launching armed struggle, the party usually forms armed squads in areas with favourable terrain and goes for armed activities, from the very beginning. In most cases, the squad members are recruited from distant places and very often unaware of the language, culture, customs etc. of the local people (mostly belonging to tribal communities inhabiting in forest areas where the Maoists find favourable terrain to conduct armed activities). So there is hardly any scope for the squad members to initiate armed activities basing on the consciousness and active participation of the local population.

The role of the people becomes extremely marginalized as they have no control over either of the two forces. The Maoist Party decides its war strategy at the party level and execute the same with the armed forces at its command. The people have no command whatsoever on the 'people's war' being conducted by the party. The CPI(Maoist) spokesman Azad admitted that the party had deliberately annihilated Swami Laksmanananda, the Hindu leader in Kandhamal in Odisha, which triggered a communal violence killing at least 35 people of the Christian community. There are scores of such instances that clearly show that the Maoist-armed actions are planned at the party level and the people have nothing to do about the decisions while they suffer the consequences most. The party's press statement on 5 November 2008 on election boycott urged the "entire party ranks, the heroic fighters of PLGA and members of all revolutionary mass organizations....to throw out reactionary parliamentary party leaders who come for votes in the areas of our struggle."

No Quest for Land Reforms

Agriculture has turned non-productive is the common refrain. This is not wrong either. But it is not the agriculture which on its own has ceased to have productive value. In fact, it is utter neglect of the primary section by the governments which has been primarily responsible for agriculture acquiring subsistence value. With the emphasis shifting to crash crop and Bt Cotton and other cash crop gaining currency, the farmers were not encouraged to experiment with production of food grain.

Agriculture or farming is still a profitable avocation. Look at the two major agriculture-based states, Punjab and Haryana. Notwithstanding some decline in production level and slight tilt towards diversification, the economy of these two states still revolves round the agriculture. In recent years, these states have seen dearth of labour, the working farm hands, but that has not been a major deterrent. The political class of these two states has been quite agile to the needs of the farming sector. Land conversions have been taking place but still utmost care is ensured to protect the fertile agriculture land.

Though land reform has been a forgotten agenda in state policy, it is a bare fact that the future of the people of the country depends on agriculture. India cannot aspire to sustain its economy and future development and growth purely based on services sector. The west-looking economists might have been pressing the government to go for strengthening the growth, but they too could not deny the fact it has its own limitations. Beyond a certain stage, these reforms and liberalization would not work. The reason is India still depends on agriculture for its economic sustenance. Even big corporate houses are finding it difficult to completely divorce the agriculture.

The inability of the corporate sector and the services sector in creating and providing new jobs to the unemployed has been exposed. The frustrated youth in the 2014 Lok Sabha elections voted for Narendra Modi's promises and assurances. But the fact remains no Modi can do anything to salvage the situation. Modis may create some jobs but they cannot ensure jobs to all the youths. This fact has to be realized. Given the jobless growth of the Indian economy and the spurt in rural violence, with people protesting lack of access to land, water and jungle, it is the land that would provide livelihoods to everyone; to labour attached to agriculture and also to the surplus unemployed people.

It is better the policymakers should realize the fact at the earliest that India at this stage of development and growth desperately needs a sound and consistent land reforms. No doubt, this would hurt the interest of the corporate and capitalist section. But it has to be done. This in the long run would also serve the interest of the corporate sector. The corporate industry needs a big market to sale their products. In this regard, one aspect ought to be closely watched. Even today the corporate products find their purchasers in the states of Punjab, Haryana and Rajasthan, in Western Uttar Pradesh and to some extent in Bihar and eastern UP. One thing is significant all these states are agriculture-based economies. In Bihar and eastern UP, the agriculture activity is not so productive even then these two regions are famous of sale of new luxury and costly cars. Even today Bihar has been dubious distinction of being the launching state for new cars in India. These states are the dumping ground for the consumer goods. Eighty percent of the population of these states have mobile phones.

Obviously, for the future expansion of the corporate sector and market economy, it is imperative that the government should undertake thorough land reforms. It will also empower the 70 percent of the people living in villages and turn them as the future target groups for consumption of the consumer goods. So far there has never been any serious discussion on the mode and relations of production in agriculture. Now the time has come primarily in the interest of the crony capitalists that it should be given priority. Unless agrarian relations are conducive, the market forces cannot expect to gain.

The urban middle class and political class ironically nurse wrong notions about the liberalization, globalization and reforms. They ought to realise that these measures would not create jobs which can cater to the Indian youths and unemployed. In fact employment figures for the organised private and public sectors present a dismal picture. In 1991, total employment in this segment was 267.33 lakh. It went up to 282.85 lakh in 1997. Since then it had been continuously dropping. In 2004, the figure was 264.43 lakh, 3 lakh less than the figure for 1991 when liberalisation was initiated. There is a gradual squeezing out of regular employment and simultaneously increasing the quantum of the urban unemployed. What is also happening is that regular jobs are being 'casualised' in the organised sector. Women are encouraged to grab these jobs behind the facade of empowering them. This is in fact an attempt to feminise the casual employment. The ILO has described this situation as the "feminisation of poverty."

Let us look at the benefits of the land reforms measures undertaken in West Bengal. Once the Left Front Government implemented land reforms, the face of the state has transformed. Bengal is now considered as an agriculturally advanced state. Till 1981, the agricultural growth rate in Bengal varied between 0 percent and 1 percent per annum. The land reforms unleashed the stagnant human and social forces. The rural areas of Bengal which primarily survived on *panta bhat* could look beyond that. The rural areas witnessed a new yearning for development. The farmers could come to realize the values of their lands. This point is often ignored by the agriculture pundits: land reforms in West Bengal played an important role.

No doubt, the overall economy of the state did not shine. But this owed to lack of penetration of investment in the industries and urban sector, especially in Calcutta. The growth of urban Calcutta was slow. But it grew. The pace was less. In fact, with the rural areas acquiring wealth, consumer products found their way to the rural people. One development deserves mention. Recently, the biggest ever scam in India, the Sharadha Scam of Bengal, was unraveled. The CBI, Enforcement Directorate, the Income Tax and other government agencies are yet to find out the real amount involved in the scam. Sharadha has been a chit fund scheme. So far the Fodder Scam of Bihar was supposed to be the biggest ever scam that had taken place in the country. According to the estimates, the total amount involved in the scam is not less than 3500 crores. Name any one, whether politician, journalist, intellectuals, sports person, cinema, media or sport organization, and you will find him involved in the scam. This money belonged to the rural people.

The rural people had deposited their cash money with the Saradha chit fund. Obviously, question arises from where did they get such huge amount of money? After the land reforms, the government pumped crores of development funds in the rural areas and the farmers were the eventual beneficiaries. The flow of the fund boosted their purchasing power. Unfortunately, their purchasing did not get corresponding support from the urban conglomerate, primarily from Calcutta to that extent.

In the quagmire of the nasty localized politics, this development lost its relevance. Though some of the CPI(M) leaders had come to realise this development and growth of a strong rural economy, they could not channelize the latent force as they lacked correct economic perspective. This was the reason that the rural poor had alternate than to dump their money with the chit fund operators. It is a study in contrast that while Calcutta has been groping for its survival, most of the towns, even the district towns have been thriving.

Ironically, the protagonists of the neo-liberal economic policies could not fully utilize and exploit the existing situation. They could not comprehend the impact of the land reforms in totality. As a result, the land reform went off the radar of the Indian polity. Unfortunately, they even did not bother to assess the observations of the market forces. They considered the land reform laws as detrimental to the free play of capital in the land market. They wanted to do away with the peasantry and the peasant way of life. But they were wrong. They could not comprehend that the success of liberalisation, privatisation and globalization lies through the dusty and dilapidated roads of the rural India.

Had the government undertaken the task of land reforms, probably the contentious issue acquisition of land for industries would not have arisen. The situation has been worsened in the rural areas due to almost mindless 'landgrabs' in the name of Special Economic Zones (SEZs). This is something different from a Zamindar grabbing the land of poor farmer. It is a direct attack on the economic interest of the rural people. This land grab has witnessed popular resistance as in Nandigram in West Bengal and Jagatsinghpur in Odisha. The matter of fact is the Indian bureaucracy and political class do not like the rural poor. They treat them as usurpers. They intend to keep them under their thumb else they will lose their authority.

The Maoist document 'Strategy and Tactics of the Indian Revolution', which is said to be a blueprint of the Maoist revolution, fails to look into the issue of land reforms in the right perspective. The document ought to be examined for two major reasons: firstly, to understand the psyche and thought process of the Maoists; and secondly, to make an assessment of the document and compare with the existing ground realities.

The document, with 13 chapters, covers strategy and tactics in two different parts, was conceived by the joint central committee of the PWG and the MCCI prior to their merger in September 2004. The political and military strategy is based on three broad factors, which include a detailed and objective analysis of (a) the class character of Indian society, (b) the character of the Indian state, and (c) an in-depth analysis of the uneven economic, political, social and cultural developments in the country. Though Maoist theory has undergone change from 'Land to the Tillers' to the present anti-globalisation and anti-reforms, ironically, it has failed to understand that the theory adopted by Mao in the 1930s cannot be replicated in the current scenario. Over these years, the global scenario and relations have transformed.

While the Maoists claim to have carried out the demographic mapping of India to identify and exploit the weaknesses in the political, social, economic and cultural dynamics of the country, they have failed to measure and map the mood and feelings of the people. As such they have not been successful in evolving the mechanism to align with the aspirations and feelings of the common people. They should have given importance to the social and economic inequalities, issues pertaining to governance, implementation of land reforms, land acquisition for industrial or mining purposes. But they miserably failed in this task. Incidentally, the Home Ministry's Annual Report 2010-11 underlines that left wing extremists operate in a vacuum created by the functional inadequacies of field-level governance structures. Nevertheless, a detailed study of the Maoist document suggests that there is a lack of flexibility in the thought process. The document appears to be aggressive and ambitious in spirit but lacks pragmatism in its long-term vision and design for execution.

One of the recent phenomenon in the tactics of Maoists has been to use the children, women and innocent civilians as human shields to protect themselves from the security forces. This certainly could not be described as a true and correct Maoist line. Obviously, they have adopted this tactics where they are weak.

Maoists claim to becoming less adventurous in their operational strategies and discreet about their bloody actions. After some major reverses and losses, they have started joining popular protests against neoliberalism. But the fact remains that their presence is not felt in the sphere of democratic movements against the neoliberal policies and programmes. Like the other left outfits, CPI(M) and CPI, they too have not been clear about the nature and content of the democratic movement. Economic reforms and consequent social changes have led the Maoists, influenced by class relations, in a state of indecisiveness. While their emphasis now is on a defensive approach, for protecting preserving and consolidating their gains, they are at the same time extensively using armed insurgency and guerilla actions for expanding the organization.

It is the compulsion for survival that has made them reconcile. The middle class intellectual think-tank has to a major extent prevailed upon the leadership to keep a check on the whimsical decisions to resort to violent actions. Maoists are now far more convinced that a revolutionary communist party should not be impetuous and adventurist in its organisational work. During the last five years, the Maoists have lost most of their politbureau and central committee members due to the indiscreet actions. The organization which barely a year back was averse to pursuing the principle of waging democratic movement and described the Naxalites outfits taking to this line as neo-revisionists, is now keen to fall in line. There is a general feeling that the Maoists must adopt the tactics of advancing step by step, slowly and surely keeping to the principle of waging struggle on just grounds, having select cadres working underground and never adapt empty clamour and reckless activity that would never lead to success.

Though the party claims to have adopted this strategy in Nandigram, it is a wrong assertion. During the days of Nandigram-Singur-Lalgrah land struggle in West Bengal, party pursued the policy of indiscreet killings. Had the Maoists actively participated in the struggles under the banner of the 'People's Committee Against Police Atrocities, (PCAPA) and allowed the forum to grow, the situation might have been entirely different. Their decline in the Junglemahal and Nandigram primarily owes to the fact that they chose wrong tactical line, resorted to excessive violence and forged alliance with the wrong people. They in fact had worked out strategic alliances with different groups and organisations including those ideologically opposed to them only with the intensions to use them. But they unfortunately became the victim of their own machinations.

If they were against the indiscriminate use of violence then why did they carry out the dastardly act of derailing the Jnaneswari Express in Midnapore district in May 2010, resulting in the death of almost 150 people? It is sad the Maoists are not speaking truth and confessing their guilty. Certainly, Mao Zedong had not taught his comrades to speak lie and resort to falsehood. Who were Ganapathy and his comrades trying to fool? They were deceiving their own conscience. Maoists also claim that their leader Kishenji had claimed that "the mass Naxalite movement in Lalgarh had given the Naxalites a major base in West Bengal for the first time since the Naxalite uprising in the mid-1970s." If at all what Maoists claimed was correct, then the movement should not have fizzled out within a short span of a year! Why it happened? Maoists must have some explanation. They had also claimed that Kishenji was neither being rhetorical nor exaggerating and the Maoist resurgence was likely to shape political trends in Bengal. What Bengal and not only its people but people across India witnessed; the movement died down and almost all the entire rank and file of the Maoists joined the neo-bourgeoise Trinimool Congress. This development had in fact made the CPI(M) accuse the Maoists of working at the behest of the Trinimool Congress with the aim to weaken the Marxists.

They have not been honest in describing the Bengal development as partial success. It was in fact a complete failure and they ought to do some introspection. While the movement has virtually decimated in Andhra Pradesh, its citadel for many decades, due to the Maoists' "impetuous and adventurist actions" it has also been completely finished in Bengal and has not lived upto the claim of the Maoists that it would give new impetus for the party to pursue this line in other areas, particularly in the South where the movement had taken roots in the past.

The political bankruptcy of the party and its think tank could be gauged from the simple fact that they recently opened new fronts in the inter-state tri-junction of the three southeren states, where they have been organising campaigns on macro- and micro-level socio-economic and political issues and have expressed solidarity with the agitation for a separate Telengana as part of its strategy to re-establish its control over North Telengana region. They want the people believe that the people of Telegana would vouch for them more than Chandraehekhar Rao. Indeed a ridiculous proposition! They should have turned to the pages of history. If they had done this, they would come to know that this strategy has failed to serve the interest and cause of the Naxalites and Maoists. Instead of broad basing their organization, they have been decimated. Most of their comrades and cadres in fact joined the bourgeoise organizations.

While the Maoists in the Andhra-Odisha Border (AOB) claim to build a mass base by taking up neoliberal issues, like opposing the Special Economic Zones, acquisition of tribal/agrarian land and the signing of a large number of MoUs with multinationals, they have not come out with a concrete action plan for Bengal, Bihar and Jharkhand, which they claim to the their strong base area. What does it imply? Why they have been not keen to use the fertile region where they have considerable following! The Maoists in the AOB have also begun moves to re-build their bases in parts of Andhra Pradesh, taking up some of these issues, while political parties, environmental activists, NGOs and agrarian bodies are at loggerheads over the recommendations of the Western Ghats Panel.

In the recent past, the Maoists suffered serious setbacks in their efforts to rebuild their bases in the AOB region, which is unique for its dense forests and difficult terrain. Their docile posture makes it explicit that they have no mass base in these states and have been simply surviving on the strength of their fire-power, their resorting to armed action in trains or extorting from the private construction companies. There is no denying the fact that Robin Hoods and mercenaries use this mechanism to survive. It is not that these three states are heavens in India and lack issues on which a popular democratic pro-people movement could not be built. But they are reluctant.

After the Lok Sabha elections, the BJP and RSS has been spreading its fang in the rural areas and trying to woe the rural masses, specially the people from the backward classes. In some cases, these people have even adopted aggressive postures against the dalits and harijans. In Gaya district, these people forced the dalits to flee their village. While the administration took the initiative to bring the dalits back, the Maoists acted like a passive spectator. Significantly, Gaya has been their base area and they have killed many police constables, irrespective of the fact whether they belonged to the state police or to the CRPF. They killed the police constables accusing them of being exploiters. Strange are the working styles of the Maoists. They lamented and despised the High Court verdict of exonerating the killers of Laxmanpur-Bathe. Will they speak out what measures they pursued to bring justice for the families whose members were killed by the Ranvir Sena marauders? It is a known fact that the police and a section of the lawyers connived with the Sena and white-washed all the evidences and pressurized the witnesses to turn hostile. What did the Maoists do to set the issue straight and counter the machination of the police? In a recent press statement the Maoists condemned the High Court order, but they did not spell out whether they plan to approach the Supreme Court for justice to those killed. This will clarify their approach and attitude to the existing means of democratic weapons to launch a sustained campaign.

Interestingly in Karnataka, their strategy is to exploit issues such as the socio-economic disparities among the tribal population and the rural poor in districts such as Dakshin Kannada and Kodagu, and the eviction of the tribal inhabitants from the Kudremukh National Park area, to make way for more iron-ore mining.

Their actions to build bridges with the people make clear that they are more inclined to pursue reformist programmes than taking up the fundamental issues. On June 12, 2014, Maoists in Gaya of Bihar, took to distributing books, notebooks, pens and pencils to the children of the poorest of poor in the bid to win over the confidence and sympathy of the people in rural areas. Prior to this, they had already distributed books among hundreds of children in over a dozen villages on the border of Jamui and Lakhisarai districts, both of which are considered to be their strongholds. This was part of their exercise to win over the poor people, who are not happy with them.

This nature of programmes are organized by the NGOs. A Communist Party, that too a party committed to agrarian revolution never indulges in such kind of frivolous actions. They usually leave these tasks to their front organizations. They identify themselves with their day to day struggle and organize them for democratic movement with the aim to spread their area of operation and prepare a strong base. By providing free books, Maoists in fact tried to send the message that poor children also need education. But ironically they continue to target the dilapidated schools on the plea of CRP and BSF using these structures for carrying out oppression. This nature of dichotomy should not do good to the party. They must change their approach of targeting schools in rural areas. In the last five years, nearly 47547 schools have borne the brunt of Maoist attacks in different parts of the state. The Maoists say the schools were targeted because they were used to shelter paramilitary forces during their operations against them. They are likely to distribute books among children as it is part of their agenda to spread literacy in villages, known to be their strong base.

The May 25, 2013 ambush was perhaps their most brazen attack on politicians. On June 13, 2013, Maoists attacked a passenger train in Bihar, killing three people. On April 6, 2010, the rebels killed at least 75 policemen in Dantewada district of Chhattisgarh. It is difficult to arrive at an exact number but available data shows nearly 8,000 people have been killed during the decade. Various estimates suggest Maoists a strong cadre of nearly 40,000 personnel. Of these, thousands are supposed to be armed with weapons ranging from AK-47s to light machine-gun raided from police stations or bought from dealers in Nepal. The cadres mostly comprise landless labourers, tribals and the extremely poor, including women and children.

While the Maoists have been trying to fine-tune their strategies and tactics in order to maintain their relevance, the state too has been making concerted efforts to crush the movement using 'security and development' measures. Unwarranted fatalities from Maoist violence and the destruction of infrastructure have also reached fairly high levels in recent years. If the people looked at the Naxalites as their savior, they dread the Maoists. Why should this happen? A document of the Ministry of Home Affairs (MHA) stated that the Maoists killed 5,467 civilians and destroyed 281 schools between 2001 and 2011. Another set of comparative statistics relating to 2006-2010, in a different document, reveals that the number of civilians killed by Maoist violence (2,237) is far more than in Jammu and Kashmir (J&K) (661). It is an indicator of the intensity of the violence and level of expertise gained by the Maoists. True enough notwithstanding initiating reformist programmes, the Maoists have not announced abdication of the killings of the innocent people. Their style of functioning makes it clear that they are more dependent on the gun power for their survival than the strength and prowess of the people's might.

From 2005 onwards, the Maoists carried out a large number of attacks on police posts. Some of the significant incidents of Maoists violence are the Jehanabad jail break (2005), the Dantewada jail break (2007), the killing of Jharkhand Mukti Morcha (JMM) MP Shri Sunil Mahato at Jamshedpur (2007), the Rani Bodli Post attack in Dantewada district (2007), the Nayagarh attack (2008), the attack on an East Frontier Rifles (EFR) post at Silda (2010), the ambush at Tadmetla (2010), the Dantewada-Sukma bus massacre (2010), the kidnapping of District Collector Malkangiri (2011). In 2012, they kidnapped Italians, the Biju Janata Dal (BJD) MLA in Odisha and the district collector of Sukma in Chhattisgarh. Spate in Maoists' violence and abductions are believed to be part of their tactical counter-offensive campaign.

After the death of their charismatic leader, the Naxalite movement faced various challenges. Disagreements within the party CPI(ML) persisted. The issue of participating in elections was repeatedly raised. Moreover, the changes within the Communist Party of China (CPC) after the death of Mao Zedong 1976 had also a direct effect on the Naxal movement. Members of the CPI(ML) differed on the new line of the CPC. One section remained loyal to Beijing, another split off the main party and demanded a course correction. The group called themselves CPI(ML) Liberation. They claimed to be the preservers of Charu Mazumdar's thoughts and true successor. Their aim was continuing armed struggle while broadening its efforts by establishing mass organizations. The Chinese role model of guerilla warfare had been customized to Indian conditions and many former CPI(ML) cadres joined the Liberation group.

In 1980, around 30 Naxal groups existed in the country. The most affected states during that period were Andhra Pradesh and Bihar. Kondapalli Seetharamaiah, a former CPI(ML) leader in April 1980 formed the CPI(ML) People's War that became known as People's War Group (PWG) the major partner of the Maoist. PWG tried to give Maoism in India a new life and new characteristics. Seetharamaiah again was following Mazumdar's line of armed strife but was also expanding the struggle to economy and politics by mobilizing the masses and establishing front organizations.

Landmine operations have been the deadliest weapons of the Naxalites and are also their brand mark. From 1990 onwards, an increasing growth in violent clashes between security forces and Maoists was observed. The peak of violence was reached in 1991, where several attacks on telephone exchanges and railway stations were carried out by them, numerous kidnappings and killings of police forces and state authorities took place. In 1992, the PWG experienced several setbacks due to a large counter-insurgency campaign that was led with strong hand and accompanied by interior disagreements. Naxalite cadres were killed, 3434 arrested. Due to demoralization, around 8500 cadres gave up voluntarily. In 1993, several violent attacks proved that the PWG still existed. In 1998, the PWG merged with another Naxalite group, the CPI(ML) Party Unity.

Among the Naxalite groups in the respective state, the Maoist Communist Centre (MCC) was the dominant force in Bihar. The MCC had a similar strategy as the PWG. They abstained from elections, and followed the ideology of people's war while establishing front organizations. Their armed cadres were well trained and equipped. The MCC was also able to establish liberated zones that cut-off the influence of the state.

Thirty years after his death, the thoughts of Charu Mazumdar, the intellectual father of the movement, play an important role for the Naxalites. In his "eight historic documents", he points out the necessity of setting up an armed group in rural areas and to establish liberated zones in order to capture state power. The participation in the electoral process within the Indian political system was rejected categorically. In contrast to the CPI(ML) and the Liberation group that by now participate in the parliamentary system, the CPI(Maoist) regards themselves as the true successor of the movement that started in Naxalbari. Instead to the parliamentary process, the seizure of power shall be accomplished through the armed struggle.

The official line of the CPI(Maoist) focuses on the underprivileged, basically poor peasants and tribals, rejects any caste systems and supports all national movements striving for independence and self-determination, with a special reference to India's North East as well as Kashmir. The success of the Maoist movement is deeply rooted in the weakness of the Indian state. Social elites like high castes, landlords and loan sharks dominate the rural population and benefit from their exploitation. State-aided rural development programs in these areas have often not reached the bottom of the society and instead contributed to the persistence of landlordism.

"Revolutions never proceed in a straight line. The history of all successful revolutions are a proof to this. The path is zigzag, there are ups and downs, there is victory and failure; repeated a number of times before the final victory. Of course, there is no final victory until the stage of communism is reached." This statement drafted by some senior leaders of erstwhile PWG, explains the state of affairs within the contemporary Naxal Movement.

Increased number of deaths among the security forces during 2009-10 seriously questions the rationale of the Operation Green Hunt. The security forces deployed to carry out the Operation Green Hunt were certainly on a disadvantageous side in the absence of real-time intelligence and jungle warfare training. This period 2009-10 witnessed some of the deadliest attacks on the security forces meticulously and mercilessly executed by the Maoists; the worst being the killing of 76 security personnel in Chintaland in Chhattisgarh. Another reason for the increased Maoist violence during 2009-2010 was their ability to penetrate in to people's resistance movements. Lalgarh in West Bengal is a clear example where the focused infiltration by the Maoist forces in to the tribal movement enabled them to inflict maximum damages to the security forces. West Bengal registered 26 deaths in 2008, while 158 and 256 deaths in 2009 and in 2010, respectively.

Similarly, out of the 39 member Central Committee which also includes the Politburo; 18 have been neutralized, 5 killed and 13 are in custody. Those killed include Sande Rajamouli, Wadkapur Chandramouli and Patel Sudhakar Reddy, Azad and Kishenji. Among those arrested include Sumanand Singh alias Sumanda, Kobad Ghandy alias Rajan, Sridhar Krishnan Srinivasan alias Vishnu, Balraj, Chintan, Varanasi Subrahmanyam alias Sukanth alias Srikanth, Vijay Kumar Arya alias Yashpal alias Jaspal and Jantu Mukherjee alias Sahebda alias Ajay.

The Maoists have lost at least 150 of their leaders at various levels just within the past few years. The most recent of these losses was Mohan Vishwakarma, a senior member of the Maoist's Central Technical Committee and Technical Research and Arms Manufacturing Unit, who was arrested in Kolkata (West Bengal) on July 26, 2012. Past few years have also witnessed large number of Maoist cadres either being arrested or surrendered in different parts of the country. As per the available statistics, 905 Maoists have been arrested in 2012, in addition to the 1003 arrests of 2011, 1281 of 2010 and 836 of 2009. Similarly, 414 CPI(Maoist) cadres had surrendered in 2012, as against 227 in 2011, 150 in 2010 and 73 in 2009.

All the recent losses definitely have its impact on the course of Maoist movement. This is also one of the reasons for the significant fall in the volume of the Maoist violence. West Bengal saw an extraordinary upsurge in Maoist violence under the leadership of Kishenji. His killing has largely left the movement clueless which subsequently weakened the impact and the base of the movement in the state.

Death of Kishenji was a major blow to CPI(Maoist) particularly in Bengal-Odisha-Jharkhand region. There may not be another Maoist leader of his stature but the party has already nurtured a second-level leadership that can take control in the event of a major setback. There are experienced leaders like Prashant Bose alias Kishanda, Katakam

Sudershan, Nambala Kesava Rao, Kadari Satyanarayana Rao and Ramakrishna who have now swiftly positioned themselves to oversee the course of Maoist Movement. Politburo members Malla Raji Reddy and Misir Besra, who were arrested by the police, have rejoined the organization after escaping the police net. The crisis of leadership faced by the CPI(Maoist) cannot be ignored, but the real strength of this guerrilla organization lies with a large number of leaders who have not yet appeared and are unknown.

The most prominent effect of the crisis of leadership has been the rising dissent within the CPI(Maoist) and creation of several new fractions within the broad tradition of Maoism. As per the available statistics, Jharkhand has seen emergence of at least eight splinter groups in the recent past; most prominent among them being the Tritiya Prastuti Committee (TPC), the People's Liberation Front of India (PLFI), and the Jharkhand Jana Mukti Parishad (JJMP). Inter-organizational and intra-organizational feud apart, the cycle of competitive violence has sucked entire Jharkhand which now is grappling to tackle the Maoist violence from multiple fronts. The internal friction between various rival LWE groups in Jharkhand is the principal reason for the alarming Maoist violence in the state.

The Telugu leadership of CPI(Maoist) came under severe attack from the top Odisha Maoist leader Sabayasachi Panda. On 1 June 2012, Panda wrote two letters to CPI(Maoist) General Secretary Ganapathy, politburo members Prashant Bose, Narayan Sanyal, and other Maoist leaders. In the two letters, which ran upto 39 pages, he leveled serious allegations against the party leadership of mindless violence, dictatorship, financial irregularity, tribal exploitation, sexual harassment, big brother attitude of the Andhra Odisha Border Special Zonal Committee (AOBSZC), discrimination against minorities and Christians and so on. Further, in an audio tape released to the media recently, Panda declared to have severed all ties with the CPI(Maoist) and announced the formation of his Odisha Maovadi Party (OMP). Since then the Maoist Movement in Odisha has been experiencing certain new conflict dynamics which could have serious implications in the future course of the movement. In retaliation, the Maoist leadership has been unsparing of Panda and in a recent circular described him as renegade. What was really surprising was the Maoist did not take pains to rebut point by point the allegations and charges leveled by Panda against them.

Little doubt the war of wits between the Telugu and other leadership has acquired a nasty dimension. Apprehensions are expressed that some of the prominent leaders became victim to this bickering inside in the party. It is also feared that some prominent people informed the police about their activities and they fell to the police bullets.

□

6

Myth of a Protracted Battle

Whenever the people try to defy and raise their voice against the oppression, exploitation and challenge the barriers put up by the state to express their anger, they are described as the Maoists! Dalits and adivasis are the worst victims of this machination. Adivasis in Bastar refusing to leave their habitat in defiance of the state's desire are all Maoists; when dalits gave up their 'given' framework and came to the streets of Maharashtra in protest against the Khairlanji killings, they were described as Maoists for simply to be battered ruthlessly; when the dalits of Bihar and Jharkhand challenged the hegemony and repressive rule of the landed gentry and upper caste feudal lords, they were accused of being Maoists.

Notwithstanding the sustained propaganda and projecting the challenge of Maoism out of proportion, the state has been manifesting its obsession with the Maoists. The Maoists surely pose a formidable ideological challenge. They have been holed up into the forests of Chhattisgarh, Jharkhand, Odisha and Maharashtra with most of their important leaders incarcerated in various jails. Ideologically, of course, their influence extends beyond these tracks but certainly not to the extent the state projects. But for the help from the state, in the form of alienating vast masses of the people with its elitist neoliberal policies, deceitful misdemeanor towards masses and harassment of innocent people, the Maoists would not have be in a position to attract as many people as they do. As such, the state with its dismissive attitude towards majority of the people and repressive apparatus is proving to be the biggest recruitment agent for the Maoists.

Desperate Maoist groups are now adopting apolitical means to achieve a non-existing political goal. Killing a poor tribal on suspicions of being a police informer, abducting foreign tourists and govt. officers and gunning down unarmed lower-ranking policemen are the part of the so-called revolutionary struggle. One might argue that in a war this kind of collateral damage will happen on the way to a social revolution. I have also heard many Maoist sympathisers calling such acts a 'silly mistake' or a 'political blunder'. Can we just ask them, how many innocent lives do you need take before you stop making these 'silly mistakes'?

Maoist movements, despite of its militant nature and bloodied history, draw great sympathy and support of the Indian middle class. The sympathisers rightly feel that the Maoists at least brought many pertinent issues to the table for debate and discussion in the neo liberal economy.

The Maoist document released on the eve of the tenth year of formation of the CPI(Maoist) unequivocally accepts the fact that the movement is facing a critical situation. This statement coming from the hierarchy of the party simply endorses the fact that the influence and operation of the party has been on decline and Maoists have been losing ground.

It would be ten years since the formation of CPI(Maoist) by September 21, 2014 and the Maoists would celebrate this occasion on a grand scale all over the country. A yearlong new enrolment campaign should be taken up to expand the party. They plan to utilize this occasion to place before the party, PLGA, mass organizations, RPCs and the masses the successes and the positive and negative experiences achieved by the new party in various spheres; the tasks before them is to advance the movement and educate them.

Incidentally, it is for the first time the Maoists have confessed: "Though our countrywide revolutionary movement is facing a critical situation, there are several differences in the social conditions in various states and in our subjective conditions therein. So our tasks in various states should be formulated keeping these conditions in view. Our tactics, methods of work and style of work should also be formulated accordingly. They should be creatively implemented. Keeping in view the changes occurring in the course of the movement and in the situation in the world and in our country, we must make the necessary and timely changes in them."

The party leadership has so far not clearly spelt out the mode and nature of the changes they intend to bring about in the organization. But one thing is absolutely clear that if they at all want to survive in the Indian scenario and want to contribute positively they ought to reform themselves and also the organization. There is no doubt that even today the party apparatus has been badly split on the line of regionalism and casteism. Often allegations are leveled by lower-level cadres of harassment by the leaders having Telugu base. These Telengana-based leaders still nurse some sort of chauvinist approach and style.

Little doubt the organization must preserve subjective forces, to fight back the enemy forces and to build guerilla bases with the aim of establishing base areas but they should made to rest. The political commisseur should have the last word. Before ordering any armed action, the party should evaluate the ground realities. The indiscriminate use of armed action must stop. In all the states and areas party committees should come to a correct assessment about the actual objective and subjective conditions and formulate the tasks.

The document also emphasizes to Bolshevize the party so that it can efficiently wield the two basic weapons of People's Army and United Front and lead the revolution to victory. They reiterate to expand and strengthen mass base adhering firmly to class line and mass line. One thing can be safely inferred that the Maoist leadership is still immature and it mainly owes to their disconnect with the ground-level reality. It was surprising to read their assertion: "Let us grasp in depth the two Marxist principles – 'No revolution without a revolutionary party' and 'People are the makers of history'.

Grasping the true meaning of these guiding principles and implementing them in practice would help us tide over the critical situation we are facing at present." It is beyond comprehension how could the Maoists have been running their party over the years without grasping the true spirit of Marxism? Does it imply that they have finally come to accept the fact that Maoism is not a parallel ideology or philosophy to Marxism-Leninism, as so far they have been claiming? They claim to work for raising the levels of ideological and political consciousness of the vast masses, build and consolidate wide ranging movements and fight with determination to bring about a notable turn in our revolutionary movement. Obviously, this raises the question what they have been doing all these ten years? Why this sudden emphasis on mass movement?

If the government is to be believed, the greatest possible threat to India's progress is posed by Maoist movement. With this assertion, the government has intensified its military operation against them. In fact, the situation has been created by the Maoists themselves who have had the habit of mouthing, "Our aim is to overthrow this 'democracy' and 'parliamentary rule', which are nothing but means for the dictatorship of the feudals and comprador bureaucratic bourgeoisie, which stand in complete opposition to 95 percent of the population's interests, using armed force, to establish a new people's power. We feel it is a wonder of wonders to say that these elections and the parliament are sacred and that the present rule is the highest form of democratic rule."

The reality is notwithstanding a psychological boost in favour of the Maoists, they are not at all in the position to take on the armed might of the state with some splintered and disorganized groups of guerilla squads belonging to the PGLA. We have been witness to these units losing their dedicated cadres in police actions. Even the Maoists confess of huge human resources loss. But unfortunately they have not learnt lessons from their past mistakes. Maoists must realize only Dandkaranya or Lalgarh do not constitute the whole of India. Moreover, they have lost Lalgarh. There is no remnant of any guerilla squad. The 2011 statement of the Union Ministry of Home Affairs is worth recollecting; "CPI(Maoist) philosophy of armed struggle to overthrow the Indian State is not acceptable in our parliamentary democracy and will have to be curbed at any cost."

The Maoists must not hesitate in accepting their failures. Recently, I happen to scan through an official document of the Maoists. It was full of rhetoric and self-eulogy. This is not Marxism-Leninism or Maoism. The Communists are supposed to be self-critic. The Maoist strategy to overthrow the Indian State revolves around the simple, utopian idea of exploiting the contradictions in the polity, economy, and society. The protracted people's war to realize a 'New Democratic Revolution' is to be fought by exploiting and deepening the contradictions. Though the Maoists claim to use the contradictions, it is really sad that so far they have not succeeded in defining the character of India in the post reforms and globalization era. The country has changed, but it could not actually identify the nature of the changes. The fact remains despite India's remarkable growth story over the past two decades, it faces serious challenges: A big question mark looms over its ability to sustain eight to nine percent growth and development in the future years. Though irony it is significant the economic development and growth of India is looked through the narrow prism of sensex.

The Maoists must do some amount of self-introspection and ask questions: why have we been carrying out indiscriminate killings? Can in India a guerilla action is the effective weapon to coerce the government? Does in the era of globalization and liberalisation the tactics of using guerilla squad is enough?

The Maoists' Strategy

The aim of Maoist movements remains the same: overthrow the Indian State, seize political power through an armed revolution, and install a 'new democratic revolution', or a 'people's dictatorship' through a 'protracted people's war'.

Though they derive their ideological strength from the Mao Zedong's ideology, the fact remains that they have not worked out a concrete ideological approach to apply to the existing Indian situation. It can be claimed that the Maoists do not have any idea of the social relations of the Indian society. It would be wrong to infer that the Indian State is perhaps unable to determine the nature and scope of the Maoist movement. This perception is entirely wrong. The fact of the matter is the Indian rulers and the democratic structure is quite convinced that the present political order, parliamentary system of the country, is capable enough to embrace the movement and Maoists. Look at what happened to various Naxalite organizations and groups. Baring a few almost all of them are now defunct and their hardcore comrades and activists have embraced the present system.

This Indian phenomenon ought to be analysed and studied in depth. Look at the way even the saffron diehards have been changing. They have been clamouring for many utopian actions and policies but the day they came to power they have mellowed down. Indian political system and establishment has no parallel in the world. The Indian establishment analyses the problem using two indices, the welfare state and the market view. The first one subscribed to by a large section of the civil society, political leadership, and a portion of the government sees the Maoist movement as a result of the state's failure. The Maoist movement is nothing but a reaction to the lack of social and economic development arising from deprivation, lack of employment opportunities, and abject poverty. The Maoist problem, according to this view, is a result of the state abdicating its role as a guarantor of welfare.

Obviously, the solution should lie in addressing the socio-economic development deficit. Even the Maoists can partner the state in addressing the deficits. But the protagonists of the market forces are for all out offensive against Maoists. They look at the Maoist movement as a challenge to the manner in which politics and governance is organised in India and, therefore, needs to be addressed as enemies of the state.

They and their political lackeys in fact argue for military action against them. This has helped the Maoists in the crucial fight against the state.

Though the Maoists claim that the current strategy of the party has been much more refined and sophisticated, the fact remains that there is no fundamental change in their approach and implementation of the programme and ideology. In early years, the leadership believed that only the armed action will bring about changes. The same is even shared and nursed by the party leadership. Yes of course there is one change. Earlier the leadership held that the people will spontaneously revolt without being organised, but now they have learnt the hard lesson that people are by and large averse to the Maoist actions; in fact in most of the cases they voice their protest and oppose it.

For the Maoists, there are four major contradictions or chasms in Indian society: (a) The contradiction between imperialism and the Indian people; (b) The contradictions between feudalism and the masses; (c) The contradictions between capital and labour; and (d) The internal contradictions among the ruling class. The first stage of the people's war comprises establishing 'liberated zones' in the countryside, and then moves towards a gradual expansion till cities are surrounded, followed by a final push into urban areas. It is to this end that the Maoist strategy says, "The revolutionary war has to begin in those regions that are relatively more backward and where the social contradictions are sharp." Not surprisingly, therefore, the primary concentration of the CPI-Maoist is on poor rural communities in remote areas, and the tribal populations that predominantly stay within or on the fringes of the forests. "The inadequacy of the transport and communications system and isolation of the remote countryside" also make them an ideal base for a nascent Maoist guerrilla army.

It is really surprising that even today the Maoists are yet not clear how to begin the work of revolution, though they claim to be in the midst of the ideological war against the Indian State.

The Maoist document, strategy and tactics of the Indian revolution, issued by the Central Committee of the Maoist in 2004, clearly says that the path followed by Lenin in Russia, that of "capturing the urban area, establishing revolutionary authority in the urban area, and thereafter, capturing the villages and establishing the revolutionary authority in the whole country is not suitable for India." The document says that the Indian revolution will have to start in just the opposite direction – from the far-flung backward villages towards cities. The idea of building bases in the rural areas, and then encircling cities is a well-known tactic advocated and adopted by Mao Zedong. But, what is different in this movement, is that, unlike Charu Mazumdar, who in 1971 famously said that the 'Indian liberation' would happen in just four years – the present leadership of the Maoist advocates a protracted people's struggle that will stretch over decades, going through these phases: 'stage of strategic defensive', 'stage of strategic stalemate', and 'stage of strategic offensive' indicating a much more pragmatic and meticulously planned approach. If the disconnected rural areas of India form the initial setting for the Maoists' agenda, contradictions found in the urban centres provide the second stage. And supporting the many separatist movements in India based on identity, religion, and caste politics is their third area of concentration.

Façade of Peoples' Assertion

It is a general allegation that Maoists target only those areas and people for armed action which are vulnerable as these attacks will fetch good money. Usually, the project sites of the private companies had to bear their attack. Once the scared employees of the companies flee the work will come to standstill and the companies have to suffer huge financial loss. Obviously, in order to avoid any loss, they are eager to pay the amount the Maoists demand. Recently, the Maoists attacked a work site at Riga in Sitamarhi district of Bihar. This is one of such attacks planned by the militants in areas where large mining, irrigation or industrial projects are to be set up. This is suggested by the fact that an annual report of the Maoists, seized by security forces recently, had listed several upcoming projects in Bihar, Chhattisgarh, Jharkhand and Andhra Pradesh for attacks. The Riga attack may just be a symbolic call for battle to create Red terror in the nearby region, where the proposed Kosi irrigation project is to come up. Incidentally, the Kosi project is on top on the Maoists' hitlist.

The Maoists had made their intentions clear nearly six months ago when they met to observe the sixth anniversary of their armed wing People's Liberation Guerilla Army. In their annual report (October 2005-September 2006), they specifically listed sites for attacks having proposed bauxite mines of Jindals near Visakhapatnam and Polvaram irrigation project in Andhra Pradesh, projects of Tatas, Essar and Jindals in Chhattisgarh, Rajghara-Raoghat-Jagdalpur rail line, steel plants of Posco and Tatas in Odisha, power plants of Reliance and ongoing Narmada projects in Madhya Pradesh.

The ultras, in their eight-page report, asked their cadre to put up a brave front against these projects and initiate a Kalinga Nagar-type of agitation. The Kalinga Nagar incident had witnessed killing of 12 tribals during a protest against Tata Steel's proposed project in Jajpur district in Odisha in January last year. Thousands of tribals, backed by Maoists, had opposed the plant fearing displacement. Besides touching upon their future plan, Maoists also listed their successful operations, which included the Jehanabad jailbreak in Bihar, killing of 11 Naga jawans and attack on Salva Judum camps in Chhattisgarh, killing of 14 cops in West Singbhum in Jharkhand and attack on Malkangiri-Udaigiri jail in Odisha.

Though the government has launched a massive offensive against the Maoists, the fact remains that in most of the cases the states have not been following the defined directions and guidelines for operations issued by the Union Government. Reports indicate that at least Jharkhand has not being following the directions laid down by the Union Government for countering Left Wing Extremism. The Jharkhand Police has an alarming vacancy rate of 29 percent and there has been little attempt by the State Government to recruit additional personnel. The state also has a poor police-population ratio of 85 per 100,000, compared to the national average of 122. Similarly, the density of police personnel (policemen per 100 square kilometre area) in Jharkhand is 30.8 against an all India average of 42.4. It makes clear that nearly 30 percent of the state's geographical area of 79,714 square kilometres is forested and poorly policed. Obviously, with this preparedness Jharkhand police can hardly make the task of countering the Maoists easier.

The malaise is deeper. The State Government is known to have failed to utilize the central assistance released under the Police Modernization Scheme. According to the MHA, ₹ 1.827 billion were provided to Jharkhand in six financial years between 2000 and 2006. Utilization has, however, been abysmal. The official documents reveal that the utilization has been not more 12 percent of the total amount. Significantly, Jharkhand represents all that is currently lacking in most of the states affected by Maoist activities.

The fallacy of their revolutionary claims is also perceptible in their documents. At their 9th Congress in March 2007, the Maoists had adopted 'Resolution Against Hindu Fascism', it said: "The CPI(Maoist) pledges to fight resolutely against each and every instance of the trampling on the democratic rights of the oppressed minorities and others by the Hindu fascists. It pledges to do its best to defend the sections of the population targeted by the Hindu fascists. Our party is willing to unite in a broad front with all the genuine democratic forces which would be willing to fight back the Hindu fascist offensive."

After the 2014 Lok Sabha elections, the country witnessed with complete disbelieve that Hinduva forces have captured power and ascended to the Delhi throne. How it happened is immaterial. The fact remains that they have succeeded in their mission to distort the peoples' mandate. The Congress no doubt has been the representative of the bourgeoise and oppressive forces, but the fact remains that it at least maintains the façade of being secular, anti-Hindutva notwithstanding following the policy of soft Hindutva. The socialists failed to counter the juggernaut of the Hindutva forces. They perished.

But what about the Maoists! They had pledged to fight united and resolutely against the Hindutva fascist forces. Now is the time they should come out the explanation what they did to unite these forces during the last seven years? The Maoists even did not try to bring the Leftist and Naxalite forces on a common platform on this particular issue. They continued to practise the hate politics. The only instance of their direct assault on the Hindu fascist forces was the killing of the Vishwa Hindu Parishad leader Swami Lakshamananda in Kandhamal in western Odisha on August 23, 2008. Ironically, the person who led the action, Sabyasachi Panda, was later disowned by the party and recently he was arrested, exactly after six years, for the killing of Lakshamananda. After the killing of the Swami, the Saffron outfits communalized the issue by blaming the local church. They carried out a massacre of dalit Christians in Kandhamal from August 25-28, 2008. What was most surprising was the much touted guerilla squad of Maoists was not present around to protect and defend the poor dalit Christians. While it raises questions on the relevance of the guerilla squad, it also strengthens the belief that the squads are not the military apparatus of the Maoists. They are something else.

During these years, many incident had taken place, but the Maoists did not intervene either politically or through their guerilla squads. Surprisingly, the bullets or Maoist landmines did not take the life of even one member of the Sangha Parivar. Even Sumanta Banerjee in a recent write-up questions the party general secretary, Ganapati: "Is there any tacit understanding between your armed squads and the local BJP politicians, and corporate houses in your areas of control? There are enough grounds for such suspicion. In fact, immediately after the formation of your party in 2004, your Bihar-Jharkhand Special Area Committee came up with a report warning against such practices: '...a huge battery of contractors and middlemen in the rural area...maintain links with organizers (comrades at zone and even higher levels), appease them....That relation with such type of contractors have been maintained by party organizers is a matter of concern..." (Quoted in Gautam Navlakha's *War and Politics: Understanding Revolutionary Warfare,* Setu Prakashani, Kolkata, 2014. pp. 165-66). Despite the warning against the prevalence of this trend among Maoist cadres, you have failed to stem it during the last decade. In fact, this tendency towards making deals with agents of industrial houses has been reinforced by your cadres in your base areas in Chhattisgarh, as revealed by a contractor, Dharmendra Chopra (Re: *Indian Express*, January 24, 2014). After his arrest, he confessed to his role as a middleman who, in the Kanker district of Bastar, helped top mining firms, and BJP MPs and MLAs to forge deals with the local Maoist party leaders and squads who, in exchange for money, allowed them to engage in mining and extracting mineral resources from the tribal heartland – a corporate project which your party's programme opposes. Will you investigate into the role of your party leaders and cadres in this area?"

Let us look at their election boycott call. Maoists knew that the 2014 Lok Sabha election was not a common election like previous ones. This was in fact very crucial. This was set to alter the political culture and colour of the body politick of India. But they ignored the threat and continue to stick to their boycott call. What ultimately they got? Nothing at all substantial. They simply facilitated the victory of the BJP in Chhattisgarh, Jharkhand and Bihar, the three electorally important states for the BJP. Maoists not only threatened the common voters in their areas of control but also attacked a number of polling officials, innocent government employees who were simply performing their duties. What kind of class struggle has been this? The most surprising development was the victory of the BJP candidates from the liberated areas controlled by the Maoists. The simple explanation could be either the Maoists perceive the saffron as the future hope of India or are scared to confront it.

The Maoists instead of taking lessons from their past mistakes have been committing mistake after mistake. They must strictly adhere to the three major contradictions – (i) between imperialism and the Indian people; and (ii) between feudalism and the broad masses of the people; (iii) between capital and labour; but at the same time must properly evaluate the role of the ruling classes in the background of the deepening crisis of religious fundamentalism. The Maoists must stick to their 9th Congress resolution: "unite in a broad front with all the genuine democratic forces which would be willing to fight back the Hindu fascist offensive."

Some Bitter Questions

Why do the landlord and the greedy moneylender still corner the major chunk of the peasants' surplus? Why is most of the land still in the hands of few, while the vast majority eke out a meager living either selling their labour or trudging on scraps of land? Why are women fettered in obnoxious customs? Why is the dalit still preyed upon? Why are the adivasis scorned? Why is the inhuman caste system still alive and strong?

It would be naïve to believe that the government would come out with a reply to these questions. These questions are the fundamentals of building a peoples' movement against the establishment. It is the duty of the Maoists and Naxalites to rouse the consciences of the people, especially the present urban middle class, which has been hostile of various government welfare programmes and measure for the poor. No doubt, these people nurse a strong anti-class feeling towards the tribals, dalits and rural poor, yet they constitute the section of the petite bourgeoise and they ought to be kept in the loop, though not in that historical perspective. This will have an effective impact on the bureaucracy and the rulers. At present the governments instead of coming out with a definite reply to these questions have been resorting to ruthless use of armed forces to gag the voices seeking the answer.

The Indian rulers have been quite adept with the art of double speak. While they respond to the needs of the rural poor and proletariat, they also retaliate to their democratic struggles through violent means accusing them of indulging in violence and destruction. But what about the violence of the society they protect?

Maoists claim that in the villages under their control a new society has emerged. The outdated authority of feudal lords has come to an end. The bondage of caste has been smashed and ground prepared for its annihilation. This new democratic power is the Revolutionary People's Committee (RPC) popularly known as Krantikari Janata Sarkars, Krantikari Jan Committees or Viplava Praja Committees in the guerrilla bases of Central and Eastern India. The committee is directly elected at an interval of every two/three years by all adults, except those who support the state and its armed forces. The voters have the 'Right to recall'.

The RPC addresses all aspects of the people's lives through its defence, finance, agriculture, trade and industry, judicial, education and culture, health and social welfare, forest protection and public relations departments. On the basis of 'Land to the Tiller', forest lands were distributed by the RPC to all those who have no land or have scant land. Where people are well organised, women own half of the proprietary right over land. 'Equal wages for equal work' is being implemented. Bazaar committees are working to end the indiscriminate exploitation in weekly bazaars. Mass struggles demanding fair wage rates were successfully waged and there was an increase in fund collection to fulfil the needs of the people. All kinds of restrictions and taxes on collection of forest produce were annulled. Forest produce can be freely collected and consumed. The slogan of 'All Rights to the Adivasis, Local People over Forests' has been realised. There is a ban on taking away any kind of resources from the forest without permission from the RPCs. New entry of imperialist multinational companies (MNCs) and comprador companies has been blocked.

Apart from creating irrigation facilities for crops to increase the average yield and encouraging the usage of organic manure and high-quality local seeds, the RPCs assist the poor peasantry in all possible ways to cultivate their lands. Where conditions permit, with the purpose of raising living standards, fulfilling the masses food needs and those of the PLGA, all efforts are made to develop agricultural production and thus ease dependence on the market. The RPCs are themselves establishing agricultural farms. Mutual aid/work teams are formed to fulfil various productive tasks and services. Grain Cooperative Associations are formed. The effort to provide nutritious food to people through planting orchards and growing vegetables and greens has begun. Encouragement is given to fish rearing in ponds. The party and PLGA participate in productive labour as a responsibility.

The Maoists want us to believe that their programme has been a grand success. If it be so then by now almost all the rural areas of Bihar, Jharkhand, Odisha, West Bengal should have turned to Maoists. But the fact is otherwise. Yes they have formed the RPC but in some villages of Chhattisgarh, not in Jharkhand or Odisha or Bihar. Even the RPCs in Chhattisgarh have been pursuing reformist programmes. RPCs are opposing forceful religious conversion of adivasis into Hinduism and Christianity. They also inculcate scientific thinking and atheism. Overspending in marriage ceremonies and death rituals has been reduced. Schools are opened as part of fulfilling the basic needs of the people. For the first time in history, in Dandakaranya, education is imparted in 'Koya', the majority people's mother tongue. Syllabi were prepared in the light of democratic-socialist ideas. In Bihar-Jharkhand too, special emphasis is laid on reaching education to the adivasis, dalits and other sections deprived of it. Indiscriminate felling of forests and the robbing of valuable timber by the government and the timber mafia was stopped. Instead of people felling trees according to their will and wish for their agricultural and domestic needs, RPCs are striving to fulfil the needs of the people and are regularising the felling of trees.

Maoists claim that more than three decades of hard sacrifice had already made significant advance in the war zones of Dandakaranya, Bihar-Jharkhand. In these two regions, the RPC is always guided by the politics of new democratic revolution. While in Bihar-Jharkhand there still remains the need for struggle, backed by arms, to break the bonds of caste-feudalism paving the way for the development of Krantikari Kisan Committees, in Dandakaranya, the grounds were laid through struggles in which the adivasi peasantry was mobilised, with arms in hand.

Besides carrying out armed actions, the ruling classes are also indulging in psychological warfare, as Maoist leaders are running away taking huge amounts of party fund, women are being exploited in the party and that forceful vasectomies are being conducted, hundreds of party cadres are surrendering. They are propagating through posters that they would give lakhs of rupees to those who run away from the movement with weapons. On the other hand, the police and paramilitary are distributing materials in the name of civic action programmes. This is nothing unusual. They usually indulge in disinformation campaign.

Nevertheless, Maoists owe an explanation why the government should indulge in this nature of vilification campaign. The only plausible reply is, the Maoists have provided this opportunity to the rulers. If they had not been secretive in their actions and involved in open actions, this situation must not have been created. Undoubtedly, the aim of this attack is to decimate the revolutionary movement, destroy the people's political power developing in the various revolutionary movement areas in the country and get rid of the hurdles in their machination to facilitate the MNC to usurp natural resources.

Yet another reason for this disinformation is the MoUs worth lakhs of crores of rupees signed with the comprador, foreign corporate companies such as Tata, Mittal, Jindal, Essar, Al Khaima and NECO Jaiswals but they are not getting implemented due to the resistance of the people. In some cases, the Maoists led the movement which is why the Maoists movement became the 'biggest threat' for the ruling classes. But ironically allegations are also being leveled against the Maoists of being hand and glove with the corporate houses. The allegations have come from the cadres and leaders once associated with the Maoists operations. They allege that the Maoists leaders take cut money from these big houses. If they are not paid, in that case, they create all kind of hindrances for them. Their offices and machines are also set on fire or destroyed. These cadres also claim that while other persons, even the government officials, cannot dare to move inside the forest areas, the representatives of these companies move around freely. They have free access to the forest areas.

The Maoists owe an explanation to the rural poor and particularly to their rank and file. If there is no iota of truth in these allegations, why have they not taken initiatives to steer clear such allegations? Why have they been silent?

While the MNCs are putting pressure on the Indian ruling classes to implement the MoUs signed with them, the people are opposing their implementation braving all odds. The Jayalalitha Government in TamilNadu trampled the movement opposing the Kudankulam nuclear plant and started work. In Jaitapur in Maharashtra, some NGOs withdrew the agitation after getting a promise of increase in compensation. One after another the gram sabhas are rejecting bauxite mining by Vedanta in Niyamgiri. Though the state ruthlessly suppressed the anti-POSCO agitation in Odisha, they have not succumbed and are continuing to fight. But it would be wrong to credit the Maoists for all the successes the people's movement got in these specific cases. In Odisha, the Maoists taking the initiative have not been tune with the Maoist Party.

It is strange that the Maoists even failed to acknowledge the contribution of some of the anti-poverty programmes of the government, though it is again a fact that the fund meant for these projects are siphoned off by the government officials and middlemen. Nevertheless, the fact remains that measures like MNREGA, food for work, right to education and health, right to information, increase in minor forest produce rates,

Forest Rights Act have helped the poor. In fact, based on the success of these programmes, the UPA could come back to power in 2009 in spite of BJP launching an intensive campaign against the Congress. The Maoists must refrain from rejecting any thing outright. They have to evaluate and analyse government measures in proper perspective. In fact, their frontal organizations could associate themselves with such programmes and force the government agencies to function in a more transparent manner.

The most unfortunate development that is being witnessed is the emergence of right opportunist and post-modernist trends in party in some places. The danger of such trends arising would be present particularly at this juncture when the offensive of the ruling classes is increasing and unfortunately there is utter lack of a popular mass movement to face the situation.

The obsession of Maoists to armed actions is so acute that they have forgotten the primary task of building a political movement. Though their documents speak of need for giving priority to politically mobilize the working class, landless and poor peasants they seldom implement it. They even talk of rallying the middle peasants and urban petty bourgeoisie these sections are scared of the Maoists. They abhor the very idea of sharing platform with it.

They always speak in future tense; we should do, we must strive, etc. But they never try to give their plans a concrete shape. This is primarily due to their over reliance on gun power. It would not be exaggeration to say that the elements having faith in guns and goons have overshadowed the political commissars and pushing the organisation towards isolation. The Maoists expressed the opinion to build appropriate united front forums on various issues that would bring together revolutionary and democratic organizations, forces and individuals. But they are yet to make a sincere effort. While the ruling class is resorting to all kinds of offensives to isolate them from the people, they are yet to build bridges with the friendly organizations and forces and integrate with them.

It is interesting to watch that while the Maoists have been identifying mobilizing people on land and displacement as the main direction of their agitations, they are still to launch the movement in the right perspective. The basic thing of putting efforts to carry on propaganda and agitations around the issues is yet to start. Maoists claim that more than ten thousand of their cadres, supporters and leaders are languishing in the jails. They are facing severe inhuman conditions and lack of any kind of rights. They should have been given priority to provide legal aid and build movements for their early release. The Maoists plan to put extra efforts to strengthen the civil liberties movement.

Their political document underlines: “Following our general political line we should give priority to politically mobilize the working class, landless and poor peasants. We should put all efforts to rally the middle peasants and urban petty bourgeoisie. The worldwide financial crisis is negatively impacting the rich peasantry and the national bourgeoisie who are a part of the four-class alliance. So the time is more favorable to bring to the fore their demands too. According to their attitude towards the people and PW, we must take up tactics that would win over a section of these classes, make a section at least neutral and isolate the other. We should pay particular attention to forming appropriate united front forums on various issues that would bring together revolutionary and democratic organizations, forces and individuals. When the ruling classes are resorting to all kinds of conspiracies and fascist offensives to isolate us from the people, friendly organizations and forces, our practice should be centered on integrating with them further.”

But in reality these are utopian postulates. They have been consistently alienating every section of the society. The petit bourgeoise and middle peasantry perceive as their worst enemy and more than that a gang of criminals. Why these people form this notion? Did the Maoists ever try to find out the real reason? In Jehanabad region of Bihar, they have succeeded in implementing some of their programmes but this is not wide ranging. This initiative primarily owes to the local unit of the party which is not split on the caste line and also enjoys the patronage of the ruling party. In fact, this is described as Shikaria Model.

The main problem of their lack of initiative owes to their dearth of clarity about the measures they contemplate to adopt and pursue. They claim that in all the movement areas we must intensify anti-imperialist, anti-feudal struggles based on the agrarian revolutionary program. But how to carry out is not clear before them. They in fact admit: "Though we are taking up struggles, there are severe shortcomings since a long time in continuing them consistently. Other important shortcomings are – not consolidating the forces that emerge from these struggles, not establishing our leadership in UF forums and not developing proper methods for legal-illegal coordination. These shortcomings should be rectified. In this class struggle we should not confine ourselves to secret and illegal activities. We should carry on broad-based UF activities that would rally the various oppressed classes and social sections. In UF activities there is lot of significance to establishing our leadership, preserving our independence and advancing by basing on our own strength. We should utilize both open and secret forms of organization and struggle. In UF forums we should always adhere to democratic methods and avoid any kind of sectarianism and bureaucracy. We should expose and fight with such tendencies that may arise from other organizations and forces in these forums. We should pay attention to mobilizing the support and solidarity of vast masses particularly that of intellectuals and democratic elements as it is very crucial for the fighting people and organizations."

Surviving Adversity

Only in April 2013 the Central Committee (CC) of the Communist Party of India-Maoist conceded, "the condition of our countrywide movement is critical." It also accepted "in DK (Dandakaranya) mass base decreased in considerable area, the intensity and expanse of the resistance of the PLGA (People's Liberation Guerrilla Army) and people decreased;

non-proletarian trends increased in party and the PLGA, recruitment decreased; number of people leaving the party and the PLGA increased...the movement in North Telangana and AOB (Andhra Odisha Border) is in ebb. We are striving hard for their revival. Gondia division is continuing in a weak condition since a long period of time. Due to series of arrests in the past few years the Maharashtra movement is facing setback."

This was the time when the Maoist leadership came under attack for indiscriminate violent actions and killings of the innocent people. Those killed could not at all be classified as the enemies of the proletariat. It was the whim of the gun-tottering Maoist guerillas that prevailed over the party. What could have been the rationale of killing more than 200 innocent rail passengers of the Gyaneshwari Express?

The Maoists mentioned, "Due to betrayal of Sabyasachi Panda and enemy onslaught the Odisha movement weakened a lot. Due to heavy losses to the leadership and subjective forces and due to decrease in mass base the BJ (Bihar Jharkhand) movement suffered setback at present. Due to Comrade Kishenji's martyrdom, arrests of state and district leadership comrades and dent in the deluge of Lalgarh movement the West Bengal movement suffered a setback. Further, between 2009 and 2012 their central weapon manufacturing and supply departments; the political and military people's intelligence departments, the central magazine department, central Sub Committee on Mass Organisations and the international department were completely damaged."

Though the Central Committee of the CPI(Maoist) had rejected all the allegations leveled by Sabyasachi Panda as vicious, baseless and sham and accused him of betraying the party, the fact remains that he raised most pertinent and important mistakes the party leadership was consistently committing. Panda, the secretary of Odisha State Organizing Committee in his 16-page letter addressed to the General Secretary Ganapathy on 14-07-2012 had alleged of deviation. On their part Maoists charged him; "In cahoots with the ruling classes he spit venom on the CPI(Maoist) and the revolutionary movement led by it and hurled several baseless, sham allegations and fabricated lies. He released this letter with the evil intention of liquidating the party and the revolutionary movement, discarded the ideology of Marxism-Leninism-Maoism and left the vanguard party of the proletariat. He openly declared that he is completely disassociating himself from the People's War line and revolutionary practice and exposed his modern revisionist face. In the most abominable, crooked and conspiratorial manner he betrayed the party and revolution and the great cause of the toiling masses, particularly of the oppressed masses of Odisha and proved himself to be a renegade."

Sabyasachi Panda was initially with the CPI(M). After that he joined the CPI(ML)-Liberation. In 1998, he joined the CPI(ML) [PU]. Due to the merger of parties he continued to work in the erstwhile CPI(ML) [PW] and later in CPI(Maoist). He worked as a member of the AOBSZC between 2003 and 2005, as a member of Odisha State Organizing Committee from 2005 and as its secretary since 2008.

The Maoists allege that in his 15-year long practice, though he worked in a revolutionary party, he failed to transform himself into a genuine proletarian revolutionary and was criticized several times by his colleagues, cadres and the CC comrades for his anti-revolutionary opportunist political views, stands and practice. If the Maoists charges are correct then in that case the Maoists are to be blamed for it. The Maoists should answer why they failed to transform in a revolutionary? If he was not committed to revolution why then the Maoist leadership appointed him as the general secretary of the Odisha unit? Obviously, it implied that Maoists did not discretely follow the Marxist process in selecting a leader. In fact, the charges against Panda are of general nature.

Panda had in fact openly questioned the leadership of Ganapathy which was obviously not acceptable to the leadership. How can the general secretary, the top leader, of the party tolerate a person criticising him?

Some of the allegations Panda made were:

1. Violence for no reason and killings of innocent persons has become the norm for the Maoists; cadres are being ordered to kill innocent and unarmed policemen indiscriminately.
2. There is domination of Telugu and Koya comrades in the Party.
3. Adivasis are exploited the most by the Maoists, they are made to cook and carry luggage; cadre are not allowed to meet their families even during festivals; Adivasi women are being exploited sexually by the Maoists.
4. Ganapathy wants to establish a dictatorship based on terror and fear.

Nevertheless, the Maoists alleged, "his 16-page letter is full of lies, distortions and twisting of facts. There is not an iota of truth in them whatsoever. They were hurled with the most awful intention of liquidation and destruction of revolutionary movement in Odisha and damaging the image of our party that is serving as a ray of hope for the toiling masses and renowned for dedication to a great cause, the cause of liberation of our country and selfless unparalleled sacrifices. It is an open secret that he hurled them with the evil and appalling intention of fulfilling his selfish political motives that serve the ruling classes. Ruling classes bring to the fore people like Panda to gain legitimacy for the foul propaganda they carry on about the revolutionary movement and such phenomena occur frequently in history. The enemy has been hurling such fabricated lies on several of our leaders like comrades Charu Mazumdar and Kanhai Chatterji, on our party and the revolutionary movement ever since the launch of the revolutionary movement by keeping opportunists likes Panda in the front."

"Before going into the allegations made by Panda and the reasons behind them, we want to clearly state the fact that our party conducts meetings, plenums and conferences in order to correct and improve our practice and to advance with higher tasks. It realizes its mistakes and corrects them through criticism – self-criticism, reviews and rectification campaigns taken up specifically. This is a continuous process. Panda's evil intentions can be gauged from the fact that in spite of knowing all these things, he placed before the people his 16-pages of sham allegations. The actual fact is that he decided to leave the party as he was not ready to rectify himself in such a process."

The Maoists alleged, "Panda resorted to the age-old cheap 'divide and rule' tactic of the British colonialists and the Indian ruling classes who are retracing their steps by making the allegation that Telugu and Koya comrades are dominating in Odisha. The revolutionary movement led by CPI(Maoist) follows the path of Protracted People's War and builds the revolutionary movement to finally seize political power all over the country by spreading from smaller areas to vaster areas, isolated areas to all over the country, and by developing from a small force to a mighty force. From the beginning with a strategic outlook, it deploys its forces in various areas accordingly and carries on the work. It develops local mass base, develops party and army and establishes area-wise political power. By following this line, it brings a change in the strength of forces, finally surrounds the cities and captures political power all over the country. Keeping this in view, every member of our party must be prepared to go to any part of the country to work. Moreover, as internationalists communists must be prepared to go any country or area and work shoulder to shoulder with the people there for their liberation."

Panda was even accused of being narrow minded with nursing regional chauvinism towards comrades from other states who came to work in Odisha. It accused Panda of behaving in a domineering, undemocratic and sectarian manner with them. "The fact is Odiya people and the Odiya comrades have happily welcomed and accepted the comrades from Andhra Pradesh, Jharkhand and Chhattisgarh coming to work with them. We hope that those handful of cadres who are with Panda would rethink about the People's War path, see through the lie and expose him by realizing his conspiracies."

Panda had alleged that Ganapaty wanted to have complete control on the party and did not allow the lower rank leaders to put their views. He had even alleged 'exploitation of adivasis' by the Maoists discarding the aim of liberating the adivasis as part of people's revolutionary movement. Nevertheless, Maoists clarified the culture in a Maoist party is a democratic, socialist culture that does not discriminate between man and woman, literate and illiterate and cadres and leaders. This is one of the major factors in attracting a huge number of Adivasis towards our party. The allegation that Maoists are raping and sexually harassing women in the party are useless and false. The party said, "In what other manner can we expect the newly turned renegade to attack the Maoists than in the heinous manner of the ruling classes? The answer given by our party several times in the past is the answer to this allegation now too. But the best answer to this allegation is being given by the hundreds of women comrades who are joining the party."

It said the allegation that Ganapathy wants to establish a dictatorship based on terror and fear is so ridiculous that it in fact does not even deserve an explanation. CPI(Maoist) is not at all any bourgeois party. Its immediate aim is to overthrow the present semi-colonial, semi-feudal system in our country and establish new democratic revolutionary rule, i.e., the democratic dictatorship of four classes – workers, peasants, petty-bourgeoisie and national bourgeoisie under the leadership of the proletariat and based on worker-peasant unity. Its ultimate goal is the establishment of socialism and communism. Panda is fully aware of this. Panda is making false allegation on comrade Ganapathy and our party with the selfish motive of gaining a place through compromise in the dictatorship of the comprador bureaucratic bourgeoisie and the landlords that are in collusion with the imperialists and carrying on an unprecedented despotic rule wearing the mask of parliamentary democracy.

In reality, it was Panda who was trying to establish his dictatorship inside Odisha. After seeing the reviews and decisions made in the Special Plenum he realized that the party cadres are no longer prepared to accept his domination. They criticized his bureaucratic behaviour and his undemocratic and sectarian attitude towards comrades from other states. Realizing that he can no longer carry on his bureaucratic methods, this opportunist decided to quit the party and doubled his preparations for the same since then. Panda in fact took a right opportunist stand regarding some political issues that came to the fore in the course of the Odisha movement and finally degraded into a revisionist who rejects the line of Protracted People's War. His sectarian, bureaucratic, ultra-democratic, factionist attitudes, careerism, craving for name and fame and organizational indiscipline caused severe damage to the Odisha party and the movement.

Not One Sided Affair

Nevertheless, Odisha's Maoist Sabyasachi Panda, accused in several cases including the killing of VHP leader Laxmanananda Saraswati in 2008 that triggered a fierce ethno-religious conflict in Kandhamal and adjoining districts, was the poster boy of revolution. In Odisha, they called him Che Guevara. Tickets were offered to him by political parties, but he said he had gone off too far to be in the mainstream. Odisha's deputy leader of the opposition once called him the "voice of 57 percent in Odisha, who have only ₹ 12 to spend per day." He was arrested in Berhampur in Ganjam district in September 2014. Police said Panda did not resist arrest despite being armed with a revolver. Police also seized the bullets, 10 cellphones, ₹ 1 lakh in cash, 500 g gold, a laptop, two hard disks and five pen drives. Panda had in August 2012 formed his own extremist outfit, Odisha Maowadi Party, after he was sacked by the CPI(Maoist). He used Sunil and Sarat as his aliases in the Maoist circuit.

Panda is accused in 61 cases and he is believed to be involved in the abduction of two Italian nationals in March

2012 and killing of at least 25 cops apart from looting of the armoury in Nayagarh in February 2008. He is also accused of killing 34 civilians. Of late Panda's support base had weakened and he had limited his area of operation to Ganjam, Kandhamal, Gajapati and Rayagada districts. Police had arrested several of his associates while some others surrendered. In March 2013, police killed his deputy, Govinda Majhi alias Pradeep, during an encounter at Mohana in Gajapati district. Describing Panda as a 'dreaded Maoist', DGP Sanjeev Marik said his arrest was a "very big success for Odisha police." The Odisha Government admitted that Panda was directly involved in the killing of 59 people, of which 24 were security personnel and 34 civilians.

After the attack 84-year old Swami fissures in CPI(Maoist) surfaced on the issue of sharing the supari amount. There are unverified accusations that Sabyasachi appropriated the entire amount meant for the killing of Swami Lakshamananda Saraswati. Around this time the CPI(Maoist) Organisation was also said to have split into two major camps – the Odisha camp and the Andhra camp. As the fissures between the two groups widened, the Andhra camp asked Sabyasachi to own up responsibility for Swami Lakshmananda's killing. Six months after the brutal killing of the Swamiji and four of his followers, Sabyasachi owned up responsibility for the killings.

In 2012, from his hiding place in the forest hinterland in Jirakua Mangadakhari in Ganjam district, Sabyasachi Panda masterminded the kidnapping of two Italian nationals – Paulo Bosusco and Claudio Colangelo. Panda first released Bosusco, the Italian who was working as a tour operator in Puri. It is worth mentioning that Bosusco is a member of the Italy-based ultra-Left outfit Party of Committees to Support Resistance for Communism (CARC). Soon, Sabyasachi Panda's cadre started deserting him and he became forlorn. It was around the same time that Panda became vulnerable to attacks from the Maoist leadership in Andhra Pradesh and Chhattisgarh, who tried to kill him with the intention of gaining control over his territory. In February 2014, Panda was injured in an encounter with Ganjam police.

Panda's expulsion was a face-saving act of the Maoists. Days before the party announced his expulsion, 43-year-old Panda had written a long letter. In fact, he had written two letters – the first, a three-page letter addressed to party comrades in general. The second was longer one, 16 pages in Panda's own hand. It is addressed to the Maoist supreme commander Ganapathi and two senior leaders currently in jail – Narayan Sanyal (Vijay Dada) and Amitabha Bagchi (Sumit Dada). Panda raised serious questions over the functioning of the Maoist leadership. The letter also brings to the fore issues the Maoist leadership has been brushing aside as "enemy propaganda."

Panda wrote: "Dear comrade GS (Ganapathi Sir), Vijay Dada and Sumit Dada. With much sorrow I am writing this letter to you. After some developments of debatable questions in our state, I have no way but to write the letter. Leaders are thinking them as masters and cadres have no courage to oppose the leaders' mistakes. They (some CC members) want to politically eliminate me, if they cannot do it physically. They want to take some important contacts and other things from me, which they are not able to create but are much needed in war. Kill the dog after it becomes old – which is exploiter ideology? After arrest of Vijay Dada and Sumit Dada, Comrade BR and Bhaskar (Balakrishnan) had tried to convince me that the [guidance] of Vijay Dada and erstwhile PU leaders in organisational matters and their approach on women cadres was not correct." Panda writes how BR did not even spare Kishenji. He quotes BR as saying that He (Kishenji) is not doing anything, not killing a single police[man] and giving statements. As if killing police is only job for revolutionary."

Panda refers to repeated clashes with a Central Committee member Manoj, alias Bhaskar (Modem Balakrishnan) and BR (Basavraj, party name of Nambala Keshava Rao, in-charge of the Maoists' Central Military Commission). He quotes Balakrishnan as saying: "In communist party for faults of a party member we may suspend/expel and if need kill him/her." He also reveals that a Maoist unit was sent to his area of operation after he had abducted the two Italian tourists. His fear is that the 25-member squad, perhaps led by one Suresh, may have been sent with 'bad intention'. He points out that 'superiority complex' of the PWG cadre (essentially Telugu) and their disregard of members of other factions like the PU or the MCC has vitiated the atmosphere inside the party. He refers to certain comments made by BR about Narayan Sanyal and Amitabha Bagchi (both from the PU).

Panda strongly opposes the practice of 'unnecessary class annihilations'. According to him, "Beating and burning or eliminating someone by simply stamping him/her informer is not the solution." He cites how six villagers from Sambalpur who were killed by the party in 2004 on wrong presumptions. 'I alone opposed this. BR had given wrong information by saying that there was a Salwa Judum campaign in Sambalpur." He questioned the rationale of calling someone as police informer. "We are too weak in trade union movement despite our repeated views on this. But we had killed one CITU leader, Thamaso Munda, on Odisha-Jharkhand border and demolished the TU office. We can stamp anybody as informer and kill him without convincing people of our action." Panda's biggest grudge is what he sees as the hegemony of the Telugu-dominated AOB leadership. "Our AOB leaders are always for their superiority and tried to keep Odisha committee as subordinates. Politically, they never think about Odisha, its people's condition and political acceptance."

The most shocking was the allegation that AOB committee was only demanding the release of Telugu cadre in exchange of Malkangiri Collector, R. Vineel Krishna (kidnapped in February 2011). "They had given false answers that they demanded for Ganonath Patro and Tapan Mishra of Narayanpatna movement." Panda recounted how Telugu food habits are forced upon other cadres, which was responsible for many members quitting. He also alleged that shaving private parts is prevalent among Telugu cadre and writes: "Women cadres are regularly advised to do so. And it is also said that all should bathe without clothes. What is the relation [between] revolution [and] such stupid theories, I could not understand."

Panda also questioned the attitude and approach of the leadership towards the tribals. He writes, "in spite of having worked with tribals for 30 years, the CPI(Maoist) has not developed a concrete model for development of tribal zones." He writes; "Your janatana sarkar (people's government) is not the tribal autonomy body or it is not governed by traditional tribal rules, not even partially. What type of tribal autonomy do you want to give after revolution? "They have to hope for one good heaven only after their death. As we cannot think [of] a better tribal autonomy as we have promised, we are taking the help of such theories of wrong class lookout to exercise our authority over the backward tribes by using the tiny and non-antagonistic contradictions among them."

The Maoists are in fact scared of the declining graph of their party. A document reads, "No official or outside assessment has been as devastating as the 4th CC's resolutions, reiterated in the Revolutionary Greetings for the 9th Anniversary of the party (September 21-27, 2013). Unsurprisingly, given the acknowledged weakening of the party, fatalities linked to Maoist violence across the country have remained relatively low, at 421 in 2013 [including 159 civilians, 111 Security Force (SF) personnel and 151 insurgents], less than 36 percent of the peak fatalities in 2010, at 1,180 (626 civilians, 277 SF personnel and 277 Maoists), according to the South Asia Terrorism Portal (SATP) database. The 2013 figure, however, represents a significant escalation, after three years of continuous decline, from 367 fatalities in 2012 [146 civilians; 104 SF personnel; 117 Maoists]. Initial data for 2014 suggests a continuation of this escalating trend, with 81 already killed by March 17. Union Ministry of Home Affairs (UMHA) data, however, indicates a continuance of the declining trend through 2012-13, with 394 fatalities recorded in 2013, as against 415 in 2012, 611 in 2011 and 1,005 in 2010."

The Maoists have pinned some hopes for a revival in the Telangana region of Andhra Pradesh, where they had spearheaded the movement for the formation of a separate state, with the legislative separation of the Telangana and Seemandhra regions receiving Presidential assent on March 1, 2014. The 4th CC Meet Resolutions observed, "In Telangana the movement for Separate Telangana is developing in militant forms. Revolutionary political and propaganda agitations are ongoing widely in AP, NT and AOB. People are getting consolidated through various people's movements." Maoist optimism on Telangana, however, is likely to be belied by future events. Even if a politically sympathetic regime is installed after the formation of the new state in June 2014, sheer administrative imperatives will eventually make it necessary for the government to eventually restore anti-Maoist operations in the region – a pattern that has been repeated on several occasions in the past.

After sustained leadership losses since 2007, the Maoists appear to have taken some effective measures to contain this trend. Only one Central Committee member from Assam was arrested in 2013, while Maoist fatalities through the year included no leader above the level of state committee members. However, in a major shock to the system, the high profile spokesperson of the Dandakaranya Special Zonal Committee (DKSZC), G.V.K. Prasad alias Gudsa Usendi, surrendered to SFs on January 8, 2014.

The Maoists have devised a 15-point two-year plan for the revival of their 'countrywide movement'. The losses they have suffered over the past years have tempered the euphoria and adventurist expansionism that followed the unification of the People's War Group and the Maoist Communist Centre, and the formation of the CPI-Maoist, in September 2004. Despite defections, losses and a visible degree of demoralization, however, the core leadership remains committed to its radical project of revolutionary violence, and its conviction that the present reverses are only part of the inevitable cycle of 'advancing and retreating' that is the essence of the 'revolution'.

Maoists: Cash Crunch

The Union Ministry of Home Affairs on July 22, 2014, said, "The Left Wing Extremists groups, particularly the CPI(Maoist) are reported to extort 'levy' from industrialists, businessmen, contractors particularly tendu patta contractors, transporters, government servants and various illegal mining mafia groups in the LWE-affected states." Though an exact quantification is not possible, a study conducted by the Institute of Defence Studies and Analysis, Delhi has assessed that the Maoist have been collecting not less than ₹ 140 crores annually from a variety of sources. Earlier, on February 12, 2014, the UMHA had also given a similarly-worded reply.

Meanwhile, media reports quoting Chhattisgarh Police suggest that Chhattisgarh was the centre of Maoist extortion, with the rebels collecting nearly INR 1 billion from the state. The June 22, 2014, report quoted an unnamed senior Police officer saying, "Numerous intelligence inputs suggested that Maoist have extorted money to the tune of ₹ 80-100 crore from various sources, like contractors, businessmen, transporters and tendu patta contractors, every year in the state." Senior Maoist leaders were primarily focusing on mineral-rich Chhattisgarh to extort money to run the CPI-Maoist organisation across the country.

Details of accounts of money extorted by Maoists have been recovered by the State Intelligence Bureau (SIB) in Chhattisgarh. Giving details, an officer disclosed that the Maoists had been extorting money to the tune of INR 30 million annually from locals, INR 100 million from businessmen, INR 200 million from contractors, INR 100 million from transporters, about INR 200 million from tendu patta contractors, INR 150 million from timber contractors, INR 200 million from industrialists based in Naxal-hit areas and INR 200 million from employees and officers. About 20 percent of total cost of any projects or development work undertaken in the Maoist-affected zones is extorted as 'protection money', to ensure the safety of the works and the people involved, a SIB document claimed. Moreover, mobile operators also pay protection money of INR 20,000 to the Maoists to ensure the safety of each mobile tower. From the locals, money is raised in the name of 'revolutionary tax', which ranges from INR 10 to INR 2,000. Of course, these figures can, at best, be taken as 'guesstimates' given the significant variation in the totals and breakup given by various agencies. Thus, while the total is given as INR 800 million-1000 million, the breakup exceeds the upper band of INR 1000 million by INR 180 million. It is alleged that the Central Committee of CPI-Maoist takes the final call on the amount to be extorted from different sources. The task of recovery is divided among the organisation's segments such as the zonal committee, area committee and local cadres.

Significantly, the spokesperson of the Dandakaranya Special Zonal Committee, Gudsa Usendi alias G.V.K. Prasad, who surrendered on January 8, 2014, in Andhra Pradesh, had revealed that the Maoists were involved in extorting large amounts of money from the Bastar (South Chhattisgarh) region. Earlier, the interrogation report (IR) of top Maoist Chandu alias Tella Anil Kumar, member of the Andhra-Odisha Border Special Zonal Committee (AOBSZC) and intelligence in-charge for the 'Malkangiri Division', 'Koraput-Srikakulam Division' and 'East-Visakha Division', arrested on February 1, 2014, had revealed that the Maoists demand at least five percent of the total cost of road contracts from contractors. While five percent is the initial demand the Maoists are at times flexible, but do not accept anything less than three percent. Significantly, in lieu of the 'levy', the Maoists demand walkie-talkie sets and tablet computers from the contractors involved in civil work in the areas. If the demand of communication equipment is not fulfilled, the Maoists ask for explosives. Lastly, money is accepted, if no other option is accepted. Kumar further disclosed that one percent of the cost of total agricultural produce such as tamarind, on the Andhra-Odisha border, is demanded by the Maoists. Chandu also revealed that the 'One Rupee a kilogram rice' scheme of the Odisha Government was being siphoned off by the Maoists, as gram panchayats (village level local self-government institutions) were required to withhold a proportion of this rice for the Maoists.

Significantly, Chandu had also revealed that the CPI-Maoist has been facing a cash crunch in recent times. His interrogation report stated that, to cut expenditure, CPI-Maoist had decided to provide tea to the cadres only once a day, because prices of milk powder and tea had gone up. "If any cadre does not like tea, he is not encouraged to develop this habit. Also cadres are encouraged to give up the habit of 'khaini'," the IR said. Other austerity measures include provision of meat only once a month. However, women and sick cadres are given one kilogram of almonds per month for quick recuperation.

Interestingly, an earlier estimate of financial strength of the Maoists in late 2009 suggested the 'levy' collected by the Maoists was up to INR 20 billion. Nevertheless, if the earlier estimates, based on official sources, and the new estimates acknowledged by the UMHA, are accepted, the decline in 'levy' collection would be by far larger than the overall decline in the strength of the Maoists.

Aware of the development, the Centre has asked the State Governments to initiate legal action whenever such instances of extortion come to notice. Significantly, the Seventh Report of the Second Administrative Reforms Commission had recommended the setting up of special anti-extortion and anti-money laundering cells by the State Police/State Governments. The Union Ministry of Mines has disclosed that the State Governments have been advised to establish such cells to prevent the nexus between illegal mining/forest contractors/transporters and the extremists. Besides, LWE-affected states have been advised to effect certain changes in policy with a view to curb the flow of funds to the Naxalites from tendu patta collection. Recent developments, however, seem to indicate fissures that may lead to critical vulnerabilities within the Maoist uprising. These include a growing aversion to continued violence among the rural population and the morphing of the Maoist organization into a centralized, hierarchical structure that is increasingly becoming susceptible to caste, class, and gender biases among the cadres.

On May 9, 2012, Union Minister of State for Home Affairs told the Rajya Sabha that the Maoists were trying to 'revive' activities deep in India's South, in the States of Karnataka, Kerala and Tamil Nadu: "The CPI-Maoist is making forays into Karnataka, Kerala and Tamil Nadu under the supervision of its South West Regional Bureau and is planning to link the Western Ghats to the Eastern Ghats through these states. Their (Maoists') plan includes creating a base on the border of Kerala and Karnataka and establishing a forest route from Wayanad District in Kerala to Mysore District in Karnataka." Singh also states that, "The CPI-Maoist are (*sic*) gradually expanding their activities in these States."

Maoist Model of Development

Maoists claim to stand for a people-oriented, self-reliant model of development. According to them, in their model, people play the central role; their initiative is released to the fullest extent possible. They are of the opinion that all wealth generated within the country should stay here and not be allowed to be drained off abroad. India is a very rich country with tremendous human power and ingenuity, together with a vast natural resource base. The vast wealth, illegally and immorally appropriated by the imperialists, feudal elements and compradors, should be seized and turned to use in developing the economy, first and foremost in agriculture and in rural areas, where the bulk of our people live.

Undoubtedly, both the observations are vague. In recent times, bringing Indian money stacked in Swiss and other banks have been rocking the political establishment. The Lok Sabha has even constituted a committee to look into it. While the political parties vehemently oppose any move to park Indian money abroad as black money, the Maoists have simply expressed opinion. They arc not opposed to it. About the second proposition almost all the parties have placed themselves in the position of crusader against such anti-people and anti-national activities of the business houses.

What is most significant is that their assertions made it explicit that Maoists are not sure of coming to power by seizing the state power. They at best could share power with other political parties in the prevailing scenario. If it is not their contention then how come they mention these lines? In fact, in a Maoist set up, these issues do not have any place. They are discarded. Interestingly, they argue that their model of development is oriented to vastly enhancing the purchasing power of the masses. This will create a huge home market in the country itself, which will act as the main engine for growth. The starting point for this is overhauling the rural economy, where 70 percent of our people live. This will be initiated through land reforms, by the redistribution of land on the basis of 'land-to-the-tiller'. Their approach is in fact reformist.

Strange while the Maoists claim to build up political and mass movements, they continue to be dogmatic about their over reliance on armed action. A recent document refutes the allegation and emphasizes that this is a misconception. It reads: "there is yet another major misconception – that 'innocent' people are being caught in the crossfire between the Naxalites and the police. First, this is not a fact. Secondly, the 'people' are not a homogeneous mass; the ruling elite and their hangers-on are with the state, while the masses of the oppressed are with the Naxalites. The former support state terror while the latter act together with the Maoists to resist such terror. The misconception of a homogeneous populace is linked to postmodernist thinking of a so-called 'civil society', which conceals class divisions within society. All the same, in conflicts involving state terror and the people's resistance to it, there will be some sections not allied to either side, but the majority are polarised into two camps – a minority allied with the state, on the one hand, and the masses backing the Naxalites, on the other."

This is ridiculous proposition. The Maoists obviously lack the moral conviction accept their misdeeds and wrongs. How could Maoists claim that the people opposed to them are not innocent. Who are the Maoists to come out such diktat? Do they want the people to believe that baring handful of people who support Maoists all the 99 percent of the Indian population are reactionary and pro-capitalist and imperialist. This poorly reflects on the intellectual and ideological conviction as well commitment of the Maoists. There is no denying the fact that by observing this the Maoists have betrayed the immature mindset.

Maoists' 10th Congress

The Maoists held the crucial 10th Congress of the party during September 2014. The mega meet of the banned outfit, which is usually held once in five years, aimed at reviving the flagging fortunes of the Reds. The 9th Congress was held in 2007 on the Jharkhand-Chhattisgarh border.

The 10th Congress was crucial for the future of the banned party as it chalked out the future course of action. The meeting, to be chaired by Maoist party general secretary Muppalla Lakshman Rao alias Ganapathy, was expected to draw the entire top brass including Maoist party's all India military chief Namballa Kesava Rao alias Basava Raju, guerilla warfare strategist Malla Rajireddy alias Sattenna among others. The meeting would also debate over the next generation leadership of the party as most of the top brass of the banned outfit are over 60 years.

The 10th Congress could not be held in 2012 as scheduled because of the weakening position of the Maoists, who have suffered grave losses over the past five years. Since the 9th Congress was held in 2007, the Maoists saw their strongest Nallamalla division in Andhra Pradesh being completely wiped out by security forces after the 2005 peace talks with the YSR Government, even as the Maoists stronghold of West Midnapore in West Bengal was declared liberated by the security forces. The last five years has also seen 25 central committee or politburo leaders either being captured or killed in encounters. While key leaders like Kishenji, official central committee spokesman Rajkumar alias Azad, military wing chief Patel Sudhakar

Reddy were killed, key think-tank like Kobad Gandhi were captured.

Notwithstanding recent assertions that they would mainly focus on political struggles and organizing the peasant and rural poor, the Congress focused on violent actions.

The Congress urged:

- Form secret party units even in prison and carry on the task of running them regularly through secret methods.
- Build action committees such as 'Jail Bandi Sanghursh Samiti' behind bars. In case comrades are kept in separate prison barracks, then form barrack committees, and press with demands to keep all revolutionaries in the same barrack depending upon the concrete situation. Such action committees are quite helpful in further enhancement of the spirit of unity and sacrifice, and in identifying vacillators and coverts.
- Transform the prisons into political universities.
- In order to enhance your own theoretical-ideological and political levels, continue holding a series of study and political classes as far as possible.
- Arouse and mobilize common prison inmates, forming cultural teams, aid committees and various types of organizations.
- Develop the prisons as centres of struggle against the ongoing widespread extortion, corruption and atrocities as well as against the attacks on democratic rights. At the same time, unite and create a huge outcry in support of the revolutionary struggles being waged on the world scale, and against the repression campaigns aimed at them.

This Congress hereby adopts a resolution to take up every possible programme so as to express solidarity with the 'struggles of prison inmates'; to lend strength to their struggles; and to form suitable organizations. The Congress resolves to:

- Form organizations such as 'Committee to Release Prisoners' along with intellectuals, democracy-lovers and members of the families of imprisoned comrades, in solidarity with prisoners' struggles and to lend them strength. Such an organization shall conduct struggles on various demands related to the jail by establishing coordination between various Prisoners' Action Committees. Employing different means, such committees shall help create public opinion about the assault upon the civil rights of the prison inmates. In this direction, efforts are already underway.

- Organize progressive lawyers to provide legal support to the prisoners. Some efforts have been made in this direction. Yet we shall lay stress upon forming such organizations in different cities. These organizations shall provide legal support to imprisoned comrades as well as generate public opinion against draconian laws.
- Mobilize 'Committees to Release Prisoners,' lawyers organizations, civil liberty organizations and the common masses against 'Fast Track Trials' and such other outright anti-people provisions.
- Pay special attention to raise protest against and organize resistance to atrocities perpetrated upon women prisoners.
- Rope in various means of propaganda in order to highlight the inhuman conditions in prisons.
- Conduct signature campaigns on various demands of the prisoners and in support of their struggles issues in order to arouse and mobilize the masses.
- Strive to punish the prison officials who carry out atrocities upon the prisoners.
- Constitute a prisoners' fund to help secure their release.

□

7

Dogmatism of a Maoist

On the occasion of the 10th anniversary of its foundation, the Communist Party of India (Maoist) observed that though it was formed on the September 21, 2004, to shoulder the tasks of revolution, the fact is even during the decade they have not succeeded in consolidating their base areas. They are confined to some pockets in some states and have been keeping the organization alive simply on the strength of indiscrete armed actions. The party general secretary, Ganapathy in the article 'Lessons and Challenges of the Indian Revolution' wrote: "In the past ten years the movement in the plains and urban areas have weakened. We have not succeeded in vast non-peasant masses. Both of these have negatively impacted the successful implementation of our central task. But we also have the experiences where vast masses have rallied in the Nandigram, Lalgarh, Narayanapatna movements, the movement for separate Statehood for Telangana and anti-displacement movements in various parts of our country. These are new experiences we must cherish and learn from. We should deeply probe them to grasp the social dynamics they reveal, new features they contain, as well as new forms of mass mobilisation they brought up and the potential they demonstrated for building broad unity of classes extending beyond rural areas into urban centres."

The document released on the tenth anniversary claims: "It has been a decade of heroic struggle and sacrifices by the best daughters and sons of this land, nearly two thousand and five hundred of them, from Dandakaranya (Chhattisgarh), Bihar, Jharkhand, Andhra Pradesh, Telangana, Maharashtra, Odisha, Paschim Banga, Karnataka, Tamil Nadu, Uttar Pradesh, Uttarakhand and Asom, laid down their precious lives. They include hundreds of great leaders of the revolution, from the topmost level of our party to its basic levels. Scores of valiant fighters of the People's Liberation Guerrilla Army (PLGA) shed their blood in battle with the oppressor's mercenaries. Many among the masses too made the highest sacrifice." Nevertheless, the document does not speak about the reasons why the Maoists have not succeeded in building a significant political movement in any of these states. They have been surviving simply on the strength of their armed squads and guerrilla actions.

The document claims of achievements and valuable experiences and building a resolute struggle in the political, economic, military and cultural spheres. But it does not provide a vivid description of any such political or economic struggle. In fact, it claims that this was a period which saw ever more militant mobilisation of lakhs of people, people at the bottommost levels of society, in mighty revolt to destroy the oppression and exploitation weighing heavy on them for ages.

Astonishingly, it claims that it nurtured the shoots of new political power through the destruction of the old power and more extensive building of a new society in a primary stage, the fact remains that in the areas where the Maoists have been waging a so-called class struggle have voted overwhelmingly for the Hindutva BJP. How the phenomenon would be deciphered? It is for the Maoists to explain. It claims to have Peoples' Militia, which is again not based on facts. During these years, the Maoists tried to build a base in Lalgarh of Bengal. But they were completely erased from their base area. The reason was they even did not trust the adivasi people for whom they claim to fight. Due to wrong handling of the ground-level contradictions and over dependence on the armed squad, they lost a number of precious lives.

They feel proud in claiming that thousands of their leaders and cadres have sacrificed their lives. But why they do not come out with the introspection under what circumstances and why they have to lose their lives? They were allowed to be butchered by the state forces by the Maoist leadership. Had they adopted pragmatic policies and followed the principles and ideologies of the Marxism-Leninism and Maoism probably they would not have lost so many lives for without any valid reason and logic.

The document underlines, "Yes, we have striven hard to fulfil the promise given to you and made advances. It is so, because we are communists. Our words are sealed in deeds, serving the people. Inheriting the finest traditions of the countless rebellions waged by the peoples of this land throughout the centuries against their oppressors, both local and foreign, drawing inspiration from the heroic struggles of a long line of patriots who fought for true independence from British colonialism, boldly taking up the banner of armed struggle bequeathed to us by the red fighters of the Telengana armed struggle, Tebhaga and Punnapra-Vayalar, forever holding high the Red flag crimson with the blood of lakhs of martyrs throughout the world, we will fight on – till our beloved country is liberated from the clutches of imperialism and its lackeys, to make it a base of the world socialist revolution, to advance through socialism to the bright future of communism. We will fight as a contingent of the international proletariat, as comrades-in-arms with all oppressed nations and oppressed peoples and broad masses of capitalist countries. It is so, because we are the children of that mighty Spring Thunder that shook up the whole of India – the great Naxalbari armed peasant rebellion of 1967."

It further reads: "The rulers tell us we are fast advancing towards express highways, bullet trains, hi-tech cities and what not. They go on and on. But look around you, look at your lives. Despite all those gadgets, smart phones, cable TVs, motor cycles and flashy dresses why do the chains of hidebound tradition weigh so heavy? Why do the landlord, old or new, and the greedy moneylender still corner the major chunk of the peasants' surplus? Why are their wishes inviolate, their words the law, when all of us are supposed to be equals? Why is most of the land still in the hands of a few, while the vast majority ekes out a meager living either by selling their labour or trudging on scraps of land? Why are women fettered in obnoxious customs? Why the dalit still is preyed upon? Why are the adivasis scorned? Why this ridiculous spectacle of Brahmanical rituals heralding the launch of high tech space vehicles? Why is the inhuman caste system still alive and strong? There are many changes, new things not seen before. But the age-old structures and values of the caste system, of patriarchy, of landlordism still remain. This is feudalism, inextricably bound up with caste, another big mountain crushing us."

Why Live in this Hell?

The document released by the Central Committee of the Maoists while trying to justify its armed actions claims, "In these villages the Indian state has been destroyed. The outdated authority of feudals and those tribal elders, who lorded over people, has come to an end. The bondage of caste has been smashed and ground prepared for its annihilation. Organs of people's political power were established. This new democratic power is the biggest success achieved by the people through people's war. The Revolutionary People's Committee at village level, with 9 to 11 members, is directly elected every three years by all adults, except a few who oppose people and stand in support of the reactionary state and their armed forces and gangs. The voters have the 'Right to recall'. Women have right over half of the political power through equal representation. The people have all the fundamental democratic rights – Right to meet, Right to form organization, Right to conduct strikes and demonstrations, Right to live according to one's wish, Right to primary education, Right to primary medical treatment, Right to gain minimum employment, etc. The RPC addresses all aspects of the people's lives through its defence, finance, agriculture, trade and industry, judicial, education and culture, health and social welfare, forest protection and public relations departments."

It also emphsises, "On the basis of 'Land to the Tiller' forest lands were distributed by the RPC to all those who have no land or have scant land. Where people are well organised, women own half of the proprietary right over land. Equal wages for equal work is being implemented. Bazaar committees are working to end the indiscriminate exploitation in weekly bazaars. Mass struggles demanding fair wage rates were successfully waged and there was an increase in fund collection to fulfill the needs of the people. All kinds of restrictions and taxes on collection of forest produce were annulled. Forest produce can be freely collected and consumed. The slogan of 'All Rights to the Adivasis/Local People over Forests' has been realised. There is a ban on taking away any kind of resources from the forest without permission from the RPCs. New entry of imperialist multinational companies (MNCs) and comprador companies has been blocked."

A look at their operational areas, the areas where they are active and their guerilla squads have the base, will make it clear that apart from Dandakaranya region, specially Rajnandangaon area, at no other place in India they have even the façade of liberated zone. In Jharkhand and Jamui of Bihar, they are active to some extent, but it would be fooling the people if a claim is made of these being liberated zones. Undeniably, they have formed RPCs in some pocket areas and they have been doing some commendable work. They have to be given credit for that. But to portray these as an all- India development would be just deceiving the people and a sort of self-consoling exercise.

The Maoists must stop boasting as they have in this case; "The development of class struggle and building of RPCs has opened doors for new developments in people's cultural life. As the free labour done for the tribal elders came to an end, people fulfilling their needs through mutual aid work teams has increased. In adivasi areas, collective hunting which used to go on for weeks together was gradually discouraged. Instead, expending labour power on land leveling and creating irrigation facilities which promise growth in yield of agricultural products is increasing. As the customs and rituals observed with blind faith are proving a hindrance to production and productive forces in the changing conditions, meetings are being held with traditional healers and priests and necessary changes are brought about through discussions. Apart from discouraging consumerism, RPCs are opposing forceful religious conversion of adivasis into Hinduism and Christianity. They also inculcate scientific thinking and atheism. Overspending in marriage ceremonies and death rituals has been reduced."

It is a fact that they have opened schools as part of fulfilling the basic needs of the people. For the first time in Dandakaranya's history, education is imparted in 'Koya', the majority people's mother tongue. In Bihar-Jharkhand too, special emphasis is laid on reaching education to the adivasis, dalits and other sections deprived of it. In fact, their effort has been a big news. Even the media expressed cheers for the simple reason that the Maoists have been blown hundreds of schools were now trying to impart education. Little doubt their endeavour should be appreciated and encouraged.

The document mentions, "More than three decades of hard sacrifice had already made significant advance in the war zones of Dandakaranya, Bihar-Jharkhand. Given the different situation in these two regions this advance took different forms, but was always guided by the politics of new democratic revolution. In Bihar-Jharkhand a stubborn struggle, backed by arms, to break the bonds of caste-feudalism, defeat upper casteist private armies, seize and distribute land, paved the way for the development of Krantikari Kisan Committees as leading centres. In Dandakaranya, grounds were laid through struggles in which the adivasi peasantry was mobilised, arms in hand, to smash the authority of the forest department, private contractors and, in some areas, feudal lords or feudalistic tribal elders and end their exploitation. Party and mass organisations were built. Revolutionary armed forces, the People's Guerrilla Army and People's Liberation Guerrilla Army, were formed step by step. Thus embryonic forms of people's power emerged.

The merger of the two revolutionary streams in 2004 made these gains, its experiences and lessons, the solid foundation for a bold, powerful, push forward. Its results are before you."

Curiously enough, Maoists have also been taking credit for creation of Telengana. The document says: "Forces led by our party have contributed much to the success of the long-drawn struggle for separate Telengana. It has also provided strong support to many other mass struggles. This has helped them withstand state repression and attempts to divide them. Through all these struggles, the right of the people over water, land and forests (jal-jangal-zameen), their right to lead a life of dignity has been asserted."

The document underlines, "The Indian state is getting ever more desperate and ferocious in its attacks. There is a macabre logic in this madness of waging 'war on people', of 'pitting the people against the people'. Day by day the true condition of the country is being revealed. With 70 percent of the population scrapping on at ₹ 20 per day, the rulers' tall claim about India entering the league of world powers is seen as a cruel spin story. In opposition to this stands the new armed force, new people's movements, new political power and society emerging in Central and Eastern India. This is beginning to attract wider attention, not only among the deprived but also among a broad section of patriots and progressives. It is increasingly seen as a real alternative to the destruction of human and natural resources by the rapacious exploitation and loot and oppression carried out in the name of development by the imperialist and Indian corporates. It holds up a democratic model where the oppressed classes and social sections – workers, peasantry, urban petty bourgeois, women, adivasis, dalits, national and religious minorities – will be freed from the domination of Brahminical caste-feudalism and all the reactionary values it promotes, serving as the social base of imperialism and colluding with the comprador-bureaucrat bourgeoisie."

"In our country, armed revolution is confronting armed counter-revolution. Combating the superior forces of the Indian state with guerrilla tactics of people's war, the PLGA fights back. Unlike the aggressor, its strength lies in close ties with the masses, in its creativity and steely determination. The annihilation of a whole company of the CRPF at Mukaram (Dandakaranya) by the PLGA was a resounding rebuff to the Indian state's 'war on people'. In a protracted people's war, it is not the control of territory but the preservation of the revolutionary military force that is decisive. Grasping this principle, the PLGA has evaded efforts of the Indian state to pin it down and destroy it. It has broken out of heavy encirclements by attacking small units of the enemy and breaching its circle. Withdrawing in the face of massive forces, it circles around to hit back with all force when an opportunity arises. The Tongpal ambush (Dandakarnya) in which 15 mercenaries were annihilated, and 20 weapons and a large quantity of ammunition were seized and the Farsagaon (Jharkhand) ambush where five mercenaries were wiped out and five weapons seized testify to the strengths of a protracted people's war, a war that is led by a Maoist party and draws in the masses in their thousands."

The document also says, "Our livelihoods, dignity and very existence are under multiple attacks by neo-liberal policies that intensify foreign and Indian corporates exploitation. In the name of mega projects, mines, power plants, dams, ports, airports, super-highways, metros, hi-tech cities, tourist spots/resorts and Special Economic Zones, etc., lakhs and lakhs of our people are being driven out of their habitats. The destructive policies of the rulers are triggering of environmental disasters which take the lives of hundreds and render thousands homeless and penniless. They are enacting laws to cut down, one after the other, the rights won by workers. They are handing over more and more sectors of the economy to the control of imperialist multinationals. Agriculture is being shaped for deeper penetration of foreign capital and technology like genetic engineered plants. Land concentration is taking place in new forms as real estate 'land banks' and SEZs. Corporate farming is being promoted. Existing laws are being amended to assure that the chiefs of MNCs cannot be prosecuted here, no matter what crime they commit. While they grab land for their projects, nothing is being done to address the cry for land from the deprived sections of the peasantry. Big landlords continue to monopolise this precious resource."

"Wherever the people protest, they are met with brute force and black laws. While the farce of democracy is enacted with elections, the ground reality is one of increasing fascisation. With the genocidal Modi, this tool of the fascist RSS, in the Prime Minister's chair, Brahmanical Hindu fascism is consciously promoted by the ruling classes and their imperialist masters. The most reactionary religious fanaticism is fanned up to instigate sectarian violence, specially targeting the Muslim minority. Narrow chauvinism is whipped up to foster illusions of becoming a world power and thus cover up the abject dependence of the country. National cultures and religious diversities and even the formal federal structure of the country are sought to be effaced by sinister moves to impose a 'Hindi-Hindu' mould as supreme."

Nevertheless, the Maoist general secretary, Ganapathy writes: "The Message of the Central Committee of our party, issued on the occasion of its 10th anniversary, has given an overall evaluation of the past 10 years. Along with pointing out the gains and advances we have made, it has also drawn attention to the weaknesses and mistakes which hinder us and the favourable and unfavourable aspects of the objective situation. This article is an elaboration of some of the issues the CC Message has placed before the whole party, focussing on a few of the important lessons we must take and the challenges we must surmount.

".... Our party is leading the PLGA and the people in carrying on PPW against the ruling classes to complete the new democratic revolution. This is a total war that should be fought protractedly in all spheres such as ideological, political, military, cultural, psychological and economic, focussed on the destruction of the Indian state and building a new state, at present concretised in the RPCs. If a small and weaker force is to defeat a big and mighty force, then it does not have any other way than waging such a war."

"Yet we did not pay sufficient and timely attention to theorising these experiences. The enemy has developed its counter-revolutionary war strategy and tactics (Low Intensity Conflict or LIC) drawing on worldwide experiences. Therefore, in our theorisation, we too should have a broad vision, not staying restricted within our own experiences. The task of summing up and preparing policy to face up to the enemy's LIC strategy and tactics was taken up later. But this lapse resulted in delay in equipping the whole party with a deep understanding about the intensity, expanse and concreteness of the counter-revolutionary war as a total war in a comprehensive manner. This hindered us in tackling the challenges posed by the enemy's new methods and achieving the successes we expected."

"Our party lost considerable number of comrades belonging to all levels, right from CC to the village level, in the offensives of the enemy. Though leadership losses began since 2005 May itself, they increased gradually after Unity Congress and the situation took a serious turn by 2011 end. The leadership failed to a large extent in defending itself and the ranks. These losses weakened the three magic weapons of NDR – the party, PLGA and the UF – quite a lot. This failure is a very severe one. Sacrifices are inevitable in revolution. However, any revolution can be ultimately victorious only by destroying the enemy's strength and developing its own strength. This is applicable to protracted people's war (PPW) too."

"When the people take up arms, rebel and set out to wipe out the rulers, they will counter-attack even more brutally. They will attack with utmost ferocity and cruelty to wipe out the revolution. The leadership that prepares to wage an armed revolution must achieve victory by fighting back counter-revolution and ultimately by wiping it out. Defending the party from the offensives of the enemy during the course of war and from left and right deviations and advancing it towards victory would be a decisive factor for victory and the responsibility of the leadership. We should advance in PPW by defeating such attacks, by wiping out the enemy bit by bit and by increasing our strength step by step...."

"During Naxalbari period, the most important reason for the setback of those days was the immense loss of subjective forces including Central leadership. This is applicable to the setback of the AP and Telangana movements too. It is true that we had formulated broad tactical guidelines in our 'Strategy and Tactics of Indian Revolution' document to build revolutionary movements in various types of plain areas, keeping in view the changes that occurred in our country. We also have a policy document regarding urban work. But it would do well to examine how much and how deeply the strategic importance of these two areas is grasped and how much effort has been made in taking forward this crucial work. Weaknesses in this regard and failure to work as needed have led to our loosing many subjective forces in these areas that were a soft target for enemy repression. The persisting lack in doing social investigation and study is one major reason for such weaknesses."

"The majority of the people who are becoming victims of imperialist feudal and comprador bureaucratic bourgeoise exploitation and oppression live in the vast plains and the urban areas.

"Several movements are raging in the plains and the urban areas. The worldwide economic crisis is crushing the people of these two areas. There is not a single problem that they are not facing. There is no alternative to them other than revolution. And there is a lot of impact of the PW on the people of these areas. The situation in these areas is thus objectively very favourable to the revolution. What is needed is a creative approach addressing the concreteness of the situation existing in such areas and the demands of various sections and classes among the masses. The experiences we gained in the past decade will also help us in working under the new circumstances. Drawing on these experiences, if we creatively work in a planned manner, employing new methods to suit the changed conditions and enemy's tactics, we can certainly create opportunities to wage guerrilla war in these vast areas as part of PPW."

"When the enemy is carrying on a severe offensive on us to isolate us from the people and destroy us, we must follow tactics allowing us to protect and preserve our forces. We preserve ourselves to fight even better and destroy the enemy. Therefore, while implementing the methods necessary to defend and preserve our forces, we should fulfill political, organisational and military tasks of the PPW and increase our mass base. The enemy's policy is to isolate us from the people and destroy us. Our policy is to go more deeply into the people, integrate more closely with them and destroy the enemy. The favourable objective condition gives us good opportunities to do this. We should utilise them and politically rally the peasantry and various sections of people who are becoming victims of intensifying feudal and imperialist exploitation and oppression and mobilise them on various political, economic, social, cultural, environmental and other issues. The advanced elements that come to the fore in these struggles should be consolidated after raising their political and ideological consciousness. We must thus increase our mass base and subjective forces. We must take political initiative to utilise the contradiction among the enemies to serve this purpose by isolating the main enemy and hastening its end.... According to the conditions in various areas, the government is implementing reforms for developing illusions among the masses and to isolate us from them and destroy us. We should formulate tactical programs based on the policy already formulated by us and on our experiences and implement them to fight back and defeat the enemy's LIC tactics. Similarly, the party, PLGA and the mass organisations should fight back the relentless psychological operations carried on by the enemy."

Ganapathy admits, "Shortcomings persist in following iron discipline, in implementing democratic centralism, secret structure and secret work methods in the party and in leadership work methods and style. These cause damage to unity of thought and action inside the party. They were also one of the reasons for losing subjective forces in large numbers include top leadership Our party's ideological, political and military line is correct. The ultimate victory of the PPW is decided by these factors. In the present conditions, the key task regarding party building is that of moulding the party in such a way that it is capable of tackling and surmounting the difficult situation we face and advancing the movement again. For this we should take our past experiences and lessons learnt from them and discuss about them at all levels. At every level our comrades must discuss their own experiences, realise their mistakes and take steps to rectify them."

Ganapathy writes, "We should study the teachings of great Marxist teachers. If we look only at successes and advances and ignore failures and difficult situations or if we look only at these and ignore successes and advances, we would not be able to prevent past mistakes and would become victims of pessimism.... Another important task regarding party building is increasing the quality of the party. While giving party membership to new recruits, while developing them as professional revolutionaries and while giving promotions we should definitely give importance to quality. We should select active members from the mass organisations and from the non-party members of the PLGA and give them membership and training according to our constitution. To the extent we succeed in recruiting new members in the party, it would not only expand but would also be infused with young blood and new experience. To improve the quality of the party we should carry on study and training of MLM like a campaign. We should make study of concrete conditions and discussion on creative application of theory a part of this ideological and political effort.... All this effort regarding party building should be done as part of Bolshevisation campaign."

Using the word professional revolutionaries is in fact the spirit of Marxism-Leninism and Maoism. It is not clear from where Ganapathy borrowed this word; from the concept of the white collar professionals or somebody else. A revolution has to be brought about the proletariat, the working class, and the poor. Ganapathy has not tried to spell out his concept of professional revolutionaries in concrete terms. Does he imply that this bunch of professionals could be imported from anywhere, from any other country and they ought to not be necessarily proletariat or poor? Probably, he has borrowed from the cadres of Maoists armed squads. It is a known fact that they have been depending upon professionals who are experts in carrying out violent actions, like killing innocent poor and blowing the government property.

Significantly, Ganapathy also writes, "By making this program successful, we would be able to increase the ideological, political level and organisational solidity of the party, and thus vastly build up its capability in developing mass base and enhancing its efficiency in leading the PLGA and the people to advance the people's war. For the development of the movement, along with favourable objective conditions it is also necessary to have sufficient subjective strength. However, even when we are lacking in this strength, if we put in correct political and organisational efforts with determination, then the favourable objective conditions will allow us to build up subjective forces in a fairly quick manner. Our past experiences stand testimony to this. If we do not take this into consideration, think with a metaphysical outlook and become passive, thinking that our subjective forces are weak, we will never be able to overcome the hurdles we face today. The PPW path is one with an orientation which teaches us that a weak force can turn into a strong force and weak movements can develop into strong ones. Before the success of the Russian Revolution, revisionism dominated the ICM and the genuine revolutionaries, like the Bolsheviks led by Lenin, were a minority. The victory of the October Revolution smashed the revisionism of the 2nd International and unleashed a huge growth in communist parties and revolutions. When Krushchev revisionism emerged, only a few parties stood with the CPC led by Mao Tsetung. But the Great Proletarian Cultural Revolution brought forth a powerful wave of new parties and revolutions. Our revolution and the PPW in the Philippines are continuators of that wave.

Once again, only a few parties stood up against the revisionists led by Teng who seized power in China. But that struggle gave birth to the Peruvian and Nepali Revolutions. While the former has suffered a setback, the latter was betrayed by neo-revisionism. But the lesson still remains. It is by making revolution that we can draw out the full potential of a favourable situation and defeat imperialism, reaction and its tool revisionism. It is by standing firm on MLM, the ideology of the proletariat, and sticking to the path of revolution that we can surmount hurdles and tackle all challenges successfully. The global crisis of the imperialist system that broke out in 2008 is continuing. The masses in both the oppressed countries and imperialist ones are time and again coming out in struggle. PPWs are continuing. The people's war led by our party has gained widespread support all over the world. The unity of Maoist forces is increasing, facing up to the betrayal of the Prachanda-Bhattarai clique and liquidationism of Avakianism. The world situation shows great potential for a powerful new wave of revolution. But here too our subjective forces seriously lag behind the objective situation. Thus we see the contradiction, the glaring gap between the potential of the objective situation and the subjective capacities of the Maoist forces. The history of the world revolution teaches us that the principal way to overcome this is by waging revolution and advancing to victory. We have a great responsibility in this regard."

Ganapathy cautions: "Various opinions combat each other in the party as a reflection of the class struggle going on in society. We should keep in mind that, generally, when movements are facing a difficult situation, the possibility of right and left opportunist trends coming to the fore inside the party would be more. If we are not alert to this and do not take up struggle against them in time, we will suffer losses. If we over assess the strength of the revolutionary forces and look down upon the enemy, our party would suffer losses due to left mistakes. If we over assess the strength of the enemy and look down upon the strength of the revolutionary forces, again the party would suffer losses due to right mistakes.

Today the latter is the main danger. We should carry on internal struggle by following correct party methods against both right and left trends. However, we should not treat every difference of opinion as a basic difference on our line or enter into endless debates. Such matters should be clearly discussed in the concerned committees following proper methods according to our party constitution. This is the correct party policy followed by us towards differences of opinion and differing views that arise in the party. Some people have lost preparedness to continue along the arduous path of PPW and the will to sacrifice. They assess the might of the enemy as permanent and the people's strength as always being weak. They are making bankrupt arguments joining hands with the enemy. We should strongly fight back against such betrayers."

He writes: "In every country and society where class contradictions and class struggles are continuously sharpening, changes continue to occur. In our country too, not only in the economic, political and cultural spheres but also in other factors that seriously impact the revolutionary war such as transport, communication, media, technology, art of war, topography, proportion of rural and urban population and in legislature, administration and judiciary many changes have taken place. Even during the LPG period, these took place unevenly in our country where uneven development is present. We should stick on firmly to our political and military line and study these changes deeply, keeping in view the dialectical relation between them and our strategy and tactics. These changes are impacting some aspects of our strategy. That is why we should implement our strategy creatively and develop our tactics. We should make necessary changes in slogans, struggle and organisational forms and priorities that do not help in mobilising the people vastly and actively into PW. This was necessary in the past and it is even more so at present when changes take place relatively rapidly. When class struggle is continuing fiercely, study and investigation of conditions and formulating tactics according to them has a lot of significance."

"So far as our country is concerned, we should study these changes from another point of view too. It is necessary to understand that the changes that occurred in various spheres in our country have occurred due to the unprecedented level of neo-colonial exploitation, oppression and control of the imperialists. It is necessary to decide the direction of our tactics keeping this in view. Our 'Strategy and Tactics of Indian Revolution' document has stated clearly that constantly studying the phenomena in the world and the country, investigating and analysing them in the light of MLM, educating the party based on the summarisations, actively and widely rallying the people into the arena of struggles and developing the necessary struggle and organisational forms are of utmost necessity. When we continue to implement tactics that are no longer suited to the conditions, to that extent the movement too would be damaged. We had already reviewed that one of the reasons for the setback of the AP movement was such a mistake. We have also realised that some such mistakes have been committed in the past decade too. The party must retain initiative where we are strong, regain it where we have weakened and develop the movement by rectifying mistakes in time. As long as we firmly grasp the ideological weapon of MLM, and develop the political and military line through its creative application, we can overcome our weaknesses by improving political, organisational and military struggle efforts. Such a correct practice will once again regenerate favourable subjective conditions in all our areas of work for achieving victory in the NDR by overcoming the present situation we face."

Analysing the post-election scene, the Central Committee of the Maoists pointed out that the formation of the RSS-dominated NDA Government and the threat of Brahmanical Hindu fascism has brought forward the urgent and important task of building broad-based and powerful mass movements by uniting all the revolutionary and democratic organisations, forces and individuals and the vast masses. Attacks on religious minorities and atrocities against dalits will increase.

Progressive intellectuals and movements will be targeted. Contradictions among the ruling classes will also sharpen as a fall out of the drive to Hindu fascism and the concentration of government power in the hands of a small coterie close to Modi. The stealthy attempt to impose 'Hindi-Hindu-Hindustan' on all the nationalities will bring up more opposition. All of this will provide new and diverse opportunities to unite a broad array of forces in struggle.

Ganapathy has earlier also mentioned about need to build a broad base and powerful mass movements by uniting all the revolutionaries and democratic organizations, forces and individuals. But he never clarified the tactics or the plan they were working out to achieve it. It is a matter of fact even in the existing situation they have not identified the forces with whom they intend to associate. In background, when they treat all the organizations and democratic forces as pariah and untouchables, how could they plan to move ahead? Their major test would be the process adopted by them to identify the democratic forces. Nevertheless, it appears that it is a simply a façade of lip service and the Maoists are not at all serious about it. If they have been serious, they should have identified one of their own open organisations to undertake the task of meeting such forces, as the Maoists cannot on their own take this course.

Interestingly, the Maoists chief mentions: "the Modi regime is aggressively pushing the LPG agenda and the neo-colonial grip is tightening. It seeks to cover this up with false talk of nationalism. This nationalist posture of the Sangh Parivar must be challenged by facts about the wholesale sell-out of the country by the Modi Government. Wide and concrete propaganda must be carried out to expose the real pro-imperialist, pro-feudal nature of Modi's agenda. A new phase of Operation Green Hunt has started. The Modi regime will also be stepping up attacks on national liberation movements and people's movements. This attack on the people will be accompanied by more draconian laws, blatant violation of even formal justice, and more brutal persecution of political prisoners and suppression of activists who take up such issues. We must energetically intervene in such issues. There is good potential for building and strengthening civil rights/ human rights movements in a broad manner. We must try to unite them with the ongoing activities against Operation Green Hunt and the defence of political prisoners' rights. The aggressive promotion of Modi's 'development' agenda will see an unprecedented level of displacement. The very existence of the adivasis will be severely threatened. This will bring forward mass struggles. We should actively intervene in these, either directly through suitable forms or by playing a supportive role. We must keep in mind that it has the potential to give rise to a massive mass movement. The aggressive neo-liberal policies of the Modi Government will intensify the hardships faced by the peasantry, workers, government employees, and various sections like women, student, and youth. We must pay attention to intervene in such issues and organise the people in struggles."

But surprisingly the Maoists did not spell out their strategy about combating the menace of Modi Government on political level. Ganapathy simply writes: "to overcome the situation we are facing today, we must protect our subjective forces, consolidate them, strengthen our mass base and thus advance the protracted people's war more powerfully. The new situation emerging after the coming of the Modi regime must be utilised in this direction. It no doubt brings up serious challenges, but it also brings even more opportunities. We must boldly go more deeply and broadly among the different oppressed classes and sections of the people, mobilise them politically and unite them in struggle. We must respond to each and every anti-people, anti-country policy and measure of the Modi Government, persistently expose them, mobilise all the people in struggles against it, and strive to link them up with the ongoing protracted people's war. We must go all out and seize these opportunities."

We shall Win the Battle

The supreme commander of CPI(Maoist), Mupalla Laxman Rao leads the most ferocious Left insurgent group of

India. He replaced the founder of the People's War Group, Kondapalli Seetharaamiah, as the party's general secretary in 1991. Ganapathy is known to change his location frequently. The police of at least six states have been on look out for him but he has managed to evade successfully.

Here are his views on different issues that confront the Maoists. They had used the resentment and anger of the adivasis and poor people of Lalgarh in West Bengal to build a broad-based Maoist movement in the state. But eventually they could not succeed and the movement fizzled out. In the initial stage of the movement, Lalgarh was even described as the New Naxalbari by the CPI(Maoist). While Naxalbari left its impact on the Indian political scenario, Lalgarh became famous for the political intrigues. While Ganapathy described Lalgarh as mass uprising, which raised new hopes among the oppressed people and the entire revolutionary camp in West Bengal and had emerged as a new model of mass movement in the country, the fact remains that it cannot sustain. It died down within a short period. The entire support base which was with Maoists shifted their loyalty to the Trinmool Congress of Mamata Banerjee.

Ganapathy also argued: "There have been mass movements in Singur and Nandigram but there the role of a section of the ruling classes is also significant. These movements were utilised by the ruling class parties for their own electoral interests. But Lalgarh is a more widespread and more sustained mass political movement that has spurned the leadership of all the parliamentary political parties, thereby rendering them completely irrelevant." The fact remains that Lalgarh movement was also utilized by the ruling class. Had the Maoists ruled their leader Kishenji probably would not been killed. No doubt, Lalgarh had some distinctive features as high degree of participation of women, a genuinely democratic character and a wider mobilisation of adivasis.

Ganapathy had observed: "we have been working in Paschim Midnapur, Bankura and Purulia, popularly known as Jangalmahal, since the 1980s. We fought against the local feudal forces, against the exploitation and oppression by the forest officials, contractors, unscrupulous usurers and the goondaism of both the CPM and Trinamool Congress." The CPM had become the chief exploiter and oppressor of the adivasis of the region. It unleashed its notorious vigilanté gangs called Harmad Vahini on whoever questioned its authority. With the state authority in its hands, and with the aid of the police, it is playing a role worse than that of the cruel landlords in other regions of the country. Experiences make it explicit that in an area experiencing mass uprising, it is difficult for the anti-proletariat forces to survive for a longer period. In Lalgarh, they survived and even turned the table. The ground realities did not conform to what Ganapathy said. The Moists even did not spare space to the anti-feudal forces. They coerced the poor people and suspected the activities of some adivasi leaders. It even killed the honest CPI(M) local leaders who were against the hegemonic attitude and actions of the CPI(M) leaders.

A detail analysis of the Lalgarh movement would reveal that there were primarily three reasons for fizzling out of the movement; first, lack of faith in the leadership of the local people, second, unwillingness to transform the discontent into a popular mass political action and movement and third, excessive reliance on the armed actions. Even while the local people were getting organized and taking to mass mobilization and movement, the Maoist guerilla cadres took resort to planting the landmine on 2 November 2008, to kill West Bengal Chief Minister Buddhadeb Bhattacharjee. He escaped the plot but this provided opportunity to the state to ruthlessly crush the movement. Ganapathy's claim that the incident was carried out by the local people and it manifested the anger of the masses was entirely wrong and preposterous.

It would not be an exaggeration to say that Maoists messed up the Lalgarh movement and killed a popular movement at the embryonic stage. The area has the Naxalite bastion since 1967. Some of the front ranking leaders of the movement worked here amongst the tribals. In fact, they had laid the foundation. But in later years with disintegration of the movement, the leaders also retreated. Later the MCC started its activities. In fact, it was the common people, with the assistance of some advanced elements, who played a crucial role in the formulation of tactics formed their own organisation, put forth their charter of demands, worked out various novel forms of struggle.

According to Ganapathy, the reason for massive offensive against them owes to the pressure exerted by the comprador bureaucratic bourgeoisie and the imperialists, particularly US imperialists, who want to plunder the resources without any hindrance. He says these sharks aspire to swallow the rich mineral and forest wealth stretching from Jangalmahal to Andhra. This region is the wealthiest as well as the most underdeveloped part of India. In fact, he wanted to underline why the Maoists are active in this zone which is eventually described by the government as red corridor. Another reason according to Ganapathy for the offensive is the fear of the rapid growth of the Maoist movement. The Central as well as State Governments have been hatching schemes over the years. But they could not achieve any significant success. He nonetheless conceded that the setback in Andhra owed to several mistakes they committed. However, he said in a protracted people's war, there will be advances and retreats.

Countering the criticism of being simply involved in violent actions, the CPI(Maoist) spokesperson Azad had refuted the allegation in October 14, 2006 issue of *Economic and Political Weekly*. But the fact remains that even while the party has completed its ten years of birth, it is yet to build up a significant mass movement which could give it a new identity. The *EPW* had devoted its special issue (July 22, 2006) to the Maoists in India. Azad wrote: "Though the *EPW* has chosen a wide spectrum of views, it would have been more constructive if the articles were linked more to the question of the alleviation of the horrifying conditions of the masses, particularly in this period of globalisation when the situation has worsened. In these nearly 60 years of so-called independence the situation has not significantly improved compared to what prevailed in the last years of the

British Raj – at least for the general masses. In the Nehruvian period, the model of development relied on the 'trickle down effect'; now, in the present phase of globalisation, there is no pretence of even that. The one lakh figure (official) of suicide deaths in rural India in the past 10 years is only the tip of the iceberg of misery that none of the writers refer to. Poverty and deprivation of the masses have continued apace, more so in the present phase of globalisation."

He writes: "The contemporary Indian economy is unduly influenced by the activities of carpetbaggers, a ruthless mafia, rapacious mining interests and giant speculators, all linked to the politics of criminality. The degeneration is so deep, the rot so acute that these same moneybags are floating thousands of non-government organizations (NGOs) in order to trivialise the ills of the system so that people are diverted from seeing that these are endemic to the very system itself and not due to just some bad individuals or policies. The semi-colonial, semi-feudal order reproduces social polarisation – a growing rich and their vast number of hangers-on, and an increasing mass of the impoverished. A small section of the middle class is moving into the first category, partaking of some crumbs from the opulent dining table; the bulk of the people are being pushed into squalor, unemployment, agrarian crisis, business bankruptcy and financial ruin. Even the local bourgeoisie and small traders are being squeezed out in increasing numbers with the entry of giant companies in all spheres of the economy."

He continues: "We Maoists stand for a people-oriented, self-reliant model of development. In this model, people play the central role; their initiative is released to the fullest extent possible. We are of the opinion that all wealth generated within the country should stay here and not be allowed to be drained off abroad. India is a very rich country with tremendous human power and ingenuity, together with a vast natural resource base. The vast wealth, illegally and immorally appropriated by the imperialists, feudal elements and compradors, should be seized and turned to use in developing the economy, first and foremost in agriculture and in rural areas, where the bulk of our people live. Our model of development is oriented to vastly enhancing the purchasing power of the masses. This will create a huge home market in the country itself, which will act as the main engine for growth. The starting point for this is overhauling the rural economy, where 70 percent of our people live. This will be initiated through land reforms, by the redistribution of land on the basis of land-to-the-tiller."

Little doubt the claim of the Maoist is utopian. So far they have not experimented with the ideas they propound. How could they say that this was the panacea for the country? Moreover, the Maoists ought to realize that their package for enhancing the purchasing power of the common people is merely like day-dreaming. The party is talking like BJP and its leader Narendra Modi and yoga guru Ramdeo. It would be nice if the Maoists spell out the strategy and mechanism to seize and bring back the money. To be fair enough, this proposal of the Maoists is simply reformist and market oriented. This is not viable any longer as there is not enough surplus land. Since Maoists claim to work for the rural poor and adivasis, will they make public what should be the total land available to a poor family? How much land the government earmark for redistribution? Did they ever try to find out how much surplus land is with the government? What should be total land with religious institutions and mutts? What quantum of land is held by the absentee landowners?

Ironically, all the suggestions appeared to be a part of the government official note. It did not reflect the urgencies of a communist discourse. "Cultural, sports and recreational activities will involve the masses, while education will be made available to all. All forms of caste and patriarchal oppression/discrimination will be fought against and prohibited. Untouchability will be abolished and severely punished. All degenerate and feudal ideas will be fought against long after the revolution through cultural revolutions. Healthcare will be freely available, and more focus will be on preventive care and hygiene."

The party spokesperson emphasized: In a nutshell, this is the model of development that we Maoists stand for. It is stated in the party programme and political resolutions issued from time to time. In Bastar, before the massive state onslaught in the present Salwa Judum campaign, extensive development projects along the above lines were taken up and have been documented in the booklet New People's Power in Dandakaranya (2000). In Andhra Pradesh, Jharkhand and Bihar, it was the just struggles of the peasantry under Maoist leadership that led to the seizure of lands from the big landlords and distribution among the landless and poor peasants. What we propose is a model of new democracy built around the axis of land reforms and a self-reliant economy. It is also this new democratic model that we seek to implement (on seizing power) in its rudimentary form in the guerrilla bases and later in the base areas. That is why in Dandakaranya the Maoists not only implemented people-oriented projects (when the military operations were not as intense) but also called for the stopping of our rich iron ore being taken away by Japan at the Bailadilla mines and supported the 400-odd indigenous small-scale rolling mills facing closure due to government policies.

Does not it sound like the government annual plan document? No doubt, it is not a violent model; it is neither undemocratic. But the fact cannot be denied that these are all utopian. The spokesperson confesses that these development programmes were implemented before the Salwa Judum attack. But they did not furnish any account of the success of the scheme. Yet another important factor is, if they had succeeded in building and putting in place an alternate model of governance which was accepted by the people, then why did the people, the tribals, stand solidly behind them and fought the aggression on the basis of a political mass movement. Down the line their assertions make it clear that like the government, they too have all their programmes and policies on paper!! In Bihar, their success owes to the Shikaria model launched in Jehanabad with the assistance and monetary support from the Bihar Government.

Azad writes: "No real communist is for violence per se. Communists are for a peaceful social system built around equality and justice. But when they seek to work for such a system they are attacked most brutally. This has been the case ever since the birth of the communist movement. It would be naïve to think that the Indian ruling classes, who have a lengthy record of violence unleashed on the oppressed masses, are any better. Besides, it is not just state violence that people face; in a class society, as in India, violence is endemic to the very system and the oppressed masses are exposed to it in the course of their daily lives – by the feudal authority and by factory managements, and also as a result of untouchability, patriarchy, etc."

He argues: "To put so much emphasis on the violence of the Maoists appears to divert the issue, where, in the present system the masses have to face violence everyday of their lives. Hundreds die each day of hunger, starvation and easily curable illnesses. Semi-feudal authority in the villages has only force as its major instrument of control. The violence of the Maoists, which is preceded and provoked by the violence of the oppressors, is not really the main issue; justice is. If Naxalite violence is to be discussed, it should be in the context of violence pervading every aspect of our system. If not seen in this framework, one falls prey to the abstract bourgeois concept that 'violence breeds violence', without understanding the structural causes of violence."

Sad enough the party instead of confessing the mistake and striving to rectify the mistakes has been suspecting the intentions of the critics. They should do it, because their operations are shrouded in utter secrecy and mystery. They blew the Gyaneshwari Express. But so far they have not come out with confessional justification for carrying out the operation in which nearly 200 innocent poor people were killed. This habit has not died. They continue to practice this even today. Only in the first week of October 2014, they kidnapped a railway guard. It is very difficult to find out the reasons since he did not represent the interest of a brutal landlord nor a feudal lord nor he represented the oppressive state machinery. He was a poor middle-class employee. Do the Maoists expect that these actions of theirs would usher India towards a new horizon. It is quite natural that the government machinery should use espionage and informers to decimate the movements from within.

Strangely, the party argued if all persons in every village are tightly organised (into mass organisations, militia, and party units), it is very difficult for an informer to survive without getting noticed. Who refrained the Maoists to take recourse to this strategy? Instead they came out the alibi, "such intensive organisation takes time and is not so easy in the bigger villages and the urban bastis." For hiding the organisational incompetence, the Maoists have been blaming the state.

Maoists also blatantly refuted the allegation of their killing innocent people. It said: "There is yet another major misconception – that 'innocent' people are being caught in the crossfire between the Naxalites and the police. First, this is not a fact. Secondly, the 'people' are not a homogeneous mass; the ruling elite and their hangers-on are with the state, while the masses of the oppressed are with the Naxalites. The former support state terror (as in the Salwa Judum), while the latter act together with the Maoists to resist such terror. The misconception of a homogeneous populace is linked to postmodernist thinking of a so-called "civil society", which conceals class divisions within society. All the same, in conflicts involving state terror and the people's resistance to it, there will be some sections not allied to either side, but the majority are polarised into two camps – a minority allied with the state, on the one hand, and the masses backing the Naxalites, on the other."

Its shocking that for justifying their actions, they have been distorting the basic fabrics of the argument. Where do the passengers of the Gyaneshwari Express stand? Did those people were the stooges of the ruling elite? There are a number of such murderous incidents where the Maoists killed really innocent people, not the stooges of the ruling class. Is it not a fact that some time back they killed one of their own supporters in a train attack? Sumanta Banerjee correctly wrote: "the Maoist guerrillas often betray an immature mindset by intimidating them, instead of patiently politicizing them." Banerjee rightly observed: "Of the two (i.e., state and communist revolutionaries), the communist revolutionaries who: claim to look after the welfare of the poor and the oppressed, are expected to be more humane in their choice of tactics and genuinely democratic in getting popular consent for them – particularly when such tactics affect the vast masses of uninvolved citizens."

Maoists cannot deny that they have been consciously attacking the poor people, the civilians. Azad refuted Banerjee's contention. But then it raises one question: does it imply that the guerilla squad of the party is not under effective control of the leadership? Had it been so then a number of indiscriminate killings ought to not have taken place. Denials by the Maoists, who usually take responsibility for the attacks, and the PCPA may be a sign of something more disturbing: a rift between the leaders and their supporters on the ground. According to an estimate, Maoists have nearly 20,000 armed guerrillas and have established pockets of resistance in forested and rural areas in at least 10 states. With the state launching the operation to flush them out, the Maoists have become more aggressive and are resorting to indiscriminate armed action. One aspect of their action is worth mentioning; their actions are mostly aimed against the poor people ironically who of them claim to represent. Take a look at all their actions, this will become crystal clean. They target and kill railway passengers, rural poor, low level police constables and after every action they pat their backs for accomplishing the Maoist mission.

This simply points to two aspects of the movement; either there is utter lack of democratic centralism in their party or the armed squads control the functioning of the party with the political leadership relegated to the position of mere passive observers. An insight into the party functioning and a look at their documents make it clear that they lack on both counts. If there is utter lack of centralized unification, implying centralization of correct ideas; based on which they can evolve correct understanding of policies, frame plans, build up organization and issue command, action, how could the leadership claim that theirs was a party of the proletariats. The revolutionary communist party lacking this element cannot aspire to make a significant impact on the political scene and culture.

Often the Maoists blame other democratic or revolutionary forces for unnecessarily criticizing them. They may be nursing the correct impression. But they ought to evaluate and analyse their failures in the right perspective. If there is no agreement and unity on the ideas and the spirit of consensus and agreement by majority votes does not have a place and respect in the organisation, how could the leadership think of taking party forward? In fact, this is the trend what is clearly visible. The manner in which the party guerilla squad has been dictating terms and not listening to the command of the political leadership is testimony to it. After the guerilla squads carry out action and plunders the government property, the party leadership steps in to issue clarification. The party leadership must abide by the democratic rules and norms. Once unity has been reached on ideas and there is agreement by majority vote, they must unite to apply the agreed upon policies, plans, etc. Applying the agreed upon ideas then proves or disproves the correctness of our decisions in practice. If proven incorrect, then they can return to democratic discussion to reach a new level of unity and revise plans, then return to practice again. Essentially, centralism means once a decision or course of action has been agreed upon through democratic discussion, debate, and vote, all members must whole-heartedly unite in applying that decision or course of action. Those who disagree with the majority decision must still abide by and apply it, but may reserve their disagreements and appeal them up to higher party levels or bring them up for discussion and debate again at the next committee session.

Mao Zedong gave an important explanation of inner-party DC: "The Party Committee at various levels is the organ which implements centralized leadership. But the leadership of the party committees is a collective leadership: matters cannot be decided by the first secretary alone. Within party committees democratic centralism should be the sole mode of operation. The relationship between the first secretary and the other secretaries and committee members is one of the minorities obeying the majority."

Mao also felt: "It is nonsense if whatever one person says goes. I am referring to important matters, not to the routine work which comes in wake of decisions. All important matters must be discussed collectively, different opinions must be listened to seriously, and the complexities of the situation and partial opinions must be analyzed. Account must be taken of various possibilities and estimates made of various aspects of a situation: which are good, which bad, which easy, which difficult, which possible and which impossible. Every effort must be made to be both cautious and thorough. Otherwise you have one-man tyranny. Such first secretaries should be called tyrants and not 'squad leaders' of democratic centralism."

By living among the people, even in times of intense enemy repression and surveillance when open meetings are not feasible they can exercise DC. They can investigate and discuss problems through observation and inquiry of the masses, drawing out informal discussions, and keeping our ears close to the ground. What one learns and experiences at lower levels should be conveyed to higher levels to inform decisions made there. The comrades should not fear and should be encouraged to speak out as we a communist is committed to truth. Those unable to accept the truth of their own actions and errors being exposed and criticized are not suited to serve as the people's vanguard leadership. A look at the incidents of reprisal against fraternity members would reveal the hollowness of this understanding. With guns in their hands the Maoists activists and leaders forget the basic tenet of the democratic operation and building the party. Recent killings of the members from Tritiya Pratuti Committee in Jharkhand are testimony to it. They are behaving more like goons; intolerant of the functioning of the rival organizations.

What should be the explanation for stopping development works? People are already denied of their basic needs even after sixty-seven years of independence. Even if now at this stage the government is contemplating to undertake some development work then why to suspect it as an anti-Maoist or Naxalite action? Besides the Maoists are being accused of collecting levies using force. No doubt, they need money. But the manner in which they collect funds is anti-Maoist strategy. Mao Zedong at no place mentioned this as the right way of collecting money. Of late levy seekers in Jharkhand have stalled over 100 road construction projects, including 50 of rural development department. Sources in both the state rural development department and road construction department confirmed that many projects have been hanging in the balance owing to problems caused by Maoists. As a contractor has to pay levy to several groups which have mushroomed over the years, no one is ready to take up this work anymore. There are at least 17 rebel outfits, including CPI(Maoist) and People's Liberation Front of India (PLFI), which are active in the state and who try to get their share of every contract that is inked here. The amount collected as levy range from ₹ 1 lakh-₹ 10-15 lakh, depending on the cost of the project.

"Since a huge amount is taken up as levy, the quality of roads that are being made nowadays have deteriorated. Our engineers don't go for inspection in remote areas, and in most cases the contractor uses poor quality material. The result is bad roads and bridges that are washed away during monsoons," observed a former engineer-in-chief of state road construction department. This situation has in fact helped the corrupt officials. They have been looting the government money but blaming the Maoists. Some time back the Special Secretary (rural development) had confirmed that some 40 projects in Chatra, Palamu, Hazaribagh, Garhwa and Chibasa have been in the backburner owing to the Maoist problem. Even after signing contracts, the contractors did not start the work. Maoists often resort to one whimsical and irrational action; burning the machines and abducting the poor staff of the contractors. The mercenary type action and behavior of the Maoists has been simply delaying the development of the state. Since the government did not undertake development work in the past years, it does not mean that no development work should be allowed to be implemented."

Undeniably, this nature of the Maoists actions have been primarily responsible for the government resorting to armed offensive. The armed forces are deployed on the plea of protecting the interest of the state. Obviously, this enjoys the people's trust and support too. On their part, the Maoists have been blaming the government of ruthlessly using the security forces against them and also the poor people. They ought to do some kind of introspection about their approach to the development and also their style of operation. The government is contemplating to establish new security bases in four major Naxal-afflicted states in a bid to prevent the CPI(Maoist) from having a free run in their so-called 'liberated zones'. The Union Home Ministry has asked Maharashtra, Odisha, Jharkhand and Chhattisgarh to allocate land to set up the bases to impart jungle warfare training to security forces. The success of Army's first Maoist zone base, Narayanpur in Chhattisgarh boosted the government's strategy to step up Army presence in Naxal-affected areas. It hopes to 'unnerve' the Maoists and instill a sense of security among villagers through the Army's outreach programmes.

Earlier the Maoists used to indiscriminately kill the constables. But now they have been bringing about a change in their style. Recently, the Maoists sought apology for killing SAP personnel, soon after the Goh operation in which the ultras got their biggest cache of arms in the state (INSAS rifles, SLRs and AK-47 assault rifles). This is a part of their new strategy to entice and win over the constables in the name of class affinity. For Maoists, earlier the constables symbolized the might of the state power and representative of their class enemy, but now the Maoists have made it clear that they treat the constables, as their allies. Nevertheless, this may not yield the result as expected by the Maoists.

The Maoists have been concentrating in the adivasi areas sheer for the geographical reason; these provide tactical security to the Maoists guerillas. A senior forest official recently admitted: "In the absence of any government support and the apathetic attitude of the forest management departments towards the livelihood of forest-dependent communities, the Naxalites have found fertile ground to proliferate." But it be wrong to construe that these areas have turned heavens for the tribals. Some of the Maoists actions undeniably have helped the tribals, not all. Maoists have between 10,000 and 20,000 full-time guerillas, many of them armed with an AK-47. These revolutionaries are also conversant with the use of grenades, landmines, and rocket-launchers. They maintain links with guerilla movements in other parts of South Asia.

□

8

Globalisation, Rural Poor and Maoists

Did the rural poor benefit from globalisation and economic reforms? The reply to the question would be uniform No. In most of the public debates, different people mean different things by globalization, but one thing is common, its 25 year journey in India has not been quite encouraging. If the farmers committed suicide during this period, it also witnessed worst type of rural migration to urban India. Obviously, if the globalisation had helped ameliorate their socio-economic condition, the poor would not have preferred to leave their homes and migrate to unknown urban conglomerates in search of livelihood.

Though the CPI(Maoist) claims to espouse the cause of the rural proletariat, they have not succeeded in evolving a mechanism to protect them from the impact of these twin factors nor they are clear about what should be done to check this migration of the rural poor. It is not the wages or better living condition that has been at the root of their poverty. Instead it is the basic issue of landlessness, which is the main reason for poverty. The rural poor of the five states, West Bengal, Bihar, Jharkhand, Odisha and Chhattisgarh where the Maoists have been quite active have been worst sufferers of this syndrome.

In rural India, an estimated fifteen million families are both poor and landless. They have no secure legal rights to the land they occupy or cultivate. Traditional poverty alleviation efforts have largely bypassed these families. With land as a foundation, the rural poor would have been able to use the building blocks of education, healthcare, clean water, and access to credit to wriggle out of the extreme poverty.

Ask Maoist leaders what they have to say about the need to organize the landless poor for getting their land rights? Astonishingly, while even the socialists have been raising this issue and spearheading struggle for land to the tiller, the Maoists have abandoned their duties. The hunger for land is the best issue to organize the proletariat and launch a sustained struggle. But the Maoists never undertook seriously this nature of struggle. Instead they only focused on guerilla actions.

Let us look at the globalization. Some interpret it to mean the global reach of new technology and capital movements, some refer to outsourcing by domestic companies in rich countries, some view it as spreading of tentacles by corporate capitalism or US hegemony. The fact remains that globalization simply does not mean as openness to foreign trade and long-term capital flows. It affects the psyche of the poor and makes them further poor. During these years, the government launched a number of poverty-eradicating programmes, but the impact of these programmes has not at all been satisfactory. In fact, the globalisation has caused devastation to fragile economies.

The New Economic Policy (NEP) is not just a government policy. More specifically, it represents demands of hegemonic fractions of the domestic and international capitalist class. This class now wants to, and with modern technological changes is able to do business in a different manner. It wants the state to clear the way for this. We have how recreated pressure in UPA govrnment to down on prople centric policies that suited its near.

Introduced in 1984 by Rajiv Gandhi and given a concrete shape in 1991 by Narsimha Rao and Manmohan Singh, NEP expresses specific demands to create conditions where domestic and foreign capital can invest to make a lot of money quickly, by using cheap natural resources of the country, like land and cheap skilled and unskilled labour. The government is under capitalist obligation to remove all the barriers to capitalist accumulation.

Neoliberalism in India is a part of the imperialist project, implemented via burgeoning 'new compradore' elements both in the business world and outside. Given the adverse impacts of neoliberalism, it has resulted in massive resistance from below which has been countered by the state. Interestingly, in spite of some opposition it has offered, the Left has been, overall, a conduit through which NEP has been delivered. Neoliberalism has, however, opened up interesting possibilities by renewing the classical political questions: national-democratic question and the agrarian question as well as the question of socialism itself.

Specific demands of business politically expressed as NEP include: deregulation of private business; privatisation of government-owned businesses, trade liberalisation, allowing entry of foreign capital to own business in India; tax cuts and other incentives for business, and withdrawal or reduction of meagre government benefits for the poor. The NEP therefore is the neo liberal program of the bourgeoisie.

The intervention of major anti-poverty policies is primarily like the check valve. The anti-poverty policies are focused at assuaging the hurt sentiments and feelings of the exploited and deprived poor, adivasi and make them survive in the utopian world that are the integral part of the development and growth. This is in fact a machination to deceive the poor, particularly the rural poor and adivasis. It is not that the pre-globalisation and reforms era was golden age for the masses. Mass poverty, exploitation, oppression and (petty) bureaucratic heavy-handedness were rampant. Resources were in the hands of the state and were used by the rich and feudal classes.

It is a wrong notion that the NEP is an economic issue; Not at all. It is in fact a political and ideological condition for capital accumulation. The NEP is a class project and it produces an enormous amount of class inequality. The reality is the NEP has multiplied and heaped miseries on 70 percent of the Indians, the proletarians and semi-proletarians and vast numbers of small-scale business/landowners. It has produced a massive amount of economic inequality, insecurity, unemployment and under-employment. It has produced what Utsa Patnaik calls 'a republic of hunger' and what Jean Dreze calls 'a nutritional emergency'.

Peasants are turning paupers as they are forced to leave their land because farming is not viable: costs of cultivation are going up due to denial of adequate government support. Highly indebted, many have committed suicide.

Professor Utsa Patnaik (2007) has correctly documented, food production and availability per capita is decreasing, in part because land is converted to non-food crops both by big companies and smaller owners attracted by the prospect of making a little cash. This is a grave danger to food security. The NEP also resulted in an enormous amount of unevenness between regions, as neoliberal investment, whose main motive is profit making, tends to be geographically concentrated. Little doubt neoliberalism is a process of production of spatial inequalities and spatial displacements. A most important form of this unevenness is between rural and urban areas; urban areas grow 500 percent times faster than rural areas.

India's NEP is part of global neoliberalism, whose history is connected to working-class struggle in the West and anti-colonial struggles in the periphery. Capitalism, has been seeking to withdraw, since the 1970s, many of the concessions (the welfare benefits) it had conceded to the working class.

The implication of malaise of NEP should have been used by the Marxists and Maoists to organize the poor and proletariat to build a massive mass movement. But unfortunately they could not comprehend the nature of the onslaught of the NEP. The Left ironically prefer to exhaust much of their precious time and energy in debating the futile issues on the name of entering into polemical discussion. This has ironically acquired the character of fashion. The more you debate, the more prudent and wise leftist you would be acknowledged and revered. These intellectuals and think-tank never look at the NEP, as the instrument of class struggle. Given the devastating impacts of the NEP it is not surprising that there should have been massive resistance against it in India. Globally, millions of people have gone on strike many times since the 1990s.

Significantly, the main opposition to the NEP has come from the NGOs. Precisely, this was the reason that once the NDA Government headed by Narendra Modi came to power, it decided to crack on the NGOs. The bureaucracy prepared some flimsy grounds and pretexts for clamping down on these organizations. Latest attack on the NGOs has been in the form of putting under scanner their source of foreign funding. It is noteworthy that the UPA 2 had to slow down the pace of the reforms because of the resistence from below.

Though Maoists took to resistance in some areas against dispossession of tribal peoples and intensification of poverty exacerbated by neoliberalism, it was not well-organized resulting in little impact and fragile pressure on the government. The Maoists resistance did not have the desired result; it even could not send the right type of message amongst the tribals. In most of the states, they could not repose their faith in the Maoists. It again owes to the gun tottering image of the organization; most of the tribals in Jharkhand, Bengal and Bihar perceive the Maoists as a conglomerate of the caste leaders in league with the big industrialist houses. In fact, this averseness of the rural proletariat and tribals is effectively used by the state to project the Maoists as the biggest energy to their interest as well as to the nation. The government uses it to suppress any legitimate democratically organised protest against neoliberalism.

In a neoliberal economy with the government providing all kind of facilities to the capitalist and industrialists, the state as well as police administration is always ready to crack upon any democratic movement against the state. They even refrain from taking action against the goons of the industrialists as was witnessed some years back in Gurgaon.

It is a bare fact that the Left parties have not succeeded in putting pressure on Central or State Governments to implement certain pro-poor measures and to slow the pace of neoliberal measures. Unfortunately, from early nineties, the parliamentary Left, the CPI and CPI(M) have virtually become the vanguards of reforms and globalization. Though they have been pretending to fight against it by observing annual festivity of observing India bandh, they utterly lacked seriousness.

It is beyond comprehension how could the Maoists and parliamentary Left ignore the fact that the neoliberalism is for changing the balance of class power in favour of the capitalist class. It is a matter of concern that the private sector and industrial houses have been completely opposed and hostile to even implementing neoliberal measures favouring the proletariat, tribals and rural poor. They made a big issue of the right to food. It was basically adoption of these measures that turned them towards the BJP for solace. The rout of the Congress in the Lok Sabha polls primarily owes to this. The fact remains that the Congress was simply providing lip service to the poors and was not at all sincere in their commitment to them.

The lack of commitment was clearly manifest in the ambivalent stand of the Congress leadership towards programmes meant for the inclusive growth and empowerment of the dalit and poor. This approach was primarily responsible for the rout of the Congress in the 2014 Lok Sabha elections. The rout of the Congress needed deeper and inclusive diagnosis of the malaise that inflicted the Congress. On May 16, 2014, the Congress witnessed its worst defeat since the first general elections.

After this nature of drubbing what Sonia Gandhi as the president of the party should have done? Her response would have been directly proportionate to the magnitude of the defeat. Though the Congress admitted disconnect with the people and said the party needs to introspect and rework its strategy, the basic reason still missed the self-introspection. Congress has been the political organ of the liberal bourgeoise and democrats following the political line of left to the centre. Its primary target group and support base has been the poor and marginalized section of the society.

A vibrant political outfit reshapes and changes its approach and ideological contour suited to the changing times. But no such initiative was taken by the Congress. Though the globalization and reforms were introduced in India in late eighties, the Congress leadership preferred to follow socialist mode of politics and programmes as it felt that the rural people still deserve the preferential treatment. Though it helped the Congress gain power in 2004 and again in 2009, this time the party was not lucky enough. There were certain very important reasons and factors. Neither Sonia Gandhi nor the collective Congress leaders ever thought of giving a new shape and colour to the ideology in the background of the changing global scenario and precisely during the phase of reforms and liberalization in India. In its desperation to have both the worlds, Congress continued to project Dr Singh as the reforms face of the party and brought in Rahul Gandhi as the socialist crusader to keep afloat its concern for the rural people. In the process the Congress failed to do justice to the reforms and also could not project itself as the protector of the marginalized people. In its eagerness to espouse the cause of the poor, Rahul even roughed up Dr Singh, the person towards him the global fraternity looked with high hopes and aspirations. His famous remark on bill to protect corrupt politicians while failed to win over the trust of the urban middle class it did not find takers in the rural people.

There is little doubt that the Congress had to pay for its ambivalent approach on reforms. It is irony that in its confusion the party could neither identify itself with the rural poor nor the urban middle class. The party turned suspect in the eyes of both these sections. It lost the trust and confidence of both the sections. The manner in which the food security act was derided provided the insight into the attitude of the urban middle class towards the Congress. For them Congress has lost its relevance as it was not eager to push reforms. The rural poor also turned skeptical of the Congress approach. After Jaipur chintan shivir an impression gained that the party was shifting its loyalty to the urban middle class. The rural people looked at its actions and programmes with suspicion. Now in the changed situation the Congress would have to spell out its priorities and also identify its core base. The Congress leadership could not abdicate its responsibility for the failure to carry forward the process of reforms. Singh was left to look after it as if this was his baby.

What was worse the Congress did not shield Dr Singh against the BJP attack which turned the Congress vulnerable. Why was the Congress not protecting an honest person Singh? In fact this was the hotly debated issue in the public domain. There is no denying the fact the Congress had to dearly pay for distancing itself from the programme and policies of Dr Singh and launching a parallel political initiative of socialistic programmes. This proved suicidal. Rahul campaign was more mechanical oriented and failed to catch the psyche and aspirations of the people. He failed to carry the message to the masses. Under him the Congress stood alienated from its core support base. The manner in which he insulted Dr Singh, obviously with the intentions to identify him as the symbol of capitalist and crony capital which is detrimental to the interest of the poor and downtrodden, did not go down well with the people. His style of functioning was alien to the rural people and they failed to connect with him and the Congress.

Significant the NEP has pushed the issue of the national question to the centre stage of the Indian politics. Till some time the national question veered around the issue of semi-feudal and semi-colonial character of the country. But now the issues of crony capitalism and fighting new imperialism have become the central task. A sustained campaign is being made to identify India as a part of the global capitalism through projecting it as a superpower.

Narratives of Poverty

Poverty in India is widespread, with the nation estimated to have a third of the world's poor. In 2010, the World Bank reported that 32.7 percent of the total Indian people fall below the international poverty line of US$ 1.25 per day (PPP) while 68.7 percent live on less than US$ 2 per day. According to

2010 data from the United Nations Development Programme, an estimated 29.8 percent of Indians live below the country's national poverty line. A 2010 report by the Oxford Poverty and Human Development Initiative (OPHI) states that eight Indian states have more poor people than 26 poorest African nations combined which totals to more than 410 million poor in the poorest African countries.

The latest UNICEF data shows that one in three malnourished children worldwide are found in India, while 42 percent of the nation's children under five years of age are underweight. It also shows that a total of 58 percent of children under five surveyed were stunted. Rohini Mukherjee, of the Naadi foundation – one of the NGOs that published the report – stated India is "doing worse than sub-Saharan Africa." The 2011 Global Hunger Index (GHI) Report places India amongst the three countries where the GHI between 1996 and 2011 went up from 22.9 to 23.7, while 78 out of the 81 developing countries studied, including Pakistan, Nepal, Bangladesh, Vietnam, Kenya, Nigeria, Myanmar, Uganda, Zimbabwe and Malawi, succeeded in improving hunger conditions.

There has been no uniform measure of poverty in India. The Planning Commission of India has accepted the Tendulkar Committee report which says that 37 percent of people in India live below the poverty line (BPL). The Arjun Sengupta Report (from the National Commission for Enterprises in the Unorganised Sector), based on data between the period 1993-94 and 2004 – 05, states that 77 percent of Indians live on less than 20 a day (about $0.50 per day). The N.C. Saxena Committee Report states, on account of calorific intake apart from nominal income, that 50 percent of Indians live below the poverty line.

A study by the Oxford Poverty and Human Development Initiative using a Multi-dimensional Poverty Index (MPI) found that there were 650 million people (53.7 percent of population) living in poverty in India, of which 340 million people (28.6 percent of the population) were living in severe poverty, and that a further 198 million people (16.4 percent of the population) were vulnerable to poverty. 421 million of the poor are concentrated in eight North Indian and East Indian states of Bihar, Chattisgarh, Jharkhand, Madhya Pradesh, Odisha, Rajasthan, Uttar Pradesh and West Bengal. This number is higher than the 410 million poor living in the 26 poorest African nations.

Globalisation of production, by reducing the industries in the backward has reduced the victim countries to the status of mere parts of the global factories and has led to unprecedented crisis in these economies which will worsen as the crisis in the world economy intensifies further. Globalisation has led to the massive flows of short-term speculative capital (portfolio capital) into the countries. As a consequence, these economies have become most vulnerable to every crisis in the world economy. They are at the mercy of the whims and needs of speculative capital. Any sudden withdrawal of foreign funds can even lead to the collapse of economies as was witnessed in India some time back. Though the BJP used it to malign the Manmohan Singh Government and accuse it of being indecisive and suffering with policy paralysis, the fact remains that this withdrawal has created a piquant situation and the country had to face serious economic crisis.

The so-called growth in the Indian economy as well as world economy is actually speculation-driven and does not correspond at all to the real economy. Of the four factors that seemed to buoy up the world capitalist economy, three – the high-tech and dotcom, the stock market, and the dollar build-up – have already taken a nose-dive in the three years since 2000 and the real estate bubble is about to burst anytime. Strange enough, the political class and a section of the pro-capitalist economists have been quite ebullient at the sustained rise in the sensex. But the fact remains that this rise in sensex has neither boosted the manufacturing sector in India nor benefitted the people at the lower level. There is little sign of any recovery in business investment.

The extent of globalisation of production and capital accumulation can be seen from the rapidly growing intrafirm trade, sales by foreign affiliates of MNCs, TNCs. To enhance the profitability of these global corporations and to facilitate their entry into the cheap wage areas of Asia, Africa and Latin America, the World Bank and its sister agencies launched massive programmes for developing infrastructure such as roads, railways, tele-communication, power generation, etc. The policies of the governments of these countries are being changed to suit the new requirements of international capital.

Estimates by NCAER (National Council of Applied Economic Research) show that 48 percent of the Indian households earn more than 90,000 (US$1,647.00) annually (or more than US$ 3 PPP per person). According to NCAER, in 2009, of the 222 million households in India, the absolutely poor households (annual incomes below 45,000) accounted for only 15.6 percent of them or about 35 million (about 200 million Indians). Another 80 million households are in income levels of 45,000-90,000 per year. These numbers also are more or less in line with the latest World Bank estimates of the 'below-the-poverty-line' households that may total about 100 million (or about 456 million individuals).

Significantly, during these years crores, of foreign funds under FDI has come to India and specifically to the corporate sector. But this did not find a channel to the welfare of the poor and eradicate poverty. If we measure the amount of total fund invested to eradicate poverty and eradication of poverty to the true sense, we will find the money spent on various development projects have failed to have any inclusive impact. A large part of the discussion around globalization is around its effect on relative inequality. Ironically, while the protagonists of reforms and globalization have many good things to say, no efforts have been made by the organisations and political parties claim to represent the aspirations of the poor.

Globalisation has played a decisive role in weakening trade unions and thus reducing the bargaining power of organized industrial workers in achieving improvements in their living standards, no sustained effort was made to challenge this. It might have opened opportunities in some countries, but what I feel the poor of India have generally been deprived of their due rights and also accrue benefit from it.

In 1991, an acute foreign exchange crunch brought the country face-to-face to bankruptcy. It was in this backdrop the socialist political executive of the country resorted to major structural changes, something unthinkable: they began dismantling key government controls in favour of an open and market-oriented economy, a radical departure from the socialist past. During the past two decades, the face of the reforms has hastened up but it has failed to serve the rural proletariat, the dalits and adivasis who were claimed to the targeted group of beneficiaries of the reforms. The pace of globalisation and liberalisation catapulted India into the league of the world's fastest-growing economies, the impact at the ground level was quite disastrous. Many key sectors: telecommunications, roads, ports and insurance, opened up for foreign direct investments but the poor people were kept out of the purview of the benefits accruing out of these foreign funds.

It was expected that the government reversing the socialist policies that stifled growth would bring about a major change in the lives of the common people, especially the rural poor. The government reduced export subsidies and import barriers to enable free trade, scrapped the industrial licensing regime, reduced tariffs and changed to market-determined rates. But it won't. The government move simply helped and boosted the financial needs of the private industries. It unshackled private sector enterprises from labyrinthine bureaucracy. It did away with multiple permits, licences and the red tape that gave rise to a cumbersome system derisively referred to as the 'licence raj'.

The globalisation simply helped the urban middle class. It led to the spread of unbridled consumerism. In the pre-liberalisation era, getting a telephone connection, which took months, sometimes years, was considered a luxury. Today, India, in the middle of a mobile phone boom, is the world's fastest growing telecoms market. The biggest concern nevertheless remained the uneven nature of India's economic growth.

It is an open secret that economic reforms has produced stark disparities in wealth, giving rise to social tensions and a bloody Maoist insurgency spreading rapidly across India's countryside. In a study in 2009, the Asian Development Bank (ADB), warned about the 'Latin Americanisation' of the Indian economy, a term it used to draw parallels with Mexico, where economic growth has been inhibited since the early 1980s because of large, family-run corporate concerns that unfairly influenced state policies for private gain, while the interests of the majority was ignored. In India, the number of high net worth individuals, those with assets of at least $1 million, grew from 84,000 in 2008 to 126,700 in 2009, according to the latest edition of the Merrill Lynch-Capgemini World Wealth Report. That is the fastest growth in the number of wealthy individuals in Asia after Hong Kong. The latest Indian edition of Forbes says the wealthiest 100 Indians are collectively worth $276 bn, while their top 100 Chinese counterparts have assets of $170 bn. ADB's report underlines, 80 percent of this wealth was accumulated by companies in sectors where government control is the heaviest, primarily minerals and other natural resources. These sectors can only be tapped into through lucrative government contracts.

But in sharp contrast the poor, particularly the rural poor, continue to languish. Their level of economic sustenance deteriorated to such an extent that it posed a serious problem of survival for them. A closer look of the rural areas of Bihar, Uttar Pradesh, Jharkhand, Odisha and Bengal would make it explicit that rampant poverty has turned the areas into breeding ground for human trafficking. Massive migration of rural poor was witnessed in these states. This has simply destroyed and ruined the rural family culture.

Models of Development

While participating at the chief ministers conference at Hyderabad in 2004, the then Prime Minister, Dr Manmohan Singh had suggested for adopting inclusive socio-economic measures to eradicate the menace of Maoism. He had even suggested to the chief ministers present at the meet to handle the issue carefully. But within a couple of years, Dr Singh made a paradigm shift in his perception and described the Maoist uprising as 'the biggest internal security challenge ever faced by our country' as several states, like Chhattisgarh, Jharkhand, Karnataka, Andhra Pradesh, Maharashtra and Madhya Pradesh, are facing internal insurgency by Maoists.

The Maoists on their part declared Dr Singh as the biggest threat to the security of the country. While he made it clear that the government would not hesitate to use the armed forces to curb Maoist violence in Jharkhand and other places, the Maoists asserted their desire to continue their struggles against the state. Soon after this, the Maoist struck a serious blow to the writ of the government in Lalgarh and Chhattisgarh. One thing is quite spectacular; both were correct in asserting their political lines.

In fact, we ought to analyse the positions not from the security perspective. Instead we should look at it as the fight between two models of development. While Dr Singh symbolizes the neoliberal model of development which is based on foreign investments, the Maoists are for indigenous economic model which would not destroy the life and livelihood of the rural poor, dalits and tribals. It is unfortunate that the Maoists have been so embroiled in and obsessed with their armed actions that they ignored to reach out to the people with their own set of principles and programmes. Undeniably, the top leadership of the party thought it proper to encourage the armed action instead of organizing common people on this issue. Maoists' adoption of the self-defeatist policies and programmes in fact, harmed them and created confusion among party bourjeon.

There are a number of important issues on which the Maoists could have built a poplar mass movement. Unemployment is on the increase. Misery and impoverishment have wrecked the country. Farmers in the country have been committing suicides. The neoliberal model has failed. Instead of working on an alternative model of development, in spite of the miseries caused by the neo-liberal model of development, the government continues the rhetoric of the free market. Despite having such favourable subjective condition, the Maoists were unnecessarily hedging around.

Lack of any positive initiation has failed to attract the common people, especially the rural poor in significant number to the Maoists. In July 2009, there were mass demonstrations across India demanding democracy in the forests. *Chakka jams, rasta rokos, dharnas* and *morchas* were organized in Rajasthan, Gujarat, Maharashtra, Madhya Pradesh, Chhattisgarh, Jharkhand, and Odisha. Their demands were to recognise tribal rights and power to protect and control their forests and resources; to stop illegally destroying forests and robbing the indigenous people of their resources through diversion for private companies and large projects. But this protest movement remained simply confined to tokenism. No effort was made by the Maoists who claim to work for the tribals to broad base and sustain it.

The claims of the Maoists that they are fighting for the rural poor and the landless peasants cannot be completely ignored but many things remain to be done to really make the movement effective. Since the state has embraced neo-liberalism or market economy, the Maoists simply cannot claim to survive by obsolute rhetoric of overthrow the Indian state. This appears to be simply resorting to rhetoric. Maoists must not nurse any illusion that they would match the armed power of state. This is a ridiculous proposition. The Maoists have to protect and preserve their human resources for using effectively. They have already alienated a huge section of the Indian population through their frivolous military actions. The Maoists must seriously ponder why the youngsters are averse to joining the Left parties, least to speak of the Maoists. Whatever little amount of members the Maoists manage to get is through use of terror and goading. It is unfortunate that civilians have become victims of both the Maoist violence the State Governments' plans to curb the Maoists.

Some of the studies, specially of Chen and Ravallion estimate that between 1981 and 2001 the percentage of rural people living below an international poverty line of $1.08 per day (at 1993 purchasing power parity) declined from about 79 percent to about 27 percent in China, from about 63 percent to about 42 percent in India, and 55 percent to 11 percent in Indonesia.

Yet another fall out of the globalization and reforms has been cut in the social protection and expenditure on basic services. Budgets are cut to reduce fiscal deficits. These measures are the part of the package of macro-economic stablisation prescribed by the World Bank of IMF. The government often slashes the expenditures meant for the poor as the rich do not like to share the fiscal austerity. During these years, the actual budgetary expenditure on education, health and water has been substantially reduced. This is primarily due to top-heavy administrative obstacles and bureaucratic and political corruption.

The Left parties and Maoists, with their strong cadre force, could have built a popular mass struggle against denial of public services to the poor, in their base areas, the liberated zones. But what we see is, the Maoists pursuing reformist programmes and policies in the areas under their control. Globalisation propelled by information communication technology (CT) and the knowledge-based economy (KBE) has forged the integration of cross-border transactions and interdependence to a magnitude, scale, and complexity which has appeared to tip the balance for globalisation backlash.

Globalisation is not a new phenomenon, but the current phase seems to have new elements that did not exist previously. Earlier also finance came from outside but the riders were not so demanding, as are now. In the present situation, regarding the consequences of the various aspects of globalisation at the national level, there can be both positive and negative aspects in the short and long runs. Globalisation creates both opportunities and risks, and the impacts on the rural poor will depend on the extent to which they manage to seize the opportunities while managing the increased risks. Unfortunately, the Indian rural poor have not been able to sustain the risk as the government agencies have been preoccupied with their own perceptions.

Going by economic measures, it is surmised that India is a globalisation success story. It is widely believed that average incomes, rising at 3 percent to 4 percent a year, have doubled since the mid-1990s. New industries have emerged, most visibly in the high-tech hubs of Bangalore and Hyderabad. Foreign investment, still dwarfed by flows to China, has grown substantially. But the countryside picture of these cities tell miserable stories. When we try to find out whether people's lives have improved, the figures present a different story. Poverty has fallen far more slowly than was expected, that too in the backdrop of India's economic success. One in three Indians live on less than $1 a day and India is still home to the world's largest conglomeration of malnourished people. Even UN agencies corroborate that almost half of the country's children are underweight for their age – which helps to explain the two million child deaths each year. The latest UN Human Development Report draws attention to the worrying gap that is emerging between economic growth and social progress.

The basic reason behind this lopsided economic growth has been narrow economic base of globalisation and choosing wrong priorities. The information technology sector benefitted most and has so far created around one million jobs. But side by side the net increase in the labour force has been about eight million a year. It is significant to notice that the globalisation has not benefitted much any other core sector; there has not been such boom in the main sectoral professions. Accelerating social progress will require more than sustained economic growth. Amartya Sen has written: "Even a hundred Bangalores and Hyderabads will not, on their own, solve India's tenacious poverty and deep-seated inequality." BJP had projected Brand Bangalore, through shining India, in India, during the Lok Sabha elections, but the Indian electorate decisively rejected it. The pitiable condition of the government efforts and claim could be gauged from the simple fact that across rural India, the public health system, starved of resources, has become a byword for clinics that lack drugs and trained staff. Kevin Watkins, the director of the UN Development Program's Human Development Report Office mentioned: "Changing public spending priorities is difficult. But changing the structures that consign India's rural poor, especially poor women, to a lifetime of disadvantage is more difficult still. It will require fundamental changes in governance and – more important – in public attitudes to gender equality."

Jean Ziegler, the UN's right to food advocate claimed that "After all these years of pushing globalisation and genetically modified seeds, that instead of feeding the world, we have created a food system that leaves many more people hungry.... The 'market' at least as defined by agribusinesses is not working. We have a herd of market traders, speculators and financial bandits which leaves the poorer strata completely exposed to the world markets."

According to the latest WFP (World Food Programme) Report, India is failing its rural poor; 27 percent of the world's undernourished live in India and 43 percent of its children under the age of five are underweight. The recurring World Food Crisis thus stresses the need for India to protect its millions of poor from a further deterioration in their lifestyle. The shortage of rice throughout the world was responsible for the doubling of paddy resale prices within India and resulted in decreasing levels of living particularly among the landless rural poor. Whereas in previous years most landless labourers were SCs nowadays there are also numerous landless peasant caste labourers in South Indian villages. In the past there existed hereditary labour relations between village landowning farmer patrons and their functionary and SC client labourers. This provided the patrons a secure supply of labour. This system has now disappeared because of the changing landowning pattern. The increasing numbers who therefore live below the poverty line and whose health deteriorated makes it necessary for the Indian Government to establish appropriate welfare services.

It would be wrong to look at poverty alleviation programme as an integration to global economy. It has been a domestic factor. Though some economists hold that reforms and globalisation helped to a large extent in alleviating poverty yet the facts speak otherwise. There has been virtually no impact of reforms and globalisation on the lives of the rural poor. The socio-economic conditions continue to the same which was before introduction of these twin measures. It has influenced and impacted the junkers. Yes, this is the class which has benefitted from the reforms and globalisaion to the maximum. The State Governments interestingly though have been opposed to the reforms and globalisation in reality they helped the junker, the intermediate caste farmers, as they are their vote banks. But significantly this does not owe to the foreign direct investment. Instead the money has come from financial institutions. The FIs, to some extent, liberalized their operations. But this is not a general phenomenon. The fact remains even the farmers have not benefitted from reforms and globalisation.

It would not be exaggeration to mention that no serious and sinscere effort has been made by the government to reach the reforms and globalisation to the rural sector. Leaving aside some states which had benefitted from Green Revolution, there has no sincere effort to help the farmers. But in their case the gains have not been too of desired level. Farmer's suicides in rich states of Maharashtra, Gujarat, Punjab and Andhra Pradesh is testimony to this fact. Penetration of fund, least to speak of FDI, in agriculture sector has been quite dismal. The government has been systematically reiterating to bring outside private fund in the agriculture. But so far private sector has not shown its willingness to finance the agricultural activities. As a result, the farmers are selling their lands to realtors and big houses. Even in states like Haryana and Rajasthan where agriculture has been comparatively a viable proposition, farmers have been selling their lands to real estate operators. If the fund has been available for farming and agriculture activities, the farmers certainly would not have sold out their lands.

Globalisation can help poverty eradication if the country exports products that are labour intensive. This creates jobs for the poor. But this is not happening in the case of India. The Indian farmers have failed to produce goods for export. What is most surprising is the government has been providing facilities to the import lobby. The private sector too has been in favour of encouraging import lobby. Only cash crops or fruits are produced and patronized for exports.

Since the entire rural force is dependent on agriculture, the income generated is incapable to benefit the population. In China, the population has been involved in producing exports goods like garment, toys and shoes that are all labour intensive. Cash crop is an agricultural crop which is grown for sale, for profit. It is typically purchased by parties separate from a farm. The term cash crop is applied exclusively to the agricultural production of plants. The term is used to differentiate marketed crops from subsistence crops. In earlier times, cash crops were usually only a small (but vital) part of a farm's total yield, while today, especially in the developed countries, almost all crops are mainly grown for revenue. In least-developed countries, cash crops are usually crops which attract demand in more developed nations, and hence have some export value. Prices for major cash crops are set in commodity markets with global scope, with some local variation based on freight costs and local supply and demand balance.

While the government are not too keen to help the agriculture and arrange for fund, Maharashtra has been going all out to help cash cop production. The state agriculture department has registered a decline in the area under food grain cultivation. It fell from 134.43 lakh hectares in 2006-07 to 121.10 lakh hectares in 2009-10.

Interestingly, the areas under oilseeds has remained unchanged while the area under cotton has gone up. The third estimate of the 2011 kharif season for the total area under food grain was 127.14 lakh hectares, much less than the area in previous years according to statistics provided by state agriculture department, a shift in crop pattern shows that cultivation of food grain is shrinking whereas cash crops like cotton, sugarcane and other crops like maize are preferred by farmers.

Maharashtra is not the only state to encourage cash crop products. Almost all the states have been pursuing this policy. An agriculture official of Bihar Government said: "Food grain cultivation, unlike cash crops, is not lucrative as the prices are controlled by the government. National policies on export and related matters are decided on the basis of yields of sugarcane and cotton. But this is not the case for crops like rice and wheat. Among coarse cereals, sweet sorghum and bajra have lost significant land to cotton and sugarcane."

This is having adverse impact on the land too. The farmers have to use chemical fertilizer to increase the yield. No doubt, the use of fertilizers and pesticides have enhanced production, it is deteriorating the soil quality. Every year, farmers are increasing the dosage to get more out of the land. Once the land becomes useless, the farmer has to look other way for getting some income.

A senior researcher from the College of Agriculture, Pune said, "Many farmers have shifted to cultivation of mango, pomegranate, banana, grapes and strawberry among others. These ventures demand high investment but offer higher returns. Some commodities are exported through various channels like processed food which offers farmers high returns."

In Maharashtra, about 1.27 lakh farmers have responded positively to the State Government's initiative of public-private partnership (PPP) with private firms for production and export of fruits and cash crops. Nine companies have been shortlisted to provide financial support to farmers and train them in better farm practices. These companies are into marketing, supply and distribution of fertilizers, seed production and consumable food products.

The Union Agriculture Ministry has pumped in ₹ 100 crore as partial monetary support for the initiative through the Rashtriya Krishi Vikas Yojana. Nine different projects have been sanctioned for commercial production of fruits and other cash crops like banana, pomegranate, grapes, onion, pulses, soyabean, cotton and maize. The companies that have entered into agreements with farmers have assured that their produce will be purchased at a reasonable price.

They will also provide better quality seed, fertilizers and pesticides along with imparting training on implementing good agricultural practices which will make quality of the produce good enough for export purposes.

It is irony that the government is not making any sincere effort to promote and protect labour-intensive production which would have reduced the poverty. There is a general perception and even the protagonists of reforms claim that globalisation and liberalisation has opened the avenues for more employment, boosted the labour-intensive sector, but the fact is otherwise. A number of studies point out that labour-intensive industry is not getting the right kind of impetus.

In India, globalisation has less of a role in poverty reduction because India's success story is more related to skill-intensive or capital-intensive products. Software does not employ poor or unskilled people. They are also not labour intensive. India has done significantly well in pharmaceuticals, but that industry too is not labour intensive. Notwithstanding, India has become more globally integrated and is doing well, no enough jobs have been created. China has benefitted from globalization in terms of reducing poverty. But it did not help India in terms doing something about poverty reduction.

It is expected that the regional parties would espouse the case of the rural poor. But it is not so. These parties eke out their power and strength from the rich and junkers, the kulak, the landed gentry irrespective of the fact whether it is intermediate caste political party or an outfit of dalits. Structural weaknesses and political uncertainties have also been major factors for poor not getting any benefit from reforms and globalisation. The uncertainties are more in

China than in India but there the poor have succeeded in withstanding the situation. The sad aspect of the reforms and globalisation is that they cannot identify with the aspiration and needs of the India's rural poor. They are prepared and driven by the rich people of the capitalist world.

In early 1980s, there was a big change in China's agriculture sector when the government moved from the commune system and gave cultivation rights to individual farmers. They also distributed lands' rights in an egalitarian fashion. Everyone got equal land. In sharp contrast, this issue was taken up at all. Those who raised this issue were perceived as the enemy of the state. Ironically, the Maoists who claim to work for adivasis have not been serious on this issue. They never launched a serious and sustained mass movement on this issue. This is the reason that in India a very large percentage of the rural population are landless. The landless population accounts for almost 40 percent of country population. There is no doubt that there have been economic development and achievements, but the weaknesses of the economy are underemphasized. The focus has been entirely on the urban areas and private sector. India's economic growth is service sector-led growth. This is not related to manufacturing or agriculture. The industry has been dependent on imports. Basically, this is the reason that the need to have a comprehensive view of agriculture development was ignored.

Obviously, profitability of cultivating different crops has hardly increased. As the cost of crop inputs is considerably higher than the crop prices the farmers receive, their net earning has failed to remain subsistence in nature. The farmer has to incur loss from his pocket. This has the basic reason for thousands of farmers committing suicide. While their earnings has hardly increased, they have to pay huge amount as wages to the labourers with growing shortage of labourers and the rising daily wages rate. Farmers are right in their assertion, but the fact remains that labourers also do not get minimum wages. In such situation, they have to migrate to the urban areas in search of alternate employment.

The farmers have become victims of the machinations of the market forces; whether it is sugarcane production or cotton. The falling price of sugar on the world markets in 2008 and the declining sugarcane prices has caused a devastating effect on villages where sugarcane was the major cash crop. Many farmers became bankrupt and committed suicide. This had a very bad impact on the labour situation. There was a decrease in the demand for labourers. The labourers became unemployed; poverty increased. The agriculture is a highly skilled hand in the agriculture sector. But in urban areas he had relevance as he is treated as an unskilled labourer. He had to be dictated by the terms of the market and the whim of the employers.

The rural poverty has multiplied due to the maneuverings of the middlemen. These people will never allow the benefits to percolate to the level of the poor villages. Recent exposes make it abundantly clear how these people have been usurping the welfare funds meant for the poor villagers. Whether it is opening of bank account or getting adhar card or getting the allowances, the rural poor are entirely dependent on these middlemen. The business of the middlemen thrives on the miseries of the poor. When crop prices increased in the world markets, farmers still complained that their condition continued to get worse because the middlemen who sold the crops in the world markets did not pass on the produces the higher prices. The farmer had to pay the increased cost of farm inputs also.

Farming has lost its charm to such an extent that genext is not willing to stick to the parental avocation. They want to switch over to some other trade or business. In fact, the selling of land by the farmers ought to be viewed in this background. A rural parent who can afford to finance the studies of their sons and daughters want their children to obtain a university degree.

A survey conducted in 2011 among 15-year-old village school children reveals that baring 2 percent all wanted to become a certified professional. They were asked what they would like to be doing 10 years hence indicated that only four out of 154 youngsters wanted to switch over to some other profession than to stick to the farming.

As the cost of crop inputs has risen more than the crop prices farmers receive, their net earnings have hardly increased. Farmers also complain about the growing shortage of village labourers and the resulting rising daily wage rate. Yet there is a quite considerable discrepancy between what landowners say about their farm labourers wage demands and how the farm labourers themselves describe their employment conditions.

The linkage between globalisation and rural poverty is an understudied area. Most people recognize that even the rural poor experience some level of social change brought on by the increased use of global technologies such as mobile phones and Internet. In India of late a rat race has developed to send the message that number of mobile users and Internet users have gone up in the rural areas, implying that the globalisation has benefitted these areas. When it comes to economic change, however, opinions are divided as to whether trade liberalisation leads to economic growth and through this, to rural poverty reduction. Some argue that the rural poor are not much affected by globalisation because they are not integrated in the global economy in the first place. Others assume that the rural poor are at the receiving end of negative impact as global and domestic inequality worsens due to intensified economic competition at the global level (Bardhan, n.d.).

It is beyond much doubt, however, that the impact of global economic integration on rural poverty reduction is conditioned by the country's political, economic, legal, and social institutions and the policies to address these institutional problems.

Globalisation with its free flow of finances and trade products prevents individual State Governments from protecting their own populations from any disadvantageous effects this may have on in country economic development in general and the poorer strata in particular. According to the latest WFP (World Food Programme) Report, India is failing its rural poor; 27 percent of the world's undernourished live in India and 43 percent of its children under the age of five are underweight. While India's general inflation decreased from 12 percent in July 2008 to 5 percent in January 2009 the inflation of food prices almost doubled from 5 percent to 11 percent in the same period. The recurring World Food Crisis thus stresses the need for India to protect its millions of poor from a further deterioration in their lifestyle.

Globalisation with its insistence on global free trade, increasing industrialisation and urbanisation accompanied by modern communication facilities such as the ready availability of mobiles, radio, television, and computers with access to Internet brought about radical economic, political and social changes all over the world. In India, the impact of these exogenous variables were re-enforced by the improved access to education and an official emphasis on securing gender equality and the elimination of caste differentiation. However, caste is still one of the most important aspects of an individual's place in India's society. The fact that caste identity can be hidden in the urban environment and that intra-village economic differentiation continues to increase is making class a more and more important factor in the structure of South India's societies.

Rural population increases whereas total cultivable land availability remains unchanged. Therefore, the average per household land availability continues to decrease. Moreover, the existing inheritance system and demographic accidents result in a continually increasing intra-village economic differentiation. The few large landowners usually purchase more land from those whose land no more provides even for their subsistence. Thus, the number of landless villagers who depend on their income from work as agricultural labourer increases. As there are no other income-earning opportunities in the villages, urban migration becomes a survival strategy for growing numbers of Indian villagers.

Profitability of cultivating different crops has hardly increased. As the cost of crop inputs has risen more than the crop prices farmers receive, their net earnings have hardly increased. Farmers also complain about the growing shortage of village labourers and the resulting rising daily wage rate.

The falling price of sugar on the world markets in 2008 and the declining sugarcane prices caused had a devastating effect on villages where sugarcane was the major cash crop. Many farmers went bankrupt and committed suicide. This and mechanisation led to a decrease in the demand for village farm labourers, whose poverty increased. Moreover, it made urban migration a survival strategy for increasing numbers of poor villagers. As there is still insufficient urban demand for the growing numbers of unskilled rural/urban migrants, they swelled the urban slums which in turn led to increasing urban violence and crime. Even when crop prices increased on the world markets farmers still complained that their conditions continued to get worse because the middlemen who sold the crops on the world market did not pass on to the producers the higher world market prices and moreover the costs of farm inputs also increased.

The world shortage of rice was responsible for the doubling of paddy resale prices within India and resulted in decreasing levels of living particularly among the landless rural poor. Whereas in previous years, most landless labourers were SCs nowadays there are also numerous landless peasant caste labourers in Indian villages. In the past, there existed hereditary labour relations between village landowning farmer patrons and their functionary and SC client labourers. This provided the patrons not only with a secure supply of labour but also with necessary ritual performances and the clients with a minimum of social security. This system has now disappeared because of the changing landowning pattern. The increasing numbers who therefore lives below the poverty line and whose health deteriorated makes it necessary for the Indian Government to establish appropriate welfare services.

Measuring Poverty

Policymakers and economists are badly split on the issue of following the strategy of eradicating poverty. While economists like Amartya Sen are for attacking poverty directly through poverty alleviation programmes, the protagonists of the capitalist mode of economic intervention hold the view that poverty will be eliminated only after the economy grows. In June 2012, the Government of India had appointed a committee to take a new look at the methodology for measuring poverty. It submitted its report in June 2014.

Human beings need a certain minimum consumption of food and non-food items to survive. However, what constitutes poverty varies according to the time and geo-political compulsions of that country. Nevertheless, there is a need for a measure of poverty. Measurement of poverty has important policy implications.

India has a history of studies on the measurement of poverty. But most of the studies have not been able to reflect the real ground, level situation. The easy mechanism to measure poverty is to look at it from the view of minimum consumption expenditure per person or per household. It can be derived in terms of minimum expenditure on food and non-food items.

The monthly per capita consumption expenditure of ₹ 972 in rural areas and ₹ 1,407 in urban areas is treated as the poverty line at the all-India level. This implies a monthly consumption expenditure of ₹ 4,860 in rural areas or ₹ 7,035 in urban areas for a family of five at 2011-12 prices. Based on the methodology outlined in the report, the poverty ratio at the all-India level for 2011-12 is 29.5 percent. This methodology gives the estimate for 2009-10 at 38.2 percent. This is in contrast to the 21.9 percent as estimated by the Tendulkar Committee methodology for 2011-12 and 29.8 percent for 2009-10.

There is a wide difference of dimension and intensity between the rural and urban poverty and there is imperative need to distinguish them. Conceptually, it would appear to be simple but measuring poverty is not that easy. The frequently used World Bank measure of poverty has no strong methodological roots.

The expert group headed by the former Prime Minister's Economic Advisory Committee Chairman, C. Rangarajan dismissed the Suresh Tendulkar Committee methodology on measuring poverty and estimated that the number of poor in India was much higher in 2011-12 at 29.5 percent of the population. Defending his calculation that 3 out of 10 in India are poor, Rangarajan said poverty numbers provided by him are not conservative estimates and they are at par with global standards. He held that anyone spending more than ₹ 47 per day in cities and ₹ 32 in villages would not be poor.

Yet another commonly applicable mechanism has been measuring the capability to spend on health, education and other facilities. Rangarajan held that, "All of these spendings have gone up in the recent past. That explains why urban poverty ratio is much higher in our estimation." In absolute terms, the number of poor in India stood at 36.3 crore in 2011-12, down from 45.4 crore in 2009-10. Tendulkar Committee, however, had suggested that the number of poor was 35.4 crore in 2009-10 and 26.9 crore in 2011-12.

It is irony that even 67 years of independence, India continues to battle poverty, child and maternal deaths, according to a United Nation's report on the Millennium Development Goals (MDG) that said while several key global targets have been met, more sustained effort is needed to cover disparities. India also had the highest number of under-five deaths in the world in 2012, with 1.4 million children dying before reaching their fifth birthday. The United Nation's Millennium Development Goals Report of the U.N. Secretary-General, 2012, which assesses the regional progress on eight MDGs the world promised to meet, suggests that although progress has been made on improvements in maternal health, actual targets remain far from achieving the desired rate.

India has done better on infant health but needs to focus on Assam, Bihar, Madhya Pradesh, Uttar Pradesh and

Rajasthan, where the MMR is still high. As many as 237 million Indians are still living in hunger.

If the statistics are to be believed, both the countries, India and China, have recorded the sharpest decline in poverty figures in the Asian region, but the matter of the fact is that India has to go a long way in eradicating the menace of poverty. Still in the rural areas the vast section of the people identified as mahadalits are deprived of the basic benefits. The women and children of the mahadalits are the worst sufferers. Worse, in Southern Asia, only 36 percent of the population use an improved sanitation facility and nearly half the population practises open defecation – the highest rate among all regions of the world. But, on the positive side, the region has shown strong progress on access to primary education. The sub-region reached 91 percent enrolment in 2009, up from 79 percent in 1999. Girls, however, remain at a distinct disadvantage with only 95 percent girls enrolled in primary education, 89 in secondary education, and 74 girls in tertiary education for every 100 boys.

The new poverty estimates of ₹ 29 per person per day recently released by the Planning Commission are equivalent, in PPP terms, to the new internationally accepted poverty line of $1.25. The suggestion that somehow this much money is enough for people to survive in any conceivable form has given rise to understandable public anger, much exacerbated by insensitive suggestions by some members of the ruling party that even less could be enough. What is even more important is to clarify what the poverty line does not signify.

The socio-economic caste census (SECC) undertaken by the government in 2011 to gather information on the condition of people across the country is still far from complete. It is aimed at identifying BPL (below poverty line) households that can benefit from the Centre's welfare schemes. The survey is being carried out by trained enumerators, who are mostly members of panchayats or village-level MGNREGS secretaries. The SECC has seven deprivation indicators to rank households on a scale of 0 to 7. Households with the highest deprivation score will have the highest priority for inclusion in the BPL list. Additionally, households without shelter, the destitute, manual scavengers, primitive tribal groups and legally released bonded labourers will have the 'highest priority' for inclusion. The SECC database will provide policymakers authentic information on caste-wise population break-up in the country. Based on that, the government can evaluate the performance of its past schemes and update them accordingly.

The survey is being carried out by the Centre to generate information on a large number of social and economic indicators relating to households across the country. State Governments are expected to prepare authentic lists of families living BPL on the basis of the information generated. SECC survey is also expected to address the shortcomings of the 2002 BPL survey. There have been reports of discrepancies in the survey data. There was a reported difference of one percent in the population of Scheduled Castes and Scheduled Tribes when the lists were tallied with Census results in a few blocks. Whether the consumption poverty line should remain as low as $1.25 is a relevant question. This is the internationally accepted definition of absolute poverty. There is also a notion of moderate poverty pegged at two U.S. dollars.

An analysis done in the Planning Commission reveals that the anti-poverty programmes are leaky and inefficient, unable to lift Indians out of poverty. It shows India can close the poverty gap by spending just a fraction of its annual anti-poverty budget. Poverty gap is the amount of cash given to a household to lift it above the poverty line. It is the difference in the level of consumption of the households below the poverty line and those on the line. India does not use household income levels for defining the poverty line for lack of official payroll data.

In a society where poverty is far more common than prosperity, one would expect the implications of poverty for education to be widely recognised. Instead the poverty is seldom mentioned directly in policy documents on education. Policymakers feel more comfortable using the words 'economically weaker sections", the 'marginalised' or the "deprived" to refer to the poor. The reason poverty must be treated as a factor of education arises from a basic incompatibility between the two. Education necessarily demands long-term horizons. Poverty, on the contrary, compels people to remain embedded in immediate or short-term concerns. India has now recognised eight years of compulsory education as a right of every child, but endemic poverty and social inequality are posing tough constraints in making this law a reality. The children belonging to poor families find it difficult to cope with the regularity that schools demand.

Poverty has a corrosive effect on children's health and mental capacities. Frequent illness, especially stomach-related problems, is common among children who live in conditions characterised by poor sanitation. A recent study has shown how filthy surroundings, in which faecal material mixes with water and food, weaken the capacity to absorb nutrition. There cannot be better evidence of the relationship between hunger and education than the success of the mid-day meals programme.

Education alone cannot address poverty. However, it holds an important place among the numerous strategies that a welfare state must adopt to loosen the grip that chronic poverty has on its victims. A recent British study led by Anand Mani shows how poverty saps the energy of its victims. They often fail to keep up with the effort it takes to avail the state's benefits. The daily struggles and anxieties of life reinforce the cycle of ill-health and missed appointments. In India, the state's efforts are quite often mainly symbolic.

One of the most important factors distinguishing the ultra-poor from other poor people is that it's simply impossible for the poorest to build a buffer they can draw on to meet day-to-day needs and ride out especially difficult times. Without a buffer, a household can never aspire to move forward and on the contrary are pushed further back into poverty by 'shocks' such as an illness or a bad harvest. The burden of paying back even the most modest microloan is an impossible one to bear when chronic malnutrition, poor health, illiteracy, and economic insecurity are a way of life. In fact, the hard reality is most people living in extreme levels of poverty do not qualify for microloans. They are virtual paupers.

The challenges the extreme poor typically face in their daily lives are:

- They struggle to find the means to eat three meals a day.
- They live in isolated, rural villages, typically with populations of no more than 200-500 people, in areas lacking decent roads and safe transportation to towns and cities.
- They often have to migrate for 3-6 months every year, hundreds of miles away from their families to work as day laborers in sub-human conditions to survive what is called the 'hungry season'.
- They typically live in regions that are geographically unstable and endure drought, hurricanes, floods, and other natural disasters annually, conditions that erode or damage crops, drain resources, and make food, water and basic necessities harder to come by.
- 95 percent live in homes with dirt floors and roofs that fail to keep out the rain and other elements; homes often lack basic sanitary latrines.
- Many of their communities lack basic services such as public education and health care.

It is generally perceived that working with the extreme poor is more time consuming and costly than working with other populations because their needs are so vast. For the extreme poor, it is necessary that they learn the basics of the financial skills, learn how to save, gain greater financial stability through income-generating activities and most important they need to develop the self-confidence. They often need a great deal of follow-up support in the initial stages.

A research report narrates the plight of a poor adivasi. It also underlines the insensitivity of the judicial system, the administration and the social institutions. The tribal hamlet stood far outside the main village Kanoria in Sehore district;

just a few mud huts with thatch roofs scattered among teak trees. One of the tribal residents of this hamlet, Maganlal, is sentenced to death for murdering his five young daughters in June 2010. The District Court sentenced him in eight months. It took another seven months for the High Court to confirm the sentence. The Supreme Court, four months later, rejected his special leave petition. The President also declined the mercy petition to commute his death penalty to life imprisonment; he was hanged in Jabalpur Central Jail on August 8, 2013. But a stay obtained by the human rights lawyer could avert him from being hanged.

Maganlal belonged to extremely poor section of the tribal society. Along with his family members he eked out his livelihood by selling firewood they gathered in the forests, which they sold in the village market some seven kilometres away for ₹ 40. With this money, the family could manage roti for the evening. On the fateful day his brother saw him hanging from a tree. He cut the rope just in time and saved Maganlal and found the five murdered children in the hut. He raised an alarm. Villagers as well as family members vouch that Maganlal was even-tempered, did not drink more than other tribal people, and had no previous history of crime. Obviously, the villagers were unable to make out the reasons for him killing his children who he loved more than his own life.

Nevertheless, the police personal investigating the case charged him with committing murder. The reason was cited as a dispute Maganlal had with his wives and brothers because they opposed his plan to sell their small acre of land to settle this debt. Unfortunately all the courts from the lower to the Supreme Court subscribed this police version. In the trial court, Maganlal's brothers managed to engage a lawyer for ₹ 5000, but they could not meet the expenses of the higher courts. Maganlal's legal aid lawyers unfortunately, never contacted or met them. He did not move even a step in the direction of protecting Maganlal. Astonishing, is poverty the real crime for which we are willing to hang Maganlal? This small incident has antagonised the entire tribal ghetto and the tribals nurse deep sense of distrust and anger towards the system.

The methodology for estimation of poverty followed by the Planning Commission has been based on the recommendations made by experts. The percentage of persons below the Poverty Line in 2011-12 has been estimated as 25.7 percent in rural areas, 13.7 percent in urban areas and 21.9 percent for the country as a whole. The respective ratios for the rural and urban areas were 41.8 percent and 25.7 percent and 37.2 percent for the country as a whole in 2004-05. It was 50.1 percent in rural areas, 31.8 percent in urban areas and 45.3 percent for the country as a whole in 1993-94. In 2011-12, India had 270 million persons below the poverty line as compared to 407 million in 2004-05, that is a reduction of 137 million persons over the seven year period.

During the 11-year period 1993-94 to 2004-05, the average decline in the poverty ratio was 0.74 percentage points per year. It accelerated to 2.18 percentage points per year during the seven-year period 2004-05 to 2011-12. Therefore, it can be concluded that the rate of decline in the poverty ratio during the most recent seven-year period 2004-05 to 2011-12 was about three times of that experienced in the 11-year period 1993-94 to 2004-05. The decline in poverty flows from the increase in real per capita consumption. The clear inference is that: (a) the real MPCE increased by much more in the second period (2004-05 to 2011-12) as compared to the first (1993-94 to 2004-05), (b) that the increase was fairly well distributed across all deciles of the population, and (c) the distribution was particularly equitable in rural areas.

Interestingly, estimate of India's poor is based on certain normative standards of food and non-food consumption, as well as behavioural aspects of classes concerned for consumption of some other items. The Rangarajan Committee has estimated that almost 30 percent were poor in 2011-12. It uses separate data sets for rural and urban parts. The energy requirement as calculated by Rangarajan is 2,155 kcal per person per day in rural areas and 2,090 kcal per person per day in urban areas. This is significantly lower than the

2,400 kcal in rural areas and slightly less than 2,100 kcal in urban areas used by the earlier Lakdawala panel. The reason given is that the age profile and working conditions have changed with time.

The states having the highest incidence of poverty, according to the Rangarajan formula, are Assam, Jharkhand, Manipur and Odisha, apart from Chhattisgarh. Those with the least number of poor as percentage of their population are Andhra Pradesh, Goa, Kerala, Punjab, Puducherry, and Lakshadweep. The percentage of people under the Rangarajan poverty line has been based on the national population of March 1, 2010.

While Bihar topped the list with registering highest 33.34 percent of poor people, Odisha followed with 32.59 percent by 2011-12. The incidence of poverty had been 54.40 percent and 57.20 percent in Bihar and Odisha, respectively, in 2004-05. However, Odisha has recorded the highest reduction in poverty among all major states between 2004-05 and 20-11-12 and the Odisha Economic Survey (OES), 2013-14, prepared by the Planning and Coordination Department, described the achievement as 'impressive'. According to the OES, Kerala has earned the distinction of being the number one state as far elimination of poverty by 2011-12. In Kerala, the incidence of poverty has been only 7.05 percent against 19.70 percent in 2004-05 as Punjab is the second state with lowest incidence of poverty with 8.26 percent in 2011-12 against 20.9 percent in 2004-05. While neighbour Andhra Pradesh has only 9.20 incidence of poverty against 29.90 in 2004-05, the incidence of poverty in West Bengal was 19.98 percent against 34.3 percent in 2004-05. The incidence of poverty in Narendra Modi's Gujarat has been shown as 16.63 percent in 2011-12 against the prevalence of 31.80 percent in 2004-05.

Around nine million households, or roughly one-eighth of India's urban population, live in a slum, according to the National Sample Survey Organisation. The number is significantly lower than the 14 million slum households identified by the Census in 2011. The NSSO definition of a non-notified slum was slightly more generous than that of the census; any crowded settlement with poor sanitation and at least 20 households was considered a slum by the NSSO, while the census required at least 60-70 households. The NSSO counted 13,761 notified slums while the Census found over 37,000. Notified slums formed 41 percent of all slums but housed 63 percent of the slum population, according to the NSSO. In all, the Census counted over 1 lakh slums in India which is over three times the number the NSSO arrived at. Maharashtra accounted for 23 percent of the total slum population according to the NSSO, followed by Andhra Pradesh and West Bengal. Over half of the slum population lived in 53 million-plus cities. An average slum had 263 households. Maharashtra, Karnataka and Andhra Pradesh had the largest slums. Nearly 45 percent of slums were located on private land, and 60 percent of them had pucca structures. 71 percent had tap water and over 90 percent electricity. Over 30 percent had no toilets and no drainage; similar numbers had no garbage disposal system and experienced water-logging in the rainy season.

India: Home of Hungry

It is an irony that out of the 842 million in 2011-13 in world as estimated by Global Hunger Index (GHI) about a quarter of the world's hungry, or 210 million, are in India alone. The number of hungry people appears to have declined slightly from the 870 million estimated in 2010-12, but the current GHI report says that this is due to a recalculation of how undernourishment is measured by the UN-linked Food and Agriculture Organization (FAO). Since 2006, the absolute number of undernourished people has remained unchanged but their proportion to total world population is declining because the world population is growing.

The 2013 GHI is calculated for 120 countries for which data on its three component indicators are used. The three indicators are: the proportion of people who are undernourished, the proportion of children under five who are underweight, and the mortality (death) rate of children younger than age five. Where is India in all this? The 2013 GHI says that in India the proportion of undernourished declined from about 21 percent of the population to 17.5 percent, the proportion of underweight children declined from 43.5 percent to about 40 percent and under-five mortality declined from 7.5 percent to about 6 percent. All this put together means that the hunger index for India declined from 24 to 21 between 2003-07 and 2008-12. The proportion of underweight children is an estimate done by IFPRI as the last survey was done in 2004-05.

If the reports and findings of the Planning Commission are indicators of the prevailing poverty scenario then it can be safely said that the benefits of high economic growth have not trickled to the most disadvantaged. The data based on the 66th consumption expenditure survey by the National Sample Survey Organisation (NSSO), showed that the pace of reduction in poverty has been the slowest in the bottom 15 percent of the population. The ratio of per capita income between the top 15 percent and bottom 15 percent of the population has risen from 3.9 in 2004-05 to 5.8 in 2009-10 in rural areas, according to the data. In the urban areas, the ratio has gone up from 6.4 to 7.8, indicating that the inequality between the two groups is on the rise. It can be said that the benefits of high economic growth have not trickled down to the bottom 15 percent who are the most disadvantaged in the country.

Reserve Bank of India Governor Raghuram Rajan warned against crony capitalism which he said creates oligarchies and slows down growth. "One of the greatest dangers to the growth of developing countries is the middle income trap, where crony capitalism creates oligarchies that slow down growth. If the debate during the elections is any pointer, this is a very real concern of the public in India today," said Rajan while delivering the Lalit Doshi Memorial Lecture in Mumbai on August 11, 2014.

While a person like Rajan has been concerned of the darker aspect of the crony capitalism and its imminent fall out, the Maoists it appears are not too concerned. The main problem with the Maoists is, notwithstanding having a vast group of eminent economists, sociologists and intellectuals as its think-tank they have not been able to carry out a critical and relevant analysis of the present situation and evolve a concrete counter strategy. They still hold on to their identification of the state character. It is beyond comprehension how these developments and trends have evaded their attention?

It is worth reading what Rajan says: "An important issue in the recent election was whether we had substituted the crony socialism of the past with crony capitalism, where the rich and the influential are alleged to have received land, natural resources and spectrum in return for payoffs to venal politicians. By killing transparency and competition, crony capitalism is harmful to free enterprise, opportunity, and economic growth. And by substituting special interests for the public interest, it is harmful to democratic expression. If there is some truth to these perceptions of crony capitalism, a natural question is why people tolerate it. Why do they vote for the venal politician who perpetuates it?"

Rajan continued by saying, "One widely held hypothesis is that our country suffers from want of a 'few good men' in politics. This view is unfair to the many upstanding people in politics. But even assuming it is true, every so often we see the emergence of a group, usually upper middle class professionals, who want to clean up politics. But when these 'good' people stand for election, they tend to lose their deposits. Does the electorate really not want squeaky clean government? Apart from the conceit that high morals lie only with the upper middle class, the error in this hypothesis may be in believing that problems stem from individual ethics rather than the system we have. In a speech I made before the Bombay Chamber of Commerce in 2008, I argued that the tolerance for the venal politician is because he is the crutch that helps the poor and underprivileged navigate a system that gives them so little access. This may be why he survives. India had the highest number of billionaires per trillion dollars of GDP after Russia. While excluding N.R. Narayana Murthy, Azim Premji, and Ratan Tata as 'deservedly respected', Rajan had said "three factors – land, natural resources, and government contracts or licenses – are the predominant sources of the wealth of our billionaires. And all of these factors come from the government."

Little doubt he was underlying the operation of the rich of exploiting and usurping the national wealth which belongs to the poor of the country. He said: "This is where the crooked but savvy politician fits in. While the poor do not have the money to 'purchase' public services that are their right, they have a vote that the politician wants. The politician does a little bit to make life a little more tolerable for his poor constituents – a government job here, an FIR registered there, a land right honoured somewhere else. For this, he gets the gratitude of his voters, and more important, their vote. The poor and the under-privileged need the politician to help them get jobs and public services."

A recent story of the *The Economist*, 'The New Age of Crony Capitalism' has created a wave among economists worldwide. The magazine has formulated an index named as 'Crony-capitalist index (CCI)' to measure the extent of cronyism in a country. It calculates the percentage increase in the wealth of some billionaires enjoying monopolistic powers particularly in 'rent-seeking' sectors over a period of time with respect to the Gross Domestic Product (GDP) of the country based on Forbes data.

The index was calculated for 23 countries comprising five very large developed nations, 10 large developing and eight small countries. As regards India, the report has shown an improvement in CCI – from sixth position in 2007 to ninth (2014). Does it mean India was able to restrict the phenomenon? No, this has nothing to do with government action against corrupt elements in politics and business. The ranking improved amid a slow growth rate, which had affected the fortunes of some politically connected businessmen rooted in 'rent-seeking' sectors.

Crony capitalism is not a solution but a problem in itself. One, it discourages young entrepreneurs who are otherwise equipped with skills and assets but do not have political protection. Two, as governments change, the special favours and political backing vanish. In view of this, the cronies are likely to demand a high rate of return even for small projects which stifle long-term investment. Three, the possibility of getting a favour also induces businessmen to shy away from entrepreneurial activity. Four, crony capitalism increases the income disparity as the inflow of money takes place in the higher echelons and those in the low-income groups are left to shell out a higher amount to make both ends meet. The rich get richer and the poor get poorer.

Contrary to Moists Claim

Maoists claim that revolution can be ushered in only by mobilizing the exploited people. They are obsolutely right. But it is also fact that they have not been proactive and agile to reaching out to the poor people. Though in their documents and literatures they claim to be oppose to any violent action which claims the lives of the innocent people, in reality most of those killed by the Maoist guerillas are poor and belong to the proletarian section of the society. Undeniably, the Maoist practice dualism. At a time when the government is trying to spot the poor and identify with their aspirations and needs, precisely for the electoral considerations, the Maoists who claim to represent their aspirations and feelings are not willing to identify with them.

The long-term objective of the Maoists is the armed overthrow of the Indian state and the creation of a socialist-communist government. The Maoists term this a "democratic revolution, which would remain directed against imperialism, feudalism, and comprador bureaucratic capitalism." The insurgents do not consider the Indian electoral system and governments to be democratic, but rather tools that benefit the landlord and capitalist classes. It is a paradox that seven hundred and fifty million Indians, about 75 percent of the country's population, live in poverty while the top 5 percent of Indian families hold 38 percent of total assets.

India has the third highest number of billionaires in the world, after the U.S. and China. Four of the top billionaires of the world are now Indian. These few billionaires control one-third of the Indian economy, which means someone else lost their part of the economy. The Indian capitalist class, in league with Western multinationals and governments, is perpetrating Western colonialism. The state power has been ably assisting and supporting the endeavours of the capitalist class in grabbing the mineral-rich land of the 84 million Adivasis (8 percent of the population) in India for iron. A number of violent clashes took place in Odisha, Chhttisgarh and Jharkhand, but the government is not willing to retrace. This has displaced and impoverished millions of adivasis and driven them to join the Maoists, who claim to champion their aspirations.

It is a fact that the adivasis have become alien in their own land and ironically have been surviving by subsistence farming and by scraping a living from forestry. But in recent times the government has even put a check on their activities on the flimsy plea that they were denuding and looting the forests. Even these precarious means of livelihood are threatened by the Indian state with a sustained move to confiscate their lands since 1991. This is being done on the plea of setting up of Special Economic Zones (SEZ) for economic development of the country. In his back the tribal people "risk losing everything they've ever known." In fact, the Maoist war is a resource war over land and the enormous mineral wealth under it, but also a war for the very survival of the adivasi people. Most of the fighters among the Maoists are adivasis, although the leaders are not.

Ironically, the government by attacking adivasis, has only pushed them further into the arm of the Maoists. The adivasis have a pawn in the game plan of the Maoists. Most of Maoists who have been either surrendered or left the organization accuse the top leadership of being insensitive to the needs and aspirations of the poor adivasis. Compare it with the

CPI(ML)'s Bhojpur Movement of seventies. The Harijans and dalits were the vanguard of the movement. They fought for the dignity, prestige (*IZZAT*) and economic emancipation. They carried out mass actions. They did not resort to hit and run strategy. It cannot be denied the sense of having (*IZZAT*) among them had in fact motivated the bourgeoise political parties to adopt this as their tactical weapon. In Bihar, Lalu Prasad adopted it and scored. What was most unfortunately was instead of crediting the Marxist-Leninist for emergence of this aspirational politics, Lalu was credited with the honour.

It is a known fact that the Indian political establishment and bureaucracy riles and ridicules the adivasis and mahadalits. They do not treat them as human beings. It would be worth mentioning one simple incident that took place **in Gaya district of Bihar on September 27, 2014.**

On that day over 300 Mahadalit families of Manjhi caste that the Chief Minister Jitan Ram Manjhi belongs to, fled from Pura village in Gaya fearing threats from the upper caste strongmen. The villagers took shelter in a block development office five kilometer away from the village. Though senior district officials requested them to return to their village assuring of complete police protection and security the fear-stricken villagers refused to budge. What was really note worthy was the complete lack of initiative by the bureaucracy to take action the upper caste goons. It was on September 20, Arjun, a mahadalit, aspiring to become the chairman of the primary agriculture cooperative society was killed for defying the diktat of the upper caste farmers. They had asked him to retire from the election. But he was reluctant to obey their diktats. Eventually he was beaten to death. But the officials maintained a passive attitude towards the case and were not too keen to arrest the killers. The mahadalits of the village demanded for action against the killers. After they protested, some powerful people threatened them to eliminate them like Arjun Manjhi. Fearing attacks on them, they fled the village. It was only after the intervention of the Chief Minister Jitan Ram Manjhi that the bureaucrats became active and asked them to return to their village. Incidentally villagers of Pura are the neighbourers of the Chief Minister.

In fact, the welfare schemes are merely a façade to fool the people and maintain their progressive image. The fact of the matter is the Central and State Governments are only keen to serve the class interest of the crony capitalist and feudal elements. These people are so corrupt that only about 10 percent of development funds trickle down to the people they are supposed to benefit. The face of government that adivasis see is therefore usually one of wide-scale violence and corruption.

Insurgency has wider operational area in Jharkhand. It is a known fact that the political system and the bureaucracy of the state is the worst corrupt in India. How could people forget that Madhu Koda the Chief Minister, had robbed the state of thousands of crores. The rampant corruption and acute poverty amongst the tribals have been primary responsible for state slipping into the hands of the Maoists. The state was carved out of Bihar in 2000 with the objective of serving the tribals better and take them out of the morass of poverty. But unfortunately the political executives of the state, irrespective of the fact to which party they belonged, looted the state. The fodder scam perpetrated under the patronage of former Chief Minister of Bihar Lalu Prasad is the testimony to this mechanism of loot. Its operational base was in Jharkhand. Adivasis make up 26 percent of Jharkhand's population, and depend on forests for their livelihood. The giant industrial projects have already ravaged the forests, and their increase will intensify the damage. Jharkhand contains the Saranda forest, Asia's largest sal tree sanctuary, for which the government has granted 19 mining licenses. Saranda is where the world's biggest iron ore deposit is located. At present, there is one state-owned mine operating in Saranda.

In their quest to serve the interest of the imperialists and capitalists, state security forces launched at least three major military operations in the Saranda forest, aimed at clearing the Maoist presence there for the mining companies. The government has been helping in securing land, water, and minerals for the corporate giants through military operations but what an irony was averse to mitigate the problems of the adivasis and make available fresh drinking water to them. Operation Monsoon, Operation Bravo Boy, and Operation Anaconda were launched in Saranda in June, July, and August 2011. The government gave mining leases to 19 mining companies in the region including Tata, Jindal, Mittal, Rungta Mines and others. Today Jharkhand is a fully militarized zone. There are over a hundred bases with a total of 50,000 official paramilitary troops involved in military action.

Let us look at the Maoist actions. They have been quite active and carried out a number of guerilla or military actions. It would be worth to evaluate what worth they gained from these actions? The government claims that Maoists have succeeded in spreading their area of operation. But this is simply a canard. This is a tactical ploy to bring in more para military reinforcement to protect the interest of the big houses. Unless the government prepares a strong case, it cannot deploy more and more security forces. Even by a façade it would be a tough proposition for the government to justify its action. For justifying its action it needs a strong documentary support. Today, we live in the corporate Indian state, not in a welfare state. The government makes all the laws and policies in favour of the corporate houses. The Jharkhand Government introduced the Industrial Policy of 2012, which clearly says that 25 kilometers of both sides of the four-lane road from Kodarma to Bahragora will be handed over to the corporates as a Special Economic Zone. Where should people go?

While the Maoists have been killing police and innocent villagers on the plea of fighting the class enemies, it is really surprising that they have not touched any corporate boss. Some time back they had kidnapped one boss but eventually he was released. Maoists have formed the habit of frequently giving call for strike. While the region observes strike the private companies operating in the area continue to function normally. People of the area nurse strong feeling that no mining company can operate without paying levies to the Maoists. They also link formation of numerous splinter groups to this development. Even some senior Maoists confide that Jharkhand is the place from where Maoists finance their operations in other states, too.

It is a known fact that police or army constabulary consists of the persons from the poor families. These people did not have enough resources, lacked right kind of networking to net a good job and even do not have that amount of money to purchase a nice job. In the Dantewada massacre, in which 76 CRPF personnel were killed, most of the personnel who were killed were poor tribals and villagers who had joined the force to make ends meet. Many of the dead soldiers were young men in their early twenties and they came from poor and underprivileged families. Some were reported to be the sole bread-winners for their family. In fact, the sister of a slain policeman went on record to challenge the Maoists to convince her about the cause they were fighting for. The civilians who died in Maoist attacks were mostly people whom the rebel outfit claimed to be representing the poor and the downtrodden. Will the Maoists explain what did they gain in real terms from this massacre? Did their struggle move forward even an inch in the right direction?

A leading human rights activists of Jharkhand, Gladson Dungdung is critical of the Maoists; "As far my knowledge and experience is concerned, they are not fighting for the adivasis [in Jharkhand]. Instead, they have created more problems for the democratic people's movement. It's very easy for the government to call these democratic struggles Maoist and suppress them. I think the Maoists are part of the problem, not the solution."

On Sept. 20, 2009, Paramjit, a Maoist commander in Bihar, had said that poverty is forcing the poor to turn to Maoists. He added that until India's government becomes pro-poor, they will continue their fight against the state. Paramjit also claimed that Maoists are fighting for the rights of poor farmers and landless labourers and in turn the rural people give their support to the cause of rebels.

But it is a bare fact that the Maoists have failed to articulate the miseries and plights of the poor. They are primarily concerned with the adivasis and feel more at ease in operating from the adivasi areas. Obviously, this raises the question: Why are the Maoists not willing to organize the proletariat, the dalits and harijans, in other areas? In Bihar they claim to have some operational area in north Bihar. But it is mere symbolic. Once in a full moon they carry out some action, as setting on fire the machines of the road construction companies or looting some rich. But they never tried to organize the poor peasantry and landless labourers for a protracted struggle. It is widely known fact that north Bihar is the home of the poor and at least 80 percent of the Bihari poor are inhabitants of this region. This flood ravaged region has been breeding ground for proletariat movement in the past. In fact the first Naxalite movement had surfaced in the Musahari block of the region.

Figures are quite revealing though the Maoists refute that they have been indulging in anarchy. Between 2008 and 2012 alone, there were more than 950 attempts by Maoists to destroy power plants, railway property and telephone exchanges. Over the years, the Maoists have entrenched themselves in what they call a Compact Revolutionary Zone (CRZ), or a red corridor. While India is a rising economic power, a major chunk of the population finds itself left behind. It is an open secret that the phase of economic reforms and globalisation has miserably failed to change the lives of millions of poor. But the Maoists are not at all willing to take this challenge and confront the government. They must look to the African countries for ideological inspirations. While the poor have been groaning under the exploitative pressure of the capitalists and neoliberal economic policies, the Maoists have turned passive spectators. The poor need a reply.

The Union Government has been pumping billions of funds in the rural areas for integrated and inclusive growth of the poor and adivasis. Little doubt if the money has been spent thoroughly and in a transparent manner, the poverty could have been eliminated to major extent. Since the government fund is for loot, the politicians, the babus and their henchmen are busy usurping the money. After going around the cities and towns of the eastern India states even a naive would vouch to tell from where the money has come for construction of palatial apartments and bunglows. There is a nexus of the politicians, babus, realtors and crony capitalists. They are systematically sucking the blood of the poor without any protest in sight. Instead of fighting the menace of exploitation and poverty, the Maoists are taking advantage of poverty and frustration. Absence of development on the ground is prompting other splinter ultra-left forces to gain ground in the economically backward regions of Odisha, Chhattisgarh and Jharkhand. Even as India achieves high growth rate figures, these people have not received any benefit of the economic prosperity. They are still oppressed by bureaucrats and exploited by politicians. If anything, they have only faced the negative side of the liberalised economy – land grabbing by private companies, exploitation of natural resources and a further apathy from governments.

Even Jan Myrdal, who closely monitored the Naxalites over the years feels that the movement has lost direction. Myrdal, who has been in touch with several senior leaders said it was not the Maoists' ideology but their potential for violence that is sustaining them. The present-day Maoist movement is expanding rapidly, but lacks the support of the common man, the middle class, who actually make the difference at the ballot. According to Myrdal, efforts to raise quality of life are being obstructed both by lack of trust in the government and by insurgent terror. Maoists have done little to alleviate the distress of the tribals.

Some intellectuals and academics have been projecting the Maoists as the angels of the poor. They are not politically correct. Their town locality have expand the poor, adivasi to the state repressent and torture. They are also against the basic concept of democratic centralism. They even abhor the concept of democratic functioning. Had it not been so they would not have suppressed dissension inside the party with an iron hand. An example of this is the execution of two villagers who let a steel plant commence construction work on their lands. The Maoists brutally murdered twelve adivasis who refused to co-operate with the insurgent plan of action.

The Below Poverty Line (BPL) System aims to provide at least a minimum food supply for the poorest. However, the quantities involved are not enough and for many landless villagers it is thus impossible to sustain their families as there are no off-farm income earning opportunities available in the rural areas and mechanisation of agriculture has reduced the demand for daily labourers. Moreover, the BPL system was bedevilled by a lot of corruption.

Planning Commission reduced poverty line to ₹ 28.65 per capita daily consumption in cities and ₹ 22.42 in rural areas, scaling down India's poverty ratio to 29.8 percent in 2009-10.

An individual above a monthly consumption of ₹ 859.6 in urban and ₹ 672.8 in rural areas is not considered poor, as per the controversial formula. Furthermore, the Plan panel has kept the poverty threshold even lower than it submitted to the Supreme Court last year, which created an outcry among the civil society.

The Plan panel had said in its affidavit before the Apex Court that the "poverty line at June 2011 price level can be placed provisionally at ₹ 965 (32 per day) per capita per month in urban areas and ₹ 781 (26 per day) in rural areas." As per estimates, the number of poor in India has declined to 34.47 crore in 2009-10 from 40.72 crore in 2004-05 estimated on the basis of controversial Tendulkar Committee methodology. The methodology recommended by the committee includes spending on health and education, besides the calorie intake.

But the fact is India has 33 percent of the world's poorest 1.2 billion people, even though the country's poverty rate is half as high as it was three decades ago, according to a new World Bank report. India reduced the number of its poor from 429 million in 1981 to 400 million in 2010, and the extreme poverty rate dropped from 60 percent of the population to 33 percent during the same period. India accounts for a higher proportion of the world's poor than it used to. In 1981, it was home to 22 percent of the world's poorest people. The World Bank report comes just days after it proposed a $12 billion to $20 billion plan to reduce poverty levels over four years in the Indian states of Bihar, Chhattisgarh, Jharkhand, Madhya Pradesh, Odisha, Rajasthan and Uttar Pradesh. 60 percent of the financing would go to State Government-backed projects, according to the *Business Line* newspaper.

The study showed a similar decline in the number of people living in poverty in recent years. People living below $1.25 (67 rupees) a day fell considerably from more than half the people in the developing world in 1981 to 21 percent in 2010, despite a 59 percent increase in world population during the same period. Still, there are 1.2 billion people living in extreme deprivation, and the World Bank urged the international community to increase efforts to stop this within the next two decades. China was the most successful country in helping improve its people's economic condition. Its poverty rate fell to 12 percent of the population in 2010 from 84 percent in 1981.

India with continuous and concerted efforts plans to bring down the number of people living below poverty line to 26.7 percent by 2015, but improving sanitation facilities in the country still remains a challenge. By 2015, India should be able to bring the percentage of population below the poverty-line to about 26.7 percent, which is close to Millennium Development Goals (MDG) target of 23.9 percent. The state of Uttar Pradesh has the highest BPL population at 7.38 crores followed by Bihar at 5.44 crores. In the third place is Maharashtra with half the BPL population of Bihar at 2.71 crores. The BPL population makes up 36.97 percent, 52.41 percent and 24.11 percent of the total population of UP, Bihar and Maharashtra, respectively.

As per Tendulkar methodology for poverty line estimation, 35.47 crore people in the country fall in the below poverty line (BPL) category. This figure comprises 29.8 percent of the total population for the year 2009-10. The figures are based on the daily per capita consumption of

₹ 28.65 in cities and ₹ 22.42 in rural areas. According to the Tendulkar Committee's methodology, the poverty line is fixed by factoring in the money spent on health and education besides calorie intake. In wake of wide criticisms that the poverty line figures attracted, the then Minister for Rural Development, Jairam Ramesh announced that a new committee would be formed to take a re-look at poverty line after the completion of the Socio-Economic Caste Census, 2011. The government spends only 1 percent of its Gross Domestic Product (GDP) on healthcare facilities, forcing millions to struggle to get medicines, Oxfam and 62 other agencies said in a report called: 'Your Money or Your Life' last year.

Notwithstanding, the rhetoric of there has been a fall in the rural poverty, the latest facts tell otherwise. During the phase of reforms, the actual number of rural poor has increased substantially. While rural poor parishes and suffer the Maoists continue to live in their utopian world. Works of some economists suggest that the incidence of rural poverty began to show a downward tendency from the time of Naxalbari (March 1967) movement. It is beyond comprehension how could a party of proletariat ignore these ground realities and enjoy its gun power? The Naxalite revolt of 1967 should not be seen as mere demonstration of armed strength but more than that the collective assertion of the rural poor. In fact, economists hold the view that during reforms and globalisation the actual poverty has increased. According to an economist working in the World Bank, Gaurav Dutta, this declining trend in rural poverty seems to have been halted in 1990s. In other words, the percentage of rural population in poverty seems to have remained more or less unchanged or an economist of Planning Commission, S.P. Gupta holds even increased in 1990. The process of globalisation halted the process of decline of the rural poor.

The much talked about MNREGA is nothing but a capitalist mechanism to put in check the growing resentment among the rural poor and stopping them from shaking hands with the Naxalites. Instead of setting up a mechanism that should create regular job opportunities to the rural poor, the government through, MNREGA simply doling a sum for hundred days. Does the government think that on other days the labourers would be able to manage on their own their food and livelihood. Even in this programme the implementation has been much desired. The Comptroller and Auditor General of India (CAG) has found gross is efficiencies in the implementation of the MNREGA. It called for decisive steps to improve the implementation of the scheme widely credited for returning the UPA to power in 2009. It said the scheme needs of focus on developing intensive monitoring and evaluation system.

Tendulkar argues that the sharp increase in rural poverty in 1992 was a combined consequence of the weather-related natural forces, constricted maneuverability of government action, and certain political economy factors that were influenced by reform-related policies of devaluation of the currency and the intended reversal of dis-protection of agriculture. It is important to note that had the agricultural harvest of 1991-92 been favourable, the adverse impact of the reform-related policies could have been counteracted.

The 'green revolution' made big gains in little areas. The growth process generated inequality across regions and classes, but the 'trickle down' effect perhaps did reduce poverty. However, even in the states where the 'green revolution' did not have any perceptible impact, where the growth rate of real value added per head of the rural population was low, a significant decline in poverty was recorded. Hence, one has to go beyond the agricultural sector and its linkages in the study of rural poverty.

□□□